Spells & Shadows

Witch of Ware Woods

Book Three

Spells & Shadows

SONJA F. BLANCO

FIVE &
THREE
PRESS

For my parents –
Thanks for always rooting for me, even
when I make horrible puns

What we seek awaits beneath the cherry tree.

CHARACTER LIST

Sullivan Family
White Ash
Kinetic Witches

Kane
Abigail/Abby
Thomas
Violet
Connor

Lochton Family
White Pine
Psychokinetic+ Witches

Sara
Ann* *(Sara's
great-grandmother)*
Gran/Rosetta
(Sara's grandmother)
Alice *(Sara's great-aunt)*
Charlie *(Sara's father)*
Ted *(Sara's uncle)*
Ian *(Sara's half-brother)*

Cahill Family
American Chestnut
Earth Witches

Eliza* *(Sara's mother)*
Uncle Larry
(Sara's grandfather)
Helen
Eddie
Rebecca/Becca
Caleb
(Sara's second cousin)

Atwell Family
Black Gum
Air & Water Witches

Kingsley   Lily
Orsen   James
Elizabeth   Johnny
Claire   Ophelia
Ben

Walker Family
Sugar Maple
Shifters

Albert
Bill
Shannon
Moira
Matthew
Michael

Blue Ridge Pack
Red Spruce
Shifters

Dean   Tobio
Alesha   Luke
Iesha   Wes
Moesha/Mo

Additional Characters

Mary* *(Sara's
great-great-grandmother)*
Winona* *(Ian's mother)*
Naomi* *(Ian's aunt)*
Lochton
Florine
Bettina

Lethal
Ryujin/Jin
Samson
Kira
Amira
Damon

Makwa/Tituba*
Dorcas*
Brad
Shadow Mother
Motley*
Kahn
Vasile

*Deceased at the start of Book 3
+Lochtons have a variety of magics
(named characters only)

OUTER FOREST
Atwell
CEMETERY
BIRCH GROVE
COUNCIL STAGE
Walker
Cahill
MAIN HOUSE
Lochton
Sullivan
OUTER FOREST
Ware Woods

CHAPTER 1

Sᴴᴇ'ᴅ ʟᴇꜰᴛ ᴛʜᴇᴍ alone for one hour—*one* hour—so she could have tea with Gran and consult the Book; now, half the birch grove lay decimated. Splintered tree stumps jabbed the chill air, chunks of wood littered the snowy ground, and curls of black-and-white-striped bark fluttered in all directions.

So much for a peaceful afternoon.

Sara slammed into the center of the grove, and before her impact could form a crater, she summoned magic. The answering power crackled around her, every muscle taut as she swooped her arms and commanded a whirlwind of earth and water energies. Trees regrew, damage disappeared, and a fresh layer of snow settled with a sigh. The forest's audible whoosh was comforting, but she had no time to relax and inspect her repairs.

Sara dashed into the surrounding tree line, sweat soaking her undershirt as she sprinted down a shortcut, Hells-bent on catching up with a certain dragon and mending his damage to Ware Woods.

A low groan accompanied by a series of brittle snaps forced Sara's attention to a tall pine falling across the path ahead of her. She threw out an arc of magic, pushing the tree back into place while repairing its upper trunk—smashed by a dragon tail. With another burst of magic, she healed the broken understory and kicked up her speed.

That's the fourth pine today! She vaulted over a frozen brook, dodged a glacial boulder, and grabbed the trunk of a thin elm, swinging herself around a sharp bend before facing the trail's abrupt end.

Sara skidded to a halt, snow squealing beneath her boots. In front of her, winter blanketed the Cahill common, its pristine quiet at odds with her hammering heart.

She gulped a breath and tucked herself into the trees, hidden at a safe distance from the two dragon shifters. In human form, they circled each other near the center of the snowy expanse. Not a single bird fluttered in the hazy sky and, across the common, not a single soul stepped outside the Cahills' Main House. Thank the Mother. She didn't want anyone getting hurt *this* time.

Thomas stopped circling, cracked his neck, and phased into his dragon. He landed with a thunderous boom that carried across the open field, thumping into Sara's chest.

A gasp escaped her. She'd seen him shift a dozen times, and it still rendered her awe-struck. Perhaps it always would. Thomas's dragon shone the iridescent blue of starry twilights and dazzling dragonfly wings, of glowing sapphires and dewy forget-me-nots. Spikes tipped in shimmering silver protruded from the backs of his compact arms and legs. More spikes ran down his serpentine spine from the base of his horned head to the tip of his poisonous tail. The air around him rippled with power.

Magic flared inside Sara, its intensity threatening to split her. She fisted her hands, fingernails poking through the knitted loops of her mittens, and resisted both the magnetic pull to help him and the innate urge to protect the forest from his volatility.

Though being part elysian-eyed dragon was far better than the death Thomas had almost succumbed to, learning how to control his dragon was proving a dangerous and destructive challenge. If only his struggle were Sara's single worry. One she preferred over the unease, tight as a choke collar, regarding Thomas being bound to his dragon savior and sire—Jin. But instead of ordering Thomas to his side, as Sara had feared, Jin had left his half-brother, Tobio, in charge of training Thomas. Either Jin had no patience for young dragons, or he dreaded the Shadow Mother enough to immediately beseech the Global Council's aid in uniting against her. Given the red dragon's short-fused patience and Ware Woods' dire need for help, most likely both.

A shiver snaked down Sara's spine. Memories of the Shadow Mother raking her mind with pain and fear frequently tormented her—not from reliving her trauma but from imagining a possible, horrible future in which the Shadow Mother reigned. If Jin and Lethal couldn't convince the Global Council to help them, it would only be a matter of time before the Shadow Mother's dark magic infected and controlled all elysian-eyed dragons, including Thomas. And used them to destroy every sacred site and the entire normal world as well.

Teeth clenched, Sara shook off her doomsday thoughts and focused on the current threat—Thomas. His spiked tail swept back and forth, carving a deep rut in the snow, while his gaze pinned Tobio as if he were a meal.

The cold, reptilian glint in Thomas's eyes was not promising. Energy tingled in Sara's palms, ready to blast him if necessary and *only* if necessary. The very idea of hurting him twisted Sara's stomach. She yanked off the mittens Gran had given her for Winter Solstice and dropped them onto the path behind her.

Tobio barked an order, and Thomas phased back into his human form. It was a quick and clean phase without spitting fire. It would have been perfect—had Thomas remembered his clothes. The twins, Matthew and Moira, once explained to Sara that shifters kept their clothes in a magical void. Upon phasing back into your human form, you simply grabbed your clothes as mindlessly as grabbing a jacket on your way out the door.

Sara stilled, partly enjoying Thomas's backside and partly

awaiting Tobio's reaction. She knew being naked didn't bother Thomas, but if Tobio challenged him in the slightest . . .

Tobio's golden eyes flashed. "You forgot your clothes again, *little* dragon."

Thomas morphed, his roar rattling the winter-bare branches of the nearby Cahill chestnut tree, his flames singeing their tips. He lunged at Tobio.

The half-dragon shifter, clearly expecting the attack, instantly phased. Though Tobio's black-and-gold dragon was slightly smaller than Thomas, his motions were swift and precise. A noticeable difference to Thomas's puppylike, uncoordinated movements.

When Tobio zipped aside, Thomas crashed into the ground, plowing a bank of snow and frozen dirt with his armored head. The impact rumbled across the common and shook the surrounding tree line. Billows of crystalline snow released with a soft tinkling.

Sara's cringe at Thomas's nosedive promptly turned into a yelp as snow plopped onto her head and slid down the inside collar of her jacket. She clamped her hand over her mouth, but it was too late.

Thomas snorted, his exhalation dissolving snow into water and steam, the soil beneath him now mud. He swiveled his attention toward Sara. She tensed, face burning with phantom pain from their last practice session when Thomas's fire had engulfed her. Before his molten gaze could lock on to her, Tobio headbutted him and raced across the common. His sleek, graceful body rippled through the air, skimming the snowy field before disappearing into the forest—away from Sara and the Cahill farm.

Giving another roar, Thomas charged after him, the end of his blue tail dragging like a forgotten rudder, leaving a trench of slushy snow and mud in his wake.

Relief washed over Sara, along with a touch of irritation. *Are all dragons this destructive, or is this a shifter thing?* The Blue Ridge pack often tussled with one another in their wolven forms, tearing up the forest floor and acting like they were going to kill each other before phasing back and laughing. Though Tobio could only shift into a dragon and didn't partake in such positioning romps, he was second-in-command to his half-brother, Dean, the pack's Alpha. As a fierce second, Tobio punched back any provocations, friendly or aggressive, from anyone in the pack, especially Luke. Displays of dominance and sparring were first nature to the shifters.

And now Thomas was part dragon shifter. Wonderful. As if he needed more instinctual impulses fueling his already adversarial demeanor.

Sara blew back a lock of snow-damp hair and flicked her hands, magically restoring the common. With a mental apology to the forest for yet another fiery training session, she flew to the chestnut soul tree and placed a glowing hand on its trunk. Pushing warm healing magic into the tree, she revived its burnt tips, then chased after her bonded mate. His trail of detritus was marginally narrower than the last time. It also led toward the Lochton pine—her brother Ian's sole source of medicine to regulate his heart.

"Tobio!" she mentally called out, careful to screen her thoughts from Thomas lest she distract him and become the target of his pursuit. *"Draw him into the sky and work on aerial maneuvers before he scorches another soul tree."*

A shrill response sounded, followed by a black-and-blue blur as Tobio zoomed above the treetops with Thomas dangerously close on his tail.

By the time Sara restored the forest floor and tended to all the damaged trees, the two dragons were swooping above the lake in a more playful manner than a combative one.

Good. Maybe Thomas was finally controlling his dragon instead of the other way around. Sara stretched her neck from side to side, her body aching from the magical drain of fixing the destruction. Hands stuffed into her tiny jacket pockets, elbows jutting out, she ventured to the edge of the lake. Thomas swam through the air, following Tobio's lead in performing a variety of fluid aerial stunts, reminding Sara of her first attempt at flying. It had been a terrifying and miraculous moment.

Actually, terrifying and miraculous summed up a lot of her High Witch experiences. Sara visually tracked the two dragons chasing each other in a sizeable figure eight over the frozen lake. Fortunately, Thomas had experience with flying as a kinetic witch and simply needed to get a feel for soaring through the skies as a dragon. A remarkably large, shimmery blue, silver-spiked dragon with a powerful instinct to unleash fire and incinerate anything that snagged his attention.

She puffed her cheeks, slowly exhaling. Until he could control himself, Thomas was a danger to Ware Woods, to everyone in the forest, and especially to Sara. He knew it, and she knew it. Ever since his first accidental spray of fire in the treehouse, his frustration and determination to master his dragon crept through their bond and into her. He practiced relentlessly with Tobio, and in the rare moments when Tobio needed a break, Sara gleefully stepped in to tease and test Thomas with the expressed interest of making his blood boil in all the right ways.

Her soft chuckle caught in her throat when Tobio stopped gliding the figure eight pattern and rammed into Thomas's side. Thomas screeched as Tobio hovered, baring his dagger-sharp teeth in what Sara hoped was a grin. *Don't lose it, Dragon Boy.*

With a snap of his jaws, Thomas lunged at Tobio, who instantly dove for the lake, its frozen surface glinting in the late afternoon sun. Thomas followed, both dragons racing headfirst like monstrous bombs.

Sara shot into the sky, heart racing, hands burning with white energy.

Was Tobio challenging him in a perverse game of chicken? Didn't he know Thomas never backed down from a challenge? She grabbed at the frigid air, palms up, but her attempt to kinetically slow them was futile; dragons were an unyielding force—impossible to kinetically move or whish aside. Short of blasting them with power and risking injuries, Sara could only watch as they careened toward the frozen surface.

At the last second, just before kissing the lake, Tobio pulled up, the tip of his tail slicing the ice like a whetted knife. He streamed into the sky, away from Thomas who made no attempt to slow himself.

"Thomas!" Sara screamed through their bond as he smashed into the lake. A deafening crack pierced the air as a glittery plume of ice and water exploded from the impact. It veiled Thomas's dragon as he punched through the surface, his serpentine body a smudge of silvery blue before disappearing into the depths.

She hung in the sky, dread immobilizing her while the lake and entire forest shuddered. With a high-pitched whine, the lake's ice splintered in all directions, its jagged fractures reminding her of black lightning. Of the cruel power of Brad—the sick bastard who had tried to kill her on more than one occasion and was now a dark witch serving the Shadow Mother.

Sara's repulsive memories of Brad flickered, eclipsed by stronger fears as her gaze darted between the void where Thomas failed to surface and the wave of ice spears surging across the lake, toward the Atwell island's stone wall.

Sara rushed forward. *Do I dive in after Thomas? My magic might keep me warm long enough to find him. But then what? I can't pull his dragon body to the surface. Or do I protect the island?*

Sara flew faster, her face stinging from the cold. *Maybe I have time to save the island first before searching for Thomas?* She stole a glance at the black opening where she last saw him, and in that moment, the ice wave hit the island and the wall crumbled.

CHAPTER 2

SARA THREW OUT an invisible arc of kinetic power. Lake water and ice suspended in mid-air, glistening like glass in the sharp winter sun. Her muscles screamed at casting the significant burst of magic, the island surely at the threshold of her magical reach. As she gritted her teeth and focused on drawing forth more power to fix the wall, someone else summoned a gust of wind to join her magic in holding back the lake. Sara hovered, catching her breath, relief easing her urgency. The Atwells had been ready with their air and water magics, no doubt having seen Tobio and Thomas practicing above them.

Thank the Mother.

In a flash of green light, the stone wall rebuilt itself. Sara faltered. Only earth magic could repair such damage. And the only earth witch on the island was Caleb, her cousin. Caleb, whom she loved so much she had refused to let him die, begging Lethal to turn him into a vampire despite the consequences. Now he was some combination of witch and vampire, different and hiding on the island, only seeing the Atwells and his mother, Rebecca. Though Caleb refused to acknowledge Sara and, she guessed, probably hated her for what she'd done, Sara took comfort in knowing he still had his witch powers. At least his magic hadn't been his nonconsenting sacrifice.

A high-pitched dragon screech cleaved the air. A warning.

Sara snapped her gaze from the island to the sky, finding only Tobio among the clouds. His black-and-gold dragon zipped back and forth in clear agitation, his horned head fixed on the lake below. Still hovering, Sara swung her attention to the lake, now magically smoothing and refreezing—with Thomas trapped below.

Her heart skipped as something massive writhed deep below the glassy surface. Fighting the instinct to flee, she descended closer.

Thomas?

Her bloodstone amulet pulsed. Sara put a hand over the stone buried beneath her winter layers and stared into the luminescent eyes of the dragon swimming up at her. He opened his mouth, his dagger-long teeth a sharp white contrast to the dark abyss surrounding him. And then he did the unimaginable.

He breathed fire under water.

A burst of yellow-orange obscured him from view before melting through the icy surface with a hissing fountain of steam. Sara shielded her eyes with the crook of her elbow and fell back, narrowly avoiding Thomas as he exploded from the lake with a skull-rattling roar. Freezing cold and scalding hot water sprayed her. With his slick body so close, her magic ignited around her, protective shield up, flames sizzling in her hands.

Thomas shook himself. This time, the water bounced off her shield and back onto him. His scales quivered at the contact, and he swiveled his head, setting his sight on her like a snake spotting a mouse.

Shit. Tobio had said young dragons perceived any show of magic as a threat. Sara guttered the energy in her palms. Thomas's fierce stare only sharpened. The bloodstone pulsed again, and Sara inched back in a slow nothing-to-see-here glide. Did Thomas simply need to get a grip on his beastly instincts, or did the Shadow Mother somehow control him? Rational thought screamed it was pure instinct—the Shadow Mother couldn't breach Ware

Woods' invisible barrier. Sara knew this as truth, yet her darkest fear screamed louder.

She pounded back her panic. She believed in Thomas. He just needed to gain control of himself.

"Thomas?" she projected while internally feeling the many invisible, silken strands connecting their souls. Something whisper thin, undeniably reptilian and more prone to fight over flight, brushed the inside of her mind. She resisted the urge to recoil and mentally pulled on their bond.

Thomas inclined his head. *"Sara?"* His voice, sounding as though he were still underwater, floated into her mind.

She could have kissed his snout in relief. He *was* gaining control and, bonus of all bonuses, he could communicate with her in his dragon form. She extended her hand, the desire to touch him overwhelming. Magic flickered on her fingertips.

His eyes tightened with predatory intent. A deep growl resonated inside him, the sound stopping her reach, warning her to flee—to get away from him as quickly as possible. An image of a shadowy dragon sliced its claws in her mind. *"Thomas?"*

No response beyond the pulsating growl.

Sara slowly pulled back her hand, sweat icing the sides of her face. And when Tobio swooped in and body checked Thomas, momentarily distracting him, she took her opportunity and flew toward the meadow.

A furious roar slammed into her back, shoving her out of the sky and onto the meadow's shoreline.

Sara skidded through snow, her arms flailing for balance, her boots grinding for purchase before she stopped and pivoted to face Thomas barreling at her. She bent her knees, ready to take to the sky again, when Tobio shrieked another warning. Sara instantly stilled. *Running triggers a dragon's predator instinct.* Another of Tobio's cautions.

In the forest behind her, wolves howled. The Blue Ridge pack responding to Tobio. Soon they would enter the meadow, ready to throw themselves between her and Thomas, eager to protect her at any cost. The thought of them getting injured by Thomas's dragon twisted her insides. Neither she nor Thomas would ever forgive themselves.

With a flick of her hands, Sara erected a wall of wind between the tree line and the meadow. It would hopefully hold off the pack long enough for her to deal with Thomas. She squared her shoulders at the blue leviathan charging at her like a runaway freight train.

No more practice. She needed to *tame* this dragon. And she needed to do it *now*.

Snow crunched as she ground her stance, arms loose at her sides. He was already too close, too fast for a barrier of ice and stone to offer any safeguard from his searing fire or sheer bulk. The only chance she had was for him to stop on his own.

"Thomas!" she hollered at him. Into the cold air, into his mind, into his soul. She mentally grabbed the invisible strands of their bond and yanked as if she could tug him right out of his dragon body.

The strands tightened and twitched. The shadowy dragon gripping the back of her mind released and disappeared. Yet Thomas continued his crash course toward her, his open maw expelling clouds of smoke, shrouding him from view. He was dangerously close now, his smoke crossing the shoreline.

Does he not want to see me because he's going to eat me? Sara ignored a bleat of panic and dug into their bond, pulling with everything she had, the bloodstone pounding in time with her rapid heartbeat. "Thom—"

Her cry broke off as he rammed into her. But instead of bones splintering and flesh burning, she flew up from the ground and sailed backward across the meadow. Warm, human arms wrapped around her, holding her against a very solid, naked chest.

"Hello, monster," Thomas's voice rumbled in her head. Distinct joy colored his words, melting her into his embrace. He

rolled, clutching her to him, then grunted as he took the fall on his back—just as he once did in the treehouse, right before a very passionate kiss. They slid through snow and remnants of dragon smoke, coming to a stop near the rear of the meadow, directly in front of the cemetery entrance.

Sara stared at his face, her lungs and mind equally empty, waiting for one or the other to kick-start her heart. Stunned. She was one thousand percent stunned, and unsure if she wanted to kiss him or punch him.

Thomas smirked, likely reading her thought, and planted a kiss on her. It was warm and spicy and too damn quick. He pulled back, his head pressing into the snow. "You can punch me later. Right now, we have an audience."

With a groan, Sara raised her head, taking in the wolf pack partially surrounding them. Violet hovered just inside the cemetery, her arms held out in a way that suggested she'd been prepared to catch Sara. From the edge of the forest, Ian burst through snow-laden pine boughs, wildly waving aside their puff of winter powder before spotting her and Thomas.

"Father of Night!" Ian leapt through the snow and halted beside the triplets—Moesha, Alesha, and Iesha—in their night-black wolven forms. His wide eyes goggled at Thomas. "Promise me that's the last time you rip through the forest, cause a glacial tidal wave, and nearly kill my sister."

Sara sat back, straddling Thomas, and flinched. Having the wind knocked out of her hadn't stung half as badly as Ian's reprimand. His tone implied Thomas had meant to do those things.

She peered up at Ian. Ice crystals clung to his curly hair. Forever the protective big brother despite her being High Witch of Ware Woods—the most powerful magical in the forest. Though, she supposed, that wasn't entirely true. With Thomas now part witch *and* elysian-eyed dragon, he was certainly her equal.

Thomas chuckled. Actually *chuckled*. The sound was music

to her bonded soul. He hadn't laughed or cracked a smile in days but had brooded, frustrated with learning to control his dragon.

A surprised yelp slipped from Sara as Thomas stood, pulling her up with him. Snow steamed off his bare torso while he maintained a firm grip on her hand, their fingers interlaced. "I could never harm Sara. And thanks to her believing in me"—a tender squeeze—"I was able to rein in my dragon instincts."

Ian frowned. Thomas had skimmed right over any sort of promise. Instead of getting into a verbal sparring match with a part dragon, part witch who was also a trained attorney, Ian wisely said, "Good."

The triplets huffed, creating clouds of wariness, their amber eyes keenly assessing Thomas. Very keenly.

Wait a minute—Sara glanced down. Thank the Mother, he had remembered his pants and boots this time. Maybe he *was* finally getting control of his dragon magic. When she had yanked on their bond, he'd tightened his grip in return. It had been completely insane to hold her ground, but she had believed in him. She would always believe in him—in them. *Fated mates ordained by the Mother and Father.* The Book—the Lochton family grimoire with spells, knowledge, and far more sass than necessary—had revealed this to her. Apparently, it believed in them too.

The chilly air of pending evening stirred Sara's hair as she dragged her gaze to the suspicious smirk still upon Thomas's face. *Dragon devil!* He had felt her tug on their bond and had *chosen* to continue charging her.

The fist she drew back to punch him fell to her side as Tobio descended over the meadow, phased, and dropped before them. Following his lead, the rest of the wolves shifted: the triplets with hands on their hips, Luke with his headphones, Wes in his ball cap, and Dean who towered behind them with Moira at his side. Matthew shifted from his russet wolf and sauntered a few paces before standing near Tobio.

If Tobio hadn't pressed Thomas so hard, perhaps none of this would have happened. With a snarl, Sara faced the all-too-calm half-dragon, hands casually in his pockets, not a bleach-tipped hair out of place from his spiky ponytail despite his repeated headbutts of Thomas.

CHAPTER 3

"Y OU INTENTIONALLY PROVOKED him!" she yelled at Tobio. "And you're welcome for it. Thomas needs to learn restraint." "He barely has restraint in his human form," she seethed, ignoring the tug on her hand, the soft laugh beside her.

Tobio grinned, the gold in his eyes like liquid metal. "I know. And he must learn not to be so hotheaded, especially as a dragon. However . . . he did manage to shake off the base dragon impulse far quicker than I had." He gave an approving nod to Thomas before drawing his golden gaze back to Sara. "And you . . . ." His nostrils flared in the exact same manner as his half-brother, Jin, when he was exasperated with Sara. "Rather bold of you to face a charging dragon."

Not what she had expected him to say. *Stupid* was more on point. She snorted. "Yeah, well, that's me. Bold, reckless, and a touch infuriated at the *both* of you."

"I deserve your fury," said Thomas, dropping her hand and reaching into his back pocket. "And yet, look at the progress we made today." He brought forth her mittens, holding them out like an offering, while magically conjuring his shirt and coat into place. For once, they were on correctly, not a button on his jean jacket out of alignment.

Sara narrowed her eyes at him. She supposed he'd magicked

his clothes the same way she had once witnessed Jin summon a tea setting in his secluded garden lair. Crafty dragons.

Thomas smiled, the last light of day shimmering in his blue eyes—elysian eyes matching Tobio's and Jin's with swirling color and vertical pupils.

Sara's ire melted. She accepted her mittens, a spark of light-blue energy snapping between her and Thomas, and slipped them on. They were still warm from his touch. But just to let him know he wasn't completely off the hook, she projected, *I may still punch you later.*

I'm looking forward to it. His grin deepened.

Someone cleared their throat. Probably Dean.

"I told you their bond is stronger than dragon impulse," said Matthew, leaning into Tobio and giving him a nudge. His red hair was also pulled back, ends curling in a small ponytail similar to Tobio's. The half-dragon huffed a patch of smoke, his expression relaxing. "Come on," said Matthew, angling his head toward the south side of the forest. "Moira and Dean are running patrol tonight while the rest of us are eating and gaming at Ian's. The Cahills made us a ton of pizzas, including your favorite—Hawaiian." Matthew flashed a foxy grin.

Tobio quirked a brow at him, a hint of amusement on his usual stoic face, then shot Thomas a severe look that shouted, *Behave yourself!* He and Matthew took the nearest forest path, loping off, shoulder to shoulder, in the direction of the Lochtons' brown house with Ian's gaming empire in the basement. The rest of the pack followed except for Moira and Dean. The two phased and ran off in the opposite direction, Dean's massive black wolf chasing Moira's russet tail.

Sara wrapped an arm around Thomas, who returned the embrace with a firm hold. She turned to the last person in the meadow.

"You're welcome to come hang out too," said Ian, pushing back his curly hair, one of his nervous habits along with tapping. He gave a wary glance at Thomas before jutting his chin at Sara. "I know you orchestrated tonight's game night to keep me busy. Which I'm grateful for because it beats another night of Gran, Dad, and Ted doting on me. Lily and Violet promised to come"—Ian gave Thomas a nod at the mention of his sister, whose eyes matched her name—"but I doubt Caleb will show."

When Sara flinched at the mention of Caleb, Thomas's grip tightened, his chest pressed against her side. His voice, a tad huskier since becoming part dragon, thrummed through her as he responded, "Thanks for the offer, but we have plans tonight."

"We do?"

"Most definitely."

A tingle of energy raced up Sara's spine and heated the tips of her ears.

Ian's face lit up, his eyes brighter. "Are you—are you going to look for Kira?"

All warmth instantly evaporated, replaced by cold, crushing guilt. Sara flinched again, this time leaving her face as contorted as her gut. Less than a week had passed since their encounter with the Shadow Mother, when Sara had killed Dorcas and further upset the balance between light and dark magic. Then Brad had swooped in, taking Dorcas's and Makwa's bloodstones and, it seemed, taking Kira as well. She had been missing ever since.

To Sara's dismay, Kira's father, Samson, had disappeared shortly after in the search for his daughter.

"I've tried, Ian, but I can't locate her." Despite trying various spells and pleading with the Book to share anything that could be of help, Sara's efforts had yielded nothing except for one cryptic clue. Some High Witch she was.

Ian put a hand over his heart, the brightness in his eyes dimming. "It *hurts*. Not the ice splinter pain from the Shadow Mother. A different type of hurt—an ache that squeezes my soul."

Sara's own heart constricted at her brother's anguish—both

physical and emotional—and through their bond, she felt Thomas tense as well. "The Book said, '*The clever half-vampire, half-witch you seek is safely waiting*,' and Gran had a premonition of Kira and me laughing. I'm sure she's fine. We just need to trust Lethal and Jin to convince the Global Council to help us find her." The Book had refused to elaborate on Kira's whereabouts, which had infuriated Sara into grabbing a candle and holding it coercively close until Gran had shrieked and whished the candle into the kitchen sink.

Of course, Gran had been no better at providing details about the location of Kira or Samson. Her premonitions were notoriously vague at best and frustratingly false at worst, as if she couldn't tell the difference between the future and an indigestion-induced dream. Hells, Gran had once hinted that Sara might have children, which was *completely* impossible.

"Hmph. I'll believe the Book over Gran. And I know you're right." Ian's palm and long fingers pressed harder against his barn coat, his nails scraping the canvas fabric. "I'd feel it if anything bad happened to Kira. All the same, I want her back in Ware Woods where she's safe. Before he left, Samson said if another magical found her, they would kill her for being a half-breed."

Sara stiffened as Ian's last words hung like poisonous fog in the cold evening air. *Half-breed.* Ware Woods harbored many half-breeds, from Lily and her siblings to Tobio and now Caleb and Thomas. The Global Council wasn't exactly welcoming of magical anomalies.

She pursed her lips and looked past Ian, toward the center of Ware Woods.

They were all worried about Kira and their tenuous predicament with the Global Council. A predicament so fragile that Lethal had insisted Sara *not* approach the Council composed of Magi from other sacred sites. The Death Vampire had been firm in first securing an agreement from all Magi for the factions to unite against the Shadow Mother *before* revealing any of Ware Woods' secrets. Which apparently included Sara, a much-too-young and unpolished High Witch.

She sighed.

While lying low pissed her off, she understood the strategy and would play along with Lethal's plan. For now. But what she wouldn't do was let her brother suffer horrible "what if" scenarios. It was obvious his vulnerable heart was quite taken by Kira.

"Ahhh," drawled Sara, stepping forward, her grasp slipping from Thomas's waist and into his awaiting hand. With sibling affection, she slung her other arm around Ian and steered all three of them into the cemetery, toward the oak treehouse. "If any magical even *thought* to harm Kira, Lethal would dismember them, and Samson would crush their pieces into ash. And this would be *after* Kira was finished with them."

Ian chuckled. "You're right. She's as feisty as you."

"Father above," Thomas mentally murmured. *"One of you is enou—"*

Sara jabbed him with her elbow just as Lily popped out of the backside of the oak's trunk, stepping through the deep groove they'd recently discovered looped to the forest's other soul trees.

The platter of cookies in Lily's petite hands swayed, her gray eyes wide upon nearly running into Ian. "Oh," she exclaimed, "I thought I was looping to the pine tree."

Ian grabbed the platter before any cookies could fall.

"Thanks." She paused, squinting at him. "But what are you doing here? Sara said we were getting together at the brown house tonight. Or did something change?" She tipped her head quizzically, her mouth partly open, pale blonde braid swinging over her shoulder. Though Lily was half-vampire, half-witch like Kira, her teeth were perfectly straight. Her delicate, serene appearance belied her vampiric speed and strength, her hugs often bruising Sara's ribs.

Thomas rubbed the back of his neck. A lock of sable hair

still wet from the lake stuck to his forehead. "Sorry about my . . . destruction. It won't happen again."

"No worries," sang Lily, her voice light and carefree. "We were all watching and ready. Even Caleb." She swung her gaze to Sara. "He's making progress, even helped me make the cookies, but he's not ready to leave the island."

"Progress is good," said Sara, resisting the pull to glance at the island, wanting to see her cousin happily baking cookies, smiling and laughing the way he used to before he nearly died and she begged Lethal to turn him.

Ian linked an arm with Lily and tugged her with him toward the oak. "Let's go before the shifters eat all the pizza. Sara and Thomas aren't coming because they suddenly have *'other plans.'*"

When Ian and Lily disappeared faster than Sara could snag a sweet, she turned to Thomas. "What's more important than pizza and cookies?"

He nipped a kiss at her jaw. "You. Me. Together. Alone for an evening without Tobio hovering like I'm about to eat you and set fire to the entire forest."

Heat flushed her insides. They hadn't been alone together in *forever*. Perhaps it would be *her* setting the forest on fire tonight. She leaned into him, enveloped by his warmth and scent of musk and ash and—eww, lake water.

He shook his head, spattering her with droplets.

"Thomas!"

"First, I'll shower while you check on Caleb. I know you've been to the island every day, even though Lethal and Lily told you not to." He ignored her grumble. "I don't fault you for trying, my monster." He kissed her brow and disappeared, leaving behind a compact puff of silken dragon smoke.

Cold crept over Sara. Gone was Thomas's heat, the pack's presence, and Ian's worry, leaving her in a quiet cemetery with guilt twisting in her belly. *And I'll keep trying until Caleb finally agrees to see me.*

From the forest behind her drifted the powder-soft tinkle of snow falling from branches. To her left, lights flickered on inside the stone cottage, Thomas bathing here instead of at his studio. Sara swept her gaze to the recessed island. A wisp of smoke from the Atwells' chimney curled up into a sky now pewter with twilight.

Taking a shaky breath, Sara stepped into the static hum of the oak. Darkness caressed her cheeks and gently lifted her hair. For a moment, she felt weightless, unsure which direction was forward or backward, then the humming stopped, and she was standing beneath the Atwells' soul tree—a tall and regal black gum atop a small knoll dusted in snow.

Numerous sets of footprints led from the tree toward the Atwell homestead. Instead of following them, Sara approached a copse of hemlocks along the backside of the knoll. Here was where she always sensed Caleb, a heavy presence smelling of chestnuts and moss. Yet she hadn't seen him. Whenever she had drawn near, he'd eluded her, either streaking away with vampiric speed or, she now realized, burying under the frozen ground with earth magic. According to Lily, Caleb wandered the island's small forest alone at night, his need for sleep gone with his transformation.

"Caleb?"

Nothing but the hush of wind blowing through the trees and the far-off lowing of the Atwells' milking cow.

She took a step closer to the tightly knit hemlocks, wringing her mitten-clad hands. "Lily said you helped her make cookies today. That's good. I bet they taste amazing."

Silence fell as heavy as the boulder that seemed to be crushing her chest.

Mother below, Sara had no idea what to say or how to comfort him, and she was dangerously close to starting a friction fire with her wool mittens. "And, um, thank you for repairing the wall earlier. Thomas didn't mean to do it. He's still adjusting to his new . . . powers. Like you. I mean, I think you're still adjusting. That's why you're avoiding me, right?"

She cringed at her rambling. More than anything, she wanted to believe he simply needed time to adjust, time away from her and others to control any bloody vampire urges. Not because he loathed her and himself for whatever he now was. Though Sara had made a pitiful peace with the idea of him not forgiving her, the thought of him hating himself gnawed at her conscience. Lethal had warned her of the high cost of turning into a vampire, stating Caleb would lose the one thing he loved most. She had no idea what her decision had cost him, but she would do it again if it meant saving his life. Better a part-vampire, part-witch than wholly dead. Right?

"It's fine," she blurted, her voice ringing from atop the knoll like the last desperate call of a failed search party. "I deserve your hate. I just—I just hope you'll be happy again. Someday." Her last word came as a whisper.

The shadows beneath the hemlocks stirred, yet he did not reveal himself.

Sara lingered, hopeful, for a few frozen breaths before turning away. "I love you, Caleb. No matter how you may have changed or what you think of me. You're family, and I'll always love you." She reached for the soul tree, grateful for its comforting resonant hum and gentle darkness as she looped back to the oak.

After popping out at the base of the oak's trunk, she glided through the cemetery toward the cottage. Its inner light spilled across the meadow, calling her to Thomas and, hopefully, an evening free of worry over the Shadow Mother.

CHAPTER 4

Sara cleared the cemetery gate and rushed along the snow-packed patio, past the apple tree and its web of indigo shadows. In a blustery gust, she threw open the cottage door and entered.

Cozy heat from the floor-to-ceiling fireplace rubbed her cheeks while the steady patter of a shower floated from the bathroom on the far side of the central sitting area. Ever since becoming part dragon, Thomas took excessively long showers, saying the water both mesmerized and soothed his acute dragon senses. The only person—and she used that term loosely—who took longer showers was Lethal. When Sara had asked the centuries-old vampire what they could possibly be doing for so long, Lethal had said, *"It's habit for washing off the blood."* The implication of real and figurative gore had rendered her speechless. She doubted a tsunami could cleanse their murderous soul.

With Thomas enjoying his hydrotherapy, Sara kicked off her boots, tossed her mittens and jacket to one of the room's side chairs, and entered the adjacent kitchen, eyes narrowed in determination. Given the current contents of the fridge, dinner would be a challenge.

By the time she'd made a simple red sauce and added ravioli—a surprise find no doubt left by the Cahills—Thomas exited the bathroom. He wore his signature black jeans and T-shirt, this one heather gray, the sleeves snug around his biceps. A line of diamond-shaped tattoos marked his outer forearms, each diamond an indicator of a deadly dragon spike. Running a hand through his damp hair, he paused beside the couch, his luminous blue eyes studying her over the kitchen counter.

Sara's heart skipped.

In a measured tone, he said, "I'm sure Caleb appreciates you stopping by and will see you when he's ready. He hasn't even left the island yet, so don't take it personally."

She groaned. "How can I not take it personally? I'm the one responsible for his *condition*."

"We've been through this. You made a decision with the best of intentions, and now you need to let go of the guilt and move forward. Here, let me help." Thomas glided beside her, two plate-sized shallow bowls appearing in his hands.

He'd reassured her of this many times, speaking from his own tangled experiences and tossing back the advice she'd once given him when he'd made a crap decision on taking poison from Makwa. Sara knew he was right, and yet she couldn't let go. Not this time. She wanted to keep her guilt as a permanent reminder—a stamp on her soul—that she was responsible for the safety of everyone in Ware Woods.

She could live with the guilt. What grated her nerves the most was her recent dependence on Lethal and Jin to win over the Global Council, coupled with everyone else helping her and not allowing her to fully do something on her own. It was suffocating.

At least let me make dinner. Sara pointed her cooking spoon at Thomas. "Sit," she said, the single word a curt command.

His blue aura flared at the challenge in her tone. In a huff of smoke, the bowls wobbled on the counter and Thomas sat at the wooden dining table, the sides of his mouth curling up, a faint growl in his chest. "There's the aggressive witch I love."

Half frowning at him, she dished the ravioli into the bowls, plunked them on the table, and sat across from him.

His smile vanished, his confident expression slipping into one of perplexity. "Are you angry we didn't go to Ian's? Even with our bond, I get confused by your thoughts and emotions."

That makes two of us. Her mind was a tornado, always twisting with worry about every little thing while feeling deeply in all directions. Sometimes she even caught herself carrying others' emotions as though they were her own. It was exhausting and gave Ian headaches if she forgot to keep up her mental shield. While Charlie said empathy was a sign of a natural leader, Sara knew her emotional sensitivity often resulted in actions *not* becoming of a leader. Her frown deepened.

"You're still confusing me, Sara." Thomas stole a glance at her mouth, and his smirk reappeared. "I wanted to be alone with you, and I *know* you wanted the same. I felt it when I kissed you." He picked up his fork and took a cautious sniff of his ravioli. "No onions?"

She dropped her doubtful leadership ruminations. "Of course not. We haven't had any onions in the kitchen for weeks." Thomas knew she was aware of his disdain for onions, and he was right; she wanted to be alone with him. Ever since he woke as part dragon and she got a taste of his new power flaring in equal to her own, she craved him even more—their bond practically a physical connection. Maintaining a safe distance took an iron-willed effort, her magic reaching for him as she knew his did for her.

But without control of his dragon impulses, Thomas had hurt her, unconsciously shifting and spearing her with his dragon spikes. It had devastated him, and so they'd agreed to limit their physical connection until he could master his dragon.

Given his motivation and natural instinct to attack any challenge, Thomas had worked relentlessly with Tobio. The two had been practically attached to each other. The only time Sara had been alone with Thomas was when they'd slept together in the treehouse, exhaustion and the threat of dragon spikes—as well as Tobio sleeping in one of the treehouse's spare rooms—keeping them on opposite sides of the bed.

Thomas devoured his meal, any inhibitions over stray onions apparently gone. Despite her own meal growing cold, Sara narrowed her gaze, studying him. He seemed fine, at ease even, and though she would be a fool to think he'd mastered his dragon so quickly, maybe he had enough control to cuddle without painful consequences. But first, she needed to test him and perhaps mess with him a wee bit as payback for scaring her half to death and barreling into her full throttle.

"Father above, you have that devilish gleam in your eye." He wiped his mouth with a cloth napkin, his molten gaze leery.

She took a bite of her dinner, leisurely chewing and swallowing. "Why were you under the ice so long? Did you intend to give me a heart attack?"

"No. Never." He sat back, a trace of his earlier confusion flashing in his face. The single log in the fireplace shifted, emitting a series of pops.

Sara resumed eating; not giving him a chance to catch her smile. But when she dropped her eyes to avoid his intense stare, she must have looked left—one of her tells.

Blue energy sparked around him, the only warning before he smacked his hands on the tabletop, palms down. The bowls bounced, his fork jangling on the earthenware as Sara halted her fork midway to her mouth.

"Careful," they projected in unison.

She held his gaze as his warning rumbled through every inch of her, right down to her curling toes.

He leaned forward, sliding his hands across the table, closer to her, as if wanting to grab her. Faint scars from years of fighting laced his knuckles. Sara knew every nick, having memorized them on the rare occasion when she woke before he did, his arms wrapped around her. She fought to hold her neutral countenance. *"I'm still eating."* The nonchalance in her mental voice was not convincing.

"Eat faster."

A tingle of energy danced up and down her spine like deft fingers playing an instrument. *Damn him.* She gripped her fork tighter, determined to fully test his dragon restraint. With a casual one-shoulder shrug, she popped another ravioli into her mouth and chewed. Slowly.

The blues in his eyes swirled with the tension of a building storm about to let loose. *"Wicked little monster."*

"True. And you love me for it. So, what happened to you under the ice?"

He huffed, and Sara whiffed the distinct scent of his dragon smoke—a velvety mix of musk, ash, and spice. His hands relaxed, fingertips no longer threatening to carve the tabletop. "I was . . . distracted. Being in the water felt *amazing*." He cocked his head, aura radiating a wondrous silver. "Did you know there's a whole town at the bottom of the lake? Well, remnants of a town. Nothing magical down there. I checked."

Sara sat back, half-empty bowl before her. "Ian mentioned it to me once." Hundreds of years ago, local townspeople flooded the forest in an attempt to drive off their great-great-grandmother, Mary, because they feared her witchy powers. But Mary, along with the Cahill, Atwell, Walker, and Sullivan families, held her ground to protect the forest and its inherent energy. According to Ian and the Book, this was when the families were gifted magical powers and the stone wall barrier grew into place, protecting them all from normal and magical threats.

Sara sucked on a tooth, remembering a clear summer day when she peered over the edge of the rowboat and glimpsed the submerged town. Her memory skipped to hovering over the lake, ice thickening, trapping Thomas in the darkness below. A wave of fear washed over her. The many candles illuminating the cottage snuffed out.

Thomas drummed his fingers on the table, snapping her attention back to him, stopping her from unraveling. Through their bond, his magic nudged her. She met his eyes, his vertical pupils wide in the soft, dying glow of the fireplace. Now was not the time to indulge fear. Mother below, this was the first time they were truly alone, and Thomas hadn't so much as hiccupped a ball of flame since tackling her in the meadow. If he kept this up, tonight held spectacular promise. Her ears burned as she considered him, his infernal grin returning, his eyes boring into her. His hands slid closer.

"Wait," said Sara, staring back at him, at his ethereal eyes. *Not so fast, Dragon Boy.*

Thomas raised a brow at her.

"You could see in that black water?"

His grin grew wider. "Yes, Sara. I see everything." The tone of his voice was seductively low, reverberating in her core. "I see the mittens you drop to come to my aid. I see the trust in your eyes when my dragon races for you. And I see the game you are playing with me right now."

She froze. The log in the fireplace crumbled into embers with a satisfied hiss as she dragged her gaze to his hands and arms on the table. Not a hint of a talon from his fingernails nor a spike from his diamond-shaped tattoos. He had known all along that she'd been testing his control and had laid himself bare before her.

His aura flared so great she could see its luster from the corners of her eyes. "Are you prepared to lose?" he challenged, when really she knew he meant, *Are you prepared for me?*

What a silly question. "Does a bear sh—"

Her smartass response was smothered by Thomas's fierce kiss. She had no idea if he whished the plates away or if he physically swept the dining table. All she knew was that she was now sitting on the table, jean-clad legs wrapped around him as he stood before her, hands buried in her hair, lips pressed to hers while his tongue quite literally stole her breath.

Something within her ignited. It could have been their bond, her magic, her heart, or all of them combined. It didn't matter. All that mattered was her love for him. A love so strong it was all-consuming, infinite, capable of destroying and rebuilding entire worlds. The strength of her pull toward him was both blissful and devastating, a wickedly perfect balance of delicious contrasts similar to the honey-and-spice taste of him. And she needed more.

With a groan like the lake's dam giving way, she returned his claiming kiss, her hands fisting his T-shirt. Heat tore through her, a bonfire fueled by stars, as his magic filled her and hers poured into him—an endless, glorious circle of give and take.

Light-blue energy exploded from them with a *BOOM*, shaking the cottage's stone foundation.

Sara pulled back, eyes wide as their combined kinetic power caught every jostled item within the cottage, from the pots on the stove to the pine-scented pillow on the couch. They gently lowered everything back into place, all except the table she sat upon, which was definitely askew, hovering a cat's whisker above the stone floor.

Thomas tightened his grip, fingers digging into her sides. "Everything is fine," he ground out.

"We just rattled the *entire* cottage with one kiss." What else could their pent-up desire affect? She glanced at his forearms, muscles tense beneath his still circle brand and starry tattoos. No spikes.

A low thundering, like a storm on the cusp of torrential release, vibrated from him. "Then let's shake the forest to its core." The promise in his tone melted her insides.

Father above, they were *perfect* for one another. They'd also been *behaving* for far too long. If they destroyed the cottage, they could build a new one.

She pulled him flush against her front, feeling just how much he ached for her, and kissed him with the force of a lightning bolt.

Energy erupted, filling the cottage, their powers seeking, grabbing, entwining, drawing them closer and closer until their hearts beat as one, their souls wrapped together.

Thomas moaned a deep-chested rhapsody and whished them to the couch with Sara on top, straddling him.

"Are you sure you're up for this?" she mentally projected, slowing down their kiss and holding his forearms, dormant spikes like rivets of bone beneath his skin.

"Yes! Wait—no." Thomas jerked beneath her.

"What?" she panted, pulling back just in time to see his pupils widen and fix on something she couldn't see.

"It's Jin," he whispered, then vanished.

CHAPTER 5

S ARA FELL FACE first onto the couch, Thomas's scent and smoke curling around her. *Oof.* She reared back, darting her gaze about the empty, dark room, the fire having died out. *Jin? He's at the Global Council.* Had something gone wrong? Her heart raced, uneasiness replacing desire.

"Thomas?" she called out to the quiet room, before mentally yelling his name into the Aether.

"*Sara!*" His instant response had the muffled echo of being terribly far away.

"Where are you?"

Nothing.

With Thomas bound to Jin—a result of Jin shedding a dragon tear and saving Thomas's life—he was obligated to obey him. Jin hadn't seemed interested in ordering around Thomas before he left for the Global Council, so something must have changed. If the meeting had ended, Jin and Lethal would have both returned to Ware Woods, which meant the meeting must still be under way. What if it wasn't going well?

Sara threw open the cottage door and flew for the treehouse. As part dragon, Thomas was now something *other*—a magical with powers outside of a sacred site. Given this change, perhaps she could locate him through their bond and loop to him through the oak tree, the only soul tree in Ware Woods that could transport her anywhere she wished.

She rushed into the main room, past the furniture crafted by Caleb, and hovered on the far side with one hand on the oak's gnarled trunk. If Jin had summoned Thomas to the Council, she would follow despite Lethal's warning to stay away. No one took Thomas from her.

She closed her eyes and envisioned the many threads connecting her with Thomas. In the soft darkness of the Aether, the silken cords vibrated and glowed creamy pink, the same hue as the cherry blossoms in Jin's garden.

Okay, not at the Global Council. But why would Jin leave the Council and summon Thomas to the garden just when she and Thomas were *finally* having a moment?

Only one way to find out. She patted the oak and mentally made her request: *"Take me to Jin's garden."*

The thump of the oak's heartwood filled the treehouse, filled Sara's being. Satin darkness swirled around her like petals caught in an eddy before wholly engulfing her. Cool mist brushed her cheeks, and the scent of rain tickled her nose before the darkness lifted, leaving Sara in the center of the garden, directly between two fuming dragon shifters. Had they been in their dragon forms, she bet they would have been locking horns.

"What's going on?" she asked, her voice heavy with the calm worry her father, Charlie, used whenever he approached a dicey predicament.

Her stomach flipped as Thomas whished her to his side and gripped her hand as if he had no intention of ever letting go—something he had once promised her. Faint drifts of smoke snaked around him. She dragged her gaze to Jin, clad in a red wraparound tunic and black pants, hair pulled back into a severe bun, absolute fury on his face.

"What happened at the Council? Did they agree to help us?

Did you find Samson and Kira yet?" Her questions, her worries, spewed forth, Thomas's clasp her only restraint from witlessly shaking Jin for information.

Jin roared, quaking the garden's manicured trees and new teahouse pavilion—an exact duplicate of the one his anger had destroyed the last time they were all in his garden. "The meeting just started. And can you *imagine* how it reflects on me—on *all* of us—when I have to disappear because my scion cannot behave himself?"

Thomas snarled. "I can control my dragon."

"I know, otherwise you would have attacked me by now."

Sara's turn to snarl. "Then what's the bloody problem? You should be proud of him!" She hesitated at Jin's withering glare, at the grateful squeeze of Thomas's hand. Or was it a warning? Her mouth was always faster than her brain and common sense. "Wait. What do you mean '*the meeting just started*'? You've been gone almost a week."

Jin huffed smoke out his nostrils. "It takes a while for most of the Magi to *decide* to show up. And no, we haven't heard anything about Kira or Samson. The entire situation is far too delicate, and I cannot have any more distractions." He paused, his mouth a thin line as he leveled his gaze on Thomas. "Because you are choosing dangerous behaviors, you leave me no choice but to forbid you from desiring this witch."

Sara forced a chuckle. If she didn't laugh at his preposterous statement, she would explode. "You can't be serious."

The liquid fire in Jin's eyes was answer enough. Why in all the stars would he . . .

She tilted her head at him. "Are you *jealous*?"

"No." His response was too quick to be convincing. He dipped his chin and added, "Male dragons cannot desire female witches."

Thomas's aura flared pink with spots of sickly green and indignant indigo. Sara merely chuckled again before she said, "Jin, don't be ridiculous. We're bonded mates." Though the Global Council frowned on the mixing of factions, Sara had never thought Jin felt this way. Something else must be bothering him. She raised her brow in silent demand.

Jin sighed, and Sara swore she heard him murmur a plea to the Mother and Father. "When you asked me to save his life by shedding a tear, I warned you I did not know how it would affect your bonded future." He softened his gaze on Thomas. "You continue to surprise me, and while you have learned to control your dragon, there are other ways in which you can hurt her."

Thomas stiffened. His bristling shock flooded their bond, followed by the twisting pang of guilt and fear.

Sara opened her mouth to protest, but Jin held up his hands, silencing her. "Just behave for now, and we'll discuss it *after* the Global Council meeting." He dropped his hands, bringing down a ring of shadowy ash around Sara and Thomas, which promptly swallowed them.

After a quick yet significantly unpleasant moment of feeling sucked through a keyhole, Sara landed on the stone floor of the cottage's shower with Thomas beside her. And before she could berate Jin to all Nine Hells, cold water blasted them, soaking their clothes and drowning out her roar.

Sara shimmied under the covers of the four-poster bed, her sleep shirt—one of Thomas's tees—riding up as her bare legs slid through the cool sheets. Keeping her arms above the coverlet, she looked up at Thomas and patted the space beside her.

Thomas, clad in gray sweatpants and a white T-shirt, pursed his lips. When she patted his side of the bed more firmly, he took a step back, his gaze drifting to the bedroom's small table. On its wooden top lay the colorless fragments of a gemstone. Sara silently cursed herself for leaving it out. To her, it was a reminder of

Thomas's thoughtful love—a Winter Solstice gift of the amethyst ring she had admired while on their summer beach trip. Now, she realized it reminded Thomas of his dangerous dragon impulses. Shortly after they'd exchanged gifts—hers had been a sketch of his dragon—Thomas had huffed in surprised delight, releasing a cloud of flames, which incinerated the sketch and smelted the ring. Its silver band had evaporated, its stone fractured and leached of color.

A muscle ticked along his clenched jaw. "Now that you're settled, I'll sleep at the studio." Satiny smoke crept up his legs.

"If you leave this room, I will follow you, so lie down and we'll try to *sleep*."

His smoke halted, his body trembling, clearly at war with himself. "Ordering me is not helping our situation."

Sara's heart fluttered.

He held her stare for a long moment before extinguishing his smoke and easing onto the bed. He stretched out atop the covers, arms folded over his chest, hands fisted.

It took a conscious effort not to touch him. "This isn't forever. In fact, *technically*, Jin amended his command to behave until we can talk some sense into him after the Council meeting."

Thomas remained quiet.

Sara traced the quilted coverlet with her fingertips, considering Jin's pointed words: "*Male dragons cannot desire female witches.*" He had said desire, not love. And Jin had once confessed to her that the only love he knew was mating. *And* he had pulled Thomas away just before they . . .

Oh! Sara turned toward Thomas. "I think Jin is being over-protective. He has limited knowledge of love and probably has never heard of contraceptives. And he certainly has no idea that I can't have children." She snorted a laugh. "Why would he even care about that?"

Thomas rolled to his side, facing her, and gently gathered her hands in his. "I'm not sure." His gaze fixed on his thumbs as he brushed the tops of her knuckles—where the ring had briefly been placed. "You've told me you can't have kids, and I know *nothing* will change my love for you, but . . ." He inhaled deeply, chest swelling. "Gran told my folks that she saw us having a family far off in the future." Brilliant blue eyes met hers.

Sara was speechless. It was one thing for her grandmother to offhandedly mention such a premonition to her, but to tell Thomas's parents was brash—even for Gran. Which meant she believed it. Hells, Sara wanted to believe it too—that she and Thomas could have this gift of a family and long lives ahead of them. But she couldn't pin her hopes on what was likely a false premonition. There was too much stacked against her—in more ways than one. And though she knew Thomas, like most of the forest, humored Gran's forecasts, there was a hopeful lift in his expression. Her gut twisted. Just yesterday she'd overheard her loose-lips grandmother telling Ted that Ian would someday be High Witch. And if that premonition were true, Sara would certainly not be living a long life with Thomas and "*having a family far off in the future.*" No, Gran's second sight was hazier than a blanket of soupy fog.

"Relax," sighed Thomas, tucking back a lock of her hair. His fingers lingered on the sensitive curve of her ear before returning to her hand, this time with a tighter grip. "I'm grateful for any future with you, and I know we'll win our case with Jin." He flashed his overly confident lawyer-in-training grin and, without taking his eyes off her, kissed her palm. "But," he added with a sudden change in tone, "I'm concerned about Jin's warning that I can hurt you."

Her chest tightened as their bond pulled her closer to him, energy the palest of blues emanating between them. She placed a hand on his cheek, dusky stubble brushing her palm. "Thomas, you would never hurt me." Not intentionally.

"I know *I* wouldn't. But the Shadow Mother would." His face turned stricken, his aura a grievous shade of puce green.

Sharp-toothed worry bit through their bond. Like brimstone

briars, it squeezed and cut deep into Sara's heart. Thomas had learned to control his dragon, but how long did they have until the Shadow Mother controlled him? The very idea of that insidious entity latching her icy hooks into Thomas lit a fuse of rage inside Sara. Their grasp sizzled with her white energy. "I won't let that happen."

"I wish I could say the same," he whispered.

"It won't happen," she said more forcefully, her defiant tone pounding her statement into a promise. The treehouse shook as if in agreement. "Lethal and Jin are meeting with the Council right now. They *will* convince the three factions to unite against the Shadow Mother. With every magical working together to destroy her, she'll be gone so quick I bet Ware Woods won't even need to be involved. We can sit back and clink birch beers, safely keeping our unique little site a secret. All dragons will return to normal, leaving Jin busy overseeing flat-eyes. Kira and Samson will return. Ian's heart will finally be healed. And I'll find and slowly kill Brad. Then we can all live in glorious peace."

Thomas studied her, his vertical pupils thick slices in the dim light. "Peace sounds wonderful." With a kiss to her forehead, he completely diffused her fury.

"It will be." She snuggled into him, her head tucked under his chin, their hands enfolded beside her bloodstone. The treehouse swayed, gently rocking the bed. Sara closed her eyes, cherishing the steady rise and fall of Thomas's chest. Stars, her love for him was infinite, and she would do everything in her power to keep him safe.

As tired as she was, Sara couldn't stop her mind from wandering, from planning. With Thomas in control of his dragon and no longer an immediate threat to Ware Woods, she could double down on her efforts to find Kira and Samson. She had to. Since Jin had said no one at the Council had seen them, and since the Book had only revealed page after page of undulating shadows for Samson and a vague account of Kira's well-being, Sara needed a new method. Perhaps Ian had something of Kira's that she could use in a locating spell. Or maybe she needed to find Samson first. Because if Brad did indeed have Kira, Sara would need Samson's help to rescue her.

She sighed softly so as not to wake Thomas, who seemed to have instantly fallen asleep.

Father above, she hated to admit it, but she missed that wily witch. Samson's barbs pushed her buttons, and she still hadn't forgiven him for eating her finger, *but* he was incredibly knowledgeable and had successfully harbored the Hills children and his own daughter. Plus, his powerful presence alone drove Sara to do her best.

Pfft. Samson. While Sara may not have Gran's foresight, she knew when her inner compass was pointing her in the right direction.

She needed to find Samson first. But how?

"Whatever you're scheming can wait until morning." Thomas's sleepy voice distantly caressed her mind. And either he used dragon magic or the long day finally caught up with her, for a wave of soothing nothingness numbed her senses. She let it take her under, comforted by Thomas beside her, their magic wrapped tightly around them.

CHAPTER 6

H ER DREAMS FLOWED lazily, rippling and overlapping one into the next with occasional glimpses of Kira pacing a dark room, Lethal drawing their Death daggers, and Samson prowling amid smoky shadows. The thump of the oak's heartwood drummed around her, through her, strumming her being. Eventually, the images faded into the rosy glow of dawn. But instead of comforting dragon smoke, Sara smelled the tang of spent forest fire.

She wrinkled her nose. The watery remnants of sleep receded. The oak's heartbeat stopped. At the spongy give of soft earth beneath her feet and brisk air upon her skin, Sara opened her eyes. Instead of lying beside Thomas in the treehouse, she was standing on a patch of apple-green grass before a giant pine tree. Surrounding the island of grass were the snow-dusted remains of the Hills' forest.

"*Sara!*" Thomas's panicked voice shouted in her mind. He gave a firm yank on their bond. "*Did you just loop to the Hills' site?*"

She rubbed her eyes and surveyed the landscape again, just to be sure. "*Yeah. The oak must have looped me here.*"

A relieved huff. "*Give me a minute to grab some clothes and then I'll smoke to you.*"

"*You'll do no such thing! You need to stay in Ware Woods.*" Where it was safe. The last thing she wanted was for the Shadow

39

Mother to discover Thomas outside of Ware Woods and sink her claws into him.

The strands of their bond vibrated with his disapproving growl. *"Is this part of your midnight scheming?"*

Not exactly, but close enough. *"Yes. You, Dean, and Tobio are to keep watch on Ware Woods while I search for Samson and Kira. If either of us encounters trouble, we'll simply shout through the bond for help."*

Another growl, followed by an exasperated sigh. *"Next time, tell me your plan* before *you vanish from my arms."*

She winced at the hurt in his voice. It had been her intention to tell him when they woke. But it seemed the oak felt her role as High Witch and the urgency to find Samson trumped a sweet goodbye. *"I will. I'm sorry."*

Warmth flooded her through the bond. *"I know you meant to. Just be careful. Please."*

For his sake, she forced a grin. *"I'll be extra sneaky. No one will notice me,"* she projected with as much playful swagger as she could muster.

Thomas's responding grump faded as she rounded the tree and spotted Samson sitting on the grass, knees bent, with his head in his hands. When a surprised squeak escaped her, he bolted to his feet.

"Did you find Kira?" they asked at the same time.

"No," blurted Sara. "I thought it best to find you first. Have you been here the whole time?" She eyed the grassy island, surprisingly warm given the surrounding winter landscape, and the gargantuan tree, its trunk larger than Tobio's gray muscle car. *Why didn't the oak loop me here sooner?*

"I've been searching everywhere, probably too fast for you to find me."

Sara folded her arms. *"Did you just read my mind?"*

Samson casually brushed a blade of grass from his dark blue jacket, not deigning to answer. "I stopped here to restore my energy and properly mourn Motley."

Her stomach knotted at the name of Samson's right-hand Taker, the curiously kind henchman who'd fought back-to-back with Sara against two flat-eyed dragons under the Shadow Mother's control. The Taker who died, likely in this very spot, because Sara couldn't save him in time. She bit her lip to stop it from trembling.

Samson pierced her with his onyx eyes. "None of that," he said firmly, but not unkindly. "Wasn't your fault." Without skipping a beat, he snapped his fingers and Sara's nightshirt was replaced by her standard clothes: jeans, thermal shirt, black zippered jacket, and ass-kicking boots.

Sara yelped. She hadn't realized she'd only been wearing Thomas's shirt. When he said he'd grab some clothes, Thomas had meant *hers*, not his. *Too late to be embarrassed now.* She smoothed her hands down her torso. Samson even remembered her belt and folded knife from Gran. How did he do that?

Like an actor slipping into character, Samson's face relaxed into the smug grin she knew all too well. And in the taunting voice he *had* to know incensed her, he drawled, "Rookie, you really should dress your part for saving the world."

She spluttered, arms waving, open jacket flapping around her. "I'm not saving the world! I just wanted to find you and Kira."

His grin deepened and, with a crinkle of his nose, turned into a grimace. "Why do you stink of dragon?"

"I don't smell!" She took a cautious sniff of her jacket. Well, maybe a little musk-and-ashy. When he lifted a brow at her, she launched into a condensed explanation. "After the Shadow Mother slunk off, I killed Dorcas, and Thomas nearly died. Jin saved him, but now Thomas is part dragon."

Samson raised both brows.

"Oh, and Jin and Lethal are at the Global Council, asking the Magi to band together against the Shadow Mother. Lethal wouldn't let me help because they said if the factions can't agree to work together, then they won't be willing to accept how special

Ware Woods is." Sara gulped a breath, watching Samson's reaction to their dire status.

He pouted. "I wanted to kill Dorcas. I hope you made her suffer."

"Not nearly enough. She played me for a fool, letting me kill her so her death would further upset the balance and give the Shadow Mother more power. As if *that* wasn't bad enough, Brad swooped in and took both Makwa's and Dorcas's bloodstones. It had to have been planned, and I bet the bastard also took Kira."

Samson paled. His concern caused Sara to sway; she needed him smugly sneering and figuring a way out of this mess because she certainly had no idea what to do. His focus snapped to her, his concern taking on a fatherly furrow in his brow. "You look peakish. Sit and eat."

With a twirl of his hand, Sara found herself sitting on a blanket, a tray of tea, flatbreads, cheeses, and fruits before her. She swallowed her indignant yelp, suddenly hungry and grateful. "Heroes need sustenance," he scolded.

"I'm *not* a hero! I just want to destroy the Shadow Mother and live in peace." She tore off a chunk of bread and stuffed it in her mouth.

"Exactly," replied Samson, back to his devilish self.

Sara threw him a halfhearted glare before diving into the cheeses and fruits.

Ignoring her, he marched around the tree muttering, snippets of his self-dialogue drifting to Sara: "A dragon at the Council . . . No one takes Kira, unless . . . She's going to castrate me."

Sara choked at the last comment. Taking a swig of the strongest tea she'd ever tasted, she gazed up at the tree. It was far taller than the Lochton pine and appeared hundreds of years old, yet Samson must have just grown it along with the swath of grass. She squinted at the bright, surrounding snow. He had created the entire living memorial out of season. It must have taken a considerable amount of magic—not as much as the underground retreat he had created to hide the Hills children from the Shadow Mother, but far more than a simple twirl of his hands. Clearly, Samson mourned Motley, a Taker who had been confoundingly courteous and loyal. All other Takers Sara had ever encountered were little more than beasts, strung out on the very dark magic that poisoned them.

Her curiosity getting the better of her, Sara asked, "Motley wasn't a normal Taker, was he?"

Samson halted his ponderous pacing, his many bloodstones swinging outside of his jacket when moments before they had been concealed as usual. "No. He was a good man who'd been tricked by a dark witch. I killed the dark witch and let Motley follow me. I even gave him a little of my magic, which made him more powerful than your average Taker."

Sara stopped chewing. "You can gift magic?" Her mind spun. Brad had said the Shadow Mother *gave* him everything he always wanted. And when Ian had explained how Ware Woods was formed, he said the families had been *gifted* magic. This seemed important, though she couldn't put her finger on why.

"Yes. But it's rarely done. I've only done it once, to save Motley's life. And even then, it was a scant amount."

"Selfish much?" The fact did not escape her that Samson hadn't given her any of his power when she'd mistakenly drained herself and gone into magical stasis for weeks. Maybe she was a tad jealous but then again, she hadn't been dying. Perhaps giving away magic was only for extreme situations.

Samson tugged at his cuffs. "I prefer the term *conservative*." He gazed upon the snowy wasteland for a heavy moment, one of his hands grasping the sole red bloodstone around his neck. "Yet I'd give it all up to ensure Kira's safety."

"Well, let's go find her." Sara sprang to her feet, done inhaling her meal and ready for action.

He released his red bloodstone and clapped his hands together once. "Good, you're finally finished. You eat slower than a bear without teeth. But there's no '*us*' on this venture. Given all you've told me, I'm paying an overdue visit to the Council. Kira is less at risk if I reveal exactly who she is. And you cannot come because Lethal wisely told you to stay far, far away."

Sara scowled. She desperately wanted to check out the Global Council, observe the Magi from other sacred sites, and witness firsthand their reaction to Lethal and Jin's petition to unite against the Shadow Mother. Surely there was no harm in popping in and being a bystander at the back of their crowd. They wouldn't know she was from Ware Woods. She'd be so quiet they wouldn't know she was there at all, and now was her best opportunity. "I'm sure the Council will be too occupied with you to even notice me."

"Doubtful." Samson jangled his bloodstones and combed a hand through his wavy, shoulder-length hair. He seemed nervous. All the more reason for her to tag along, on the off chance he actually needed her help. So when he twirled his hands and smoky shadows enveloped his tall form, Sara lunged for him.

CHAPTER 7

SARA DUG HER nine fingers into the front of Samson's wool jacket, shadows pulling her in all directions, threatening to transport her to the four corners of the world. *Maybe this wasn't such a good idea.* She looked up at him, meeting his wide eyes.

"Must you always be so reckless? Don't answer that. Just stay quiet and don't move." He shoved her behind him. The shadows stopped pulling and settled over Samson in the form of a cape, concealing Sara against his back as they landed on supple earth. Through the cape's undulating smoky curls, Sara gawked at the surrounding spacious dome composed of the thick branches, trunks, and dripping roots of an enormous banyan tree.

Like the main attraction at a one-ring circus, Sara and Samson stood center stage.

She pressed against him, barely breathing while hoping his smoke magic worked the same as a one-way mirror, keeping her hidden from the dozens of Magi staring at them. Their shrewd gazes and blazing auras reminded Sara of owls with razor-sharp beaks and talons, silently waiting to pounce.

Similar to birds of prey, many of the Magi perched directly overhead among the banyan's massive, smooth, gray, lateral branches. And where the dripping roots and trunks formed a ring around the earthen arena, more Magi reclined in bulbous, smooth-barked chairs.

"Sara?" Thomas's voice rang in her head. *"Where did you go now? I can sense you through the bond, but I can't locate you."*

"I'm with Samson at the Global Council," she projected, her voice calm, as if this had been her plan all along.

A disgruntled huff. *"Okay, first, I'm glad you found Samson. And second, why are you at the Council? Did they agree to help us?"*

"I'm not sure yet." She waved at the Magi peering down at her and Samson, their stares a mix of despisal, fury, and fear. Nothing. She stuck out her tongue, making the face that always sent Ian into giggles. Still nothing. Thank the Mother they couldn't see through Samson's shadows.

"So why are you there?" Thomas's admonitory tone had the familiar sting of his father—Kane.

"I need to see this Council for myself. To know who'll fight with us against the Shadow Mother." That was plausible and much better than *I impulsively tagged along with Samson.* She swallowed, her back flush against Samson, her arms tucked in, hands pressed tightly to her chest, trying to shrink as small as possible. Hopefully these intense Magi, radiating confidence and deadly magic, were on their side. *"Don't worry. No one can see me. Samson and I will leave as soon as he asks them about Kira."* She threw up her mental shield, blocking him out of her head. Later, she'd deal with his frustration; right now, she needed to focus on remaining hidden and not getting herself killed for imprudence.

Samson expanded, somehow growing bigger, taller, inky black tendrils unfurling from the edges of his cape. Power radiated from him, shaking Sara and the earth beneath her feet to the point soil levitated off the ground. A few Magi leaned back. One Magus—a female with glowing-umber skin and a fanged grin that probably stopped hearts right before she ate them—inclined forward. All regarded him warily.

From somewhere in front of Samson, a voice dripping with disdain and arrogance demanded, "Where have you been?"

Sara stiffened. She knew that voice, beautifully smooth and sharp like cut glass. Lethal.

"Here, there, everywhere," teased Samson, his tendrils jutting in all directions. "I've had no reason to attend for quite some time. *But*, drama lover that I am, I couldn't resist seeing a dragon at the Global Council."

Murmurs fluttered among the Magi.

Sara frowned. *What game is he playing?*

"Then take your seat," Lethal commanded, each word a bite.

Shit. There was no way Samson could move, much less sit, without exposing her.

"Ah," drawled Samson with all the surety of a ringmaster extraordinaire, "but there's another reason I dropped in, and I'd rather remain standing as the center of attention for the exciting announcement I have to share." He raised his arms, an oracle addressing his flock.

In spite of his magical strength and his flippant tone, pressed against him as she was, Sara felt a faint shudder.

"I'm a proud poppa," he exclaimed.

Harsh whispers peppered with a few snorts of disbelief rolled through the assembly. From someone out of Sara's sight, a gruff laugh followed by: "What witch would be brazen enough to raise your spawn?"

Samson chuckled, deftly turning the jab into a compliment. "None. I raised her myself. She is a beautifully vicious creature and, like most teens, prone to scampering off with her own wicked agenda. As a model parent, I'm on the hunt to reel her in. So"—he paused, and Sara visualized his signature sneer growing in tandem with his spreading shadows—"if anyone has seen or heard of a murderously darling half-vampire, half-witch who goes by the name Kira, now is the time to tell me."

The heart-stoppingly stunning vampire gasped, her hand flying to her décolletage, while the rest of the Council exploded with furious shouts.

"Half-breed!"

"Impossible!"

"Halflings are to be exterminated!"

Sara cringed. Though Lethal had told her a mixing of factions was despised, this level of hatred and ignorance was far worse than she'd feared.

"Make no mistake," thundered Samson, silencing the crowd, "I'm not telling you this for her protection. I'm telling you this for *your* protection." In a lower, obsequious voice, he said, "Tell me, Kahn, why does your striking face have an unhealing wound?"

From the branches before Samson, out of Sara's sight, boomed the gruff voice. "No half-breed did this. They are powerless abominations." A war cry of a growl sprang and landed to Sara's left. The ground quaked and the entire Council tree wavered. Magi grabbed the banyan's sleek branches and roots to steady themselves.

Sara's scalp prickled, her magic coating her with protective white flames in response to the threatening witch beside her. He was a mountain of a warrior, long hair tangling with a thick beard, metal breastplate magnifying his already hulking chest. A nasty cut oozed from his reddened forehead. His flinty eyes fixed on Samson, his clenched fists flickering with black energy. Dark witch.

From beneath the smoky cloak, Sara reflexively shoved a wave of power at him. It seemed time stood still, giving her a pulse-pounding moment to reflect on what was either a good decision or a horrible, irrevocable mistake. All too soon, the moment ended. And the unexpected happened.

Samson's tendrils latched on to her magical outburst, pulling it back and crushing it in an explosion of sparks as he spun to the side, taking his now ribboned cloak of shadows with him.

Before Sara could blink, much less throw another round of energy, Lethal loomed before her, holding a Death dagger to her throat. Surprise quivered through her, the slight movement causing her neck to burn as the blade nicked her skin. The vampire's distinct scent of frankincense choked her sinuses, their icy eyes searing her with a silent reprimand.

Sara dared not breathe as Lethal placed their perfect lips to her ear. "This tree is neutral territory. Do not force me to make an example of you. Understood?"

Her body flushed with a mix of fear at the promise in their voice, embarrassment at being a newbie and violating Council protocol, and guilt at defying Lethal's warning to stay away. She guttered the magic flickering around her and blinked her compliance, not daring to utter the faintest of curse words. Remaining still, she raked her gaze past the dark witch seething with contempt, past the Magi watching with rapt attention and, with Samson no longer blocking her view, spotted Jin on the far side of the open arena. Though he was in his human form, the red dragon's elysian eyes glowed with ire.

Wonderful. She had managed to piss off both Lethal and Jin with her unexpected visit. She fought the urge to grimace.

Unlike the seated Magi, Jin stood at the base of the banyan's main trunk. Beside him towered a high-backed throne of twisted roots. Sara's eyes widened at the vacant seat. Leaning against the side of the righteous chair rested Kindness, Lethal's sword, in its scabbard.

Never trust a vampire. Lethal's number one rule.

Father above. Lethal presided over the Global Council. And she had just directly disobeyed them. A bead of sweat traced the side of her face.

"Calm yourself," Lethal whispered for only Sara to hear. "I'm on your side." The Death dagger pressed against her throat eased, its burning cold relenting its torment. Sara sucked in air, grateful yet unsure what to do next. Apologize and leave? Surely no one here knew who she was. No harm, no foul. She could just—

"Samson," scolded a voice from overhead.

Sara snapped her focus to the gorgeous vampire leaning from

a branch, the cleavage above her slinky red dress positioned as precariously as she.

"Amira." Samson played out her name like a fine instrument and gifted her a wink. "You look ravishing as usual."

She cocked a brow at him, her grin spreading with the slow deadly heat of lava about to swallow a trapped victim. "You said Lethal killed the child." Even her flowery accent was alluring.

Samson shrugged one shoulder. "I fibbed."

Now would be a *really* good time to disappear, but this conversation riveted Sara in a grisly train-wreck kind of way, and there was no shimmery hum of the banyan tree to throw herself at and loop back to Ware Woods. She was stuck at the end of Lethal's dagger until Samson finished his exchange and used his shadows to loop them both away.

Lethal grunted. Without lowering their dagger or, unfortunately, taking their attention away from Sara, they said, "You framed me?"

"I merely leaned into your sanguineous reputation."

Amusement flashed in Lethal's gray eyes, perceptible due only to Sara's terrifying proximity.

The tree rustled, a fresh wave of murmurs rippling among the Magi.

"Enough!" bellowed the dark warrior witch—Kahn. He clapped his metal vambraces together, the resulting clang assaulting Sara's ears. Samson chuckled while Lethal remained a statue of indifference, their attention still on Sara as if she were the greater threat.

"Lethal, you neglected to tell us this Kira is a half-breed," Kahn roared. "And I bet the supposed threat of the Shadow Mother has everything to do with this *girl*." He jabbed a finger at Sara as he spat his last word, letting it hit her in the face.

Anger tore through Sara, but before she could do something truly stupid, she felt the reminding burn of the dagger at her throat. She exchanged furious glares with Lethal.

The vampire gently shook their golden head at her before

declaring, loud enough for everyone to hear, "Mind your tongue before I remove it, Kahn. I act in the Council's best interests. Now take your seat so the High Witch of Ware Woods can explain herself and what she knows about the Shadow Mother."

Kahn jerked back, gaze fixed on Sara. A glint of fear in his dark eyes betrayed his growly confidence. Without a word, he flew to the branches, which were now quaking, the entire Council in such an uproar Sara could barely hear Lethal's warning: "You are surrounded by light, dark, and all shades of gray. Proclivities mean nothing because everyone here wants the same thing—power. And what everyone here fears is power. Be careful how you wield yours." A blur of movement, and Lethal was reclining on their throne. To their right, Jin folded his arms, an ashy semblance of a tail lashing behind him.

Crap. Gone was her chance to disappear with Samson. She touched her hand to her neck, gently probing her sticky skin. Just a scratch. Given Lethal's advice and the many eyes on her, Sara decided against healing it. And instead of scowling at the arrogant full-of-secrets vampire, she inhaled to the slow count of three. *Think.*

Okay, maybe this wasn't so bad. As her optimistic father would say, here was a splendid opportunity to tell everyone about the Shadow Mother. Smart Magi that they were, of course they would band together and defeat her, and Sara would retreat into anonymity, keeping Ware Woods' power a secret.

She lifted her chin and took in the agitated Council seated around the perimeter of the arena and hanging from the canopy overhead. Sharp-grinned vampires, shimmering witches, and amber-eyed shifters were tightly clustered by faction. And except for the translucent dark flames around Kahn and a male Elder Vampire with villainous handlebar eyebrows, it was impossible to tell who was morally light, dark, or prone to gray. Not a black-stained hand in the group because none of these quarreling Magi were poisoned. They freely chose their actions.

The bloodstone hidden beneath her thermal shirt thumped against her breastbone in time with her brain finally processing Lethal's warning. Light, dark, or gray, it didn't matter. Power radiated off each and every member. They wanted and feared power. All Sara wanted was peace. And quiet. *Yeesh, when would they stop arguing?*

Since she couldn't shout over the ruckus, she fidgeted and glanced at Samson, hoping for a smug smile of encouragement. At least she wasn't completely alone in the center of the arena.

"Thanks for taking the heat off my little announcement." His grin didn't meet his eyes. And instead of cracking another joke like she needed him to, his forehead puckered in the same worried manner as her Uncle Ted. "Keep your chin up, don't show any magic, and Father above, do not say or do anything rash."

Sara groaned. All Hells, this was going to be sudden-death–level hard.

CHAPTER 8

AFTER FAR TOO many minutes of excruciating awkwardness, most of the shouting died down enough to make out what the Magi were saying.

"Inconceivable!"

Sara whirled for the source. *What is? Me or the Shadow Mother?*

"She is too young to be a High Witch. Even if she has any magic, she wouldn't know what to do with it. She is incapable."

Partially true.

"Ware Woods has always been a problem. As their High Witch, *she* is a problem."

Okay, definitely not true. Is it?

"Hush now, the lot of you. It's a wonder we can ever get anything done to maintain the balance," stated a clear, pleasant voice. A branch, creaking with growth, extended into the central open space. Glossy leaves at the tips of its twiggy ends waved at Sara. Seated along the branch, her long skirts draping over the edge, perched a tan-skinned woman. Two long braids of thick white hair woven with flowers of all colors cascaded into her lap. "What is your name?" asked the woman. Faint wrinkles feathered from the corners of her hazel eyes as she smiled down at Sara. No fangs pressed into her lips, and her scent was distinctly floral. Soft orbs of magic flitted around her like moths drawn to a flame. A High Witch.

The unexpected kindness lessened some of Sara's tension, her face softening in the woman's glow. "Sara Lochton." To her relief, her voice rang proud and clear throughout the banyan.

A new breeze of whispers drifted among the Magi. "Lochton . . ."

The woman's smile deepened. "Lethal tells us of a threat to all magicals. They say we must work together—something we have never done before—to defeat this threat and protect the balance. I think you know how to achieve this. So I must ask, why didn't you willingly beseech the Council on this matter and offer to lead this crusade?"

For a moment, Sara stood entranced by the witch's melodious voice—until her words sank in. Sara stepped back, head swiveling to take in the separately clustered Magi and their expectant faces. Even within the safety of the Council tree, they were rigidly divided. Sara had no experience or desire to lead anything, much less a fractured group of highly suspicious and dangerous magicals. And she certainly had no idea *exactly* how to defeat the Shadow Mother. That's what this Global Council was supposed to do for her. Not the other way around. A memory of Caleb tossing a raw egg at her in the Cahill barn popped into her mind. "*Think fast,*" he'd sung. She had dropped that egg.

Sara shook her head. "I—I'm just High Witch of Ware Woods. I'm not capable of leading a *crusade* and mending centuries-old hate and mistrust."

Samson chuckled again. Under his breath, he said, "Oh, I think you are."

She threw him a scowl, equal parts annoyed at his casualness and anxious for his help in digging her out of this mess.

To Sara's surprise, he rushed to her side. But her flash of relief dissolved into full annoyance when he patted her shoulder, whispered, "You're doing a great job of letting them think you're harmless," and flew into the branches. The angry-browed Elder Vampire hissed as Samson alighted beside Amira, a seductive smirk on her painted lips.

Sara fisted her four-fingered hand at her side. Assuming she survived this inquisition, she would rip into Samson later for leaving her completely alone in the arena. Some mentor he was.

The kindly High Witch overhead hummed in thought. "Start with explaining what you know of the Shadow Mother."

Finally, a request Sara could answer. She'd have to be careful not to reveal Ware Woods' unique power, including the shield Ian and the Hills children created to drive away the Shadow Mother. And of course, she couldn't tell them about killing Dorcas and further upsetting the magical balance. That mistake was firmly on her conscience and not something she wanted to reflect on Ware Woods. To protect everyone, she had to secure the Council's aid in defeating the Shadow Mother. Everything hinged on Sara convincing them to believe her.

Sara swallowed around the knot in her throat. "She thrives on discord and deceit. And she has infected flat-eyed dragons. They are now under her control."

"Impossible!" snarled an amber-eyed Magi, his broad shoulders draped with a mane of animal pelts. Definite Alpha Shifter.

"It's true. She destroyed the Hills site and attacked Ware Woods. We needed Jin's help to fight her off. She is growing stronger every day and plans to control elysian-eyed dragons and kill us all. We must work together to defeat her, to protect our sacred sites, and to save the dragons." *To save Thomas. To save everyone I love.*

"You spout lies," yelled the Elder Vampire who had hissed at Samson. "The Shadow Mother does not attack magicals, and if she is taking over dragons, she is doing us a favor. It has been a reprieve to see so few dragons lately. Why would we want to save the dragons who kill us? In fact, this very Council was formed to help us avoid dragons. One should not even be in this sacred space." He shot a poisonous look at Jin.

"Dragons keep the peace," thundered Jin, gold-tipped spikes protruding through the sleeves of his tunic. "We only kill when necessary. Without us, you would destroy one another. Do you dare question the Mother's rules?" His pulsating hiss rocked the banyan. Magi gripped their smooth-bark seats, snarls on more than half of their faces.

"Of course not," bellowed a shifter seated at ground level. His rooted chair groaned as his massive hands clutched the knobby arms. Sara retreated a step, studying him. This Alpha Shifter with silver locs, ebony skin, and blazing eyes reminded her of Dean. Yet, unlike Dean's warm, friendly demeanor, this Alpha exuded a cold, ruthless, predatory temper. "Perhaps this is a trick, and the Mother is testing us. She divided us into factions and gave us separate sacred sites. Why would she want us to work together now?" He paused, reveling in the many grunts of agreement. "If the Shadow Mother is stirring, it is because of Ware Woods. She attacked Ware Woods, not any of us. We should let her *purge* the site. Surely this will correct the current imbalance. I'll even help her rid us of the abomination."

Oh no.

Sara felt the blood drain from her face. *Oh no no no. This cannot be happening.* She had made a grievous error in appearing before this Council. "No! You don't under—" Her plea died as Lethal rose from their throne with murder in their glimmering gray eyes.

In a tone that froze the marrow of Sara's bones, Lethal slowly stated, "Ware Woods will be left alone. The Global Council agreed to this long ago."

The Alpha Shifter pounded a fist on the arm of his chair, chunks of bark spraying in all directions. "And yet you went. And you are not telling us what you witnessed." He pointed a claw-tipped finger at Lethal. "The great Death Vampire either has a weakness for atrocities, or they are hiding something for their own gain."

And before Sara could rush to Lethal and beg for a recess—for a moment to gather her splattered thoughts and form a plan to redirect the disastrous proceedings—her bloodstone thumped a warning.

The banyan tree quaked. Everyone stilled.

From behind Sara came a frigid gust. It slammed into her back, icing the nape of her neck and churning her silvery-gray hair. She spun, gasping with the rest of the Council as black smoky chains snaked along the ground at the edge of the arena. The chains wove through a section of vertical roots, bending and twisting the wood into a blackened chair equal in size to Lethal's.

The Elder Vampires to the right of the disturbance hissed while the Alpha Shifters to the left growled and bared their teeth. The mass of ashy chains contracted upon itself and disappeared, revealing Brad on the chair, a smirk on his punchable face.

Fury ignited within Sara. Blazing hot witch fire sprang up around her, the piercing snaps a sharp contrast to the gentle energy that usually sizzled in her palms. Flames burnt her skin and obscured her view as she struggled to gain enough control to launch them in Brad's direction.

"There is NO magic here!" roared Lethal, and either their admonishment broke her focus or they compelled her, for Sara's flames vanished.

From the branches overhead came whisperings of, "Witch fire."

Sara seethed at Brad and at her slipup of showing magic. And not just any magic, but rare and difficult-to-control witch fire. She glanced up at Samson for any hint as to what to do next, but his gaze was pinned on Brad. The faint outline of ashy tendrils writhed around Samson, unquestionably readying to crush the stained witch like the cockroach he was. On the far side of the arena, Jin paced, a line of golden dragon spikes jutting through the back of his tunic.

Lethal demanded, "How did you find us?"

Instead of immediately responding, Brad reclined, resting his head on the high back, spreading his legs to physically take up as much space as possible. *Disgusting.* He wore a sleeveless, studded leather tunic, proudly displaying the black ink that coated his hands and snaked up his forearms. "One of your own told me."

Brad tapped the side of his head before gesturing at the branches above—at Kahn. The dark witch scowled, facial muscles straining with contempt, his wound oozing.

Lethal pointed a dagger at Kahn. "I'll deal with you later." In a smooth arc, the vampire leveled their weapon at Brad. "I assume you have something important to say on behalf of the Shadow Mother. Speak and leave."

Brad grinned. "Gladly." He swept a stained hand through the air, addressing the entire Council. "Her Dark Glory has risen. She seeks to correct the wrongs caused by Ware Woods. Anyone helping Ware Woods, or its High Witch, will be eliminated along with them."

Gasps and harsh whispers erupted among the Magi.

"Liar!" shouted Sara. "She wants to destroy us all!"

Brad inclined forward. "Tell them the truth, Sara. Tell them how you killed two powerful witches so you could be High Witch. Tell them it's *you* who's upset the balance."

Sara stumbled back as if struck by Brad's ink-black hand. She *had* killed two witches and played right into Dorcas's scheme to upset the balance. It was her fault. And this Council meeting, gone horribly wrong, was *exactly* what the Shadow Mother wanted. More discord and imbalance so she could grow stronger—and wipe them all out.

The impulse to vomit and disappear howled at Sara, but she stayed her ground, jaw clenched. While she had never intended to be High Witch, he was right about everything else. Damn it.

The banyan tree buzzed, the Magi arguing and stirring like angry bees.

Triumph shone in Brad's red-tinted eyes. He rose, his chair disintegrating into ash as he stepped toward Sara.

Her bloodstone pulsed. *Think! What can I say to turn this around? To fix—*

All rational thoughts ceased as Brad took another step closer.

She faced him, her blood boiling. Clever words would never stop him or the Shadow Mother. And since Sara had already ruined her opportunity to gain the Global Council's favor, she unleashed the rage she kept on a short leash. Let the Magi have their spectacle. Magic may be forbidden in the banyan, but physical violence was all she needed to end Brad. Kane had taught her to be ruthless with both magic and hand-to-hand combat. Indeed, she'd once nearly gouged out Brad's eyes. This time, she'd make him confess where to find Kira; *then* she'd crush his windpipe and watch the smirk melt from his face.

She tightened her fists, readying to rush at him. "You bastard! I'm going to kill *you* next. Where's Kira?" A tooth cracked in her clenched jaw.

He sneered, shadows gathering behind him. "Come at me and find out."

Sara flew at him, her skin burning with anger and suppressed witch fire. But instead of her fists connecting with his soft neck, she was met with a mass of biting-cold black chains. They wrapped around her, halting her advance, suffocating her physically and magically.

Time slowed, every scrap of this appalling moment being committed to memory. Another irrevocable mistake.

He had baited her, had wanted her to come to him, had counted on her recklessness. Regret seized Sara, paralyzing her far deeper than Brad's numbing chains of ice.

Distantly, she felt Samson's smoke curl around her ankle, its hold tenuous, slipping. And through the Magi's uproar, she heard the sing of Lethal unsheathing Kindness. Brad yanked her to him, away from Samson and Lethal, headbutting her in the face before everything fell dark.

CHAPTER 9

PAIN THROBBED IN Sara's head, a relentless war drum beating her into consciousness. She tried burrowing back into oblivion. Anything was better than this pain, but the sound of labored breathing ratcheted her heart rate, dragging her awake. Acutely, painfully awake. She strained to suck in air through what felt like a wet towel over her nose and realized it was her own gasps grating on her nerves.

Sara squinted, fighting through mental haziness to focus on her surroundings and remember what the Hells had happened to her. Given the agony stabbing the front of her face and considering she could only breathe through her mouth, her nose was undeniably busted. And given the leering bastard before her, Brad had caused her current Hell. *Ah yes, the headbutt.*

She tried to move, to throw an atomic bomb of energy at him, but her arms were restrained across her chest, overlapping as though she were prone in a coffin. Yet she was upright, ashy black chains wrapped around her torso from her shoulders to her knees, and excruciatingly alive. Freaking fabulous. *Why can't I heal myself?* The magical warmth that normally flooded her veins was gone, replaced by the draining cold of the chains. *"Thomas?"* she called into the Aether. Nothing beyond hollow darkness. She pulled on their bond and found the invisible strands taut and unyielding, frozen in place.

Her gaze darted, taking in the square concrete room, the caged fluorescent lights overhead, the corroded metal door behind Brad, and the rust stains on the floor. At least, she hoped they were rust and not bygone puddles of something else. Panic squeezed her. Had Kira been imprisoned in this room? Or was she suffering a similar fate in a separate cell? Sara wiggled, her feet kicking at nothing as she swayed in the air. Her head pressed against the ashy chain suspending her, a network of fine roots connecting it to the low ceiling.

"Squirm all you want. I enjoy it." Brad's eyes glowed red.

Sara instantly stopped. "You son of a—" Her body froze when he held up his palm, magically silencing her. *BITCH!* she internally roared.

He laughed something wet and raspy. "I'll give you plenty of time to cry and beg later. Assuming you make the right choice."

Sara held his stare, hoping he felt her visual daggers twist in his rotten soul.

"Blink once if you wish to be delivered to the Shadow Mother, bound and frozen. She will slowly feed on you and your bloodstone, using your energy to destroy Ware Woods. Of course, she'll force you to watch her destruction before killing you too. Or, blink twice if you wish to help me destroy her. I'll even let you keep your bloodstone." His slippery grin triggered a deafening clang from her internal bullshit detector.

Crap. The first option definitely sucked, and the second offer, which was a surprise, reeked of deceit. *Think.* If she blinked once, there was the infinitesimal chance she could overpower the Shadow Mother on her own. After all, she had pushed back at the Shadow Mother with witch fire once before. But Sara would need all of her power as well as a magical miracle to summon and control enough witch fire to end her, which would be impossible in her current trussed-up state.

Her eyes stung, the need to blink building as she studied his face. A speckle of black stain marred one corner of his smug mouth. Poison. The same fatal infection the Shadow Mother had once gifted Samson. Did Brad know she had healed Samson, or did he seek to destroy the Shadow Mother to cure himself?

His lecherous grin deepened while he waited for her response, her eyes now watering. *Bastard.* Regardless of his reason for turning on the evil hand that fed him, he intended to use Sara as a weapon. *His* weapon. And, gluttonous bloodsucking tick that he was, he wouldn't stop at destroying just the Shadow Mother. Like the Global Council, Brad wanted power and would do anything for it.

But choosing to help Brad put him on her side of the chessboard and, since she'd pissed off the entire Global Council, she needed as many magicals on her side—no matter how dark—to face the Shadow Mother. The fact that Brad hadn't already taken her bloodstone was a good sign. She hoped.

Fine. Let him think he could use her. Helping him was a craptastic option and barely a shade preferable to being served up to the Shadow Mother. She blinked once. Twice.

"Good choice, pet."

Her stomach curdled at the lustful dominance in his voice.

Brad approached and pressed his thick index finger into her nose. Stars of pain exploded inside her head. If she could move just a fraction, she'd bite off his finger and rip out his throat. "If you behave, I might fix that." He grabbed a fistful of her hair, leaned in, and inhaled deeply. "Remember when I took care of you in the hospital and promised we would have fun together?"

Sara's heart stuttered. He was deranged. She had been at a mental ward where she'd been drugged and held against her will. He'd been a predatory orderly. Had he forgotten how she nearly killed him? Or was this a sadistic trick?

Perhaps she should have chosen the Shadow Mother.

He yanked Sara's hair, sending a fresh stab of torment through her skull. "But first, we're gonna play a game where I keep you as my lovely secret until the Shadow Mother gets rid of *all* the elysian-eyed dragons. They're more trouble than they're worth. Then, you'll help me destroy the Shadow Mother and that asshole goldilocks vampire, leaving me in charge of the Global Council and all magicals. If you step out of line"—he ran his finger down her cheek—"I'll take your bloodstone and set every flat-eyed dragon on Ware Woods. Even if the barrier holds, their fire will cook the forest and everyone in it. Blink once if I've made myself perfectly clear."

The audacity to think he could control her for long! Sara silently screamed into the Aether—and blinked.

She definitely should have chosen the Shadow Mother.

Brad released her and stepped back, satisfied like a rat who'd eaten a whole wheel of cheese. Little did he know the cheese was laced with poison. Sara's rage flared. For threatening to let the Shadow Mother end all elysian-eyed dragons—including Thomas. For threatening to cook Ware Woods, for plotting against Lethal and the Global Council, and for calling her *pet*, she would kill him. No way in All Hells would she help Brad. And while they shared a common goal, Sara could never trust him, not even as her sacrificial pawn.

He laughed again. "I'll give you time to cool off while I tend to other matters. And don't ruin anymore of your pretty little face trying to escape. Only shadow magic works down here." Clearly rubbing her bloody nose in her crappy situation, a plume of dark smoke expanded around Brad, then clapped together, swallowing him. The magical hold on Sara released, the rotten scent of sulfur permeating her swollen nose.

Sara closed her eyes, internally grasping to calm herself. She envisioned her mother's encouraging spirit and inhaled for the slow count of three, held it for three more, and released. Her body went limp, her head hanging forward, defeated.

What a monstrous mess she had created. By killing Makwa and Dorcas, she'd upset the magical balance, and instead of letting Lethal and Jin gain the Global Council's support, her foolish curiosity had upset the apple cart. Maybe that was putting it too lightly. *Detonated* the apple cart, rather. Blew it sky high. Thanks to her outburst, the Magi were fighting among themselves and turning against Lethal and Jin. Sara had screwed their chance of banding together to defeat the Shadow Mother. Plus, *everyone* knew she was at fault and that Ware Woods was hiding something. Oh, and she was suspended in Brad's rank prison with a massively painful broken nose.

She blew out her frustrations, spitting drool and blood. The droplets sizzled when they hit the chains wrapped around her chest.

But, she mused, Brad's bold presence at the Council, coupled with his confirmation of the Shadow Mother's rising power and his flagrant use of magic to abduct her, surely would give the Magi pause to consider her side of the story. And even before Brad had arrived, the kind High Witch with white braids had asked Sara if she were willing to lead a crusade against the Shadow Mother. She wouldn't have asked if she hadn't believed in Sara. Perhaps other Magi felt the same.

Sara sagged in her bindings. The Global Council had been her hope for defeating the Shadow Mother. They were older, wiser, experienced Magi, a blend of vampires, shifters, and witches, who simply needed to come together and destroy the evil imperiling them all. That was what was supposed to happen. Not them arguing over Ware Woods, threatening to join the Shadow Mother, and suggesting Sara lead a crusade. She had barely come into her own powers, and making mistakes seemed to be her specialty. How could she possibly lead them against the Shadow Mother? Especially when most of them believed *she* was the problem.

And maybe Sara was.

She sighed. The Global Council was not going to swoop in and save the day. But it didn't matter. To save Ware Woods, she would face the Shadow Mother alone if she had to. And if saving

Ware Woods meant saving the magical world and the normal world as well, Sara would do that too. She would find a way to fix her mess—or die trying. Hopefully there were a few magicals brave or heedless enough to join her. Though the Shadow Mother wouldn't stand a chance if everyone fought against her, perhaps a few open-minded Magi and all of Ware Woods would be enough to defeat her. It would have to be. First, however, Sara needed to free herself.

CHAPTER 10

Sara cracked open her eyes, wincing at the effort, and studied the concrete room. Given the heavy air and Brad's *"down here"* comment, she guessed it was a bunker. Its thick, unnatural walls were somehow blocking her magic and communication with Thomas, who was probably beside himself. She had to escape and get back to him, back to Ware Woods, before the Shadow Mother grew any stronger and attacked elysian-eyed dragons. And before Brad returned to play.

Without considering the consequences, she threw her head back against the chain that suspended her and immediately cursed in pain, then shouted in glee as some of the fine roots grafting the chain to the ceiling lost their grip. Apparently, even shadow magic had its limits against unnatural surfaces. Thank the Father, Brad was a moron.

She swung herself, feet kicking dead air in a vain attempt to control her back-and-forth direction while jerking her body. The ashy chain stretched and groaned. A few more jerks and the fibrous web pulled back until only a single cord clung to the concrete. "Come on," Sara gritted out, giving another lurch. The cord snapped. She fell onto the hard ground, her face smacking with a wet crunch.

A sunburst of pain exploded inside her, unconsciousness pulling at the ragged edges of her being. Sara concentrated on remaining awake, using the earthy taste of blood in her mouth as an anchor. Moaning from the depths of her soul, she rolled onto her back. Warm blood flowed down her nose, down the sides of her face and neck, and seeped into her jacket and shirt. A sizzle like eggs on a hot pan tickled her ears, reminding Sara of Helen cooking breakfast at the Main House.

With a harsh pop, the crushing chains around her torso loosened. Sara forced her eyes open, tucked her chin, and spied the top chain broken—her blood-soaked clothes having dissolved the dark magic. *Ha!* Brad was *such* a moron.

Liquid-steel resolve surged through her. She lifted her head off the floor and shook more blood onto the chains. Two more cracks. Two more chains dissolved and broken. A spattering of blood-rich drool weakened the remaining chains around her torso. Sara wiggled her fingers against her chest. If she could break just a few more chains—

Footsteps echoed outside her door. *No no no.* Sara struggled to quiet her raspy breathing. Her arms weren't free yet, and the only weapon she had was the folded knife—a gift from Gran when she first arrived at Ware Woods—clipped to the inside of her jeans. It dug into her hip, trapped far beneath the ashy bindings.

The footsteps stopped. With a screech, the rusted door swung open. A Taker with oily black bruises around his bloodshot eyes stood at the threshold.

Not Brad. She rested her head on the floor, letting it loll to the side. A pathetic whimper arose from her, its authenticity inviting the Taker into her cell. And just as she wanted, the black-stained lackey entered the room.

And left the door wide open.

"You're not supposed to move until he gets back. He—" The Taker halted, his gaze fixed on Sara's chest.

Seriously? Is my shirt ripped open? She glanced down at herself. Her bloodstone had jostled loose during her fall. Instead of being concealed beneath her layers, it now lay above her thermal shirt, shining like a ripe piece of fruit.

"Mine," he snarled, and lunged for Sara. Faster than she could lift her head and bite his blackened hand, he grasped the stone—and disintegrated.

Sara's black bindings vanished, the squeezing pressure around her lungs gone. She drew in precious air and scrabbled away from the Taker's sooty remains. With one hand pushing herself upright, Sara clutched her bloodstone, its familiar pulse calming her frayed nerves.

All Hells. Gran and Thomas hadn't been joking when they'd said bloodstones were deadly weapons. She squeezed the stone. Was this why Brad hadn't taken it from her? Because it'd kill him too?

Her pondering ceased at the thin sound of a faraway voice drifting into her room. She rose to her feet, stumbling against lightheadedness. More Takers or even Brad could walk in at any moment. A flick of her hands yielded nothing. Still no magic. Still no healing power. She unclipped her palm-sized knife and swung the blade open, feeling it click into place. With a quick wipe of her nose on her sleeve, she left the room and stepped into a vacant hallway.

Similar to the room, the concrete hallway was splotched with brown stains. Its low ceiling and many turns created a maze leading Sara past multiple dark, quiet rooms. As she crept along the corridor, knife in hand, silently pleading for the Mother to help her find a way out, she heard the voice again. Stronger this time and unquestionably female.

Kira?

Sara edged around a bend and stopped at a rusted door with chipped yellow paint and a sizable gap at the top, light seeping from all four sides.

"Oh no he didn't," said the voice. Its light tone, balanced with a touch of huskiness, was definitely Kira's.

Sara jiggled the door handle. Locked. "Kira?"

"Father far above. Am I imagining voices now?"

"Kira, it's me, Sara," she hissed, keeping her voice low in case more Takers were down there with them.

"Sara! What are you doing here? Wait—did you let Brad take you too? Damn. Only one of us needed to be the mole."

"Wha—no! I didn't *let* him take me. Are you bound in chains?" Sara eyed the ancient hinges of the door. Grooved bolts. Excellent. She attacked one with her blade, using it as a screwdriver to painstakingly torque the bolt.

"Nope. I was reading, just getting to the yummy climax, and biding my time until Brad comes back from whatever '*super important meeting*' he has and spills the beans. He has such a big mouth. But now that you're here, I'd bet my left fang it's time for both of us to leave. Which is fine by me. The accommodations here suck, and I miss Ian."

Sara's blade slipped, its chewed edge cutting her palm. She ignored the pain and started on the next bolt, her intense concentration muddying Kira's words.

"Ian and your father are worried sick about you!" She paused, her mind processing Kira's admission. "Are you telling me you intentionally let Brad take you so you could gather intel?" Sara huffed in astonishment. "You're crazier than I am. How'd you know he wouldn't serve you to the Shadow Mother?"

"He's power hungry and already double-crossed my father, so of course he's trying to do the same to her. His type is textbook predictable." She paused. "Wait. Please tell me my dad didn't think Brad *took* me. He should know better. Don't get me wrong; Brad is powerful, but he's still an idiot. No amount of magic can fix stupid."

Sara's chortle morphed into a groan of pain.

"Why do you sound funny? And whatever you're doing to the door, stop and stand back. I'm gonna kick it down."

"Hold on, I have a few more bolts to—" Sara yelped and jumped aside as the door flew off its frame and slammed into the opposite side of the hall. There stood Kira, looking as perfect as when Sara met her in Samson's secret refuge under the Hills sacred site. Behind her was a cot with a fluffy blanket, an empty bag of Cheetos, and a pile of books. Sara's jaw dropped, so did Kira's.

"Whoa. Your pert nose is totally busted. Why don't you heal yourself?" The half-vampire, half-witch stole a worried glance at the ruined knife in Sara's bloody hand.

"I can't. My magic doesn't work down here. But it seems you have full vampire powers." There was a faint twist of envy in her statement.

Kira angled her head at the room behind her, the many braids of her hair sweeping to the side. "I compelled the Takers to give me a few comforts. Brad has no clue that I have magic—my father was adamant about not showing him any of my power. The dork thinks I'm a useless half-breed and stole me to get back at my father and probably you too. Brad gobbled up my helpless act and peacocked by spilling a whole lot of Shadow Mother beans." She snorted a laugh, fangs flashing in the hallway fluorescence.

Sara stood, transfixed. Like father, like daughter. Samson was right; Kira was a beautifully vicious creature with her own wicked agenda.

"Why are you staring at me like that?" Kira didn't wait for an answer. She gently took the knife from Sara, folded it, and slipped it into Sara's jacket pocket. "This little knife isn't gonna cut it for what we need to do next."

Sara paled. Somewhere in the maze, a door slammed open and multiple footsteps ran in their direction. "You do realize I have no magical powers. Can't you compel all of them to let us go? If we can get to the surface, I should be able to reach Thomas—"

"I can only compel one person at a time, which will be the biggest Taker. She's the only one down here with a pendant, and she'll be the first one on us. I'll have her toss the pendant to us. We catch it and smoke back to Ware Woods. Piece of cake." Kira winked at Sara before shifting her gaze to the end of the short hallway—to what sounded like a legion of combat boot-clad monsters storming toward them.

"Riiight," Sara muttered, nudging in front of Kira. If the big Taker got too close, she'd vaporize her with the bloodstone.

Shadows flickered at the end of the hall. In a pounding of footsteps, a Taker rounded the corner with astonishing speed. His booted foot connected with the wall, propelling him toward Sara, his ink-stained hands clawing for her.

Not the big Taker. No pendant of freedom around his stocky neck. No matter. Nothing would keep her from Ware Woods—from Thomas.

Sara launched herself at him, slipping past his hands and grabbing his torso in a bear hug. The bloodstone, aglow like a branding iron, pressed against his chest. He disintegrated into ash. Sara stumbled forward into the arms of another Taker. He clamped his hands onto her upper arms and, with a hiss, leaned back, keeping his distance from the bloodstone. Sara kneed him in the groin, then smashed her elbow into his temple, her swift and punishing action an instinctive result of Kane's ruthless training.

As the Taker crumpled aside, Sara stared up at a gargantuan female charging around the corner. Her eyes turned glassy; her stride slowed. She ripped the black jagged stone pendant from her neck and tossed it. The cording caught on her stained fingers, and instead of arcing toward Kira, the pendant fell short.

Sara dove for the black stone, her four-fingered hand clasping it, while twisting and blindly reaching her other hand behind her. She clamped on to Kira's forearm, the half-vampire, half-witch grabbing Sara's arm in return. *Cahill common* was Sara's one thought and plea.

CHAPTER 11

A N EXPLOSION OF black smoke blotted out everything but the feel of Kira's tight grip. The pungent scent of sulfur stung Sara's eyes and crammed down her throat, its bitterness coating her tongue. A force pulled at her center, giving the sensation of being turned inside out and pushed through a meat grinder. And just when Sara questioned releasing the stone and returning to the less painful bunker of Takers, the smoke cleared.

Sara let go of Kira and sank to the ground beneath the Cahill chestnut tree. Gulping crisp air, she thrust her fingers into the snow, seeking the forest's energy to replenish her magic. Blood dripped from her nose and seeped from her cut hand, marring the white as she slowly began to heal herself.

On her right, Kira stood, leaning forward with her hands on her thighs—and laughed. Her radiant joy resounded across the common. Trees along the far edge shook, snow falling from winter-bare and evergreen branches. Sara huffed her own relief, grateful to breathe with minimal pain through her nose, and welcomed a surge of warmth through her bond with Thomas.

The splintering of wood and the thunderous crash of felled trees drowned out their laughter as something massive barreled through the forest. In a cloud of snow, a section of trees flattened, and a blue-and-silver dragon burst through.

"Oh Hells no!" cried Kira. She hauled Sara upright and tugged her toward the chestnut.

Sara dug in her heels, pulling Kira back. "It's okay. It's Thomas," she shouted over his roar—over his internal cry of, *"Sara!"*

Kira's jaw dropped, her fangs on prominent display, as Thomas shimmered and phased into his human form in midair. Distress etched his face, and instead of being fully clothed, he wore only jeans.

He dropped before Sara, his elysian eyes widening at the ruby-red blood on the snow and at the blood she knew still smeared her face and crusted the front of her shirt. Their bond flooded with his emotions: heartbreaking relief at having her back, twisting guilt for not having been by her side, and blazing fury at whoever had hurt her.

The air thrummed with barely restrained energy. Kira released Sara's hand and shuffled back a few steps, her eyes still on Thomas.

Sara trembled, her own guilt threatening to crush her at having caused him such anguish. It had been impulsive of her to follow Samson, and yet she'd do it again. She'd beg every single magical—light and dark—and she'd face Brad as many times as it took to gather any scrap of allegiance or information against the Shadow Mother. The dark entity had to be defeated before she could "*get rid of*" Thomas. Sara choked back a sob. "I'm sorry for—"

Thomas kinetically snapped her into his arms and kissed her, silencing her apology. Energy crackled around them. His physical warmth enfolded her, the heat almost painful as his magic coursed into her, wrapping around her bones, her heart, her soul. She hadn't realized how cold she'd been, how much magic Brad's chains had stolen from her, until Thomas's fire filled her.

He cupped the sides of her face, his thumbs gently swiping her cheeks, and pulled back. His swirling eyes bore into her. "Do not apologize for being you. I love every bit of your wicked self."

She pressed her brow to his. Father above, he always knew

how to diffuse and ignite her at the same time. But as much as she wanted to kiss him again—to hold on to him until the world corrected itself and peace blanketed Ware Woods—she simply murmured, "Thank you." As High Witch, duty called for her to reassure everyone of her safety and to convey what had happened at the Global Council before she could fully melt into his embrace.

Giving him a soft, knowing smile that Thomas immediately mirrored, Sara turned in his arms. She leaned her back against him, her body still chilled, her legs weak, and faced everyone rushing toward her: Cahills streaming from the Main House, Thomas's family flying in from the edge of the common, the Walkers and Blue Ridge pack in wolven form bounding through the snow, and the Atwells and Lochtons popping out from the base of the chestnut tree.

"Kira!" shouted Ian as he sprang from the tree and flung his arms around her. Sara could have sworn she saw a flash of energy, but her vision wavered, fatigue setting in. Thomas's grip around her waist tightened as Gran and her father appeared at her side. Their concern was evident as they took in her bloody appearance. Also evident was the myriad of questions about to rupture from their open mouths.

Sara held up her hand, frowning when she realized her cut still had not healed. "I'm all for having an emergency Council meeting. But first"—she swallowed, everyone's conversation sounding muffled and far away—"I need a minute." The voices snuffed out, along with her vision, as she collapsed into Thomas and lost consciousness.

Sara was vaguely aware of Thomas carrying her to the cottage, bathing her in the wooden tub, clothing her, and laying her to rest on the couch with her head in his lap. The tenderness of his touch quelled Sara's embarrassment. Besides, he'd seen her naked many times. He'd seen her drool in her sleep, covered in gore, laugh and cry at the same time, and make countless mistakes. Her heart expanded to near bursting for her bonded mate, her best friend, and so much more.

She floated in and out of awareness, a leaf bobbing along the surface of a brook, never going fully under yet never catching on a dry rock either. The cold inside her gradually thawed, drip by drip, as Thomas's love and magic flooded her like liquid dragon fire. She sighed, her power growing stronger, its tendrils seeking and wrapping around Thomas's, their magical fibers combining and fortifying, their bond strengthening.

"*Rest, Sara,*" he projected to her over and over.

"*I love you,*" she mentally whispered, wishing she could return his feather-soft kisses, wishing her body weren't so heavy, wishing she could kill Brad and the Shadow Mother right that instant.

"*I know.*"

A door opened and closed. The scents of peppermint and pine teased her nose, her body tingling as her magic continued to heal her physical injuries, the pain in her hand dispelling.

"How is she?" asked Charlie. Sara noted a touch of anxiety in her father's typically calm voice.

Thomas shifted, his slight movement wobbling her head. "She's growing stronger every minute, and when she wakes, I'm sure she'll be ready to destroy the world."

You know me well.

Charlie cleared his throat. "Kira said Brad had them in some underground facility. Seems there was too much concrete and metal for anyone to find them. Kira wasn't harmed, but Sara was somehow drained of her magic."

"*I'll find Brad and torture him for decades.*" Thomas's inner voice curled around Sara's consciousness, a vicious promise in his tone.

You can have what's left of him after I make him regret calling me "pet."

"We're lucky she didn't fall into stasis for weeks like last time," said Gran's distinct, no-nonsense tone. A cool, smooth hand brushed Sara's forehead.

Thomas tensed, a deep-chested growl of pure possession radiating from him.

Gran laughed. "So it's true. Dragons are intensely overprotective. And," she added, "prone to tantrums. You ripped up half the forest with your worry."

Oh, really? Sara tugged on their bond.

Thomas groaned. "Apologies."

"None needed. The Cahills already fixed everything last night. And I'm grateful to have dragon magic save my granddaughter."

"Actually," offered Charlie, his scholarly inflection replacing any hint of his earlier anxiety, "I think it's their bond that allows Thomas to share his energy. As part dragon, he might even have a limitless supply to offer her."

"You're right," said Thomas, the confidence in his voice strumming Sara's heartstrings. "It's the bond. Our connection has been strong since the first time we touched. Innocently," he added, to which Charlie huffed and Gran snickered. "But now, I have this bottomless well of power that seeks her—*needs* her—to pour my magic into. And when I give to her, she shares it back and our bond grows stronger." He paused, and Sara felt the telltale prickle of all eyes on her. She didn't intentionally share in return; she just did what felt right. "How did you know Sara and I share magic?" asked Thomas. His arm settled along Sara's side, his hand clasping hers, sending a pulse of energy through her. She focused on her hand in his, on pushing through her immobile state to *squeeze* his hand in return.

"Her mother and I were bonded. We shared magic only a few times and in small amounts. Our connection was special but not as strong as the connection between you two." Charlie hesitated, and Sara imagined the soft smile he wore at mentioning her mother. "She'll wake up soon. When she does, come to the Council stage.

Everyone is gathered there, including Samson, Lethal, and Ryujin."

Someone tucked a lock of hair behind Sara's ear.

Thomas growled again, which was instantly followed by Gran's laughter.

"Ma, stop teasing the boy." Charlie's mental scolding sounded in Sara's mind.

The cottage door opened and closed, a gust of wintery air skimming Sara's face.

"Your father's intuition is never wrong. And I felt you squeeze my hand." Thomas's voice rang in the empty cottage. "Should I tickle you until you wake and punch me, or should I rouse you with a kiss?"

I'm going to punch you for even asking the question.

"I heard that, and I look forward to you trying. Now, say something pleasant if it's a kiss you want."

"Thomas," she mentally projected, tugging on their bond as if she could tug his face to hers. She felt him shift on the couch.

"Yes," he sighed, his lips grazing hers. Energy jolted through Sara, skittering along every inch of her skin, her body light and warm, her senses on fire and fully awake.

She opened her eyes to see the cocky smirk on his face. Stars, how she loved him, and he knew it, just as she knew his fierce love for her. "You're mine. Now and forever," she said into him, and planted a fiery kiss on his lips.

CHAPTER 12

SARA CRESTED THE Council clearing with Thomas flying by her side. Below them, a crowd sat at the round banquet-style tables, their attention on a central table with Samson, Kira, Ian, Jin, Dean, and Lethal. Playing in the snowy edges of the clearing were the children, each one wearing a knitted hat and mittens—Winter Solstice gifts from Gran. Among them bounded Bailey—Ian's yellow Lab—her tail high in the late afternoon sunlight filtering through the bald branches of the maple soul tree.

Instead of landing atop the old maple stump stage and conducting a formal meeting, Sara alighted beside the central table and whished two additional chairs for her and Thomas. Despite winter surrounding them, the clearing was comfortably temperate, most likely thanks to Samson's magic.

While Thomas settled into his seat, Sara visually panned the crowd again. Everyone except Caleb was in attendance. Trying not to let her disappointment show, she pushed back her shoulders and addressed the crowd. "Thank you all for coming. While I have important news to share, first I want Kira to speak. She has valuable information on the Shadow Mother—information she intentionally risked her life to gather." Sara's appraising glance at Kira was met with a halfhearted grump from Samson, his feigned disapproval belied by his proud smile. Of course he would be proud. Not only had his daughter bested Brad and a cadre of Takers, she had also briefly fooled him too—the king of deceit. Someday, Sara would rub in the irony and revel in Samson's eye roll.

She motioned for Kira to rise. "Please tell us what you learned from Brad." Sara lowered to the edge of her seat, hoping Kira had knowledge of the Shadow Mother's weakness or location—or both.

Ian, who sat beside Kira, pulled out her chair so she could stand. Samson raised a respectful brow at Ian from his seat on the opposite side of the table and twirled his hand in the air—the casual gesture suggesting Kira had already told him everything that had happened to her and what she knew.

Kira swung back her long braids, an unsettling purse to her lips. Her clothes were different from the last time Sara had seen her: a white puffy jacket borrowed from the 'Esha triplets, a crimson knitted scarf from Gran, and a rosewood glow to her umber skin—most certainly from Ian. "The Shadow Mother is planning to destroy Ware Woods. But she is afraid of us. We weakened her, and she needs time to recover and form a new offense. At the moment, she is focused on controlling flat-eyed dragons, creating new Takers, and seeking a way to eliminate elysian-eyed dragons."

Uneasy murmurs rippled through the crowd.

Jin folded his arms. "Impossible. She cannot *eliminate* dragons."

Something oily squirmed in the back of Sara's mind, a distressing thought she hadn't dared voice. Until now. She glanced at Tobio, who sat beside Matthew at the next table over, and at Thomas beside her, and then at Jin. "There are only three elysian-eyed dragons awake at this time, and they are all in this clearing. What if the other dragons are not sleeping? What if the Shadow Mother has somehow infected them already?"

"No!" snapped Jin. "They are in a deep sleep along with the Mother. If any harm came to them, I would feel it. So would Tobio and Thomas. Elysian-eyed dragons are few and connected through magic. It is how we communicate with one another."

Sara opened her mouth to argue that they weren't doing a smash-up job of communicating with one another right now when Thomas grabbed her hand and slowly shook his head at her. *"Don't argue with him. Remember when he destroyed his own garden?"*

For once, she clapped her mouth shut.

Jin narrowed his gaze at Thomas, snorted, and turned his attention back to Kira. "Do you know why she is afraid of Ware Woods and what she has planned?"

"I don't know why or what, but I do know when she plans to attack us."

Sara straightened in her seat, as did everyone else, dreadful tension muffling the creaks of wooden chairs. Even the surrounding trees seemed to lean in, listening.

"When day and night are equal on the Spring Equinox," said Kira.

"The Equinox?" shouted Gran, her face puckered in disbelief. "That's three months away. And there's a damn bloody eclipse coming sooner."

Gasps and whispered pleas to the Mother drifted among the gathered. From a nearby table, Wes—the youngest wolf shifter—whined.

"My dad questioned the Equinox too," said Kira, with a glance at Samson. "But the Equinox was the only date Brad mentioned. Maybe the Shadow Mother needs time to sharpen her nails." When Gran frowned in thought, Kira returned to her seat and joined hands with Ian.

Relief washed over Sara. Three months was far better than tomorrow or the lunar eclipse which was in a few weeks. Hopefully it gave her enough time to repair the damage she'd caused by visiting the Global Council and losing her shit. If she could meet with some of the Magi, like the kind High Witch with white braids, maybe Sara could persuade them to join Ware Woods against the Shadow Mother. And if persuading didn't work, she'd beg for the Magi's help.

Sara's gaze drifted to the children playing in the snow. Rather than a jolly snowman, they had built an impressive serpentine dragon with icicle spikes glinting in the sun. Flanking the dragon was a massive wolf and the slender form of who could only be Lethal, icicle daggers in their hands. The children's rosy cheeks and innocent smiles fanned the guilt smoldering in Sara's belly. Her soul instantly burned, consumed by flaming regret. Everyone needed to know what she'd done. The upheaval she'd caused.

"I'm sorry," she cried out. "I shouldn't have gone to the Global Council. Instead of securing their aid to help us, I pissed them off. They think Ware Woods is a problem and that if they let the Shadow Mother *purge* our site, she will be appeased, and the magical balance will correct itself. The Magi don't believe all magicals are in danger." Sara didn't mention the outspoken Magi's insistence that she was a problem. By killing Makwa and Dorcas and now upsetting the Magi and playing right into the Shadow Mother's need for discord, Sara *knew* she was the problem. And to prevent bringing Ware Woods and all magicals down with her, she needed to remain calm and find a solution. The Book had once provided her with a powerful spell for help in learning her magic. Perhaps it would pull through with an epic spell to save the world.

A fresh wave of whispers halted, the clearing pin-drop quiet as Lethal spoke up. "I told you not to go."

Their *told you so* sliced into Sara far deeper than a Death dagger ever could. Thomas rumbled a warning, which the vampire completely ignored.

"That said," drawled Lethal, "negotiations weren't going well before your unexpected arrival. The Global Council has always been divided, and I doubt your outburst caused much harm. In fact, by flushing out Brad and having the Magi witness him abduct you—from the banyan, no less—I believe you have garnered more allies than you think."

Sara jerked her head at Lethal, a seed of hope sprouting inside her.

"Agreed," said Jin. "After you disappeared, many Magi demanded that I bring you back and eliminate Brad for his insolence. They were surprised when I informed them that I cannot locate Brad or the Shadow Mother. If I could, I would have already taken care of them. With this knowledge, I believe they are starting to see that we need to come together."

Samson shook his head, his black wavy hair skimming his shoulders. The top of his midnight blue military-style jacket was unbuttoned, revealing his chains. Unlike at the Global Council where he showcased his bloodstones, they were now conservatively stashed away. "While you were distracted by amiable delegates, I fraternized with some old, murderous friends. Kahn and Vasile are *not* on the pro-dragon wagon, and they are convinced Sara is responsible for the imbalance by killing Makwa and Dorcas. These fiends dominate many witch and vampire sites through fear and could easily coerce a small army of magicals to aid the Shadow Mother."

Sara slumped back in her chair, the hope seedling crushed. She *was* responsible, and now all of Ware Woods would pay the price for her recklessness. *If I hadn't killed Dorcas—*

"*Chin up, Rookie,*" Samson's voice coaxed in her head, interrupting her thought.

With a jolt, Sara lifted her gaze and met Samson's dark eyes. An encouraging smile stretched across his face. "I've killed plenty of magicals and have never upset the balance. Plus, there is the *significant* fact that the Shadow Mother used me to attack the Hills witches long before Sara came to Ware Woods." Samson placed a hand over his heart and shot an apologetic glance at Ian and the children playing in the snow. "There must be a reason why the Hills witches can shield against her and why she is threatened by Ware Woods."

Sara tuned out the din of conversation from the surrounding tables, her mind reeling. He was right. There *must* be a reason why everything had led to their current circumstance. Even though Sara had contributed to the imbalance, she wasn't entirely responsible for the Shadow Mother's presence. The dark entity's murderous uprising started decades, if not centuries, before Sara. Regardless of what started the Shadow Mother's destructive campaign, she had been very methodical, and Sara was unequivocally her current target. To have any chance of standing against her—either by herself or joined by anyone as reckless as she was—Sara needed to know why. Because if she knew the reason, maybe she could use it against the Shadow Mother.

She chewed her lip. Between the Shadow Mother, Brad, and her Global Council debacle, she had far too many fireballs to juggle alone. As usual, her inexperienced self needed help, and lots of it. She chewed harder while contemplating the many faces of friends and family staring expectantly at her.

"We all know you're plotting something," Thomas projected. *"Care to share before you ruin your lip?"*

"Am I that obvious? Don't answer that." Sara squeezed his hand, releasing a spark of energy between them, and stood. "Here's what we're going to do," she said.

CHAPTER 13

Sara drew her gaze across the crowd and put a hand over her bloodstone, bolstered by its warm, steady pulse. "We'll find out the Shadow Mother's motivation *and* we'll approach the amiable sites. If we tell them everything we know about the Shadow Mother, I'm sure we'll gain their support."

Ian gave her an encouraging thumbs up while many of the tense faces in the clearing eased.

Sara twisted her shoulders toward Gran and Alice at the table behind her. "The three of us will consult the Book and focus on finding the root cause of the Shadow Mother. There's got to be something inside Ware Woods, besides Ian and the kids, that we can use against her." Confirming her grandmother's and great-aunt's assistance with an exchange of tight nods, Sara turned back to the central table—to the Magi she needed to approach the other sites.

"Dean, will you loop to other shifter sites and ask for their help in joining us against the Shadow Mother?" She held her breath as the massive Alpha Shifter leaned back in his chair, his face expressionless while considering her request.

"Yes," he responded, voice solemn.

Sara whooshed her relief.

"But my pack comes with me," he added with a tilt of his head toward the Blue Ridge pack reclining at the table behind him. The pack members grinned, sharp toothy smiles. Of course they would be eager to go. Adventure and danger were their daily breakfast.

Before Sara could thank them, Jin spoke. "Not Tobio. He stays here."

Tobio hissed. "You do not order me. This is my pack and—"

"I am senior dragon here, and I forbid it. It is not safe for you!" Jin's body shook, threatening to shift and put genuine fire behind his order.

Spikes popped through the sleeves of Tobio's jacket.

More than half the clearing pressed back in their chairs—away from the dragons. Samson, on the other hand, spouted a laugh.

"Duuuude," said Matthew, putting an arm around Tobio's shoulders, breaking the half-dragon's concentration. "Your big dragon bro is worried the Shadow Mother will get you. Stay in Ware Woods." On a breathed whisper, he added, "With me."

To Sara's surprise, Tobio's spikes retreated. He inclined his head toward Jin, accepting his command, yet instead of anger in Tobio's elysian eyes, there was a gentle glimmer.

Matthew chuckled, his arm still around Tobio, who leaned into him.

A collective sigh and a moment of quiet followed. Before Sara could continue, someone flicked their red hair.

"I'm going with Dean," said Moira. Her determined tone carried through the clearing, making it obvious no one could stop her. "We'll start by visiting my siblings. They'll listen to us, and other packs will follow."

Dean whipped his head from her to her parents. Moira's mother, Shannon, smiled warmly while patting the musclebound arm of Moira's father, Bill, who sat beside her. Bill's amber eyes crinkled at the corners as he regarded Dean before lifting his chin at Moira. "You make an excellent point, and I know Dean will protect you with his life. You have my blessing."

Sara hesitated. *Well, that was very . . . formal.*

Moira's response was a feline grin. And when she tossed her fiery hair again and turned her grin to Dean, dimples cratered his cheeks, his mountainous chest expanding with pride.

A series of high-pitched whoops erupted from Matthew and the pack.

"Shifters," muttered Samson, bringing Sara's attention back to the central table—back to her plan. He winked at Sara, a sly tilt to one corner of his mouth. "Great plan, Rookie. We'll divide and conquer. I'll visit the witchy sites and charm them with my good looks. Kira and Ian will go with me."

Sara raised a brow at him. Had he been thinking of approaching the other sites all along and simply waiting for her to come to this idea? And why would he want to take Ian? Taking Kira, keeping his daughter close to his side, made sense. But Sara didn't agree with Ian leaving Ware Woods. He needed daily medicine from the Lochton pine, or he would fall into a deep sleep caused by the Shadow Mother's ice splinter in his heart. And while Ian was part Hills witch and could shield against the Shadow Mother, his magic also made him a target. Sara opened her mouth to protest when Samson raised a finger, magically silencing her.

"We'll take plenty of medicine with us, and we'll ask the other High Witches if they know how to cure Ian. With Ian's shielding abilities, we'll be the safest envoy." He lowered his hand and, ignoring Sara's glare, tipped back in his chair to view the table behind her. "Charlie and Ted, you're welcome to come too. It'll give you both a chance to get to know Kira better."

Sara spluttered. *What in All Hells was going on here?* This wasn't a Sunday afternoon picnic they were planning but a dangerous endeavor to secure aid while Brad and the Shadow Mother salivated over them.

Sara scowled. Ian and Kira were giddy and ready to go—ready to make a difference. *Sigh.* She knew that feeling and couldn't possibly stand in their way. Plus, it was an opportunity to finally cure Ian.

"Firecracker," said Charlie. "We know the danger, and we want to go."

Sara dropped her shoulders, cracking under their willingness and knowing she couldn't stop them. Stubborn Lochtons. "Okay. But if there is any hint of the Shadow Mother, everyone immediately returns to Ware Woods. This includes all shifters"—she swung a finger at Moira and the Blue Ridge pack—"and you too," she added, pointing at Lethal. "That is, if you'll visit the vampire sites."

Tense silence filled the clearing. Sara quickly stuffed her hand into her pocket, hoping her finger jab hadn't crossed a line with the thousand-year-old Death Vampire. Like, say, the line between life and death for High Witches who foolishly overstepped their bounds.

Lethal scrunched their flawless nose. "While I detest looping, I'll gladly terrorize the Elder Vampires into helping us. Lily will go with me as an ambassador so they can see for themselves that Ware Woods is not an atrocious threat. And I'm sure Lily will stop me from *unnecessarily* drawing Kindness."

Sara stared down at the vampire. Their easy cooperation was more than a tad jarring. By publicly favoring Ware Woods, they would jeopardize their neutral role presiding over the Global Council. Plus, there was the cold, sharp fact that Lethal had, not so long ago, pressed a dagger to her throat and had been ready to make an example of her. Of course, it had been her fault for breaking Council rules. But still. And while Sara could have kissed Lethal for their cooperation, she couldn't stop herself from poking them. "You could ask Lily instead of assuming she'll go."

Lethal kept their ice-gray gaze on Sara and called out, "Lily?"

From Sara's right, Lily and Kingsley Atwell snickered. "I'll go," sang Lily, her delicate voice full of amusement.

A four-fanged smile graced Lethal's angelic face.

Arrogant vampire.

And just as quickly as it appeared, their smile vanished. "We cannot act too soon, or we will appear desperate. We must give the

Magi a few days to reflect on the significance of your abduction and to discuss the presence of the Shadow Mother with their sites. Then we will approach them."

Good point. Though Sara wanted to immediately send her misfit team to the other sites, she trusted Lethal's advice. The Death Vampire had oodles of experience in dealing with other magicals, and they had been acutely correct in warning her to stay away from the Global Council. Sara would begrudgingly wait and let the others ponder their collective fate. A few days could be afforded when they had almost three months. And while they bided their time, Sara would consult the Book. Since the family grimoire had yet to answer a direct question about the Shadow Mother, Sara would need to employ a covert approach. It shouldn't be *that* hard to outsmart a book. If she were lucky, the Book would divulge enough information to defeat the Shadow Mother without involving the other sites. And if not, Sara would still have time to join Dean, Samson, and Lethal in visiting the others long before the Equinox. It was a perfect plan.

Sara opened her mouth, but before she could speak her approval, Samson interjected. "Stop overthinking and agree. Lethal's strategy is sound."

Gaa! Samson could be so infuriating. Sara frowned at him. "Of course I agree. I was just about to—"

"Was that a compliment?" Lethal said to Samson, a two-fanged half smile on their lips.

"Don't let it go to your pretty head." Samson twirled his finger at the children's snow figures behind Lethal. Gasps and giggles twittered among the kids as Samson's likeness became a markedly handsome snow statue, complete with power pose and radiant smile; while Lethal's effigy now sported walrus-sized icicle fangs.

"Okay!" Sara shouted, grateful when everyone, including Lethal, focused on her. Did Samson have a death wish? How could he joke around at a time like this? Did he think it would be easy to sway the other sites and defeat the Shadow Mother? Or was his jesting simply meant to relieve their ominous predicament? The slight pinch to his brow worried her.

Sara pushed down her fears and, in a voice sounding more confident than she felt, stated, "It's agreed. We wait a few days before looping to the other sites while Gran, Alice, and I consult the Book."

"What about the rest of us?" asked Uncle Larry. His booming voice filled the clearing. "How can we help?"

Sara turned to her grandfather, noting the spectrum of emotions in his aura before taking in the rest of the gathering. Silence fell as everyone focused on Sara, their earnest eyes seemingly repeating his question.

She placed a hand on Thomas's shoulder. "I ask everyone to go about their daily activities. Trips outside the wall are to be limited if possible, but otherwise there should be no changes. The most important thing we can do now is continue being ourselves. Have fun, care for the forest, and enjoy each other's company." She glanced at the children chasing one another with snowballs, Bailey excitedly darting among them, then dropped her gaze to Thomas. His elysian eyes swirled as light-blue energy snapped between them. "We can't stop living today for what may or may not happen tomorrow."

Thomas grinned. *You're getting a lot of mileage out of that saying. Maybe I should trademark it.* She squeezed his shoulder.

"Agreed," said Helen. She rose from her seat beside Gran and rubbed her hands together. "Now that we have a plan, it's time to party and celebrate Kira's and Samson's return—Sara's too, of course. Dinner is ready and simmering at the Main House."

A chorus of cheers and a few howls exploded from the gathering as everyone pushed in their seats and headed for the Main House. Shifters and vampires disappeared into the woods while the Sullivans took to the sky. The remaining crowd of witches moved toward the maple tree.

When Jin lingered, quietly admiring the snow dragon, Thomas rushed to his side. "I can help you search for the other elysian-eyed dragons," said Thomas. Sara jerked back. How could he suggest this? It wasn't safe for him—for any dragon—to leave the safety of Ware Woods.

Jin adjusted his quilted tunic. "That isn't necessary. I have already searched for them and the Mother. Wherever they are sleeping, they do not wish to be found. I'd suggest we visit other magicals, but they are frightened and mistrustful of me—of us. Until Sara discovers more about the Shadow Mother, I must return to my garden."

Sara's scalp prickled. Did the elysian-eyed dragons and the Mother not wish to be found? Or could they not be found, buried under layers of concrete and metal? Her bloodstone pulsed in time with a dreadful thought.

What if they were buried under layers of the Shadow Mother's dark, icy magic?

Panic spidered through Sara's veins. If anything happened to Jin, the same would happen to Thomas. Bound as sire and scion—if Jin died, Thomas would too.

"Jin, stay here in Ware Woods. You can help me search the Book," Sara blurted, raw fear twisting her words into a plea.

He studied her, a weary glaze in his silver eyes. "You do not need my help for this."

"Then stay and train Thomas. Show him how to be quicker, how to be more accurate with his fire." *How to stay alive.*

Jin took a step back, an ashy tail already curling around him. "If Thomas would like to train, he can come to the garden. Otherwise, summon me when you have more information on the Shadow Mother." Smoke plumed, and Jin was gone.

Sara gawped after him. *Well, that was odd.* She didn't think Jin liked visitors *or* to be summoned. As she waved off his departure, Thomas pulled her into an embrace.

"Hey," he sighed into her hair, his hands rubbing her back. "Jin is safe in his garden, and I'm fine. Although my pride is hurt that you think I need more training."

Sara leaned back and gently punched his chest with both fists. "How could you even think of leaving the forest?"

His grin vanished, his mood flipping faster than a thrown blade as he growled. "Because I can't stand being useless. It's incredibly frustrating to have all this power and not be able to do anything with it, especially when my bonded mate is constantly putting her life on the line." He paused, muscles feathering in his clenched jaw, grip tightening on her waist.

She held his intense stare, knowing he didn't share this lightly and wishing for all the world to spare him this anguish.

Thomas continued, "I was out of my mind when you disappeared, and I'm willing to do *anything* if it means keeping you safe and bringing us peace."

His declaration squeezed her heart. A soft smile stretched her lips. They were so alike it should have terrified her to know he would do anything, including sacrifice himself for her. But she already knew this. They *both* knew how driven they were, and respected each other for it.

Sara placed her hand on the side of his face, his stubble grazing her palm as she smoothed her thumb over the tension in his jaw. "Thomas, you're not useless. I need you by my side. Now and forever."

His eyes sparked. A fierce wave of emotion surged from him and crashed into her, a jet of phantom dragon fire melting her insides. He turned into her touch and kissed her palm, his gaze never leaving hers.

Energy crackled around them. Sara's heart thundered, her white flames twining with his blue magic as she pressed against him. *More.* She tilted her chin, brushing her lips against his.

Thomas stiffened. "Don't kiss me," he warned, the hammering

of his heart causing his chest to tremble against hers. "Dragon impulse wants to claim you. Right. Here. And if that happens, Charlie, Ted, and Jin will have my head."

Her flames vanished. Sara stilled, not daring to move and send him over the edge. From the corner of her eye, she spied Charlie and Ted watching them with curious expressions while waiting their turn to loop through the maple tree.

Dragons do *see everything.*

Slowly, she pulled back and locked her gaze with his, commanding his attention so he wouldn't see her magic reaching behind her, gathering what she needed to extinguish his heated impulse. If she was lucky, maybe just this once, he wouldn't see what was coming.

Thomas's eyes narrowed, an ardent rumble building inside his chest. And before his spikes could ruin his clothes, she kinetically smashed a snowball in his face.

He released her, stumbling back a step, his utter shock priceless. She'd pay for it later, probably with snow down the back of her shirt when she least expected it, but his reaction was worth it. She rocketed into the darkening sky.

"Monster!" Thomas's laughter joined hers, their bond vibrating as he chased her to the Main House.

CHAPTER 14

AFTER EATING HER fill of hearty stew—Kira's favorite, according to Ian—and losing several rounds of Rook cards with the gang, Sara let Thomas pull her away to sink into one of the main room's many couches. The grand staircase to their right and the overhead second-story balcony were still decorated in evergreen garlands, their crisp scent mingling with the smell of savory foods. Bowls filled with candies, from star mints to chocolate snowflakes, adorned the many dining tables and oversized kitchen island.

Sara propped her booted feet on the coffee table before her and kinetically summoned another birch beer for herself and a stein of ice water for Thomas. He grabbed it, downing half before leaning his head back and closing his eyes. Ever since becoming part dragon, he guzzled his weight in water every day as if trying to quench his compulsion to breathe fire.

Sara took a swig of her beer and set it on the battered table, a table Caleb made before she showed up at Ware Woods. Her chest ached for her cousin. Caleb should be here. He loved family get-togethers, all the food and laughter.

She sighed all the way down to her toes, a futile attempt to lessen her guilt, and glanced around at the room's merriment: Dean, Moira, Violet, Luke, and the triplets played an animated game of cards; Matthew and Tobio talked by the stone fireplace; and Ian,

Kira, and Wes hovered over the dessert trays. Lily had long since eaten a quick meal and disappeared with Lethal. Sara twisted her mouth in thought. Maybe they went to check on Caleb and bring him some food, something Sara should have offered to do. She cursed her thoughtlessness and scanned the kitchen full of Cahills talking, laughing, and eating sweets.

From the opposite side of the kitchen island, her father turned to face her, his direct focus suggesting he'd picked up on her thoughts. She winced. She really should work on her mental shield.

Charlie cracked a smile. *"Caleb is getting better. He visits his family regularly and even helped them repair the forest after Thomas's outburst. I'm sure he'll be ready to talk with you soon. Just be patient."*

She rolled her eyes all the way to the leafy ceiling, the inside vegetation of the Main House a seasonal mix of dark greens and deep garnets. Patience was definitely not one of her strengths, and her father knew it.

"Everything okay with Thomas?" Humor played in his tone.

Oh, her father *clearly* knew something had been up before she'd hit Thomas with a snowball. Her cheeks flamed. *"Um, yeah."* She stole a glance at Thomas, his eyes still closed, and whished his stein to the table before it could tumble from his hand. *"He was on fire after the meeting but is half asleep now."*

Charlie's smile grew. He whispered a tender, *"Be careful,"* in her mind before he returned to his conversation with Uncle Larry and Helen.

Sara tucked a leg under her and twisted on the couch to face Thomas. Indeed. She was debating the best way to wake him without risking a surprised blast of fire, when Samson strode near and paused. His brow rose at her pretzeled position beside Thomas, her chin in her hand as she stared at him.

"Tut, tut. You know the saying: 'Let sleeping dragons lie.' I'd read him a bedtime story, but my services are already booked for the evening." He chuckled at his own joke and gestured toward the second-story balcony. "I'm off to read to the kids before I hit the sack myself."

"The kids?" Samson acting as a surrogate father still struck her as odd. She turned her head, once again surveying the main room aglow with clusters of flickering candles and dancing flames in the fireplace. The children must have scampered upstairs while she had been engrossed in the card game.

"Yes. Remember the Hills children in their glorious loft filled with toys and books? While I was gone, your grandmother and the pack spoiled them rotten for Solstice. I'll never get them to work the salt mine again."

Sara frowned. Sometimes she couldn't tell if he was joking or not, her mind reconciling the real Samson with the dark witch she'd once believed him to be. The kids genuinely loved him, forgiving his transgressions with an admirable maturity beyond their years, and had missed him over the holiday. They all had. Solstice had been a whirlwind of gifts and tight smiles with everyone concerned over Samson's and Kira's whereabouts and the distinct possibility of Thomas engulfing the Main House in dragon fire.

Samson shook his head. "You must be exhausted too, Rookie. I suggest you and your mate get some rest." With that, he bounded up the stairs two at a time.

He was right; she was tired. But she also wanted to fly to the blue house and consult the Book. She'd stay up all night if it was in a cooperative mood to share information about the Shadow Mother and the other sacred sites.

Sara startled when Thomas snaked an arm around her. "You're not consulting the Book tonight. It's probably sleeping and will bite you if you wake it."

True.

His eyes fluttered open, his vertical pupils blown wide in the low light. The way his molten blue color barely swirled, combined with his head still tilted back, resting on the couch, conveyed he was far more fatigued than she'd thought.

Guilt washed over her. "I think you shared too much magic with me."

"No." He leaned forward and kissed the tip of her nose. "Sharing my magic with you made me feel stronger. I'm only physically tired because I stayed up all night with you in my lap."

From his following grin, Sara knew he had no regrets and would do it again. She placed a hand on his firm chest and whispered, slow and seductive, "Do you want to go back to the treehouse?"

"I thought you'd never ask," he said, and in a clap of dusky smoke they were in the treehouse's four-poster bed.

"Thomas! At least give me a warning before you do that." Sara sat up, her legs bare beneath the quilt-topped covers. Instead of her clothes, she wore one of his shirts—her favorite, a downy-soft gray tee. Thomas lay beside her, on top of the covers, clad in sweatpants and a tight T-shirt. His eyes closed again.

She plopped against her pillow and snuggled against his side, the covers keeping her from wrapping her legs around him. With one arm above the quilt, she slid her hand under his shirt, savoring the ridges of his abdominal muscles before tracing a still circle above his heart.

He clamped a hand down over hers, pressing her palm to his hot skin. In a strained voice, he uttered, "Lily and Lethal are reading in their room, Moira is on her way to her room in the west canopy, and Jin's ridiculous order forbids me from *touching* you. I wasn't kidding when I said he'd take my head."

She scowled at the night. "I'm going to talk with Jin right now. We're bonded! He can't possibly think—"

"He's resting. Exactly as you should be doing. And I'm fairly certain waking Jin would result in imminent death."

"Pfft!"

"Sleep, Sara." Thomas's rumbly request cast over her like a silken sheet, quelling her mind and whisking her into a deep slumber.

Something hard nudged Sara's shoulder, rousing her from a blissful dream of lazy snowflakes falling in a vibrant garden.

Mmph. Five more minutes.

Poke. Poke.

Something better be on fire. Sara cracked open an eye. Sunlight filled the room. Beside her lay Thomas, still asleep, their hands clasped together. With a faint creak, the oak retracted its outstretched twig and shook itself, jiggling the bed.

"Hello?" called a familiar, assertive voice from the main level below.

Thomas jerked awake and, as Sara anticipated, expelled a ball of fire.

She pushed back against her pillow, flicking her arms in the air, summoning water magic to squelch his flames. Her reaction was part of her morning routine. With a silent apology to the oak and another flick of magic—also part of her routine—she grew a new bedpost and called a puff of air to disperse the smoky steam. The tree shook itself again and settled with a sigh.

Sara sat up with Thomas. "Violet?" she called out to his sister.

"Is Thomas with you? He didn't show up for sparring with Connor this morning."

"Shit!" Thomas hissed through his teeth. He sprang from the bed, and with a slip of dragon smoke, magically changed his clothes.

Sara gaped at him. Dragons and their fancy magic. She threw back the covers, stumbled to her pile of clean clothes, and jammed her legs into a pair of jeans. "Yeah, we'll be right there," she hollered.

Thomas glanced at the sunny day outside the window opening and raked a hand through his disheveled hair. "I never sleep in," he muttered.

After yanking on a clean shirt and heavy wool sweater, Sara grabbed him by the arm. She tugged him past Lily and Lethal's empty room—those two were early birds, even on the rare occasion when Lethal rested—and down the narrow staircase. They tumbled into the main room and came face to face with Violet, her namesake-colored eyes wide, her long raven hair in a pair of simple braids. Unlike the kind witch from the Global Council, Violet would never weave flowers into her hair. Bones of her victims perhaps, but never flowers.

Thomas and Sara flopped onto the couch as he whished their boots from the treehouse's hidden coatroom. "I'll go now," he said, kinetically tying his laces, his shoulders angled toward the nearest window opening.

"Don't bother. Alesha and I already gave him a good workout." Violet collapsed into one of the adjacent chairs.

"Oh?" inquired Sara, using her father's inquisitive tone to pull more information from Violet. She must have another reason for popping in on them. Sara finished lacing her boots, pushed back her silvery-gray hair, and slumped against the couch, pulling Thomas to her side.

Thomas eyed his sister. "So why are you here?"

Sara pinched him. Hard.

He didn't even flinch. *"What was that for?"*

"She doesn't need a reason to visit us, and if she wants something, give her time to ask in her own way."

Hmph. *"Have you forgotten my family is all attorneys? We welcome blunt questions. No wiggle room."* He tickled her side, then looked at his sister expectantly.

"I came to ask Sara if I can help her consult the Book," said Violet, keeping her focus on the throwing knife she toyed with in one hand. "Lily and Moira get to visit other sites, so I thought I'd at least get to see the Lochton grimoire." She shrugged and glanced up at Sara.

Sara wanted to slap her own forehead. Of course Violet felt left out. She, like Thomas, could not stand to be inactive. Sullivans.

"Hells, yes," said Sara, delighted at the immediate excitement glowing in Violet's face. "I'd love to have your help. Let's fly to the blue house and get started. I'm sure Gran will have breakfast—er, lunch for us. Thomas, you can come too." She started to rise from the couch when Thomas grabbed her arm.

"Wait," he said, his tone low, his eyes fixed on something she couldn't see. "Caleb is here."

CHAPTER 15

LIKE A GHOST manifesting out of thin air, Caleb appeared on the deck. He stood a hairsbreadth outside the main room's open double archway, his gaze averted.

Sara's chest tightened. Her cousin looked the same as he did before becoming a vampire: sandy hair, green eyes, tanned complexion, wide shoulders, and brawny build. Yet there was something *other* about him now. His preternatural calm and his too-perfect features were as alluring as they were unsettling.

The back of Sara's neck tingled in tandem with a pulse from her bloodstone. But she didn't need the warning. It was evident Caleb was powerful. And if he could move as fast as Lethal, she'd never see him coming if he wished to strike any of them. Sara chastised herself for the thought. Her cousin would never do such a thing, even if he was pissed at her. Right?

She studied his face, her efforts to read his emotions meeting the same adamantine wall that stopped her from reading Lethal. Her heart clenched. Instead of Caleb's customary cheerful self, there were hints of pain and sadness in the tightness of his expression.

"Come in," said Thomas, waving a welcome and inviting him to take the vacant seat across from Sara. His tone was pleasant, yet his grip on Sara's arm tensed.

Violet slid to the edge of her seat, fingers pinching the tip of her throwing blade, her gaze darting between Caleb and Sara.

Without making a sound, Caleb entered the treehouse. His smooth stride was quieter than an owl hunting prey, the opposite of his once thunderous footsteps. He crossed the room, casting a wary look at Violet and Thomas, his eyes slightly narrowing on the latter, and eased into the wooden chair. It swelled and sighed as if in appreciation of seating its maker, which Sara had never noticed it doing before, adding more awe to the part-vampire, part-witch Caleb package. She had no words, her brain torn between relief and alarm.

When he finally regarded Sara, her heart stuttered. In lieu of the anger she'd expected—and deserved—he flashed a gap-toothed smile. Bright white fangs pressed upon his lower lip.

"You're hard to get alone," he said. Even his voice was the same yet different. Still deep chested, but his usual husky edge had been replaced by a polished resonance.

Sara merely stared. This dazzling version of her cousin wasn't the bloodthirsty creature she'd expected. And instead of latching onto her jugular with vengeance, he had offered a sliver of humor. Something inside her cracked, releasing a flood of relief.

"I'm sorry," they exclaimed at the same time.

Sara pulled back with a frown. "You have nothing to be sorry for. I'm the one who decided this for you. I'm the one who begged Lethal to turn you. I'm the one who should bear the consequences—not you."

He shook his head. "I'm sorry it took me so long to *adjust*. I heard you every time you came to see me, every time you begged for my forgiveness. But I was hurting and needed time to control urges and sort through my feelings. I'm still trying to figure things out, but I want you to know I don't fault your decision. I would have done the same for you." He shot her a watery look.

"Oh, Caleb," Sara choked out. She jumped from the couch and hugged him, her sideways angle awkward as he remained sitting in his chair. The rock-hard firmness to his body was a surprise, and when he returned her embrace and patted her back, her ribs threatened to shatter. Powerful was an understatement. At least he still smelled of moss and chestnut rather than Lethal's cloying frankincense.

"Let's not get too close to the newly minted vampire," projected Thomas. With a kinetic tug, he whished Sara back to the couch and put an arm around her, folding her into his side.

"You look good," said Violet. She bounced the hilt of her knife at him. "No urge to kill anyone?"

His faint smile vanished. "No." Caleb popped a knuckle, the sound identical to stone snapping. "How about you?" he asked Thomas, glimmering eyes assessing elysian eyes.

"Just the bad guys. Same as always," said Thomas with a wicked grin. "It's nice to see you. Alive," he added, and leaned forward to bump fists with Caleb.

"Likewise," returned Caleb.

Though Thomas didn't wince at the crack of contact, he gave a slight shake of his hand as he retracted it.

"We were on our way to the blue house for some food," said Violet, rising and sheathing her knife with the rest of the blades in her tactical vest. Sara swore she slept in it. "Care to join us?"

Caleb's face rumpled in pain, and guilt twisted inside Sara. Eating had been one of Caleb's favorite activities. He loved food. Maybe too much. Was this what he'd lost because he loved it most? The thought of food suddenly made Sara nauseous.

"Can you eat food like Lily?" asked Sara, hopeful Lethal had been wrong—maybe Caleb hadn't paid a terrible price for her decision.

"I can," he said, his response giving Sara a beat of relief that was immediately skewered by a sharp glimmer in his eyes. "But it's pointless since I can't taste anything. It's my consequence for being turned, although you'd think the All Hells' burning process was price enough. And then there is the *pointedly* obvious fact that

I can't even try to blend in with normals anymore. No more beach trips for me. No more meeting someone special. No more family of my own like I wanted." He frowned, his fangs cutting into his bottom lip. Two beads of berry-red blood welled and disappeared, the cuts immediately healing.

Violet's jaw dropped, and through the bond, Sara felt Thomas's anguish for Caleb twine with her own agony. Caleb had never talked about his feelings or what he wanted. He'd always been her happy-go-lucky, go-with-the-flow cousin with a smile and joke to brighten her day. How could she have never asked him what *he* wanted in life? And being turned into a vampire took it all away.

Or did it? She tucked her chin.

Losing his sense of taste was a terrible price, but that didn't seem to be what Caleb loved most. From his emotional gush, it seemed family was what he cherished. Death had spared him what he truly loved, only he was so distraught he couldn't see that his future hadn't been stolen—it had simply been altered. Sara pursed her lips, unsure if she should point this out.

"Sorry," he added with an apologetic glance, misinterpreting her silence. "I don't mean to make you all feel bad. I don't want anyone's pity. It's just—I guess I don't know who I am anymore." His gaze settled to the floor, seemingly searching for answers in the rug's vining pattern.

Sara slid from the couch and sat on her knees before him. Taking his hand in hers, she said, "You're Caleb, and you're family to all of us." His fingers curled around hers, his grip cool and solid, the same as Lethal's stoney touch.

"I know, and I'm grateful that everyone accepts the new me. And maybe I'm selfish or jealous, but I still want a little more." His gaze flicked between Sara and Thomas, his unspoken words hanging heavy in the treehouse: *Like what you have.*

Tears clouded the edges of Sara's vision. "I want the same for you." And with her spoken wish, a tremor rocked the oak.

Velvet darkness swirled around the main room, constricting closer and closer around the four of them as the oak's double-thumping heartbeat rattled Sara's chest. Caleb squeezed her fingers to the point of pain, his eyes wide on the approaching smoke. Violet grinned, positively delighted at the treehouse's antics.

"Sara!" Thomas shouted over the oak's heartbeat. He lunged from the couch, linking hands with Violet and grabbing hold of Sara's waist as darkness consumed them.

Feathery whispers brushed Sara's face and hair, her sight filled with pitch-black Aether. An invisible force thrust her side to side and upside down through nothingness. She blindly clung to Caleb's hand and pulled at Thomas through their bond, imploring the Mother below for his grasp on her and Violet to hold lest they break apart and loop to separate destinations.

With a stomach-dropping dip and a burst of light, Sara rolled to a stop beneath a massive tree, its above-ground roots prodding into her back, its knobby branches stretching toward a cerulean sky. *Ouch.*

Thomas hauled her up. "Are you okay? What happened?"

"I'm fine. The tree looped us somewhere, and I have no idea why." She swiped back her hair, her mouth twisting in thought. Well, she had wished happiness for Caleb . . .

Violet cackled with laughter. "Nine Hells, that was crazy! Is looping through the oak always like that?" She spat out a lock of raven hair, her braids undone, and patted her chest and upper legs, checking her weapons.

Beside her, Caleb stood in a knee-deep hole, soil pushed back in a concentric ring as if he had dropped from the sky. "We looped somewhere?" He glowered at the hole, stepped out of it, and with a gentle tap on the soil, magically repaired the damage.

"Ayup," replied Sara, imitating Uncle Larry's comical inflection.

Finding humor in their hijacking seemed a far better idea than arguing with forest magic.

She peered up at the branches and slowly dragged her gaze down the length of the tree. Small silvery-green leaves, bumpy bark, twisted trunk pocked with hollows, and ropey surface roots. An olive tree. An *ancient* olive tree judging by its girth, which was thicker than the oak's. She debated grabbing everyone and looping back to Ware Woods when a smoky cloud appeared before the trunk and Samson stepped out.

Thank the Mother. He must have sensed them leave the forest.

Samson tugged on his cuffs while looking Sara up and down. "I thought we agreed not to go anywhere for a few days?"

"We didn't mean to loop. It just happened. Do you know where we are?" asked Sara.

Samson scrutinized the olive and surrounding clearing edged by smaller trees with glossy green foliage. "This is Florine's site. She doesn't care for me." He blew a laugh through his nose. "I once pursued one of her daughters, but it was only a fling. She was too darned nice. It never would have worked out." His roving gaze stopped on something behind Sara. "Well, it seems you've been spotted. This is a nice site. You should do fine."

Should? "Wait, you're leaving?" spluttered Sara. She needed him to smooth over their unexpected appearance and sweet talk whoever Florine was into supporting Ware Woods against the Shadow Mother.

He swished a finger at Thomas and Caleb. "Try not to eat anyone," he advised, and disappeared in a clap of smoke.

"Oh, I—I don't do that," stuttered Caleb. He jerked his chin at Thomas. "Do you?"

"Only when necessary."

Sara scowled at Samson's dissipating presence. She was going to throttle him the next time she saw him.

"Finally!" boomed a voice behind Sara.

Shit. "Everyone act normal. Caleb—don't smile. Thomas—keep your eyes down. And Violet—no knives." Sara whirled to face the young woman striding toward them.

CHAPTER 16

A POLOGIES," CALLED OUT Sara. Samson's quip that she *"should do fine"* wasn't a rock-solid endorsement, not to mention their presence defied Lethal's advice. "We didn't intend to pop in. We'll just be going now."

"Oh no you don't. I've been waiting all day and then some." The woman halted before them, hands on her curvy hips. Her ample bosom heaved beneath a laced bodice embroidered with a garden of flowers. Layers of gauzy white skirts skimmed the ground beneath her. A crown of slender entwined twigs graced the top of her head. Her deep brown hair matched her doe eyes, and a smattering of freckles kissed her creamy cheeks.

Sara guessed her to be a witch a few years older than herself. And she had been expecting them. Was this Florine?

"Eyes up here," the woman directed at Caleb with a stab toward her twinkling eyes.

"I wasn't—I swear—" Caleb slapped a hand over his mouth.

She busted out with laughter, straining her bodice even more. "I'm teasing. It's nice to meet another earth witch. I saw you fix the crater you made upon entry." She winked at him. "My name is Bettina."

Caleb stared before remembering himself and quickly looking away. A knuckle cracked. "I'm Caleb," he mumbled. Keeping one

107

hand in front of his mouth, he used his other hand to indicate the rest of them. "This is Violet, Thomas, and Sara." He kept his eyes on Sara, green and gold flecks asking her if he should say anything else when Bettina gently pulled his hand away from his face. Caleb stiffened, lips pressed together.

Energy tickled Sara's palms, her magic ready to pull them all back into the tree. Even if Bettina hadn't seen Caleb's fangs, she would surely know from his cool, hard skin that he was different. And from Sara's Global Council debacle, she knew magicals outside of Ware Woods didn't approve of half-breeds, of mixing factions.

"Caleb, you don't have to hide yourself from me. I know you're also a vampire. And you"—she nodded at Thomas—"are part elysian-eyed dragon. I don't need to be a seer to figure that out. You radiate energy, your eyes glow, and you smell ashy. No offense."

"Um, none taken," said Thomas, rubbing the back of his head, his response sounding like a question.

What was going on here? Bettina wasn't afraid of them. Nor did she hate them. Samson was right. This was a friendly sacred forest. Hope blossomed in Sara's chest.

"It's an honor to have such special guests, including the High Witch of Ware Woods. We've been expecting you. Follow me, I'll take you to my grand-mama—Florine." Bettina marched for the edge of the clearing, tugging Caleb along, her hand still holding his. In a quieter voice, she said, "Oof, you're a stout one. Are you made of boulders?"

Violet sniggered as she joined Thomas in closely following the pair.

Utterly gobsmacked by Bettina's candor, Sara remained rooted by the tree until Thomas glanced over his shoulder at her and she scrambled after them.

"Where are we, exactly?" asked Sara, scanning the thick vegetation. She didn't recognize the trees surrounding the grassy clearing, and the temperature was far warmer than in snowy Ware

Woods. A sparrow of sorts, its head gray instead of brown, flitted from a nearby shrub.

"You're among friends," answered Bettina. She turned and gave Sara a smile as bright as a sunflower.

Okaaay. That wasn't the answer Sara had been fishing for but its simplicity told her all she needed to know. Though the forest had a positive energy and Sara wanted to believe Bettina, she couldn't help her natural inclination to be suspicious of strangers, especially magical strangers. Super kind magical strangers. Perhaps Florine hadn't been at the calamitous Global Council meeting and by some magical miracle didn't consider Ware Woods to be an abomination worthy of purging.

The trees parted with a swishing sigh, exposing a tree tunnel with deep green foliage. Sunlight filtered through woven canopies. Plush grass extended before them like a welcome carpet. Birds twittered and darted among the tunnel's dense vegetation. Despite being unable to see beyond the tunnel, Sara took comfort in the casual demeanors of Thomas and Violet as they studied the peaceful passage. Sullivans were born and raised to assess and eliminate threats. If they were relaxed, then Sara could chill as well.

Her contemplations were interrupted when Caleb muttered something followed by Bettina's spirited laughter. A cluster of gray-headed sparrows startled from the surrounding branches and flew toward the sunny glow at the end of the tunnel.

Sara peered around Thomas and Violet. Bettina certainly was friendly, and Caleb didn't seem to mind in the slightest that she still held his hand.

Sara narrowed her eyes. Bettina had said she was a seer. Maybe she knew what would happen with the Shadow Mother.

"So," inquired Sara, hoping her tone sounded coffee casual and not disaster desperate, "you're a seer. Are your premonitions accurate?" If Bettina had expected them to pop out of the olive tree, her insight must be more accurate than Gran's, which could hardly hit the broad side of a barn.

"Premonitions are tricky," answered Bettina. "I only share what I know will be helpful and only when the time is right." The grin she shot Sara over her shoulder kindly said, *Trust me to tell you what you need to know and don't ask questions.*

Pfft. Apparently, it was rude to ask seers to spill the magical beans. "Got it."

The tunnel ended, depositing them in a sunny patch of forest with a giant, lumpy-barked tree to the right. Hanging from the tree's lower branches were dozens of potted plants, lanterns of all sizes, and charms woven with natural elements from pinecones to crystals. Before the trunk stretched a long stone table cluttered with stacks of books, pottery canisters, multiple mortars and pestles, baskets of fruit, and dozens more potted plants. A woman wearing an all-white dress of flowing fabric turned away from the table and faced them. Kind smile. Hazel eyes. And two long braids of white hair adorned with flowers.

Sara gasped.

"What is it? Do you know her?" Thomas's gaze swirled faster, as if seeing the entire forest and the intentions of everyone within it.

"I saw her at the Global Council," projected Sara, staring agape at the High Witch—Florine.

"Come in, come in," welcomed Florine, waving them into her space. Bettina stepped aside, releasing Caleb's hand as Florine approached him. "It is a pleasure to meet you, Caleb. You are quite special to many."

Caleb's dumbstruck expression matched Sara's own shock. Either Bettina had mentally spoken to her grandmother, providing their names, or Florine was a powerful seer as well.

"And you must be Violet," Florine said, dismissing Caleb with an affectionate pat on his shoulder and fixing her attention on Violet. "A warrior witch with a tender heart. We are relieved to have you here."

Relieved? Warm fuzzies danced inside Sara.

Violet jerked, ever so slightly. "I wouldn't exactly say '*tender*.'"

"It'll be our secret." Florine chuckled before approaching Sara and Thomas. Her aura shone in golden rays, her happiness palpable. "It's nice to see you again, Sara, and to meet Thomas. Such an epic pairing by the Mother." She gave a knowing smile and gestured to the surrounding forest. "I know why you're here. My site believes in you and supports you against the Shadow Mother. We are humble earth witches, but I'm sure we can be of some help to you."

Sara stared, her insides doing flips. Well, that was easy. Though Florine may be kind and humble, she emanated power. Plus, any premonitions shared by her and Bettina could be valuable help. Their assistance would be an asset against the Shadow Mother.

"Thank you. We're grateful," gushed Sara, unsure if she should give her a hug or if High Witches were supposed to keep a cool demeanor. She hung back, awkward and overthinking.

Since Florine was eager to help, maybe she would share whatever she knew about the Shadow Mother. It was the smallest of prospects, but Sara needed as much information as possible so she could stop her before the Equinox.

Feigning a laid-back tone, Sara asked, "What do *you* know of the Shadow Mother?"

Florine leaned against the table, taking a quiet moment before answering. "She has come and gone over the years, a tide of discord inciting petty battles and upsetting the balance before retreating, beaten back by momentary peace. The only time she has ever grown strong enough to attack was long ago, when all magicals lived together and fought for dominance. This was when the Mother stepped in and stopped the Shadow Mother's chaos, first by separating magicals into our factions—witches, vampires, and shifters—and then by giving us separate sacred sites to protect and nourish our magic." She waved at the tree and surrounding forest. "To ensure peace, the Father gifted her elysian-eyed dragons to oversee the balance. But the system isn't perfect. Magicals still find ways to fight—each of us believing we are better than the other. Light, dark, or indifferent, it doesn't matter, for we all battle for dominance and power. We always will. The current imbalance and the rise of the Shadow Mother have been inevitable."

A chill washed over Sara. *Inevitable.* Perhaps she wasn't entirely at fault for the Shadow Mother threatening to destroy Ware Woods, all magicals, and even the normal world. Yet, if what Florine said was true—if history was repeating itself—where were the other elysian-eyed dragons to put a stop to this? Where was the Mother? Did she not care about them anymore?

Sara swallowed the panic burning at the back of her throat. "Do we even stand a chance? Has the Mother forsaken us?"

Florine's answering smile embraced Sara, settling her nausea. "Of course we have a chance to make a difference. We always do. The Mother works in mysterious ways, but she is always by our side. We simply need to believe in ourselves. Do you understand?"

Sara numbly nodded. *No, not really. I could use a straight up answer instead of "mysterious ways."* She needed to get back to Ware Woods and consult the Book. There had to be a chink in the Shadow Mother's armor that they could use against her. Some tiny handhold to pull themselves out of bottomless doom.

She retreated a step toward the leafy tunnel and olive soul tree. "Thank you for your support and information. We'll be going home now. I'm sure—"

"No!" cried Bettina. "You're supposed to stay."

Sara lifted a brow, as did Violet and Thomas. Caleb's glittering gaze remained on Bettina, his mouth turned up in the lively manner he used to wear.

Bettina's cheeks flushed scarlet as Florine admonished her with a gentle shake of her head. "What Tina meant to say was the day is getting late, and we insist you spend the night with us. You must visit our hot springs. They are quite energizing."

Sara glanced at the cloudless sky, the sun well to the west but still above the horizon. It wasn't that late.

"Hot springs?" exclaimed Violet, rising onto her toes as if she wanted to fly over the treetops, find the springs, and dive in. Sara couldn't blame her. It did sound inviting, but—

"Let's stay," projected Thomas, brushing his arm against Sara. *"One night will be fine. It solidifies our alliance and appeases Violet and Caleb, who seems dazzled by Bettina. Plus, I really want to check out the hot springs too."*

Soothing warmth clasped Sara through their bond, melting the last of her resolve to immediately return to Ware Woods.

With lips quirked, he answered for them all, "We would love to stay the night. Thank you."

Bettina beamed.

Florine tilted her head, studying Thomas. "Something is amiss," she said, drawing out her words. She darted her gaze between him and Sara, clicking her tongue. "Ah! Your sire, the red dragon, is mistaken." Florine snapped her fingers and held out her palm, offering a golden hazelnut to Thomas. "Take this to him before joining Sara at the springs. You are welcome to use your smoke travel in and out of our forest."

When Thomas, equally stunned as Sara, hesitated, Florine thrust the nut into his hands. "Go, now!"

His molten eyes rippled. "I'll be right back," he promised, and vanished, a drift of smoke curling in his place.

Florine snapped her fingers again and extended another golden nut to Sara. "This spell is for you. Open it when you reach the springs."

Sara eyed the shimmering hazelnut. *Humble earth witches, my ass.* Florine had exceptional powers and seemed to know far more than she was letting on.

Alrighty, then. Sara scooped up the nut. It pulsed, releasing a pleasant heat and soft glow. Though she wanted to examine the curious spell, she slipped it into her pants pocket and thanked Florine.

"I have something else for you," announced Florine, peering up into the branches laden with magical trinkets. "It's not here at the moment, but I have no doubt it will show up in the morning for breakfast. You can stop by and pick it up on your way home tomorrow." Florine turned to her table, grabbed two apples from a basket of fruit, and tossed them to Sara and Violet. She then plucked up a large, lidded canister and gave it to Bettina. "Stop at the northern bosque on your way to the springs and replenish the yew berries. Something or someone tested the wards last night."

"Yes, Grand-mama," said Bettina, accepting the canister before heading toward the thick vegetation at the end of the long table. The grasses and shrubs parted, and a new tree tunnel appeared.

"Follow me," she sang, her skirts swishing as she led them into the tunnel.

CHAPTER 17

SARA GLANCED OVER her shoulder, catching Florine's goodbye wave before the end of the tunnel closed. The High Witch hadn't seemed concerned about whatever had disturbed their wards. Perhaps it had merely been the wind or a bear—or whatever lived in this pocket of the world.

From up ahead, Bettina hummed a cheerful tune with Caleb close behind her as she led them down the cozy forested tunnel, sunlight dappling its worn path. A mild breeze stirred Sara's loose hair. She turned over her thoughts while trailing Violet, who was already munching her apple. Did Florine have another spell to give her in the morning? A glowing nut or—Sara huffed a laugh—a golden olive branch that held the secret to the Shadow Mother's demise? And what had Florine given Thomas that was so important it had to be delivered immediately to Jin?

Sara internally searched her soul, her spectral fingers testing the many strands connecting her with Thomas. Their bond remained strong and warm, no tug of tension or disaster. As much as she wanted to mentally call out to Thomas, she left him alone, trusting he would return soon and hopefully with some insight into whatever Florine had given to Jin. With any luck, it had been a spell to wake the other elysian-eyed dragons. The thought relaxed Sara, and she bit into her apple. Juice dribbled down her chin, the sweet nectar akin to honey. She took another bite, and an explosion of fresh spring, heady summer, and crisp fall flavors danced on her tongue. Her lashes fluttered. Father above, it was the best apple she'd ever tasted, pure ambrosia. Out of respect for Caleb, she withheld her groans of enjoyment, nibbling away at the core until there was nothing left.

After Bettina hummed a particularly long yet catchy song, the tree tunnel emptied into a wooded section of old-growth trees. The gathering of gentle giants continued to their left while a dense wall of blue-tinged juniper stood to their right. Separating the two sections was a wide, meandering border of pebbled soil and age-worn boulders.

Bettina set her canister on a flat-topped boulder, opened the lid, and withdrew a glove, which she promptly put on. Using her gloved hand, she reached back into the container and pulled out a handful of red, waxy berries. "We protect our forest boundary with spells and charms. No one has ever breached our wards, but occasionally a wretched Taker or rogue shifter will try." She sprinkled the berries among the boulders, shuffled a few steps, and sprinkled some more.

Spells and charms, mused Sara. She scanned the juniper, growing together like soldiers in a tight shoulder-to-shoulder formation, and squinted at the clear blue sky. An icy finger of fear scraped down her spine at the thought of dragons blotting out the sun and descending upon them.

"Can we help?" offered Caleb, picking up the canister.

"Oh," exclaimed Bettina. She snatched it away from him, her cheeks flushing again. "I should have thought to grab more gloves. These berries are deadly."

Caleb's hurt expression lifted into a sheepish grin. "Berries can't hurt me. I'm a stout vampire-witch, remember?" He flashed a fanged, gap-toothed smile.

Bettina froze. Birds twittered by and still she did not move.

"All Hells, Caleb. What did you do to her?" said Sara. *Did he compel her without intending to?* She whished the canister out of Bettina's hands before it could crash to the ground.

"Nothing! I just . . . smiled."

Bettina blinked, then fanned herself with her gloved hand. "I'm okay, just not used to a vampire smile." Her nervous laugh was more of a schoolgirl giggle, her cheeks still pink.

"That will go straight to his head," muttered Violet. She whished the can from Sara and peered into it. "You need to distribute *all* these berries before we can go to the hot springs?"

"Well, yeah. My grand-mama said it had to be done on our way."

"But she didn't say *how* it needed to be done," challenged Violet. She whished the berries from the jar, hovering them in the air like a swarm of red bees. With a swish of her hand, she aligned the berries above the row of boulders for as far as the eye could see, and dropped them.

Bettina gaped at her. "That was certainly efficient."

Violet stuffed the canister under her arm and strode toward the tree tunnel. "My pleasure. Now, on to the springs."

After chasing Bettina, Violet, and Caleb through the tree tunnel, which had inclined uphill and over more boulders than she cared to count, Sara panted atop a ridge. Below them was a pool as vast as the Ware Woods Council clearing, its edge neatly aligned with smooth, rectangular-cut stones. Wisps of heat shimmered above the water's milky surface. Beside the pool, tucked among a stand of tall pine trees, congregated a few dozen people at tables laden with food. Buttercup-yellow cottages peeked out of the forest behind them. Similar to Bettina and Florine, everyone in the gathering wore white, flowing clothes. A few had crowns of twigs and flowers. They stopped eating and conversing and looked up at the ridge with welcoming smiles. When they waved their hands down low, Sara waved her hand above her head in return. The standard greeting among magicals.

A male and female, appearing a year or two younger than Sara, left the tables and began hiking a trail toward them.

"Those are my brother and sister," said Bettina. "They'll take care of Violet at the main pool while Caleb and I hang out at the mid pool." She wagged her thumb at an outcropping of stones and a cozy hut along the top of the ridge. The location overlooked the larger hot springs while still offering privacy. Sara craned her neck, glimpsing the creamy mid pool and a table setting for two. A platter of food, a clear glass carafe of what appeared to be water, and a dark wine bottle similar to Lethal's graced the top. "I thought you might like to dine privately," offered Bettina to Caleb.

"With you?" said Caleb. A grin began to spread across his face before Bettina's breath audibly hitched and he stopped himself. "It's perfect. Thanks," he added, taking a polite yet reluctant step away from her and dragging his gaze to the intimate table setting.

"Go on and help yourself while I get Sara settled." Bettina tried to shove him, grunting with the effort until Caleb chuckled and ambled toward the mid pool.

Settled? Sara furrowed her brow.

"I'm sure my sister has extra swim clothes for you," said Bettina to Violet, who needed no more encouragement. She took off down the ridge in a scattering of loose pebbles, wisely choosing not to fly and possibly freak out their hosts.

Sara decided the same. She started to follow her down the trail, eager to meet the other magicals, when Bettina gently steered her in a different direction. "I have a special location for you."

"But—" Sara's protest ceased when a tree tunnel appeared and Bettina pulled her into it.

"Everyone wishes to give you and Thomas a respectful distance. No High Witch duties tonight, just relax. Consider it a gift from our site." Bettina's smile was ear to ear as she hauled Sara up more boulders, the trees along the path rippling with their haste, before finally nudging her out of the tunnel. "Remember to open your spell when you get into the spring and simply ask the forest for a tunnel to Florine's tree in the morning." She winked, vanishing as the tunnel closed.

But— Sara stared after her. *What just happened? Is this how they treat all guests? Or just me?* While she wanted to meet everyone else and felt a slight unease over being separated from Violet and Caleb, Sara was also grateful for a quiet moment. She blew back a lock of hair and magically tapped into the forest's energy, confirming its benevolent nature. With a resigned sigh, she whirled around and nearly tumbled into a milky pool.

Steam floated over the hot spring, its warmth tickling her face, beckoning her into the water. A faint sulfurous scent hung in the air, rich with minerals and not unpleasant. At one side of the pool welcomed a stone cottage, potted plants flanking its lichen-flecked corners. The structure's double doors hung open, showcasing its single-room interior, empty save for a large bed. Worn cobblestones, the same gray as the building, covered the floor. In a seamless fashion, the stones flowed into an exterior patio that extended to the water's edge. On the patio sat a round table, piled with food, and two chairs.

Sara's stomach grumbled. She sidled along the narrow edge, hopped onto the patio, and grabbed an apple from the table. *"Thomas?"* she projected.

Nothing.

She internally yanked on the silken strands of their bond. *"Thomas!"*

"Sara? Everything okay?" His voice echoed as if Jin's garden were impossibly far away.

"Yeah. Vi and Caleb are off having fun with others. I'm waiting for you at a private hot spring with dinner ready for us. I'm hungry and I miss you."

A dragon snort of laughter. *"Then eat without me. I'll never get between you and food. Too dangerous. I'll be there soon."*

Such a wise boy. She devoured the apple, sating the edge of her hunger, and left the remaining food to share with him later. Giving in to the temptation of the hot spring and reassured by the privacy of the dense vegetation surrounding the water and cottage, Sara stripped off her clothes.

When she dropped her jeans to the floor, the golden hazelnut fell out of her pocket. She snatched it up, chiding herself for forgetting the spell. A spell that could give her insight into how to defeat the Shadow Mother. A spell that could bring her the peace she so desperately desired.

Hazelnut in hand, Sara approached the edge of the spring, shivering in the cool evening air, and dipped her toe into the sediment-rich, opaque water. Luscious heat rushed up her leg, through her torso, down her arms, and into her hands. She clutched the nut, half expecting it to fragment and release Florine's melodic voice chanting a spell that would change the world. It merely dug into her palm.

Maybe I need to fully be in the spring.

Sara eased herself over the edge, expelling a blissful moan at the water's temperature and the soft, tingling sensation on her skin. Careful to keep the nut from getting wet, she navigated the slick rocky bottom with shuffling steps until the water lapped against her bloodstone necklace. She held the bespelled nut in her open palms, just above the steamy water.

The hazelnut trembled so gently Sara thought the steam wavered her vision, until it trembled again and a seam cracked its shell. Light pushed through the fissure, splitting the shell in two, and where a tender nut should have been, a small orb of golden light rose and hovered. The orb bobbed playfully and looped a sideways figure eight, casting a dreamy image of a still circle. Seemingly satisfied to have her attention, it traced through the air in a concise manner and, in golden light, wrote:

What you seek is before you and within you.

The shells in her hands disintegrated, their glittery dust blowing away with the fading words.

Sara scanned the water before her, but there was no magical object floating up from its murky depths, no images portrayed on its pearly surface. There was nothing before her.

She put a hand over her bloodstone, palming its steady pulse. *Within me?* What kind of spell was this? It seemed more like a fanciful quote to be found inside a cookie or hanging from a tea bag, not the monumental magic she had expected. The magic she *needed*. Perhaps Florine wasn't as powerful as she'd thought.

Sara narrowed her gaze at the water, contemplating searching the bottom of the spring in case she'd missed something, when Thomas suddenly appeared with a splash—directly in front of her.

CHAPTER 18

For a surprised moment, time seemed suspended, the spring and Thomas frozen as Sara stared at him, her mind whirling at light speed. If Florine's fortune telling of a spell was accurate, and what she needed was before her, Thomas was essential in her quest to defeat the Shadow Mother.

A wave of water smacked Sara in the face. She fell back, nearly going under before Thomas grabbed her and pulled her to his chest. His bare chest. Her eyes widened as he embraced her, his nakedness evident beneath the water.

Now was *definitely* not the time to tell him about the spell. Besides, telling him he was essential to her would state the obvious. Of course she needed him. Maybe golden nuts were meant to tell you what you already knew as a reminder of what was important.

"Hello, monster," he said and kissed her brow. "Stars above, this feels amazing."

Sara's ears burned. Their slippery embrace did feel amazing. It had been far too long since they'd hugged this intimately. She lifted her chin to return his kiss, but he released her and drifted backward, dipping the back of his head into the water, eyes closed, pure ecstasy in his open smile.

Seriously. "I thought you meant me!" She swiped her hand through the water, splashing him.

He lifted his head and gave her a half-lidded stare, his grin now seductively lazy.

Oh, hello. Maybe he had meant her.

Electricity zinged through her core.

Sara flicked more water at him, the droplets sizzling on his exposed shoulders. Dragon scales glimmered on his skin and vanished. Had she not known better, she would have believed it a trick of the tree shadows casting across them.

Thomas sank to his neck and slowly circled her. Wisps of gray dragon smoke mingled with white steam. Sara drew in a breath, every sense heightened. His elysian eyes glowed with animalistic intent, and while that was exciting in itself, his decidedly playful mood was what piqued her interest. Whatever happened with Jin must have been favorable.

"I take it things went well with Jin. What took you so long?" She maintained her poise as he glided behind her.

"Apologies, my love, but Jin had been asleep. It took me forever to wake him, at which point he almost ripped off my head. Literally." He huffed a laugh. "When he finally calmed down, the hazelnut opened and—get this—sky wrote: *'Bonded mates are compatible. The Mother never makes a mistake.'*" Thomas slid back into her view. "Jin was silent for so long, I thought he'd fallen asleep with his eyes open. Then he blitzed me with a million questions about you. If any of your nails were black, if you were obsessed with water, or if you had any unusual tattoos."

Sara frowned and studied her nine fingers, the wet pads starting to wrinkle. "My nails are normal, I don't drink gallons of water a day like you and Tobio, and the only tattoo I have is the still circle I got while we were at the beach."

Thomas stood, water streaming down his torso, and approached Sara. He wrapped his arms around her, placing his hand over the still circle on her upper back. "While I love this tattoo, you have another mark that is my favorite. Same as you, it is most unusual and incredibly beautiful." He slid his fingers down her spine, one vertebra at a time, sending a shiver through her despite the steamy water.

Sara had forgotten the faint line down her back—the line she'd always dismissed as a birthmark. Was he suggesting she was part dragon? But she had no dragon abilities. She had no shifting magic, no matter how hard she tried. And she had no fire-breathing magic unless you counted the heartburn she suffered while Thomas had been away at university.

Her mind raced, a jaw-dropping realization bubbling to the surface. She had witch fire and perhaps that was related to dragon fire. Her great-aunt Alice also controlled witch fire and had shifting abilities. And the one time Sara spotted Gran changing her socks, she'd spied black toenails. Hells, even her father had black-striped toenails, which—she now understood—were not caused by a log falling on his feet when he was young, as he'd once explained.

Mother below.

She had a dragon ancestor.

Thomas cupped her backside, returning her to the present with a jolt. In a slow, deliberate manner, he dragged his hand around her hip and splayed his fingers under the curve of her belly. "You have dragon blood in you. And I'd bet my life this physical anomaly is also dragon related."

She placed her hand over his, utterly speechless as she stared at him, his dazzling blue aura flaring brighter than the setting sun. Her body couldn't carry a *normal* child to term, because that wasn't her future. Her future was with her dragon mate.

Thomas's knowing grin launched her heart rate. They could have a family someday. Provided they survived the Shadow Mother and any magicals who sided with her. Still, it was a possibility. A delightful possibility she wasn't prepared for quite yet.

She glanced down, mystic water the only thing between them. "Should we be . . ."

"Extra cautious?" he drawled, amusement in the husky timber of his voice. He kept his hand firmly pressed on her, claiming their future potential. Possessive dragon. "Jin says it's very rare, and given our ordained bond, it will only happen when the time is right."

Well, that was good news. And if Jin—who personally knew the Mother—said this, then . . . "Sooo, are we no longer forbidden?" Though his demeanor shouted it, Sara wanted a swoon-worthy verbal confirmation.

Thomas delivered. He leaned in, placing his wet lips to her ear, and very slowly and plainly breathed, "Yes."

Her lower back tingled with energy, a gasp escaping her. She arched into him, seeking more connection, but he disappeared. "Thomas!" she shouted, afraid Jin had reconsidered and summoned him back to the garden.

"I'm right here."

The water around Sara stirred. A feather-light touch grazed her ribs, just below her breast. Cheeky dragon. She reached for him, only to catch a bubbling current. *What is he doing?* Another touch, this one a swiping caress down her back. She whirled, determined to grab him and put his teasing to an end but snatched at nothing, satin water slipping through her fingers.

The hot spring bubbled, puffs of dragon smoke bursting at the surface. Sara widened her stance and visually tracked a milky wave encircle her, its rippling wake lapping the edges of the pool. Thomas had been below the surface much longer than a normal could hold their breath. The thought gave way to a sliver of panic before Sara remembered the harrowingly long time he had been under the lake's ice. Clearly, he was enjoying his bedevilment. If she could have kinetically hauled him up by his ear, she would have.

The waves and gentle ripples stopped. Sara held her position, ready for him to come to her. Within a pounding heartbeat, fingers traced the inside of her ankle and slowly dallied up the length of her leg. Past her knee, up her thigh, and lingered as if waiting for permission.

"Thomas," she mentally gritted out, practically tasting the tension between them. *"Get up here right now and kiss me."*

His fingers stopped toying. *"Are you sure?"* His last word a purr. *"Because I intend to give you more than just one kiss."*

"Is that a promise?"

"Would you like it to be?"

Her insides clenched. Oh, she would get him back for all this teasing. *"Yes."*

"As you wish."

The water roiled, frothing ivory cream and pale blue. Thomas slowly emerged, eyes glowing. His arms slid around her waist, his chest pressing against her as he dragged himself up her front. "Amazing," he murmured onto her lips and kissed her, not with the fierce claiming she had been expecting, but with a tenderness that promised a lifetime of caring and unconditional love. A magically long lifetime that would one day include their own family and the peace she so desperately sought for them all. And though the Shadow Mother still loomed, there was a fraction of peace in this very moment. A gift indeed from this sacred site.

Sara let go of her worries, of the "what if" she couldn't get the majority of magicals on her side. Or heal Ian's heart. Or save the dragons, including Thomas. She let them go and focused on what was right in front of her.

Salt and the mild tang of minerals flavored their kiss. Sara slung her arms around his neck, pulling him closer, opening her mouth for him.

With a groan, Thomas deepened their kiss, his tongue sweeping across hers, his hands splaying across her back.

Being in his arms was pure bliss, everything about him singing to her soul. He was the fuel to her fire, and she burned for more.

She wrapped her legs around him, their kiss turning frantic. All those months of separation inflamed their desire to be closer, their magic straining for release.

Light-blue energy crackled, illuminating the water, which churned and bubbled around them. Steam hissed from the surface of the pool, filling the air with a translucent haze. Thomas strode forward, supporting her against him as he moved. One moment, they were plowing through the water and the next, they had smoked onto the patio.

Sara yelped at the sudden change, at the chill air biting her skin. A fluffy towel instantly enfolded her as Thomas rushed into the cottage, dim with evening shadows. He laid her on the bed with reverent gentleness, her lower legs dangling over the side. Much to her displeasure, he took a step back, a towel loosely hanging from his hips. She lit the overhead metal chandelier—curiously missing candles—with hovering flames of energy to better see Thomas. Dragon scales rippled across his chest. Latent spikes threatened to poke through the fleshy bumps lining his forearms.

Maybe they were moving too fast. Maybe he wasn't completely in control of his dragon. "Are you okay?" she panted, rising up on her elbows, her towel falling open on one side.

His swirling gaze roved her exposed skin, his nostrils flaring, his body trembling.

Maybe he was cold. She flicked her hand, magically warming the cottage and drawing the pool's steamy curtains across the open doors.

Thomas locked eyes with Sara. A bolt of energy lanced through her, tingling her entire body from the crown of her head to the soles of her feet. His voice was low, a touch shaky, as he said, "I was afraid this wouldn't be possible—that being part dragon meant I had to give up being close to you. It tore me apart because the *pull* I feel toward you is stronger than ever. It's all-consuming, Sara." He placed a hand to his chest, over his heart, his fingertips pressed against his flesh. "For months, I've wanted to bury myself in your magic, to lose my mind from feeling every part of you, and to completely fill you with this burning, infinite love I have for you."

Her heart exploded, her body and soul desperate to embrace every glorious facet of him. She felt his declaration in the fiber of her being, knew it as the same ache that thundered inside her. She had always craved him, from the first moment she'd seen him by the maple, and when he'd become part dragon, the pull toward him had only intensified.

Their connection blazed, bolts of energy skating over their skin, their love so blistering she feared they would scorch everything around them.

"Thomas," she said, his name a plea and a demand, her lips swollen with the pleasant sting of his kisses. She loved him with the intensity of all the stars in the sky, and more. "My love for you has no beginning or end. I could fill the Aether with it and still have this radiant, star-exploding *need* for you."

His eyes and aura glowed, bathing the room in iridescent dragonfly blue.

She tugged on their bond. *"Come here. Please."*

He stepped toward her. The hint of scales and spikes disappeared, yet still he trembled. Not from the cold, she realized, but from restraint. The same restraint that wobbled her arms as she held herself upright, visually beseeching him to come closer.

Energy sizzled between them, echoing in the stone cottage, which was bare save for the stately bed and chandelier. Her magic ignited, white flames fluttering around her and reaching for Thomas. A growl rumbled inside him, blue flames coating his torso and stretching toward her. Their magic striving to connect.

He took another step and stood before her at the edge of the bed, one hand on his towel, hesitating. "I don't ever want to hurt you." His face pinched. His aura morphed into blue black, conveying his unspoken worry. What if the Shadow Mother controlled him some day and forced him to do unspeakable things—forced him to harm Sara?

"No one will come between us, and *nothing* will keep us apart," she gritted out. "You won't hurt me. And right now, I insist you unleash yourself before I lose my mind."

His aura flared, returning to iridescent blue, their energy filling the cottage in bursts of white and blue fireworks. The structure quaked, bed rattling, overhead chandelier swinging.

Thomas leaned over her, his lips brushing hers, his voice ragged as he murmured, "So demanding. But"—he lightly kissed one corner of her mouth, then the other—"I insist we lose our minds together." Her heart melted, the rest of her molten as he mentally added, *Always together.*" Thomas nipped her jaw, a swift warning, before claiming her mouth as if he would indeed consume her.

Finally!

She gave his fierce ardor right back, their lips smashing, tongues tangling, hands grabbing. Towels whished away and in a frenzy for more, more, more, she took in all of who he was, filling herself with his love and magic until it seeped out of her every pore and flooded her heart and soul.

The floor of the cottage heaved, stones grinding, the scents of earth and smoldering fire mixing with musk and ash.

Thomas's grip dug into her, their magic fusing together as their love built and built. It was gloriously overwhelming, every part of her loose and tight at the same time. Lightning streaked up her spine, igniting her, and—screw the cottage, they could build another—she let go.

Sara detonated. Thomas joined her, releasing himself with a roar that blew out the cottage's single window. Dragon fire and witch fire engulfed the room. Sara's protective shield instinctively enveloped her and Thomas as the fires chased themselves along the stone ceiling and walls before racing out the blown window and open doors and into the pool, extinguishing with a sizzling sigh.

Blissful freedom washed over Sara. She unconsciously slipped into Thomas's mind just as she felt him slip into hers, the feeling like being weightless in a ray of glimmering sunlight.

"Now and forever." Their magics twined, each embracing the other in perfect balance. The strands of their bond grew thicker, stronger. They glowed with the gold of ribboned sunrises and heated honey.

Sara could have stayed in his physical and mental embrace for eternity, but eventually their shared hunger pulled them from the bed and to the table laden with food on the patio. After a meal, a second dip in the hot spring, and another fiery bout of epic magic twining, Sara drifted off to sleep in Thomas's arms.

CHAPTER 19

A PLAYFUL BREEZE stirred Sara's hair, the whisper of leaves and gentle clack of tree branches coaxing her from a deep, dreamless sleep. For a moment, she thought she was in the treehouse, but the bed felt different—more grounded some-how—and the oak didn't have leaves this time of year.

Sara opened her eyes. Sunlight streamed through a rectangular opening high on the opposite wall of the stone cottage. More light filtered in through the open double doors, the hot spring's hazy water the same as they'd left it last night—technically earlier this morning. They'd resisted sleep for as long as possible, savoring every moment of secluded bliss, pushing back their worries, if only for the night. A wondrous, divine night.

She grinned and nuzzled Thomas's shoulder, his steady breaths and warm skin a calming balm. If only there were no Shadow Mother and they could stay here forever. She placed a light kiss on his chest and slowly, so as not to disturb him, pushed back the bed coverings and propped herself to a sitting position. The room was still mildly warm from her magic—or his magic—it was hard to tell anymore where one stopped and the other began.

With a yawn, she whished their clothes from the floor, grateful their fires hadn't scorched them or the lush bedding. She studied the stone interior, the lack of flammable furnishings, and the wide-open doors. Bettina had somehow known that she and Thomas would have a heated night. Her cheeks burned at wondering just how precise Bettina's visions could be.

She reluctantly slid from the bed and shrugged on her clothes and boots. Judging from the sun's angle, they had slept in and would need to hustle to meet Violet and Caleb at Florine's tree before returning to Ware Woods. Hopefully, whatever Florine had waiting for Sara would be far more helpful than the motivational golden hazelnut.

Sara straightened from tying her laces and placed a hand to her bloodstone lying atop her sweater. Perhaps Florine's surprise was a secret weapon or a precise spell for defeating the Shadow Mother. Or even a magical immunization for keeping elysian-eyed dragons safe. Sara's gaze settled on Thomas.

She drank in the sight of him sleeping peacefully, the soft curls of his mussed hair, the content smile on his lips, and the murmured purr of a snore he'd developed since becoming part dragon. Placing his folded clothes on the end of the bed, she leaned over and gave his lips a firm kiss. He didn't move despite the zap of energy from their contact.

Well, that's unusual. Maybe she'd worn him out. She exhaled a soft laugh and shook him. "Thomas."

He jolted awake, spewing a plume of fire. She dodged and squelched it with a sphere of water. The resulting mist spattered the stone floor, leaving tiny rivulets in its grooved surface.

"Sorry." He groaned and scrubbed a hand over his face. "And good morning." He whished her into his arms, returning her yip of surprise with a nibble to her ear. She could have melted into his embrace all over again, but he suddenly tensed, his hands patting her clothes, his gaze taking in the illuminated room. "I can't believe I slept in again! We need to meet Vi and Caleb and get home. Jin was *pissed* I left Ware Woods and will probably check up on me. He's worse than my father." A low grumble.

He leapt from the bed, whished on his clothes, and rushed to the patio, pulling Sara with him. She tottered on the uneven stone, beholding the table now cleaned of their dinner remnants and reset with a platter of fruit. To their left, a tree tunnel parted open. Thomas lunged for the path, kinetically snatching a pair of apples as they entered the tunnel, the hot springs vanishing from view.

He tossed her an apple. "I know apples are your favorite and I saw you eyeing these." He bit into his. Surprised joy shone on his face, his aura flashing bright orange. "Wow. And now I know why. Any chance we can get these to grow in Ware Woods?"

She squeezed his hand, easily matching his swift pace. "Let's get through the Equinox, then we'll plant a whole orchard."

"That's a deal," he projected, his mouth full.

By the time they devoured their fruit, the tunnel opened at Florine's tree. Violet, Caleb, Bettina, and Florine sat at the stone table, eating and laughing as though they'd known each other for ages.

"There you are," said Florine, rising from her seat and coming around the table to meet Sara and Thomas, the rest of them joining her. "I trust you had an informative and energizing night." It was a statement, not a question. Her eyes twinkled with knowing.

Warmth crept up Sara's neck. Just how much did this High Witch know? "Uh, yeah. Thanks. The hot spring and *thoughtful* accommodations were . . . lovely."

Florine glowed. "I see your bespelled hazelnut was successful," she said to Thomas, who thanked her and gave a rare, unbridled smile.

She faced Sara. "And yours?"

Thomas quirked a brow at her. *"You had a golden nut too?"*

"Yes, but it wasn't anything special." In fact, Thomas's hazelnut had simply been a message, not a spell. At least not any type of spell she knew. Sara smoothed back an errant strand of hair, stalling to form a polite response. "It wasn't so much of a spell as it was a . . . fortune."

"Spells, fortunes, and wishes are all the same. You simply need to believe in them for the magic to happen." Florine waved her hand, her casualness suggesting this was common knowledge. "I'm sure you'll figure it out soon. In the meantime, the cat will assist you." She gestured to Sara's right, where a new tunnel of trees yawned open, revealing a giant lynx-like cat sitting in the center of the shady path.

Sara reared back at the sight of the cat. *It can't be.*

Her bloodstone thumped in recognition as she eyed the double-pawed creature with tufted ears, spotted coat, and short tail. Dorcas's cat. The cat who had slunk off to the Hills site with Dorcas eons ago and who Sara assumed had died as a light snack to some shadow infected flat-eyed dragon.

Sara shook her head. "I have no idea how that cat is here, but it can't possibly assist me." She whipped her gaze to the trinket-loaded tree, searching. Where was the special weapon or *real* spell to defeat the Shadow Mother? Where was the cure to save all dragons? Anything but this familiar of fangs and needle-sharp claws. Hells, Sara was a *dog* person.

"Nonsense," clucked Florine. "This cat will help you. I feel it in my bones. Now, off with you. Try not to let it out of your sight," she added with a gentle nudge as the cat turned away from them and stalked down the path.

Sara gaped at Thomas, hoping he would laugh, and everyone would join in on what had to be a preposterous joke. He merely shrugged and beckoned to his sister. "Come on, Vi."

"I'm staying," said Violet, her tone firm.

Instead of rising to her challenge, Thomas stared, his elysian eyes swirling as if seeing through his sister.

Sara stammered. "What? I—I need your help to consult the Book." She flicked her gaze at the retreating cat, then back at Violet.

"Come on. We all know you don't need my help, but this site does. Their wards were disturbed again last night, and I can quickly repair them. I can be of use here, and I'm choosing to stay—at least for a little while." She crossed her arms, daring anyone to question her.

Florine and Bettina were classical-statue quiet.

"I'll stay too," offered Caleb. "Ya know, to keep an eye on Vi and help out, of course."

Sara swung her head toward her cousin. He wore a new white button-down shirt, the gauzy fabric a match to Bettina's skirts. Happiness replaced the pain and sadness she had seen in his face just a day ago—before the oak looped them here.

Understanding clicked inside her mind. The oak had looped them here because Caleb wanted more for himself, and it seemed Violet did too. And, of course, Sara wanted the same for them.

"Okay," she relented. Smiles all around beamed back at Sara. "But come get me if anything other than a cricket sneeze disturbs these wards."

Violet saluted her as Thomas grabbed Sara's arm and flew them down the tunnel after the cat. Florine's affectionate goodbye wave was the last Sara saw before the tunnel turned and spit them out in front of the olive soul tree. And when the cat ran into a shimmering gap between the olive's gnarled roots, Sara lunged after it with Thomas at her side.

CHAPTER 20

Sara tumbled into their treehouse bedroom, sprawling across the floor in a failed attempt to capture the cat. Before she could kinetically grab it, the cat zoomed out the door and down the stairs. The oak quaked so violently, books fell off the shelf on the opposite side of the room. Sara cursed. Loudly *and* colorfully.

Thomas hauled her up and whished the books back into place. "I'll tell my parents and the Cahills about Violet and Caleb while you find the cat. I'll catch up with you later." He kissed her brow and vanished in a puff of smoke.

Sara tore down the stairs and into the main room. "When I find you, I'm going to—" She screeched to a halt, rumpling the pale green rug. Lethal sat on the couch, blood-red drink in hand, murder in their glittering gray eyes.

"Sit," they ordered.

"But, I—" She gestured toward the deck, toward wherever the cat had skulked off to.

Lethal pursed their perfect lips, and Sara's body betrayed her, plopping into the nearest chair.

"Don't compel me," she grumbled. "I was going to sit."

"Really? Because you have a knack for doing the opposite of what is expected. Like showing up at the Global Council and looping to another site when we agreed to wait." Venom dripped from their words, the truth of them stabbing Sara more painfully than one of Lethal's Death daggers.

She winced. "I admit going to the Council was a rash decision, but looping to Florine's was completely unintentional. Well, maybe not completely." She tapped her chin. "Caleb finally came to me and explained what he lost. And when he said he wanted more from life—poof, we looped to Florine's olive tree."

"More?"

"Yeah, like meeting someone special and all that."

"All that?"

Sara frowned at the puzzled vampire. "Are you parroting me?"

They took a long sip, draining half the goblet, before answering. "No. I'm trying to understand '*all that*' and the fact that Florine let a part-vampire, part-witch *stay* at her site. Caleb could destroy all of them if he wished."

Sara blanched, the abysmal blood supply to her brain leaching away. "Oh?" she squeaked. Ridiculous. Caleb wouldn't hurt them. He stayed behind to protect them and perhaps to have a chance for more with Bettina. It was so obvious Sara was certain Florine knew it and wished for Caleb and Bettina's happiness as well.

More. The idea softly turned over and over in her mind as she studied Lethal, the crease between their brows a clear indicator of their vexation. Why couldn't they understand this?

She frowned deeper. *Oh no.* Her heart stumbled, her limbs falling numb at a possible explanation. "Lethal," she gently inquired. "When Death turned you, what did you lose?"

The world fell silent. Lethal drained the rest of their glass, set it on the table before them, and stared, unblinking, at Sara. "Love."

Oh, Lethal. She froze in their cool stare. That four-lettered word was what made life wonderful—to give and receive love was one of the greatest joys you could feel. Life without it was incomprehensible. A normal lifespan would be torturously dreary, but over a thousand years without love would be . . . impossible.

"Don't look at me that way. I don't want your pity. Death did me a favor. It was a sick and twisted love that shackled me and abused my mortal body. So much was *inflicted* upon me. Death made certain I would never suffer that again." They casually crossed their lean legs, leather pants creaking.

Sara turned away, unable to meet their icy gaze without spilling the tears welling inside her. Glancing out the doorway, toward the meadow and lake beyond, she recalled standing on the shoreline and seeing the many scars and brands that marked Lethal's torso. Brutal reminders of their past. If any of Lethal's abusers were alive today, Sara would have gladly ended them. But she had no doubt that Lethal had hunted them down and exacted their own vengeance ages ago.

The oak released a long groan as if sharing Sara's thoughts. Her mind kicked into overdrive. Though Lethal likely had enjoyed every second of their revenge, had the final kill given them peace? It didn't seem so. The realization sent a shudder through her. Would *she* find peace if she could defeat the Shadow Mother? What if other magicals like Florine and Bettina lost their lives in the process? Could she live with herself afterward? Mother knew she hadn't accepted Caleb's death. And horror of horrors, what would she do if anything happened to Thomas?

Her downward-spiraling thoughts ended when a glimmer of movement on the lake's frozen surface snagged her attention. Someone was headed toward the treehouse. Given their white-blonde hair and unnaturally quick pace, it had to be Lily.

Sara glanced at Lethal, who was already watching the half-vampire, half-witch traversing the frozen lake toward them. A slight upturn showed at the corners of Lethal's flawless lips. The reaction was faint, but it was there—a trace amount of happiness. And like a thunderbolt announcing the promise of rain on a scorched field, Sara was struck by the awareness that Lethal *cared*. And caring was a form of love. Lethal hadn't lost the ability to love, because that would make life impossible. What Lethal lost was *one* type of love. And considering the vampire's alluded-to past, Death doubtlessly took the one that had hurt them the most—lust.

But it seemed Lethal had been so wounded, they hadn't opened themselves to unconditional caring love. Perhaps they'd never known such love before being made into a vampire and craved it. Maybe they assumed the love they wanted most was twistedly tied to the abuse they abhorred the most. If Lethal thought love was a singular notion, then they might assume *all* love had been taken away. And similar to Caleb's desire for *more*, maybe the cost of being a vampire wasn't the one thing you *most* wanted, but something other.

She gripped her knees, contemplating the best approach to tell Lethal, their arrogance and set ways likely keeping them resistant to such a revelation. Fortunately, or unfortunately, Sara had firsthand experience in being unwilling to listen.

Summoning her father's neutral professor tone, she commented, "When I first met Jin, he said the Mother told him that love would correct the balance. For a dragon who had only known lust and desire, he was confused until I reminded him there are other types, including the caring love of friends and family."

Lethal's gaze narrowed a fraction.

"Speaking of," said Sara, rising from her seat and fighting back a sly grin, "Lily is here. I'm sure you two have plans regarding which vampire sites you'll visit. And if you're done reprimanding me for an *accidental* looping, I have a cat to find and a book to consult." She headed for the open archway, pleased to leave a speechless Lethal to contemplate their definition of love and maybe find a new lease on life, when Lily topped the stairs. In a blur of movement, she zipped across the deck and stood before Sara.

"Morning," said Lily with her usual cheer, her cheeks tinged pink from the winter chill. "Oh good, you're coming with us." She linked arms with Sara and rushed her down the stairs.

"What? Where are we going?" Maybe Lily planned to grab a late breakfast at the Main House before meeting with Lethal. Sara scanned the surrounding cemetery, searching for whoever else was meeting with Lily and for any sign of the cat.

Lethal appeared beside Lily, their movement so fast they seemed to materialize. "Once you *took off*," they said to Sara with a half-hearted scoff, "Lily and I decided it best not to wait. If you care to join us, we're going to Amira's site. Since Lily's grandmother, Claire, is from her colony, I believe we have a chance of convincing her to join us against the Shadow Mother. We will be in and out within a few minutes. This is not a cozy site for spending the night." They peered down their obstinately straight nose at Sara.

She scowled at them. "Florine insisted we spend the night. And yes, I'd like to go with you." The cat was long gone by now, and the opportunity to visit a vampire site with Lethal was too intriguing to pass up. They would be back within minutes, leaving her plenty of time to find the cat and consult the Book before dark. She whished her jacket from the treehouse and slipped it on, guessing a vampire site would be morgue-level cold. "Lead the way, since you're the one who knows where we're going."

Instead of stepping into the humming void at the base of the oak, Lethal lingered, muttering a string of curses, their alabaster face a shade paler than normal.

Lily tugged Sara closer to her, their arms still linked, and extended her other hand to Lethal. "I don't mind if you vomit." Her voice rang with sincerity, her fingers wiggling with encouragement.

"*I* mind if I vomit." Lethal dragged their gaze from Lily's face to her open palm and stared.

Sara held her breath, hoping her assumption about Lethal's loss was accurate and that the Death Vampire was considering her words.

They slowly reached for Lily, their cautious demeanor at odds with their typically unwavering confidence. And when their palms connected and Lily laced her fingers with them, a rainbow of colors flashed in Lethal's silvery aura. "*Grazie,*" they whispered. The grateful softness of their tone squeezed Sara's heart, but before she could crow an unfiltered comment, Lethal and Lily entered the oak, tugging her along with them.

CHAPTER 21

ARKNESS VEILED SARA'S vision, her body floating, the drumming beat of the oak filling her ears, reverberating in her chest. Silken strands caressed her face, their wispy touch similar to stepping into a spider's web. Despite reading in the Book that the Father prohibited anything of ill intent to occur in the Aether, fear coursed through Sara's veins. Lily's grip on her arm tightened as they plummeted, and just when Sara thought they would surely crash into the open maw of a spider, they swung forward and gently landed upon packed soil.

The scent of damp, musty earth flooded her nose. Surrounding them was a grove of towering cypress trees, their shaggy branches twisting up to spear a twilight sky. Gossamer cobwebs clung to the grove's upper canopy while an opaque mist blanketed the ground, obscuring the lower portion of the trees. The mist stretched toward Sara, its cool fingers stroking her cheek.

Where is everyone? Sara inched forward, only to be pushed back by Lethal's outstretched arm.

The mist rippled and parted, unmasking the center of the grove. A cluster of vampires in evening dresses and fine suits, their perfect skin shining like polished stone in the dusky light, whipped their heads toward them. For a fleeting moment, shock widened their beautiful faces before they bared their fangs and hissed.

Dread pooled in Sara's stomach. This was palpably the opposite of Bettina's warm welcome.

Lethal strode into the grove. Vampires scattered, as if they couldn't get away fast enough, clawing up into the trees despite their formal attire. One vampire remained. A regal female in a sinful red dress. Amira.

The Elder Vampire sliced a deadly smile, showcasing two upper fangs as opposed to Lethal's four. Her smile and confident demeanor reminded Sara of Kira. If Amira felt any fear, she didn't show it.

"What an honor to have the Death Vampire visit my site. And you've even brought the High Witch of Ware Woods to sway me in joining you against the Shadow Mother." She swiveled her piercing gaze to Sara. "Only like factions visit one another, and even then, it is rare. How bold of you to come. It speaks of your incapability." Her sensual, flowery accent put a glamorous flourish on her disembowelment of a censure.

The dread squirmed, becoming a writhing mass of eels inside Sara's belly. She muttered, "Yep, bold. That's me." Or rather, naïve and admittedly incapable. She should have stayed in Ware Woods and let Lethal handle the vampires. Perhaps this was why Samson and Kira hadn't accompanied the Death Vampire. Sara wanted to crawl under a rock.

"I'm curious," continued Amira, tilting her head at Lily, "who else did you bring with you? Is this a snack? She smells most un- usual." The Elder Vampire casually cocked her leg, exposing its full length outside the hip-high slit of her gown, and licked her lips.

White flames sizzled in Sara's palm. "Lily is no snack!" Before she could say anything else or launch an energy ball, Lethal blurred to stand between Lily and Sara, a bone-crushing grip on her arm. Her flames vanished.

Amira studied Sara, her eyes glittering with predatory focus. From within the cypress trees, similar gazes glinted down on Sara, presumably waiting for their Elder to give permission to carve out her heart. Though Amira's perfect face was void of any emotion, warm vermillion danced in her aura. "I see you survived that cretin, Brad. Did you find Kira as well?"

"Yes," answered Sara, encouraged by Amira's distaste for Brad and concern for the daughter she had yet to meet. Maybe Sara could use this to her advantage. "Kira and Samson are safe in Ware Woods. But we expect the Shadow Mother to come on the Equinox."

Amira didn't blink, didn't give any reaction at hearing the confirmation of Kira's and Samson's safety or of the Shadow Mother's impending arrival. "You should know Brad has already paid us a visit. He was quite boastful in declaring he controls Kahn and many other Magi. He claims you and the disgraces in Ware Woods are the reason for the imbalance and that we must help the Shadow Mother correct what is wrong—or die with you."

Sara froze. She *was* responsible in part for the imbalance and rise of the Shadow Mother. And by default, she was also responsible for the well-being of all the other sites. Father above, she was in way over her imprudent head.

To her relief, Lethal drawled as if they couldn't care less, "Do you believe him?"

"No."

Sara whooshed, a trace amount of tension loosening between her shoulder blades.

Amira continued, "It is the dragons' role to maintain the balance. The Shadow Mother has no purpose other than to be a poisonous snake in our garden. I do not trust her, but I also do not understand why she concerns herself with the atrocity that is Ware Woods."

"I don't understand either," confessed Sara, bristling at Amira's comment though not deeming it bloodshed worthy. So much for asking her what she knew of the Shadow Mother.

"And you," Amira said to Lethal, "why are you siding with

Ware Woods? It is not like you to give a damn about anything other than blood."

A four-fanged reply graced Lethal's face, their purposeful display of superiority prickling Sara's scalp. Instead of reprimanding Amira for her candor, Lethal stated, with cold steel edging their tone, "Because Ware Woods is not the abomination we thought it to be." Lethal then whispered into Lily's ear, their words too quiet for Sara to hear.

Lily stepped forward, curtsied to Amira, and smiled widely at the vampires perched in the trees. Amira constricted her gaze, her tongue touching the tip of one of her fangs. On silent feet, Lily raced through the grove, winding between the cypresses with the blurred movements of vampire speed. Yet unlike a vampire, she used water and air magic to clear the mist and cover the grove with roses, their stems made of ice, their petals of pristine snow. When the ground dazzled white, not a smudge of packed earth to be seen, and the overhead cypress canopies were cleared of cobwebs and adorned with snowy blooms, Lily stood beside Lethal and said, "It's a pleasure to meet you, Elder Amira. My grandmother Claire sends her regards."

"*Mére ci-dessous.*" Amira's gasp echoed throughout the grove, the colony joining her in a crescendo of disbelief, their astonished faces peeking through the boughs. "You are half-vampire, half-witch and yet not weak but multi-magical. No fangs, yet swift as Lethal and gifted as a High Witch to turn such magic so easily." She plucked a rose, the ice stem snapping, and admired the frozen replica. "I am pleased to hear Claire and her child survived. It was a tragedy what occurred while I was at a Council meeting. Those responsible were severely punished." The whispers in the cypress trees ceased. Amira pointed the rose at Lily. "Tell me, is my daughter weak, or is she like you?"

Lily lifted her chin. "Kira and I have different abilities. She is exceptionally skilled in her own unique way."

Well played, Lily. Sara pressed her lips to hide her grin.

"So what Samson said is true?" Amira mulled over her own question. "And they both reside in Ware Woods. With more like you." Her eyes turned arctic cold. "That is a lot of power. Too much power." The sharp look she threw Sara cut to the bone faster than blade or fang.

Sara stiffened. Amira could be right. If Sara denied it, she would sound like she was hiding something. Which she was. But if she admitted to Ware Woods' uniqueness, she would put this discussion and so much more in jeopardy.

To her relief, Lethal broke the tense silence.

"Ware Woods has always had power," said the Death Vampire. "I can attest that their site vibrates with magic as if the Mother sleeps beneath their beds. Yet they do not assert themselves or terrorize other magicals."

Lethal deserved a bookcase full of whatever sordid stories they desired *and* their own private fridge for the cunningly delivered twofold statement.

When Amira's whetted gaze softened and turned thoughtful, Sara seized her opportunity and stepped forward. In a confident High Witch voice that was more authentic than summoned, she said, "We only want to end the Shadow Mother and restore the balance. Brad lies. She won't stop at destroying Ware Woods. She will consume all magicals and eventually the normal world as well. We need your help. Can we count on you and your colony to join us?"

"Hmm," Amira purred, a devilish curl at the corners of her painted lips. With a mere cursory glance at the grove's canopy, her colony descended, dropping so surefooted among the roses not a stem broke. As one they faced Sara, their finery and mesmerizing gazes causing her heart to falter. Though they appeared coldly distant, they regarded her without a show of fangs. "We will consider it," said Amira, twirling the rose in her hand.

Her formal tone held enough of a promise and a dismissal that

Sara nodded, murmured a thank you, and stepped back toward the ancient cypress soul tree. Lily and Lethal followed without comment, apparently as anxious as Sara to leave before Amira changed her mind.

"And Sara," called out Amira, a sly grin in her voice. "I suggest you visit Damon and secure his favor soon." Her parting advice, her seductive colony, and her white-rose-covered grove dreamily faded as the cypress tree pulled Sara into the static hum of its trunk.

Silken darkness coiled around Sara, all sense of direction escaping her in the soul tree's undulating caress and whooshing heartbeat. After more somersaults through liquid space than she cared to count, Sara popped out of darkness and stumbled into the cemetery, nearly crashing into her mother's gravestone.

She took a deep lungful of crisp air, replacing the crypt-like, musty scent of the vampire's grove with the oak and pine fragrance of Ware Woods. "All things considered, I think that went well," she announced. Amira's favorable response and departing advisement had planted a seed of optimism inside Sara. She ran a hand along the top of her mother's stone, brushing off the snow, and turned to Lily and Lethal, who had both alighted behind her with vampire silence.

In a blur, Lethal bolted to the edge of the cemetery and vomited, the bloody spray churning Sara's stomach.

"At least for some of us," she added, wrinkling her nose.

"*Futuo.* I hate looping." Lethal spat and, in a manner most unlike them, plopped to the ground, head between their knees.

Sara wavered, the metallic scent of blood and the possibility of being told to piss off squashing her urge to console Lethal. Asking them about Damon in their current state would be most impolite. She swallowed her question along with the sympathetic puke building in the back of her throat.

"I'll take care of Lethal." Lily rushed to them, her kindhearted ease the opposite of Sara's rooted apprehension. A twinge of guilt squeezed Sara's chest. Not that she wasn't kindhearted—she had her moments—but approaching the Death Vampire in a vulnerable state was not one of them. With one hand rubbing Lethal's back, Lily summoned a fresh layer of snow, covering the blood.

To Sara's surprise, Lethal leaned into Lily's touch, the pair pressing sides as they sat next to each other. Though it appeared a simple act of accepting kindness, Sara knew Lethal well enough to understand this was anything but simple for them. She had no doubt Lily understood this as well.

Sara cleared her throat. "Thanks to both of you for being awesome and handling Amira so well."

Neither a pale blonde nor a golden head turned in her direction.

Not wanting to be a third wheel in a private moment, Sara stammered, "Alrighty then, I'll just check in with Gran and consult the Book." *Hopefully it knows who this Damon is and where I can find him.*

Sara fled for the rear of the cemetery toward a cluster of pines already shifting to reveal a path. Though flying to the blue house would be quick, Sara needed a long moment to walk, think, and— hopefully—clear her head.

She hopped the low fence, instantly soothed by the snowy quiet of the forest and the occasional whistling bird instead of hissing vampires. Amira and her colony had been intense, yet despite their wariness, they seemed willing to help.

Sara slowed her pace. Would their willingness be enough to ensure Kira's safety? Amira said she had punished those responsible for attacking Claire, and she seemed sincerely interested in her daughter. Even before meeting Lily, Amira had wanted to know more about Kira when Samson admitted his deceit at the Global Council.

Sara slid her hands into her pockets, absently kicking up snow as she unraveled her thoughts. Amira and her site may be open-minded to half-breeds and Ware Woods, but there were still dozens of sacred sites that needed to be convinced before the Equinox. And while convincing as many sites as possible to join Ware Woods against the Shadow Mother was rationally their best course of action, Sara couldn't ignore the persistent pull in the embers of her magic to find another way. One that didn't promise bloodshed—that didn't feed the Shadow Mother more of the violence she craved.

What Sara needed was a magical miracle. She beseeched the Father above, ever watching from the Aether, that the Book would provide a spell or at least some insight on the Shadow Mother.

The path swerved around a cluster of hemlock and dipped to a frozen brook, the water's presence and ribbonous flow reminding her of dragons. Sara leapt over the water, mind skipping to her conversation with Thomas in the hot spring—to knowing she had a dragon ancestor. Her bloodstone pulsed as she chewed on this realization. A very big realization that suspiciously had never been discussed in her family. Perhaps they didn't know. But that was absurd. *Someone* along the line must have known and deliberately kept quiet about it. Kept it a secret.

She hunched into her jacket, summoning a smidge of white flames to warm her. Other than Alice's ability to shift, a few black toenails, and the faint line down Sara's spine, her family had no discernable dragon traits. Which meant whatever dragon blood existed in the Lochton family had to be inconsequential. And thankfully so. It meant the Shadow Mother couldn't control them. Of this, Sara was certain; otherwise, the Shadow Mother would have fully controlled her the first time they met.

Sara stopped walking. Not only had the Shadow Mother *not* been able to control her, Sara had pushed *back* at the entity by tapping into her rage and defiance.

Clearly, having a wee bit of dragon in her family didn't make them susceptible to the Shadow Mother's infection. And no one in Ware Woods was opposed to the mixing of factions. So why would their dragon ancestry be kept a secret? Given her clever family, there had to be a good reason, and one Sara would need to be careful in uncovering.

Pondering dragons, a Magus named Damon, and her need for a magical miracle, Sara hadn't thought much of the paw prints before her, their close-set marks suggesting a lazy gait along the snowy path, until she remembered—the cat!

The fluffy feline wasn't a magical miracle but, as Florine suggested, it might assist Sara.

She flew down the path, following the prints past the Lochton pine with snow-laden boughs, past the blueberry bushes with straggly winter branches, and into the backyard of the blue house. There it was—the lynx-like creature—sauntering up to the rear door, which opened on its own volition. The cat disappeared inside.

Sara dove after it, the door closing behind her.

CHAPTER 22

A COMMOTION OF hollers and thick claws scrambling on wood flooring arose from the kitchen. By the time Sara vaulted through the living room, the cat was sitting before the brick hearth, an expectant expression on its tufted face.

Gran set down the teapot she had been holding, a towel magically wiping up the counter around her overflowing cup. From across the kitchen island, Alice slid from her barstool and comforted Albert, her mate stuck in wolf form, who danced before the cat as if unsure whether he should attack or hide from the unexpected visitor.

"Oh my," declared Alice with a glance at Sara. "Wherever did you find Jynx?" She stroked the fur between Albert's eyes, calming him into standing still, his flank pressed against her side, his amber gaze trained on the cat.

Sara groaned. Of course the cat had to be named Jynx, because Lucky or Solution-To-All-My-Problems were too easy. "I didn't find the cat. It found me—at another sacred site, no less. The other High Witch said it would help me, but I don't see how, especially since it was Dorcas's cat."

"This cat belongs to all of Ware Woods," said Gran. "It's been around for as long as I can remember and only followed Makwa and Dorcas because they fed it."

The cat blinked.

An ageless creature motivated by food, huh? Sara eyed the counter: apple pie with lofty crust and cinnamon-flecked filling, half a brick of Cahill cheddar cheese, two plates, and two cups of tea—one filled to the brim. She impatiently flicked her hands, whishing another cup of tea and three more plates, then served them all pie and cheese—including Albert and the cat. With another groan, she sank onto a barstool. "Alrighty, let's feed the cat and see what happens."

They ate in silence, everyone watching the cat. Even Albert managed to be quiet as he scarfed down his food while maintaining his vigilance. Though not ambrosia apples, Gran's pie was exquisite, the cheese a chef's kiss. Yet instead of meowing for more, the cat stretched out before the hearth, soft flames waving from the fire's charcoaled logs, and fell asleep. Albert grumbled a whine and lay down as well. Alice gave an affectionate kiss to his silvery-white furry head before settling onto the stool beside Sara.

Jynx, indeed. Sara scowled into her teacup.

Gran gathered the empty plates and set them in the sink. "I'm surprised you went anywhere. Weren't you supposed to consult the Book while everyone else waited a few days before visiting other sites?"

Seemingly hearing its name, the Lochton family grimoire manifested above the kitchen island. With a frantic flick of her wrist, Sara whished aside their teacups as the Book whumped to the counter, clacking the silver pie server against the pottery plate. The cat swiveled a tufted ear, its eyes still closed.

"It's a long story," said Sara, placing her four-fingered hand atop the Book. It pulsed in greeting. "The good news is we've gained a couple of allies. The not-so-great news is they didn't have any useful information about the Shadow Mother. In fact, I now have more questions than answers." *Like, should I let Samson threaten to turn the cat inside out, so it'll cough up a magical miracle? And who the Hells is Damon?*

The Book swelled with a prideful puff and straightened the

haphazard edges of its worn pages. Thank the Mother it was in a good mood. All the same, Sara remained calm, nonchalant even. In the past, showing excitement or agitation often caused the Book to ceaselessly ruffle its pages before snapping shut. It was unpredictable, often cryptic, and prone to wanting its ego stroked. "Hello, Book," she greeted, giving its scarred leather cover a pat warmed by her magic. It shimmied closer to Sara.

Gran snorted a laugh. "Shall we feed it pie and cheese too?"

"Hush, Rosetta," chastised Alice. "Sara knows what she's doing."

Nope. Not really. Because if the Book had shown any interest in food, Sara would've fattened it up with her own piece of pie.

Taking a gamble that the finicky Book saw right through her, Sara laid out her cards. "The Shadow Mother is coming for us again, and she is much more powerful this time. I need to stop her before she comes to Ware Woods on the Equinox—before anyone is harmed. Is there *anything* you know about her that will help me do this?"

The Book shivered.

Muffled crackles from the dying fire filled the waiting stillness, an ominous foreboding of Ware Woods being reduced to ash if Sara couldn't defeat the Shadow Mother. Swallowing, she contemplated asking her question again when the Book opened to a blank page. Black ink bled up from the parchment and in deliberate, curly script divulged:

The Shadow Mother is afraid of Ware Woods.

Sara frowned, expecting the words to shift into something more sensical. This couldn't be right. Yet this was what Kira had said as well. The big mystery was—

"Why?" asked Gran, abruptly voicing the thought on Sara's mind. She had less patience than Sara, which meant none.

The script faded. In an explosion of color, an image of the oak tree sprang to life on the page, followed by dragons, witches, vampires, and shifters—each rendition overlapping into the next in an animated fury. The Book trembled, its pages rippling, the images dissolving into one another faster and faster. It didn't make sense. The grimoire hovered above the counter, teetering as if preparing to clap shut.

"Stop!" cried Sara.

The images vanished. To her relief, the Book softly ruffled in a literary sigh before lowering back to the counter, its page blank once again.

She smoothed her hands across the Book, its fibrous, bumpy parchment tingling against her fingertips. Continuing her calming strokes, Sara considered the previous images. Perhaps the Shadow Mother was afraid of facing them all at once. It made sense given the Book's original warning to never stand alone before the Shadow Mother and given Ware Woods was once able to turn her away. But Ware Woods couldn't do this again. They barely survived before, and now the Shadow Mother was growing stronger.

Sara drummed her fingers, her mind flashing through the images the Book had shown. There had been an enormous dark green elysian-eyed dragon that she'd only seen once before in the Book, months ago, when she'd first asked for an explanation on dragons. The various witches, vampires, and shifters, she'd never seen. Which meant . . .

She relaxed her shoulders. It was a comfort to know Ware Woods had a fighting chance *if* other magicals joined them. But this wasn't what she'd asked the Book. Sara had asked for a way to end the Shadow Mother *before* an epic battle with unimaginable casualties.

There had to be a way. She *needed* a way to fix her mistakes.

Sara looked up at her grandmother and great-aunt, their faces reflecting the same apprehension that iced her veins.

"The Book has helped you before," projected Alice, the pleasant lilt in her voice quieting Sara's frenzied thoughts. *"As I recall, that was some spell you cast on Samhain to summon the aid of Lethal, Dean, and Samson. Do you remember how you asked the Book for such help?"*

Sara held her great-aunt's amber gaze and gave a nod. Alice was right; the Book had been a significant help because Sara had asked for a spell—not general information but a specific spell.

She withdrew her hands from the Book and clutched the edge of the countertop. If the Shadow Mother was afraid of Ware Woods, then Ware Woods must still be capable of hurting her. Sara just needed a specific spell to guide her on how to accomplish this. "Can you please provide a spell that will help me defeat the Shadow Mother?"

A moving illustration of two hands wringing themselves appeared on the page. They faded, the ink crawling painstakingly slow to form three words:

Yes and no.

The answer that was not an answer vanished. Then, one curly scripted word at a time appeared:

Such a dangerous spell is not in this book.

The dark grimoire is where you should look.

Sara slumped back. The dark grimoire? Alice shrugged while Gran furrowed her brow in thought. Ware Woods didn't have a dark book.

This simple request for a spell was becoming a mysterious adventure Sara had zero time for. She folded her arms. "Where can I find the dark grimoire?"

The page flipped to a scene of writhing brimstone briars. Gran and Alice joined Sara in staring at the dark, thorny vines, waiting for them to reveal something—anything. After a few tense moments of nothing, the book shivered and flipped to a new page.

Sara jolted, slipping off her stool. On the page was a drawing of

Jynx, stretched out and asleep before the brick hearth—a precise copy of the cat's current position.

"Seems this cat is meant to help you," said Gran, pointing her teacup toward Jynx. The cat's snowshoe-like, furry, double paws twitched with sleep. "The question is when."

Indeed. Had Florine and the Book pointed Sara to Bailey, Ian's yellow Lab, she would have already had the dark grimoire and spell. A cat, on the other hand, would likely help Sara only if and when it deigned to do so. Pfft.

She turned her attention back to the Book. Since discovering the spell was at the mercy of a sleepy cat, now was as good a time as any to find out who Damon was and to secure his favor. Hopefully, he was a teddy bear of a shifter who would look past her transgressions and gladly take on the role of uniting the factions. Though Sara was capable of leading Ware Woods, she most certainly did not have the special sauce to heal centuries of distrust among dozens of magical groups and lead them against the Shadow Mother.

"Who is Damon?" asked Sara. To Gran's raised brow, she whispered, "An Elder Vampire told me to visit him."

"Of course." Gran scoffed.

A rustling of pages came before the Book settled open on a colored image of a broad-shouldered male with a fierce gaze and mane of silver locs. *Crap.* The Alpha Shifter who wanted the Shadow Mother to *purge* the *abomination* that was Ware Woods. The Alpha who did *not* want to unite the factions. The one bold enough to question Lethal.

A sudden light-headedness engulfed Sara.

"He looks delightful," said Gran, her sarcastic tone thicker than her wool cardigan. "Promise us you won't visit him alone. Take Thomas with you."

"Thomas can't go. Jin doesn't want him or Tobio leaving the forest." In a casual tone, careful to avert her eyes in case they shone with knowing, Sara ventured, "Did you know dragons were so protective of their family—even non-full-blooded dragon family?" She swore Alice stiffened, but Gran didn't miss a beat.

"Dragons are natural hoarders," said her grandmother, dismissing her question.

The quick comment temporarily squashed Sara's pursuit to know more about their dragon ancestor. There were more important things to deal with right now. Like violence-inclined Alpha Shifters.

After a sip of tea, Alice said, "Take Dean with you. Maybe he knows this Damon and can offer a smooth introduction."

"I hope so," said Sara. Surely one Alpha would listen to another, especially when so much was at stake.

She softly closed the grimoire, her gaze on the sleeping cat. It was assuredly in no hurry to retrieve the dark book and spell she needed. Fine. She'd rather visit Damon and plead for his favor before Brad got his hooks into him.

With a thanks for the pie, Sara pushed in her stool and rushed for the back door. She called over her shoulder, "Tell me when the cat does anything interesting." Albert's woofed response followed her out into the crisp afternoon, sunlight glinting on the snowy backyard.

CHAPTER 23

SARA ROSE ABOVE the treetops, zipping her jacket against the cold as she soared for the Main House. Dean and the pack currently resided there, with the unspoken agreement that Sara would help them restore their site—burnt by dragon fire—once they defeated the Shadow Mother. Lodgings aside, the pack never strayed far from the Cahill kitchen, ecstatic for every lovingly prepared meal.

She slowed her flight, narrowly avoiding a mismatched flock of birds flying away from the center of the forest, her mind on food instead of flying. If all shifters loved food as much as the pack and the Walkers, perhaps she could win over Damon with some of Helen's specialties.

Thoughts of an edible peace offering shattered when a dragon roar tore through the tree canopy. Startled evergreens shook, loosening drifts of snow.

Her heart leapt to her throat. *"Thomas?"* she mentally shouted, shooting higher into the sky before spying his blue dragon and Tobio's black dragon chasing each other around the Cahill common.

"We're just sparring. Tobio is damn quick, and I can't dodge his blows fast enough. It's frustrating." His last word was a gritted snarl before he roared again.

Seriously. They should have designated sparring times so the entire forest didn't suffer a heart attack every time he bellowed.

Sara flew closer. Tobio's lean dragon rammed Thomas in the side before zooming off toward the birch grove with a furious Thomas on his tail. In the common below, a group of wolves sparred as well. Their vicious growls spiked a dose of flight-screaming adrenaline through Sara. Despite seeing the pack playfully tussle many times, she preferred to observe their cutthroat sparring sessions from afar. Even Bailey, who often ran with them, hung back in the common, keeping a wary distance from their snapping jaws.

Sara landed on the sprawling wood deck of the Main House, multiple exterior fireplaces comfortably heating the space. On one of the longer tables, Dean and Moira sat beside each other, studying a poster-sized map. As Sara neared, she spotted its many green-circled areas in addition to a few black circles crossed out with giant X marks. The last time she'd seen this map of global sacred sites, it had been pinned to the wall in Ian's basement office.

Dean looked up at her and quickly cleared his throat. "We're planning which shifter sites to visit based on the possible locations of Moira's siblings."

Sara tapped her finger on one of the black circles. "I don't remember these concentrations of dark magic being crossed out. Has something changed?"

"When Samson went searching for Kira, he couldn't find any rogue dark magicals or their Takers. He thinks the Shadow Mother either took their magic—and killed them—or brought them to wherever she's hiding with the flat-eyed dragons."

That wasn't good news, but not altogether unexpected. Sara knew the Shadow Mother was getting stronger and amassing an army of Takers. All the same, seeing the evidence left a bitter taste in her mouth.

"Speaking of Samson, is he around?" Since he knew so much about dark magic, it was possible he knew where Sara could find the dark book she needed. She hoped so, because waiting on a cat seemed ridiculous when the Equinox was mere months away.

Moira sat back in her chair and said, "Samson, Kira, and Ian looped off to a series of witch sites this morning. Ted and Charlie went with them."

Bummer. Besides asking about the dark grimoire, Sara had also wanted to tell Samson that Amira seemed most interested in Kira. She couldn't fathom what it had been like for the three of them to be split apart because of factional differences and misunderstandings. The entire unfortunate situation was eerily similar to her own parents leaving Ware Woods—leaving Ian—because they thought it was the only way to keep everyone safe. And though Sara's mother was now among the stars, the thought sending a crushing ache to her heart, Kira's mother was alive and seemingly keen on her. Sara hoped they would have time for a pleasant reunion instead of meeting in battle against the Shadow Mother.

"Oh," was all Sara managed as she straddled the table's bench and flopped down opposite Dean and Moira.

In a clatter of claws and a chorus of phasing snaps, the rest of the Blue Ridge pack, as well as Matthew, joined them. Moesha, Alesha, and Iesha sank into three identical heavy wooden chairs while Luke crashed onto the bench beside Dean. The entire deck bounced.

Wes sprang up the wide steps and grabbed a chair by the triplets, Bailey lying down at his feet. The only one standing was Matthew. He watched the two dragons racing for the Main House, and when Tobio phased and thudded to the wooden deck, Matthew joined him in sitting at a nearby table.

Many seconds after Tobio, Thomas reached the deck in a spine-tingling rasp of scales. He phased and smoked in mid-air, then reappeared in an ashy cloud on the bench behind Sara, his chest against her back, jean-clad legs on either side of hers. He twined an arm around her waist and placed a kiss on the back of her head. Energy crackled around them.

"Feeling possessive, are we?" A smile pulled at her mouth as she leaned into him and summoned a breeze to clear his smoke.

His hand splayed on her hip. *"Luke has a wandering eye."*

"Yeah, but not a death wish."

The deck fell silent.

Moira narrowed her honeyed gaze at them. "You two seem different. More . . . glowy. Did something happen at the site you disappeared to?" Her smirk grew ear to ear, Alesha softly howling behind her.

Was it that obvious? Sara didn't dare glance down at Thomas's arm around her, at the light-blue magic that had occasionally flickered around them before but was now a permanent sheen since their night at the hot spring when their bond strengthened. She schooled her features—and judging by Moira's deepening grin, doing a terrible job of it.

Overhead, Moira's raven, Trouble, circled and cackled with laughter. Sara shot the bird a frown before answering. "A few things happened, including Caleb coming out of hiding and me coming back with a cat that I hope you can talk to because it has something I need. First, though, I must visit an Alpha Shifter named Damon and secure his favor to join us."

Dean's characteristically kind appearance hardened. The triplets stiffened, and Tobio hissed.

All Hells. They did know him.

"I—I saw him at the Global Council. He wasn't exactly giddy to help us." Not in the least. He wanted to help the Shadow Mother eliminate them, yet she couldn't tell them this. "Amira, an Elder Vampire who happens to be Kira's mother, basically told me to gain his alliance before Brad brings him to the dark side." She was rambling. Shutting her mouth was probably best given the tension radiating off Dean. Behind her, Thomas tensed as well.

"Damon is my uncle," said Dean. "He doesn't help anyone unless it is in *his* favor."

Luke growled. "Damon is a piece of—"

The triplets snarled louder, silencing him.

"Aw, come on," said Luke, "it's why you're here. He's a tyrant."

Sara looked at Moesha, Alesha, and Iesha. The scowls on their beautiful faces disclosed they knew all too well how much of a tyrant Damon was. Stars above.

"He's your father?" Sara choked.

"He sired us," clarified Moesha, a hook of disgust on her lips. "And as his daughters, he has one expectation of us—one we do not agree with. So when Dean and Tobio needed help, when it was just the two of them protecting the Blue Ridge site, we joined them."

Just the two of them?

Either Sara projected her thought or Dean read the confusion on her face. He said, "After my father passed, the pack was afraid of Tobio. They all went to Damon, making his Black Forest pack the largest shifter pack in the magical community. We are the smallest. Even when Luke and Wes joined us, Damon refused to acknowledge us as a proper pack. It's why I didn't attend the recent Global Council meeting. My presence would've launched Damon into a rampage." He scrubbed his cropped hair with one of his dinner plate-sized hands. "Convincing him to join us against the Shadow Mother will be difficult. Damon is very traditional in his beliefs. He distrusts witches and vampires and absolutely hates dragons—he still hasn't forgiven Tobio for what happened."

Dean didn't say it, but Sara remembered what Tobio had once told her: He had been young, given by his dragon mother to be raised by their Alpha father, and without any proper dragon training, he had accidentally killed their father.

Sara's heart ached for Tobio. Though she knew it wasn't true, a part of her felt responsible for her mother's death. If she had learned to harness her powers sooner, she could have saved her mother from the car crash. Sara carried that guilt, that grief and shame, in a dark pocket of her soul. From Tobio's clenched fists, the muscles feathering along his jaw, and storm clouds swirling in his golden eyes, Sara knew he carried similar crushing weights.

Matthew put a hand on Tobio's forearm. The half-dragon shifter eased, the storm ebbing in his gaze.

From across the table, Luke leaned back on the bench, arms folded, and grinned. "If we're paying Damon a visit—and Tobio is forbidden from this fun—I'll be Dean's second."

"In your wet dreams," barked Alesha, her pointed nails cutting into the wooden arms of her chair. She bared her teeth at Luke. "I'm second." Confidence pounded her words like a gavel, her stiff posture a warrior at attention.

Dean growled, the low threat vibrating the table and deck floorboards. Everyone, except Moira, shrank back. "Tobio is my second. His absence from this mission doesn't affect our pack's structure because Moira will be by my side. She will have my back." He cast her an approval-seeking glance, and when Moira smiled, a faint blush on her cheeks, Dean continued. "The rest of you have your own equally important roles. Our unity is our strength."

Mission? Pop-in visit sounded much more pleasant. Sara hoped Thomas couldn't feel her pulse escalating. Regardless of her gnawing apprehension, she had to complete this *mission* and secure Damon's aid. If Damon had the largest pack, and given his brutal demeanor, it stood he had influence over other packs. It must be why Amira suggested Sara win his favor.

The wolf shifters met Dean's cool stare and dipped their chins in acceptance before settling back as though nothing had happened.

Dean turned to Thomas. "I assume Jin also doesn't want you to leave Ware Woods?"

"He didn't outright forbid me as he did with Tobio, but he did *reprimand* me when I left the last time. So no. I will not be going." He wrapped his other arm around Sara.

"We'll protect Sara. You have nothing to fear," promised Dean.

Thomas chuckled a puff of dragon smoke. "Oh, I'm not worried about Sara. I'm disappointed I won't be able to see Damon's reaction when she puts him in his place."

Dean grinned as if he too looked forward to such a spectacle. A highly doubtful spectacle.

Their confidence in Sara twisted her insides. It'd be a miracle if she could sway Damon. He seemed to already hate her. Not that Sara gave a crap if he liked her so long as he agreed to help Ware Woods. And from what she knew of Damon, it would take all her willpower to talk to him in a calm voice instead of setting him on fire.

She clenched her hands, her palms already prickling with energy. Hopefully Dean would do most of the talking.

When Sara remained quiet, Dean slid his gaze over the pack and announced, "We'll leave at dawn. With the time difference, most of the Black Forest pack will be sleeping or on patrol. It's our best chance for a small audience with Damon."

Sara swallowed. A small audience should things get ugly. She would have to be on her best behavior.

If only she had such a thing.

CHAPTER 24

AFTER SHARING A meal with the pack and the Cahills at the Main House, and turning in early—Thomas instantly falling asleep, much to Sara's chagrin since the rest of the treehouse had been empty—Sara rolled out of bed at dawn.

Thomas already stood at the window opening, peering down at the cemetery. "They're here," he said, his voice thick with sleep despite the mug of coffee in his hand.

Sara slipped into her clothes, boots, and jacket. Her stomach queasy, she passed on the breakfast Thomas had brought her, mentally thanking him all the same before grabbing his hand and flying out the window opening. They landed beside Matthew and Tobio, Moira and the rest of the pack before them. Thomas embraced Sara and nipped the edge of her ear. With his lips against her skin, his voice low, he said, "You won over my father. I'm sure Damon will be easy by comparison."

Her knotted insides suggested otherwise, yet she sent him reassuring warmth through the bond. Kane had tried to kill her on more than one occasion before she *won him over*.

With far too many sets of eyes on her, Sara forced down her doubt and pulled out her swagger. She stepped away from Thomas and announced, "Tell Helen to expect us all for breakfast soon. We'll be in and out with favor in hand before her waffles can get cold."

Wes perked up. "Mmm, waffles."

"Waffles," chorused Moesha and Iesha, eyes glazing over.

"Don't eat them all," said Luke, jabbing a finger into Tobio's shoulder.

The half-dragon swiftly put Luke in a headlock, playfully tugging his blond hair. "Then make it quick." He shoved a laughing Luke away.

Dean rose to his full mountainous height, the simple act snapping everyone's attention to him. "We're stronger than the last time we faced the Black Forest pack. If they challenge us, we'll show them the difference."

The triplets smirked, appearing eager for a full-on brawl.

Dean faced Sara, a touch of concern in his golden-yellow eyes. "Shifters are more physical than witches. Whatever happens, don't interfere on our behalf." He held her gaze, waiting for her acknowledgement.

How could she agree to this? If they were attacked, Sara would instinctively protect all of them. Her eyes widened on Dean. The fierce independence radiating from him—rippling in his gray-and-yellow aura—implied for her to do so would be an insult. Damon would deem them too weak to defend themselves. All of them would become vulnerable, including Sara. Her mind raced with memories of nature shows about ferocious predator behaviors, brutal bits of information stuffed away for a rainy day of Trivial Pursuit—or interacting with Alpha Shifters.

Sara's mouth dried. Apex predators did not tolerate the vulnerable—they eliminated them. But if Damon thought the pack was weak and that all of Ware Woods was vulnerable, he was sorely mistaken.

She nodded.

With a flash of his dazzling white teeth, Luke saluted Tobio, Matthew, and Thomas—the trio standing with hands in their pockets and wariness on their faces. When Tobio jerked his chin at him, Luke pivoted, releasing an eager howl, and leapt into the shimmering void at the base of the oak tree. Dean murmured to Moira, his words none of Sara's concern. The two clasped hands and strode into the tree. In a series of yips and howls, the triplets followed: Alesha with the promise of violence on her face, Moesha with a casual flick of her double-plaited braids, and Iesha with a soft smile.

Wes stepped up to the tree next. He adjusted his ball cap, securing the fit, his hesitation pulling at Sara's nerves. Perhaps Wes wasn't ready. Perhaps this was too much to ask of him—of any of them. As if knowing he'd fooled Sara, Wes threw her a wink before back-flipping into the void with a howl that lingered after him.

Sara shook her head. If they all survived this mission, she'd return his trickery by salting his milk at breakfast. Caleb had done it to her once, and practically fell from his stool with laughter at her contorted face. She shrugged off the mouth-puckering thought and turned to Thomas.

His eyes blazed molten blue. *"Pull on the bond if you need me. I'll incinerate the entire site."*

She gave him a grin, partly because it was a classic Thomas reaction to go to a violent, no-questions-asked extreme and partly because she needed to keep the mood light—for his sake and for hers. *"I prefer the scent of waffles over burnt fur."* She blew him a kiss and said, "See you soon." And with a horrible imitation of a wolf howl that elicited a burst of laughter from the otherwise somber trio, she hopped into the tree.

Cool, crisp darkness like midnight in autumn skimmed Sara's face and tugged her hair as she tumbled through the Aether. The pack's howls and yips reverberated around her as if they were falling through a tunnel. Fine roots, soft as fur, brushed Sara's outstretched hands, the earthy scent of decomposing pine needles flooding her nose. She pulled in her arms, willing herself to fall faster and catch up with the rest. And just when the howls became louder, they abruptly stopped, the plummet ending in a swift yank, depositing Sara on crusty snow beside an enormous pine tree.

Beside her stood Dean and Moira while the rest of the pack phased and spread out: the triplets in front, Luke to her right, and Wes on the far left. Before them loomed Damon.

Father above, he was much bigger than Sara remembered. Then again, he had been sitting at the Global Council. He was a mountain of an Alpha, larger than Dean and Bill Walker, his silver locs a glacial mane, his bare forearms covered in scars. Behind him menaced five giant gray wolves, heads lowered, ears back, claws gripping the icy ground—ready to lunge.

A tumult of vicious snarls, setting Sara's every hair on end, closed in from the sides. Five more wolves flanked the right, five more flanked the left, terribly close to Wes. Sara's bloodstone thumped, slow and steady as though trying to calm her rabbit-quick heart rate. They were surrounded by wolves, their only escape to rush back into the soul tree, tails between their legs.

Sara forced herself to stand at her full height and raise her chin—to stop looking at the many claw-tipped paw prints crushed into the snow. If most of Damon's pack were sleeping or on patrol, he must have dozens of wolf shifters at his command—an army. Amira was right; she needed Damon's favor. Not only to help Ware Woods defeat the Shadow Mother, but also to repair the rift between Damon and the Blue Ridge pack. The thought of them facing off—of the triplets fighting their own father—wrapped tightly around Sara's heart.

She could not fail this mission.

Damon sneered at her. "I should rip out your throat for coming here, *witch*."

Are you kidding me? I should rip out your *throat!* He didn't even acknowledge her as High Witch. The bloodstone thumped again. *Calm yourself.*

Sara bit her tongue, focusing on the copper taste of blood

instead of falling for his challenge by spewing the stream of curses gathered behind her teeth.

Damon dismissed her with a grunt. "Dean, figures your group of misfits has aligned with Ware Woods." He inhaled deeply, nostrils flaring, scenting each and every one of them. His citrine eyes narrowed. "Where is the half-breed whelp that killed my brother? Too scared to tag along, or did you finally get rid of him like I told you?"

Sara's tenuous hold on herself slipped. "Tobio has more important things to do than visit you." And just to twist the knife in Damon's pride, she casually inspected her nails. It was all she could do not to glance at Damon and witness his fury, to not grin like an absolute idiot while his growl pounded her rib cage. She hoped Dean would forgive her for speaking for him and poking his uncle. After all, it had only been words and not physical interference.

Damon double-punched the air. He pointed at Luke and Wes with his clawed index fingers. His next victims. "And you still have these two mutts, driven off by their packs for being weak." Luke snarled, and to Sara's horror, Wes dipped his head, ears drooping.

Sara fidgeted, snow squeaking under her boots, her palms hot with energy. *Come on, Wes. Don't let him get to you.*

Beside her, Dean held his ground, hands on his hips, a placid, almost bemused look on his wide face. "Is that what you think." Not a question—a challenge.

Damon grinned, revealing elongated canines. He jerked his chin at the wall of wolves beside Wes, and two subordinates leapt for him. With a yip, Wes flipped onto his back. A submissive gesture.

All Hells! This mission would be over before it even started. Sara had to do something. White energy flared in her palms. Before she could flick her magic, Dean held up his hand, halting her. Sara fisted her magic, trembling with restraint. She'd consented not to interfere, but Wes—

Wes kicked, raking his attacker's stomach and throwing the wolf aside. In a flash of teeth, he leapt at the second wolf, his jaws snapping on the wolf's neck, not hard enough to maim but hard enough to deliver a message. Wes released his hold and pranced back to his position. The two Black Forest wolves whined as they limped back to their line, crimson blood streaking the snowy ground beneath them.

Sara's jaw dropped. Trickster Wes. Jokey. She was so riveted she'd let down her guard, forgetting about the wolves at her own back when Luke barked. Her scalp prickled, her protective shield sparking awake as she whirled to the gnashing of teeth behind her. In a twisting chaos of fur and fangs, of snarls and yips, Luke fought with three wolves—their constant motion making it impossible to tell who was who until three wolves ran back to their line, tails sweeping the ground. Luke barked once more before swiveling his hard amber gaze at Damon. Challenge met.

The Alpha Shifter glared at his line of wolves, and Dean gave a low chuckle. Damon snapped his attention to Moesha, Alesha, and Iesha. Though his expression remained fierce, which Sara now suspected was his natural resting face and very similar to Alesha's everyday expression, a touch of softness rippled through his features. "It's nice to see my girls. You're welcome back whenever you tire of playing with your cousins."

When the triplets didn't move a muscle, Damon shrugged it off and stepped closer, his focus already on Moira. Dean growled, his deep-chested warning shaking the ground with such force, the mighty soul tree swayed its branches.

Many of the wolves shrank back. A knowing smile lit up Damon's face. "Your scent is peculiar," he said to Moira, clasping his hands behind his back. "Wolf yet not wolf. A Ware Woods *anomaly*. And given my nephew's aggression, you must be quite special. Tell me, what is your animal form?"

Moira flicked back her hair, streams of dawn light setting her red tresses on fire. "I have many," she declared, her husky voice rich with confidence. And as if she had planned her performance, Moira phased into a hawk, taking flight around the gathering, her cry piercing the Black Forest site. She swooped to the ground and, in a flash of golden light, phased into a mighty bear—the largest Sara had ever seen—and released a deafening roar. Damon's pack retreated a few more steps, their heads bowed. Seemingly satisfied with their response, Moira phased into her russet lupine form, probably just to prove she could, before returning to her human self. She stood beside Dean, the very definition of smugness on her glossy lips.

Dean squared his broad shoulders at his uncle. "I suggest you don't test Moira further."

A muscle along the side of Damon's face ticked. "Impressive," he murmured before addressing Sara, his voice booming for all to hear. "I gather there are all sorts of anomalies in Ware Woods, which explains why Lethal was tight-lipped about your site at the Global Council—didn't want to start an uproar. Then again, you accomplished that with your outburst and rash display of witch fire." He gnashed his teeth. "But despite your blatant lack of control, Lethal has chosen to support you."

Everything he said was true. Sara was rash and lacked control.

She looked everywhere except at the Alpha, stalling for time while her brain stumbled over itself.

In the tense silence, Damon held still. Too still, while assuredly weighing the greater threat to his power and pack—the Shadow Mother or Ware Woods. And whatever he determined, would he side with the greater threat or plot to eliminate it?

Sara wasn't sure what to say, how to gain control of the conversation and tip this precarious situation in her favor. She didn't have Lethal's centuries-old cunning or Samson's suavity. But she did have her swagger.

She shoved her hands into her pockets, lest Damon see her flickering energy, her lack of control, her slight tremble. Summoning her bravado, she drawled, "Are you going to test me too?"

He whipped his head to her, and Sara grinned. Bait taken.

Damon snarled. "I know why you're here. Out of *respect* for my nephew and daughters who have also sided with you, I will let you speak and possibly leave in one piece."

Such a backhanded comment. And as much as Sara wanted to call him out for it, Dean's crinkled brow of pleasant surprise told her not to squander this opportunity. They'd passed Damon's tests, earned his respect, and he was willing to listen.

Sara rocked on her heels. Here was her moment to win Damon's favor. As High Witch of Ware Woods, her voice rang loud and clear as she said, "Brad lied to you. If the Shadow Mother destroys Ware Woods, the balance will not be restored, and she will not fade away satisfied. She will be stronger and hungry for more. She will consume all sites, including yours, and then she'll devour the normal world until nothing is left."

"The Mother will not let that happen," said Damon, folding his arms across his king-sized chest.

Sara shook her head, slowly, painfully. Pointedly. "I wish I could believe that. But when the Shadow Mother destroyed the Hills site, the Mother did nothing. The Mother won't come to our rescue because she is sleeping, as are all elysian-eyed dragons save for three, including your *nephew* Tobio. Their absence is too much of a coincidence, especially when we know the Shadow Mother already controls flat-eyed dragons. She is planning to eliminate us all. The day will come when she attacks your site. And when this happens, who will come to your aid?"

Damon's mouth was razor thin. His honed focus darted from Sara to Moira, contemplating.

Not a wolf stirred.

When Damon remained quiet, Sara nearly cursed out loud for her foolishness. Of course he wouldn't admit needing help—he was too proud. She needed to appeal to his ego by swallowing her own pride and admitting she needed *his* help. Tucking her chin ever so slightly, she added, "We're asking for your alliance. Together we have a chance of ending the Shadow Mother and correcting the balance—of having peace. To remain divided, fighting among ourselves, is exactly what she wants. It will lead to our doom."

The Alpha Shifter slowly raked his amber gaze across all the present wolves, including the Blue Ridge pack. After what seemed like an hour but was probably only a minute, he inclined his head to Sara. "I will consider an alliance."

From Sara's far left, Wes yipped excitedly, a few of the Black Forest wolves joining him, as if Damon had outright said yes. Sara took in their sharp smiles, their raised tails. Indeed, in his own prideful way, Damon *had* said yes.

"Ahh, thank you," said Sara, sounding like she was asking a question. She cringed at her awkwardness and could have sworn Damon chuckled, a low growly rumble. Father above, he seemed pleased. She took a few steps toward the evergreen soul tree, anxious to leave before she could say anything else remotely embarrassing.

To her relief, the triplets stretched out their front legs, bowing to their father, before turning and loping into the soul tree. Luke and Wes followed, tails high.

Sara headed after them, Dean and Moira matching her quick pace, when Damon called out. "Dean, congratulations on being a pack."

From over her shoulder, Sara glimpsed Damon's hint of a smile at Moira's hand in Dean's.

The Black Forest wolves howled in unison, their joyous cries deafening until the tree pulled Sara in, cool darkness whisking her away.

After a curious looping, as though she were falling up, wolf laughter rallying around her, Sara stumbled out of the oak and into the cemetery. "Well, seems we have Damon's—" *Favor*, she mentally finished, staring at seven wolves bolting for the Main House.

Who knew wolves liked waffles so much?

She took to the sky, racing after them.

CHAPTER 25

RAYS OF MORNING sunshine streamed across the main room, bathing the dining tables in warm light. Smears of syrup shone on Sara's otherwise empty plate. From his seat beside her, Thomas refilled their water glasses. At the end of their table, Wes told Tobio for easily the third time how Sara informed Damon that his half-dragon shifter nephew had better things to do than visit his Alpha uncle.

"Dude," gushed Wes, peering down the table at Sara. "I cannot believe he didn't tear out your throat for that."

Tobio hissed a laugh. "Wish I could've seen his face." He stabbed his fork into the last waffle on the serving platter at the same time as Luke. They both growled, eyes narrowed at one another, until Matthew set down another heaping platter between them, breaking their pissing contest.

"You already ate. Stop provoking him," Matthew admonished Tobio. He snatched the fork out of his hand and plunked into the seat beside him.

Luke barked a laugh, swiping the contested waffle as well as a fresh stack from the full platter. "Brother from another mother, you have met your match," crooned Luke. He raised his glass to Tobio and then to Matthew before draining the contents and digging into his food.

"Agreed," said Tobio, rising from his chair. "And now he can help me with the dishes." He put Matthew in a headlock and dragged him to the kitchen, his elysian eyes swirling as Matthew made no attempt to free himself.

Sara arched a brow at Moira.

From her seat across the table, Moira simply responded with a foxy grin. She leaned against Dean, who seemed to always be by her side, his muscular form spilling over his chair. A rumbled purr escaped the Alpha before he jerked his chin at Sara and said, "Damon respects you." To his left sat Moesha, Alesha, and Iesha. The triplets, their mouths full, nodded their agreement.

Sara's ears burned. It had been foolish to poke Damon. The only reason he hadn't ripped into her and had actually listened to what she shared was because the Blue Ridge pack and Moira had been with her. They had won his respect first. Without them, Sara doubted the fierce Alpha would have even let her speak—let alone leave in one piece. "Yes, well, we *all* earned his favor. I'm grateful for your assistance."

"We're in this together," said Dean, the shake of his head suggesting her gratitude was appreciated but unnecessary. "If you want, come with us to visit more sites today. While my uncle will spread the word for other shifters to join us, I promised Moira we would visit her siblings. Matt and their folks said they'll go with us another day." With a wooden scrape, Dean pushed back his chair and rose, Moira and the remainder of the pack doing the same.

Sara nibbled her cheek in thought. *Assuming there is another day.* Though the Spring Equinox was months away, what if Brad and the Shadow Mother attacked Ware Woods *before* the Equinox? She hadn't waited for Winter Solstice as she'd threatened last time. No. The Shadow Mother was unpredictable, and Brad was a loose cannon. Anything could happen at any time. And while gaining the support of other magicals was critical in case they faced an epic battle, what was more important was Sara finding a way to eliminate the Shadow Mother as quickly as possible.

"Thanks," said Sara, "But I need to check in with Gran and Alice. Plus, with Samson and Lethal visiting sites, I want at least one Magus in Ware Woods at all times."

"A wise choice. We won't be gone long," said Dean. He waved at the kitchen, his gesture thanking the Cahills for the meal while also informing Tobio and, Sara supposed, Matthew that the pack would be back soon. In a thunder of footsteps, Dean and the others barreled through the main room and onto the deck, narrowly missing Uncle Larry, who crested the wooden stairs. As the pack leapt from the edge, they phased and took off toward the oak tree, kicking up snow behind them. How they could flat-out run on full stomachs was beyond Sara.

"Come on," said Thomas, rising from the table and helping Sara pull out her chair. "Let's go to the blue house and check in on a certain cat."

"Cat?" wheezed Uncle Larry. He knocked snow off his boots and entered the main room, his pallor as white as his thick hair and beard, no doubt the result of nearly being taken out by seven shifters. "If you're talking about Jynx, I saw Albert and Alice stalking that cat with Gran in tow. They were last headed toward the north end of the forest."

Sara rushed past Uncle Larry, shouting a thank you before launching off the deck and into the pale blue sky, a polar breeze fluttering her unzipped jacket. Thomas flew ahead of her, aiming north—toward the marshy section.

"*Gran!*" projected Sara. "*Why didn't you tell me the cat is on the move?*"

"*Gaa! I knew Uncle Larry would say something.*" Gran paused. "*I wasn't going to contact you unless I had a reason. Jynx could be taking a crappy stroll for all I know.*"

A stroll toward the only section of forest with brimstone briars.

Sara surged faster, over the birch grove glittering with icy snow, its crystalline brilliance a reminder of fighting with Thomas when he had been poisoned by Makwa. As if he knew her thoughts—and perhaps he did through the bond—Thomas slowed, letting her catch up to him. He put a hand on her shoulder, his warmth spreading into her, and with his other hand, pointed toward the frozen marsh.

In a small clearing stood Gran, flanked by Alice in her white wolven form and Albert with his silver hackles raised, his snout pointing at the cat. Sara and Thomas landed beside them, the clearing's icy brown grass crunching beneath Sara's boots.

The cat lingered before Makwa and Dorcas's hut—well, what remained of the hut. Oily black brimstone briars nearly swallowed the dilapidated structure. They covered the walls, wove into the thatched roof, and shoved down the stone chimney. In spite of winter, the razor-toothed vines flourished, writhing and pulsating like a knot of snakes.

Albert snarled—not at the cat, Sara realized, but at the undulating hut. A foul odor of putrid entrails, of centuries of hate, and of rotten magic assaulted her senses. Sara gagged, eyes watering, before summoning a fresh breeze and clearing her head.

Never had she ever wanted to set foot in the hut—the home of two terrible witches: Makwa, whose lies split apart Sara's family, causing years of soul-deep heartache, and Dorcas, whose deceit forever changed Caleb and tricked Sara into increasing the Shadow Mother's power. Makwa and Dorcas had irreparably betrayed Ware Woods. And Sara had killed them for it. She wanted nothing to do with them, least of all to consult whatever dark grimoire lurked in their vile abode. The very idea repulsed her. She couldn't do this. No good could come from this place—she should have burnt it down weeks ago.

Sara backed away, shaking her head. Even though the Book had shown her brimstone briars and warned of a dangerous spell, she hadn't expected this pit-of-Hell level of dark magic. "This can't be right. The cat—Jynx—must be mistaken. There is *nothing* in there that can be of use to us." *Nothing is worth the price of using dark magic.*

In clear objection, Jynx lay down and slowly blinked at her.

This was madness. Sara shook her head again, her body trembling as Thomas gently clasped her upper arms. "I'll go in with you. We'll grab what you need and get out."

Before Sara could deny him, could tell him it wasn't worth it, that they should simply focus on getting more support from the other sites, a distressing holler rent the still air.

Thomas stiffened, gaze leveled on the forest behind Sara, his head cocked, listening. "Violet?"

Sara whipped around as the forest swayed, the ground quaking with such force she instinctively hovered to remain upright, pulling Thomas with her. Claws scraped the icy ground—Alice, Albert, and Jynx anchoring themselves—while Gran widened her stance, using a burst of energy to steady herself until the quake subsided.

They all stared, following Thomas's line of sight, as Violet rocketed over the tree canopy and rushed directly for them. Terror shone in her violet eyes, and when she neared, slowing her approach, Sara gaped at the black ichor splattered across her chest, at the dark smears on her bone-white cheeks.

Violet jerked to a stop above them, her raven hair blowing in all directions. "Florine's site is under attack. They need help. Now!" She dove for Sara, grabbing her arm and twisting back toward the direction she had come from—toward the oak tree.

Father above, Violet had looped and flown across Ware Woods to get her, losing precious time. Sara lurched after her, only to be snapped back by Thomas's hold.

"This could be a trap or a distraction," said Thomas, his tone clipped yet calm. He surveyed his sister, likely checking for injuries and assessing her composure. "Vi, remember your training, and tell us what happened."

Violet stopped pulling on Sara. With a tight nod at her brother, she released Sara's arm and, in the detached voice of a seasoned fighter, rapidly explained: "Takers broke the wards. Caleb and I stopped them, but dragons came—flat-eyes—too many for me to kill. Florine directed me to get Sara. They sought shelter in caves, but they won't last long. Caleb is with them."

Sara cursed. She needed to go, yet Thomas was right—it could be a distraction. With Lethal, Samson, and Dean visiting other sites, there would be no Magi to defend Ware Woods. "Wait, it's just dragons. No Shadow Mother. Can you call Jin to their aid?"

"I've been trying," Thomas gritted out, his gaze fixed on the empty sky as if he could see all the way to Jin's garden. "He's not answering me."

Well, that wasn't good. Not at all. Yet Sara didn't have time to drown in this fresh worry. "Vi and I will go. You stay."

"Like Hells I'll stay. I'm not forbidden from leaving. You need a dragon to fight dragons. It's my duty as an elysian-eyed dragon." His gaze pierced her, his unspoken words shouting through the bond: *My duty as your mate. We fight together—always.* Not giving her a chance to respond, Thomas faced Gran and Alice. "Alert the families and tell Tobio to stand guard until we get back."

Sara opened her mouth, a curse on the tip of her tongue, when thick, silken dragon smoke erupted from Thomas. It blocked her vision, choking off her protests. Within a heartbeat of simultaneous swirling, tugging, crushing like being sucked through a bendy straw, the smoke cleared, and Sara stood with Violet and Thomas in a vast field littered with bodies.

CHAPTER 26

SARA HELD A hand to her chest, her bloodstone pulsing beneath her sweaty palm. "You and Caleb did all this?" A frantic visual sweep confirmed the dozens of bodies, clothed in nondescript dark outfits, some still oozing black blood, had been Takers. Her relief at the absence of white gauzy clothing and red blood was short-lived when a thunder of dragon roars rolled across the field.

Sara tensed, her focus on a mountain of white stone towering at the opposite end of the spacious field. Five massive dragons attacked the stark stone face. Each body slam and blast of fire knocked loose giant boulders that strained to magically scramble back into position before the next onslaught.

"Caleb is quite efficient as a vampire," said Violet, jerking a hand at the slumped bodies before taking to the sky. Sara flew after her, barely hearing her next comment over the wind screaming past her ears. "We bought everyone time to retreat to the cave. When the dragons came, Caleb rushed to create a rock barrier while I left to get you."

White flames flickered around Sara. How *dare* the Shadow Mother attack such a peaceful site. Her eyes narrowed on the dragons. Innocent or not, they needed to go. "Three against five will be easy."

"More like one," said Thomas, coming up beside her with a grin.

Of course he was itching to fight other dragons. Taut excitement flooded the bond as Thomas barrel-rolled to the side, phased, and shot toward the five dragons. The plague-like shadows mottling their hides were a sick contrast to Thomas's brilliant blue scales.

The infected monsters shrieked. They abandoned their attack and raced for a cluster of dark clouds on the far horizon with Thomas hot on their tails. Tails wet with poison.

"Be careful!" Sara mentally shouted at him.

Thomas responded with a flush of warmth through the bond that embraced Sara's heart. She had half a mind to chase after him, but Violet grabbed her arm and pulled her to the base of the rock wall.

"Caleb! Florine!" Violet cried. She released Sara and flung herself against a cottage-sized square boulder, grunting with the effort to kinetically move the behemoth.

Sara joined her, sweat soon beading her forehead as she focused all her power into shoving the stone aside. How in All Hells had they moved this in the first place? She clenched her jaw and *pushed*. With a skull-splitting crack, the boulder gave way, toppling a few bumpy flips into the field. A small avalanche of loose rock trickled after it. Sara cleared the resulting cloud of dust with a stiff breeze and sank to her knees, chest heaving from exertion.

"It's about time!" hollered Caleb, his voice preceding him as he emerged from the cave.

Though he was covered in a film of dust, his green eyes glittered. Sara could have kissed her cousin for the carefree, gap-toothed, fangy smile he gave her. She hesitated, taking in more of his appearance. Under the dust he was splattered in blood, his hands and arms coated black as if he had killed the Takers with his bare hands. Perhaps he had. Sara refused to glance at the dead body less than twenty paces to her right. If the Takers had been infected by the Shadow Mother, granting them death had been a mercy.

"Those dragons almost gave me a permanent tan," said Caleb.

Behind him, dozens of witches stumbled out of the cave, coughing and waving off clouds of dust. The fine white powder caked their hair and muted the bright embroidery of their gauzy clothes.

Bettina appeared at Caleb's side and, despite the remnants of his fighting, grabbed his hand. "Caleb said you'd come, but I didn't think you'd get here so fast."

"Indeed," said Florine, coming forward over the rubble with the aid of Bettina's younger brother, his round face and freckles similar to his sister's. Florine eyed the sky. "What happened to the dragons?"

"Thomas chased them off," said Sara, rising from the ground. She levitated higher and higher until she could see the horizon behind the mountain of rock. The swath of dark clouds undulated and disappeared, leaving no trace of the dragons except for a glimmering slip of blue—Thomas. Sara could practically hear his furious roar at the dragons' escape.

And then she did hear a roar, felt it vibrate her teeth. Only it wasn't Thomas, couldn't be Thomas. He was too far away.

She twisted and stared in horror at a mass of black clouds erupting directly overhead as though a claw had ripped open the eggshell blue sky. The five dragons spilled forth, descending upon them, maws open, spraying fire.

There was no time to think, no time to plead to the Mother and Father. Sara threw out her protective shield, casting her magic like a fine net of impenetrable golden light over everyone frozen in fear at the mouth of the cave. And as the heat of a thousand suns hit her, Sara dug deep into herself, deep into the rocky soil, pulling and giving all her energy into repelling the flames. She burned, taking the brunt of the assault, her bones liquid fire.

Distantly, in the far recess of her ravaged mind, someone shouted her name. The invisible strands that wound around her heart tugged, and she heard Thomas. *Sara! I'm coming!*

"Hurry!" Her magic was waning, her grip slipping. And just

as her protective shield began to fray, the onslaught stopped. Sara dropped to the ground and sucked in a breath, the cool air like broken glass in her raw lungs. She was nearly depleted, her healing magic working excruciatingly slow to cool her insides as she scanned the crowd of witches, including Violet and Caleb, before her.

Miraculously, everyone had survived. They stood, patting themselves down, in utter amazement at the lack of injuries as the dragons retreated into the stormy clouds. When the last dragon tail disappeared, the clouds shrank and dissipated with a clap of thunder.

Where was Thomas?

Sara turned, a wobble in her stance. The field behind her was a burnt wasteland, smoldering lumps the only remains of the Takers. Thomas should be here, above the field, flying a victory loop. She whirled back to the rock mountain. There, hovering at the top, was Thomas. Curls of dragon smoke framed his puzzled expression.

Sara's scalp prickled. If Thomas hadn't chased off the dragons, why had they fled?

A plume of black smoke and shadows exploded atop the rock ledge behind Thomas. Quick as a viper, Brad shot forth, blowing an oily black shadow toward Thomas.

"Move!" she screamed in unison with Violet and Caleb, but Thomas wasn't fast enough. All that practice with Tobio, and Thomas still wasn't fast enough.

The shadow latched on to his tail and ran down his side like spilled ink.

From the cliff, Brad gave Sara a triumphant smile. He puffed his chest as though he'd slain a rival suitor, then vanished, taking his smoke with him.

Thomas spasmed in the sky, his body thrashing, his mouth a painful grimace of dagger-sharp teeth. *"Sara,"* he mentally rasped, the torment in his voice shredding her insides.

She tried to fly to him—to do what, she didn't know—but her feet wouldn't leave the ground. She'd used too much of her magic.

She couldn't fly, couldn't help him, couldn't cast another protective shield should he turn on them.

Trap, trap, trap. Thomas had been right. This had all been an elaborate trap. And Sara had played right into the Shadow Mother's insidious plan. Again.

Thomas shuddered, the shadows now creeping up the underside of his neck. His attention snapped to Sara, his elysian eyes clouding over with a blanched haze. *"RUN!"* he mentally bellowed, before spewing a savage roar.

Sara pivoted and sprinted for a bosque of trees at the edge of the field, away from everyone else.

Shit! Running from a dragon was stupid, infinitely more stupid than standing still, but she knew why he'd told her. It would trigger his predatory instinct to chase and kill. It was a chance to lure him away so everyone else could fall back into the protection of the cave.

She leapt over charred remains, stumbling a few paces when the toe of her boot caught on Hells knew what. She felt more than heard the slick scrape of Thomas's serpentine body coursing for her as she pumped her arms, willing her legs to run faster. Keeping her brutal pace, Sara reached inside, desperately grabbing at their bond. Instead of warm, elastic strands, the bond was a tangled mess of razor-thin strings, brittle cold and slippery with oil. *No, no, no. "Thomas?"*

Nothing.

She veered around another steaming briquet, her body flooded with adrenaline, and inwardly dove into the bond, clawing her way toward the core. *Come on!* The frozen strands bit and slashed her insides, yet she dug deeper. *Pulling on the bond worked once before. You wouldn't have told me to run if you thought you would hurt me.*

His shadow loomed over her, a grunt of hot breath licking her back. He was much too close, the edge of the field too far. She would never make it, and even if she did, he would find her. He would always find her. She gripped the icy strands. Their bond was strong—ordained by the Mother and Father—and it was still there despite the Shadow Mother's infection.

With all her being, Sara speared into their bond, pushing past the soul-shredding pain, until there at the very core, her virtual fingertips grazed a single golden thread vibrating with warmth. She snatched the thread, coiling her inner self around it, and in one motion, she yanked on the thread and pivoted to face him. "Thomas!" she cried, standing her ground.

He jerked but didn't stop, his eyes clouded, mouth open ready to swallow her whole. She clutched the thread to her heart, flooding their bond with love.

Thomas clapped his jaw shut and sailed over her, the plates of his shadow-stained belly skimming the top of her head. She ducked, narrowly evading his spiked tail, which glistened with black poison as it whistled past.

Unable to kinetically slow him down, Sara could only watch as he crashed, smashing into the bosque and plowing up soil until coming to a halt. His scaled body, splotched with inky shadows, lay limp among his destruction.

"Thomas," she croaked. A cold sweat washed over her, nausea turning her stomach. Sara staggered toward him, managing a few steps before her legs gave out. She collapsed, face down. In the distance, far behind her, came echoed shouts and the thudding of many feet. But they were not her concern. Her soul's focus was on maintaining her hold on their bond—on somehow fixing Thomas, her mate, her everything.

Pushing herself up onto one elbow, she extended her other arm, hand reaching for him. Summoning the very last dregs of her magic, she shot a sphere of healing energy at Thomas. She watched it cover him like a blanket, her white flames devouring the shadows, until darkness edged her vision, and everything turned black.

"Breathe," said a comforting voice, a voice Sara hadn't heard in a long while. It tethered her, stopped her from sliding into

an unconscious abyss. She inhaled to the count of three. A mix of lavender and lilac tickled her nose. Her mother's scent, its pleasantness replacing the stench of the acrid, scorched field. *"Help is coming."*

"Mom?" she called into the Aether, straining against the pull of the abyss. But instead of her mother's airy voice, a thundering shook Sara's being, followed by a thud and a warm pressure. The warmth started as a seed, somehow planted inside her. It quickly grew, roots burrowing deep, knitting and reinforcing as it wrapped around her chest, pumping her heart. It shot down her arms and legs, tingling her hands and feet. In a surge of brilliant greens and browns and golds, the magic seedling exploded. It flooded Sara with vibrant warmth, pulling her away from the abyss, shoving her back into her body.

She sat up with a gasp, her four-fingered hand slapping over her pulsing bloodstone. Beside her knelt Bettina, face glowing with elation, while towering over them stood Caleb, his brow pinched with worry.

Her mouth dry as kindling, Sara choked out, "What happened? Is Thomas—"

"I'm fine," he shouted, his voice drawing nearer with haste. Caleb shifted aside and Thomas appeared. He hauled Sara up into his arms, embracing her with a snap of electricity. His lips brushed hers before he leaned back, studying her until seemingly satisfied with her lack of injuries. "When you pulled on the bond, it broke the shadow's hold. Your healing magic, combined with mine, fought off the infection. But you drained yourself. I felt you slipping into darkness. I was still healing and couldn't get to you fast enough." His voice cracked, and she felt his anguish cut into her at not being fast enough to avoid Brad's ambush or heal quick enough to save her.

She held the side of his face, reveling in the return of his molten gaze. Through the bond, once again a thick cord of warm, elastic strands, she sent a wave of love. The entire bond heated, pulling them closer with a sizzle of light-blue sparks.

Sara turned to Bettina, now standing with Caleb's arm around her, his hand firmly gripping her waist. "Whatever you did, thank you," said Sara.

"You were falling into stasis and Thomas wasn't ready, so I gave you a bit of my earth magic."

Sara paled, as did Caleb. "Tina?" he said. "I'm grateful you saved my cousin, but—you did *what*?"

Samson had said gifting magic was incredibly rare; so rare, he'd only done it once to save Motley's life. From what Sara understood, it meant the giver freely and irrevocably transferred a portion of their magic to another—a selfless act in a magical world that coveted power. Her mind went blank, all words eluding her, at the sacrifice Bettina had willingly made. A mere "thank you" wasn't a drop in the ocean of gratitude Sara felt for the earth witch.

Bettina brushed dust from her skirts as if gifting her power were no big deal. "We couldn't let Sara fall into stasis right now. I was meant to help her and—stop with the concerned eyes—I don't regret it. I have plenty more magic. Besides, why would I need to specifically grow anything when I have you to do it for me?" She leaned into Caleb and batted her lashes.

Sara huffed. Bettina was a force to be reckoned with. It was clear she'd known she would gift some of her power to Sara. And it was clear she had future plans for Caleb. Sara held her tongue from asking what else Bettina might know about *all* their futures. It seemed silly not to share premonitions, but then again the future was always shifting, subject to butterfly wings and unspoken intentions—and shadowy entities. To glimpse certain possibilities was likely both a gift and a curse.

A grin spread across Caleb's face. He knelt and placed both palms on the charred field. With a leafy rustle, greenery sprouted, stalks grew, and hundreds—thousands—of sunflowers covered the field, bobbing their seed-heavy heads in a delicate breeze.

Bettina snatched Caleb up and seemed about to plant a kiss on him when the sunflowers parted and a crowd of witches approached, Violet and Florine leading the way. The High Witch sagged in relief at spotting Sara and Thomas, a tacit thankfulness shining in her hazel eyes.

Sara drew a breath to explain, then paused when Thomas's grip on her tightened. He tilted his head, eyes swirling. *"We have to go. Jin is calling us."* Ashy smoke twined between their legs.

In a rush, Sara said to Florine, "This had been a trap—for Thomas. Brad thinks he won and shouldn't be back, but if anything else happens, don't hesitate to come to Ware Woods. I invite you all into our site."

Florine's nod was the last she saw before Thomas's smoke engulfed them.

CHAPTER 27

Faster than she'd ever looped before, Sara landed on the deck of the Main House. Her knees, along with the wooden floorboards, groaned in protest.

Standing before Sara and Thomas was Jin, arms crossed. The dark circles under his narrowed eyes were visible even in the gray haze of late afternoon. Crowded behind him on the deck, fanning down the stairs and into the common, was most of the forest: Gran, Alice, Matt and Tobio, Kane and Abby, Bill and Shannon, a few Atwells, and all the Cahills. Sara assumed everyone else was still visiting other sites, hopefully gaining allies and not running into trouble.

Snowflakes slowly fell, seemingly suspended, catching in Jin's long obsidian hair. Their fluffy softness was at odds with the fury on his face and the concern dripping from Gran.

Heavy silence pressed upon the gathering as if no one wanted to know what had happened—because speaking it out loud would confirm the Shadow Mother was growing stronger and their days were numbered. Sara didn't blame them for their held tongues, yet someone had to say something.

"We're okay," she announced, "so are Violet and Caleb and all of Florine's site." The Cahills gave a collective sigh of relief while Kane and Abby maintained their rigid demeanors. The pair beheld

Thomas with a sharp parental gaze that suggested they knew at least one of their children remained in peril.

"Where were you?" Thomas asked Jin, the hint of an accusation earning a snarl from his dragon sire.

"I was sleeping and couldn't fully wake in time, which is probably a good thing since I have no bonded mate to fight off the Shadow Mother's infection. I felt everything that happened through our blood bond. You are *lucky*—we are all lucky," Jin seethed. People scrambled to get out of his way as he paced, fisted hands at his sides. "I should have been there. I should have instantly answered your call. I shouldn't be *tired*. Elysian-eyed dragons take turns resting to ensure the balance is always maintained."

Tired. Fear scuttled up Sara's back.

Thomas had also been tired. Unnaturally, and increasingly, tired. Jin's disclosure affirmed the niggling worry at the back of her mind—the reason why elysian-eyed dragons were all sleeping. They weren't casually resting or even hiding to avoid the Shadow Mother and her infectious shadows; in fact, they hadn't even sensed her presence, which was why they had never confronted her or even warned Jin. No. Somehow the Shadow Mother had found a way to put her greatest challenge to sleep. Slowly, carefully, so as not to be detected. Perhaps for centuries. It all made sense now. Elysian-eyed dragons had been steadily retreating to their lairs and falling asleep, completely unaware of their plight. And completely unable to stop the Shadow Mother.

This was so much worse than Sara had imagined. The Shadow Mother had methodically planned to incapacitate elysian-eyed dragons, control flat-eyes, and eliminate the Hills witches. And now she was intent on destroying Ware Woods.

Sara clung to Thomas's arm, fighting to stop her world from unraveling.

How much longer did Thomas, Jin, and Tobio have before they permanently fell asleep? And without them, if by some miracle all magicals came together to face the Shadow Mother, would the combined magic be enough to defeat her? Would elysian-eyed dragons ever wake up? Would the balance ever be corrected? Would they ever be able to live in peace?

Jin paused his pacing and held Sara's stare, silently sharing her concerns. And if Jin had also come to this conclusion . . . Sara stole a glance at Tobio, then Thomas, their grim countenances revealing they too knew their waking days were numbered.

Instead of voicing these worries, which would only stir panic, Jin clasped his hands behind his back. "It is too dangerous for any dragon to be outside of their lair right now. I will not force you"—he looked at Tobio and Thomas—"but I suggest you both stay with me in the garden. Nothing of ill intent can enter a dragon's lair."

A murmur swept through the gathering. Jin had offered sanctuary to Tobio and Thomas as a means to protect them, as well as Ware Woods. If Thomas could be infected once, it could happen again, and it could happen to Tobio. And what if the Shadow Mother's influence could somehow penetrate the Ware Woods barrier? An unhinged dragon could cause significant damage. But even more terrifying was what Sara would have to do to stop them.

Jin was right. It was safest for everyone to have Thomas and Tobio sequestered in the garden with him, especially when they might fall asleep and become vulnerable. And while Jin could have offered sanctuary to everyone, Sara knew such an offer would do no good—they couldn't hide forever. Jin knew this too.

"This isolation is temporary while you lead the other magicals against the Shadow Mother," said Jin, brushing snow from his sleeve. "Once you weaken her, whatever influence she has on dragons will wane, and we will come to your aid and finish her."

Seriously? Sara raised a brow at his confidence in her. No pressure to save the world. And without her bonded mate and best friend by her side. She wanted to release a scream worthy of waking all dragons everywhere, yet there were too many eyes on her, too many hopes.

Instead, she said, "You're right. This is temporary, and we *will* defeat her. I know Thomas and Tobio agree, but I ask that they spend the night before joining you in the garden tomorrow morning." Dean and the pack would want to see Tobio before he left, and Thomas's family would want to say their goodbyes as well.

"I'll be waiting," said Jin. Sara wasn't sure if he was referring to Tobio and Thomas or to her efforts in destroying the Shadow Mother. When she inclined her head, he added in a quieter voice, "Visitors are welcome."

Sara's eyes widened. For a hot-tempered dragon who guarded his solitude and nearly attacked her for dropping in on him—not once, but twice—this invitation was astounding. Maybe he enjoyed the company of others after all. Regardless, Sara had every intention of regularly visiting. Nothing would keep her and Thomas apart.

She smirked. "Oh, I was counting on it."

Jin's eyes flickered before he vanished in a puff of silky dragon smoke.

After a somber meal at the Sullivan house with Kane and Abby peppering Sara and Thomas with questions ranging from Violet to Jin's garden, followed by an impromptu sparring session between Thomas and Connor, Sara slid into bed.

She hummed a pleasant moan at the heat radiating from Thomas. Father above, she hoped Jin could magically conjure a bed large enough for both of them in the garden; otherwise, she would get very little sleep without her bonded mate warming her sheets. The thought of being semi-separated from him weighed on her heart, yet the thought of him being controlled by the Shadow Mother—either with infection or endless sleep—outright terrified her. She had to weaken the Shadow Mother as quickly as possible. And she would gladly do so, even if it meant seeking the vilest of magic. To protect Thomas, Ware Woods, and all magicals—to reset the balance and achieve peace—Sara would gladly become a monster to defeat a monster. Mother knew it wouldn't be the first time.

Phantom brimstone briars crept over her skin, an image of the foul hut infesting her mind. She shivered, then shoved the thought into one of the many black spots tarnishing her soul. Tomorrow, she would get her hands dirty. Right now, she wanted to enjoy this infection-free, gloriously wide-awake moment—provided someone didn't fall asleep on her.

Sensing her thoughts through the bond, Thomas slipped his arm under her and drew her on top of him, wrapping her in a tight embrace. "You're going into the hut as soon as I leave tomorrow, aren't you?" His words tickled her bare neck, her hair braided back for bed.

"Yes," she said. She had no reason to keep anything from him, nor did she want to.

Thomas slowly inhaled, his expanding chest lifting Sara like a rising tide, and paused in thought. The treehouse creaked. They were alone save for the trio of squirrels nestled together on the bookshelf and Trouble dozing in Moira's bedroom on the far side of the tree canopy. "When I told you to run, it was because I knew you would find a way to stop me—to bring me back. And you did. But I nearly hurt you. I didn't realize your magic had been depleted. It was too close. Until the Shadow Mother is weakened, I'd rather stay in the garden than risk hurting you or anyone else. You already know this, don't you, my monster?"

He pushed his head back into the pillow to meet her gaze. She gave him a soft smile, and the blue in his eyes shimmered. His voice dropped dangerously low. "You will terrorize the hut's dark grimoire into giving you whatever you need to weaken the Shadow Mother. Then I will be at your side to finish her. You will not fail, and neither will I."

His embrace grew tighter, golden warmth suffusing their bond. Stars above, he made it sound so simple. "Such confidence you have, Dragon Boy." She kissed the column of his neck, right below his ear, and delighted in his tremor.

He dragged his hands up her torso and cradled the sides of her face, bringing her back to him until they were nose-to-nose, his lips grazing hers. "I do not accept a future without your happiness."

"Our happiness," she corrected him. Not just theirs, of course, but everyone's in Ware Woods and beyond. Her muscles involuntarily tensed at remembering the magnitude of her role. At how much was at stake.

With lightning speed, Thomas crushed his mouth to hers, his fingers spearing into her braided hair, pulling her closer. The fervency of his kiss stole her breath, her heart, her soul. Pure passionate fire blazed from him, igniting her. Sara melted into him, forgetting her role, forgetting his role—no doubt exactly as he intended—until her only thought was of the two of them, burning together as one.

Electricity crackled, pale blue lights sparkling in her peripheral vision. Her magical core ached, her white flames striving to twine with Thomas's power. A deep-throated growl reverberated through his chest and into her, quivering her insides, confirming he felt the same.

Without breaking their kiss, Thomas flipped them over, the bed bouncing, covers falling to the floor.

Sara yelped into him. *Now who's the aggressive one?*

"We are equals in every way, my love," Thomas rumbled. Bracing his weight on his forearms, he slowly trailed kisses along her cheek and down her neck, each tender touch sending a toe-curling current of power through her.

Sara dug her fingers into his bare back. *Closer.*

Thomas groaned. Their nightclothes vanished with a slip of dragon smoke. *Better?*

Closer. She shimmied under him, her lips finding his again, eager for the spicy flavor of him. But instead of continuing their frantic pace, Thomas slowly, reverently kissed her as if they had all the time in the world—as if they already lived in peace.

Bliss flooded Sara, their bond glowing, blue and white flames swirling around them, her very essence wholly entwined with his. And when she thought this was more joy than she'd ever dared imagine, Thomas released himself, his love and magic filling her until she exploded along with him. Raw energy, pure as stars, flowed between them. There was no beginning or end, their souls freely giving and receiving in an eternal loop.

Their connection wrecked Sara in all the best ways. For a long while afterward, she stared out the window opening at the glassy lake. She had gotten a taste of peace, and like a wild animal, she would do anything for more.

Gently running her fingertips through the downy hair at Thomas's temple, she slid her gaze to his face, his eyes closed in a blessed, nightmare-free, dreamless sleep. Sara calmed her rapid heartbeat by assuring herself she could visit him in Jin's garden whenever she wanted—this was not a separation like when he went to university. Their time apart would be short-lived. She would go to the dark witches' hut, get whatever wicked spell she needed, and free the Shadow Mother's hold on all dragons, including Thomas. Then all other magicals would join them in eliminating the Shadow Mother and restoring the balance long before the Equinox. It was a clean and simple plan. Relatively clean and simple.

She snuggled closer to Thomas, wrapping her arms and legs around him, their chests pressed together. Although he didn't wake, he hugged her in return, a content smile on his lips. Eventually, she drifted off to sleep, lulled by the rocking of the treehouse and the steady pulse of their hearts.

It was late morning by the time Thomas finally woke. After a round of intimate "I love yous" and reviewing their simple yet dangerous plan, they flew to the Main House and devoured a quiet breakfast with Tobio, the pack, and most of Ware Woods. With a series of tight hugs, a whine from Wes, and a chorus of "See you soons," Thomas and Tobio vanished in a cloud of dragon smoke. Their departure hadn't fully dissipated before Sara took to the sky and rushed for the marshy section of the forest. For the dark grimoire and the promise of hope lurking inside the ominous hut.

CHAPTER 28

Sara slammed into the clearing, a web of fine cracks surrounding her in the ice-encrusted surface. Her eyes narrowed on the briar-choked hut. Determination sang in her veins until a nearby drift of snow with tufted ears uncoiled and shook itself.

She reared back, slipping, too startled to stop herself from falling. Her backside collided with the hard ground. Pain spiked up Sara's backbone before she healed herself and cursed the cat blandly staring at her.

"Jynx! Have you been waiting for me all this time?"

The cat simply blinked, turned, and faced the hut. Where the door had once been was now a writhing wall of brimstone briars.

Sara shuddered. A week ago, she had wanted to burn the hut down as a Winter Solstice gift to herself. Now she understood why she'd had a gnawing feeling to leave it alone. It had something she needed.

When Jynx gave an impatient short-tailed twitch, Sara scrambled to her feet. It would take an inferno of witch fire to burn her way into the hut. She thought about asking Alice for help, and if witch fire wasn't strong enough, perhaps Lethal could use a little Kindness to hack away the razor-toothed vines. She scowled at her options, not keen on subjecting Alice or Lethal to the shrill banshee screams of the briars, not to mention whatever horrors lay in wait. After all, it was Sara who had killed Makwa and Dorcas. Any dark retribution the hut sought should be directed at her.

She stood, hands on her hips, as Jynx stalked up to the undulating wall. The greasy black briars paused, seemingly in recognition, before pulling back, exposing the worn front door, curiously lacking a handle. With a haunted creak, the door swung open.

A noxious odor smacked Sara hard enough to make her eyes sting. It reminded her of carrion. Centuries-old, festering, rotten-flesh carrion. Despite the clenching of her stomach, Sara sprang after Jynx as the cat strolled into the dim hut, the only light streaming in from the open door.

Briars covered every surface inside the dwelling: the floor, the walls, whatever crude furnishings had once existed, even the ceiling. They twisted and turned like tar-coated reptiles with thorn-riddled hides. Their slithering wet squelch filled the foul air.

Sara stuck close to Jynx, tiptoeing in the briar-free space the cat forged as it approached a mound of tangled vines in the center of the hut. The vines hissed, raising every hair on Sara's body. Despite her bloodstone pulsing a warning, Sara refused to flee—not until she uncovered the dark grimoire and got the spell she needed.

The vines began to unknot themselves and slink off, gradually uncovering a tall, wooden pedestal of sorts with a hefty book on its dark-charred surface. Sara's eyes widened as the last of the thorned vines dragged itself over the book, trailing deep gouges into its scarred leather cover. To Sara's horror, the cuts bled, dripping claret onto the pedestal and dirt floor.

All Hells. The top of the wooden pedestal wasn't scorched; it was stained with blood.

Sara glanced at the open door, desperate to rush outside and guzzle fresh air—if only for a steadying moment—but Jynx sat on her feet, holding her in place while keeping the briars at bay.

The dark grimoire screeched open, riffling past scores of bur-gundy-splotched sections before lying flat on two corpse-white pages. In depthless black ink, the grimoire scratched out:

Sara Lochton.

Her blood ran cold. It knew her. Why would this dark book know her? Was she a dark witch too, or had the book been expecting her?

Dark, Light. Light, Dark.

Mother below. It knew her thoughts and was taunting her. With a flick of her hand she suspended a sphere of white light above the grimoire—partly to defy its dark implication of her, partly to better read its slashed script, and partly to let the entire hut know a new High Witch was in its presence.

The briars overhead shrieked, recoiling their hanging, reaching, rotten appendages. When a chilling laugh scraped the inside of the hut, Sara flared her light brighter. The shrieks and laughter stopped. The previous message disappeared, and in a scratching that sounded unnervingly similar to fingernails on stone, the following appeared:

You slayed my two previous owners and now you seek a spell to undo the Shadow Mother.
Such a bold, wicked witch you are.

The dark grimoire knew far too much about her. It was at once unsettling and reassuring.

"Give me the spell or you'll find out just how wicked I can be." Sara's voice punched true in spite of the bile creeping up the back of her throat. This book—this foul hut—terrified her, but she couldn't show an ounce of fear. If she wobbled in the least bit, she had the distinct feeling the book would grow more of the serrated fangs poking out its tattered edges and devour her.

A pleased purr of a growl vibrated from the dark grimoire.

Fabulous. She was speaking its bloodthirsty language. Hopefully, it would cooperate.

Careful what you wish for—it comes at a high price.

Ann used this spell and paid dearly.

Ann? "My great-grandmother tried to defeat the Shadow Mother?" This book made no sense. It was probably lying.

She provoked Her Dark Glory.
The beginning is the end;
the end is the beginning.

Sara pressed her lips together as the words melted, the ink hemorrhaging into the circular image of a snake devouring its own tail.

The grimoire was toying with her. Lying to whatever depraved end. Gran would have told Sara if Ann had anything to do with the Shadow Mother. "Enough riddles. Give me the spell."

As you will it, High Witch of Legend.
The spell you need is within this page.
Take it, for such a spell cannot be given,
and in so doing your blood will reveal
all you need.

The message dissolved, the word *blood* being the last to leach back into the thick parchment, its ghastly sheen suggesting it wasn't made of pulp paper. Sara swallowed.

Trembling with revulsion, every alarm bell of self-preservation clanging in her mind, she extended her hand until it hovered over the page. *Don't think. Just do.*

She snatched the page, crumpling it in her grasp as she ripped it from the dark grimoire.

Pain impaled her hand, went right through and out the other side like an iron stake. A scream tore loose—either from herself or the book. Sara didn't know; didn't care, her wicked pretense faltering. Warm wetness dripped from her hand, an offering to the book and its stained altar. The coppery scent of fresh blood cut through the hut's age-old stench as Sara bolted for the open door, Jynx barely a step ahead of her.

Sara ran, the spell cutting into her clenched hand as she chased the cat down a winding forest path, eager to get away from the dark grimoire. By the time the path opened into the birch grove, Jynx was long gone—vanished into the snowy undergrowth—and Sara was panting, a spotted trail of ruby red behind her. She threw her head back, pulling in a breath. Clouds scurried across the slate-hued sky, sunlight coming and going in flickers.

Well that totally sucked. Her sinuses burnt with the odor of the hut—of blood and deceit and *wrongness*—but it would all be worth it if she could weaken the Shadow Mother and break her hold on dragons. Because even if all the other magicals joined Ware Woods against the Shadow Mother, they wouldn't stand a chance if she was at full power with an army of flat-eyed dragons. They needed the elysian-eyed dragons to secure their survival. Besides, Sara had sworn to Thomas they would fight together, and she would not let him down.

Sara studied the crushed page in her hand, every blade-sharp crease biting into her palm and fingers, wondering just how much of her blood was needed to activate the spell, when someone shouted her name. She shoved her hand behind her back, clutching the page tighter in case it suddenly sprang to life and wanted more than just her blood. And though she needed this spell for all the right reasons, taking it from a dark grimoire left the sour taste of shame in her High Witch mouth.

"Sara?" Ian's voice projected in her head. *"Where are you?"*

"I'm in the birch grove, but now isn't a—"

A cloud of smoke billowed to life, licking the overhead striped branches of the central birch tree before contracting and vanishing with a clap. There stood Ian, Kira, Samson, Charlie, and Ted, as well as Gran and Alice.

CHAPTER 29

IAN SURGED TOWARD Sara, his gaze glimmering with concern, a sage-green knitted scarf fluttering with his lengthy stride. "We just got back from visiting other witch sites when Gran told us of the attack on Florine's and that Thomas and Tobio went to Jin's." He slowed his approach, grabbing Kira's hand as she caught up to him. A ray of sun hit the grove, creating a flash of sparkles. Sara squinted. When the sparks faded and the sun retreated into the cloud coverage, everyone was facing her with troubled expressions.

Samson cocked his head, his movement raptor-like. "Our diplomacy *had* been going well, with the exception of Kahn, of course. But once the others hear of this attack, they may rethink their alliance. Especially if they think Florine's site was punished for supporting Ware Woods. And what in All Hells are you hiding behind your back?"

They all leaned to the side, everyone's eyes widening at the bloody snow behind her.

"Firecracker," said her father, using his calm professor voice, though the worry in his wrinkled brow was anything but calm. "Why are you bleeding?"

"It's the spell from the hut's dark grimoire, isn't it?" declared Gran.

"Dark grimoire? Please tell me you're joking," insisted Ian.

His golden-brown complexion—the same warm color as his eyes—turned ashen.

No one said a word, Sara's recklessness obvious. Even Samson didn't utter, "Tut-tut, Rookie." He didn't have to.

She sighed. There was no way they would leave her alone now. May as well get comfortable. She flicked her non-bloody hand, whishing a pile of boulders—the same boulders Caleb once used in a futile attempt to contain Tobio—into a dry-stacked table. With another flick, she grew eight chairs, their straight backs a ladder of white-and-black birch branches. They were the best chairs she'd ever grown, rivaling Caleb's fine craftsmanship, and no doubt were thanks to Bettina's gifted magic. Someday, Sara hoped to return the favor. If they survived the Shadow Mother, maybe Sara could gift the magic back to Bettina, along with a little more.

Sara plunked her dripping fist, covered in so much red it was hard to discern fingers from crumpled page, on top of the moss-flecked stone table, and sank into a chair. The rest of them followed suit, Ted appearing on the verge of passing out, Ian's color far too waxen.

Sara's heart skipped a beat. Projecting only to her father—their father—she mentally asked, *"Did any of the other witches have a cure for Ian's heart?"*

Charlie pressed his lips. *"No."*

Crap. She tightened her expression, staring at her fist. Maybe the cure was in her palm—right before her. If the spell could weaken the Shadow Mother into losing her control over dragons, perhaps it could also weaken her enough to melt the sliver of ice in Ian's heart.

Samson broke the silence. "This spell looks delightfully dangerous. It's soaking up your blood as if it's preparing an essence doorway. What is it, exactly?" He casually leaned back, resting his foot on his knee, the portrait of composure to all at the table, yet Sara noted his aura dim to a deep, distressed purple.

"A spell to undo the Shadow Mother," she said. "To somehow weaken her so Jin, Thomas, and Tobio don't fall asleep, and so we all have a chance of defeating her on or before the Equinox." A chance. She was risking her life for a *mere* chance. And she was ready.

Silently, in a far pocket of her mind where no one but the Mother could hear, Sara invoked the four elements using the childhood chant her mother had taught her: *Earth below me; Water beside me; Air above me; Fire within me.* With her booted feet pressed against the snow-crusted ground, she released a slip of magic into the earth, secretly weaving birch roots far below the surface into a circle around them. Spell circle complete, she put them all out of their anxious misery, and opened her fist.

The page slowly uncrumpled with a series of nauseating cracks, reminding Sara of broken bones snapping back into place—something she had done far too many times on herself. She winced. Pulling her hand into her lap, she healed the deep cuts with a pulse of magic as the page finished smoothing itself atop the stone table.

Everyone held their tongues, watching her blood slither around the parchment. It crept and gathered, slowly forming the following grisly words:

When the moon is whole and wickedly red,

recite these words for which you have bled:

The Lochton dragon is who I seek,

Of true fire and blood, we must speak.

For power I have and power I dread,

It is my choice to be alive or dead.

Lochton dragon.
Her ancestor was still alive.

Sara reeled, her mind conjuring a theater-sized recollection of the ancient black-and-sea-green dragon she'd seen in the Book. The dragon that had seemed strangely familiar.

"That's it?" Samson spat. "This has nothing to do with the Shadow Mother. And why would this be in a dark grimoire? Summoning a dragon is insane, but it isn't forbidden."

"It is in Ware Woods," whispered Alice. Her amber eyes glazed over with the telltale fixed expression of seeing an unpleasant memory.

Gran reached out to Alice, who sat beside her, and gently took her younger sister's hand in hers. "Summoning the Lochton dragon was forbidden by Mary—our grandmother. She died protecting Ware Woods, but not before forbidding her daughter—our mother—Ann, from seeking Ann's father. The Lochton dragon."

Ian, Charlie, and Ted choked.

Clearly, they hadn't known this staggering fact either.

"The surprises never end around here," Samson projected.

"We're part dragon?" Ian sagged in his chair, his question seemingly aimed at himself for not realizing this sooner.

"Cool," said Kira, bumping his shoulder.

Sara's skin tingled with another revelation. "It's true," she gasped, a mental puzzle piece falling into place. "The story you tell every Samhain of the witch who sought her dragon father and died. It was Ann."

"Oh, Ma," Charlie whispered, silver tears lining his eyes. "Alice," he added with a hand to his heart.

Ted pulled on his sandy goatee, his mouth silently opening and closing before he found his words. "Why didn't you tell us this was how Ann died?"

Gran tucked her chin at her sons, Ted and Charlie. "Because Alice and I agreed not to tell you—*any* of you"—she gave a sharp glance at Ian and Sara—"about your dragon ancestor for fear you would foolishly seek him out too. Plus, we had Makwa and Dorcas watching our family too closely for any whisper of magic strong enough to challenge them. Our powers were weak, thanks to their curse, and to avoid unwanted attention, we never mentioned our dragon grandfather."

Ted regarded his booted feet. "I always wondered why I couldn't remember a log crushing our toes hard enough to permanently stripe the nails black." He quirked a brow at his brother.

Charlie huffed a laugh. "I thought the same thing." His hint of a smile vanished, replaced with pressed lips as he considered Gran and Alice. "Your story has two endings. One with the dragon being void of love and stopping Ann's heart with a fierce look. The other with Ann and the dragon having a joyful reunion until a dark witch attacked them. What really happened?"

"We don't know," said Gran, searching the sky as if the Father above had seen and would whisper what truly occurred in her ear. "When our mother looped back to the woods, she was coated in ice—too stunned and frozen to speak. She could barely form her bloodstone before she died under the oak tree beside Alice and me. We were so young. It's hard to remember. But Kingsley was there. He's always believed it was a dark witch."

Sara blankly focused on the stone table, recalling Kingsley's reaction to the Samhain tale. He had stabbed the air with a fork full of cake, agreeing that it had been a "*witch with ice in her heart.*"

Ice. Sara's bloodstone pulsed. Of course!

"Not a witch," she said. "It was the Shadow Mother. The dark grimoire said Ann had used this same spell and had provoked her." Sara met everyone's worried gaze and promptly swallowed the other thorn of information the grimoire had shared, the part about Ann paying dearly for using the spell.

"It had to have been the Shadow Mother," said Ian, rubbing his chest directly above his heart. "Dragons kill with fire, not ice."

"Agreed," said Alice. She frowned at the bloody parchment. "But Ann didn't summon the Lochton dragon. She *went* to him. There's something wrong with this spell."

Samson steepled his fingers, a brusque humph escaping his scowl. "Obviously, there's something wrong with this spell. You should never summon a dragon—much less on a blood moon when dragons are known to be unhinged and prone to destruction rather than governance."

"Oh?" commented Charlie with a look at Sara that screamed, *Did you know this about your bonded mate?*

Nope. Not at all, and Sara would bet all of her nine fingers Thomas didn't know this either. And with a blood-moon lunar eclipse coming up before the Equinox, this was potentially another reason why Jin wanted Thomas and Tobio with him in the garden. Sara twisted her lips, making a mental note to interrogate Jin about all things dragon.

"Doesn't everyone know this?" Samson glanced around the table, his jaw dropping. "Oh, my blissfully sheltered brethren. Tsk. You probably don't know that dark grimoires are notoriously famous for jumbling spells—calling for a pound of snakeroot instead of a pinch, because why kill one villager when you can wipe out the entire village?" He paused, absently waving his hand in the air. "I only did that once, by the way. Lesson learned."

"Dad!" exclaimed Kira.

Samson shrugged. "My point is"—he swung his focus to Sara, pinning her with his onyx eyes—"don't spout off this spell. We need to study it from all angles."

Sara clenched her jaw; she didn't have time to study this from all angles. Thomas was already far sleepier than his usual self. The thought of him being permanently asleep squeezed her ragged heart, not to mention the reality of *many* deaths if a fully powered Shadow Mother with extra-sharp nails attacked on the Equinox.

She tilted her head at the spell, considering Samson's advice: "*from all angles.*" Indeed . . . She tilted her head farther. Mother below, the spell *was* jumbled. And the dark grimoire had told her how to sort it: *The beginning is the end; the end is the beginning.*

The spell was backward because she wasn't meant to summon the Lochton dragon; she was meant to go to him.

Sara murmured, "It is my choice to be alive or dead, for power I have and power I dread. Of true fire and blood we must speak, the Lochton dragon is who I seek."

The slice of shadow under the parchment writhed.

Sara held her breath as the shadow grew larger, creeping forth in all directions like a nightmare emerging from under a bed. It coiled around the spell page, nibbling the razored edges.

"Didn't I just say *not* to speak this spell?" cried Samson. He jumped out of his chair, away from the table—away from the shadows consuming the spell. Sara did the same, as did everyone else.

"I barely whispered!" shouted Sara. "And I said it backward, the proper way." *I hope.* Fear crawled up her back, her eyes fixed on the shadows now slinking off the table and slithering toward her.

Charlie lunged for Sara, but Samson threw out his arm, kinetically holding him back. "The spell is locked on to her—her blood—and will kill anyone who tries to stop its course of action."

Sara averted her gaze from her father, preferring to spare them both from visually sharing their concern. But she couldn't stop his anguish from mentally slamming into her like a truck hitting a stalled car. Her heart stuttered.

Wonderful. But this was exactly what Sara wanted: no one else but her risking their life to find a way to undo the Shadow Mother. She had killed Makwa and Dorcas. She had riled the Global Council. Going to the Lochton dragon and getting whatever information or secret weapon that could be used against the Shadow Mother was the least she could do. And as High Witch, it was her duty to give them this advantage against the Shadow Mother, regardless of the cost. A cost she couldn't think of right now, of how it could affect Thomas and her father, her immediate family, and *everyone* else.

The shadows were now wrapping around her boots, licking up her legs.

Gran swore, quite colorfully. Had Lethal been there, they may have blushed.

Samson muttered something more of a plea than a curse. In a louder voice, he said, "I give you this."

Sara looked up as he tore open the top of his coat, grabbed his red bloodstone, lifted it—silver chain and all—over his head, and tossed it to her.

His *one* red bloodstone. The only bloodstone she'd known Samson to touch—to care about—despite the many black bloodstones hanging from similar silver chains around his neck. Kira's open-mouthed shock confirmed its priceless value as Sara caught the stone. Pleasant heat flooded her hand, spreading up her arm and throughout her body. She quickly slipped the chain over her head, the stone pulsing against her chest just below Mary's bloodstone.

The shadows were now at Sara's waist. Before she could stammer a thank you to Samson, Kira appeared at her side. "I give you this as well, so you can return to us," she said, placing the smoke stone pendant around Sara's neck.

Then Alice was before Sara, giving her Ann's bloodstone. Another wave of loving warmth rolled through Sara. It would have buckled her knees if the shadows hadn't already swallowed her legs, a sensation of cool nothingness where they should have been.

Sara fought to stuff down her panic, the last-minute gifts feeling more like tokens on a fresh corpse instead of survival boons.

She glanced down at herself, at the shadows now consuming her torso. Though her amulets vanished from view, she could feel their reassuring weight, their warmth against the cool nothingness. With all the swagger she could muster, she grinned—widely—intent on relieving everyone's terror and leaving them with hope. "Dragons are a piece of pie for a High Witch of Legend." Not that she thought she was a High Witch of Legend, but it sounded like something one would say.

She held her grin, forcing every scrap of her bravado into a mask of confidence.

No one said a word.

Either she had convinced them, or they saw right through her. After all, Ann had been a powerful witch while Sara barely knew what she was doing on a good day. And Ann had died.

CHAPTER 30

Darkness overcame Sara, the bright birch grove and crisp scent of snow snuffed out by the heavy nothing of a deep sleep. She had no body, no sense of up or down, no concept of time. It could have been minutes or days before a frigid wind whispered through the Aether.

The wind grew and grew like the ominous crescendo of a dark symphony until it was a howl buffeting Sara from all directions. And just when she thought her consciousness would surely freeze to death, the storm shattered, replaced by a distinct pulsating hiss that shook her very being.

Dragon. *Burning Hells.* Was she being welcomed or warned?

Sara's feet alighted on a hard, smooth surface. The relief of being back in her body was fleeting in the pressing obscurity. It was too still, too heavy to be outside. She fidgeted. The slight scrape of her boots echoed before it was gobbled up by a vast space. Wherever she was, it was teeth-rattling cold and silent as a tomb.

With a shiver, she summoned her white flames, cloaking herself. They kindled with a gentle heat that seeped through her clothes and warmed her bones. She stifled a sigh, for fear of waking anything—living or dead. Before her, illuminated by the flickering glow of her fire, was a mountain of obsidian rock, glinting with an icy coat. Sara's flames reached for the mountain, an invisible pull tugging her forward a step. The three bloodstones around her neck pulsed. Maybe the Lochton dragon was behind the mountain or buried under it.

Stars above. Please be here and not missing.

She summoned a sphere of energy overhead, casting light on a cathedral-sized cave of roughhewn stone, its granite-gray walls and ceiling splotched with sooty black, its ice-frosted floor a tamped cobble of worn stones. The opposite of Jin's heated cave and garden paradise.

Sara bit her lip, debating if she should holler a sweet hello as if she were stopping by to borrow a cup of sugar and not a weapon powerful enough to defeat an insidious evil, when a sheet of ice splintered free from the mammoth boulder and an emerald-green eye snapped open.

Sh—

Dragon fire engulfed her, vaporizing her curse and singeing the tips of her silvery-gray hair before her protective shield locked into place. *Too hot!* She willed ice into her veins, but still the flames threatened to turn her into ash.

She mentally screamed, *"Stop! You're supposed to help me, not kill me!"*

The inferno halted. Thank the Mother. Sara levitated a few feet, ready to fly away if the dragon—her *ancestor*, she recalled with a shudder of incredulity—spewed a second round of flesh-melting fire. She summoned another sphere of energy, large enough to fully illuminate the voluminous cavern, and gaped. The mountain was not a mountain but a dragon easily thrice the size of Thomas.

The dragon's rugged body lay partially curled in a serpentine S-form. His neck stretched out on the floor, his massive head smack-dab in front of Sara, his chin pointed away from her. Despite the fire, ice still encased him. Its glassy quality allowed a glimpse of spikes jutting out like shark-toothed icebergs along his spine and compact arms and legs. Black-as-night scales glinted with a jeweled green luster. The same luminous green tipped his spikes and swirled in the one elysian eye fixed on her. The eye narrowed, its vertical pupil shrinking in the glow of her energy as the dragon studied her.

She lowered to the cobbled floor and, imitating Dean's commanding pose, placed her hands on her hips. "If you know nothing of ill intent can enter your lair, why would you attack me?" There, let the dragon know she meant it no harm and that she was in charge here. She gritted her teeth at the raised pitch of her voice, at the fear radiating from her. Telling him they were related would probably end in him eating her for being weak. She slid back a step at his silence. Maybe he was more creature than magically conscious.

A puff of smoke. *"You disturbed me."* His resonant voice filled Sara's mind, the low timber as rich and dominant as a king.

Should she bow? She couldn't tell if he was annoyed or grateful.

"Ahh, you're welcome?" she hazarded. *Please don't eat me.*

A forked tongue flickered from his snout, curling toward Sara where she held her ground beside his cheek. Rooted to the ground was more like it as his tongue stirred the air around her before retracting. *"You smell of Mary and Ann, yet you are not them. My blood is in your veins, yet I do not know you. Who are you?"*

Sara raised her chin. "I'm Sara Lochton, your great-great-granddaughter. And I need your help to defeat the Shadow Mother."

His gaze widened, the green swirling a storm of emotions, before narrowing with deadly focus as a snarl rocked the cave. Fist-sized pebbles rained upon Sara, pinging against her shield and the hard-packed floor. Just as she was about to grab her stone pendant and smoke away should the lair collapse, the vibrations faded. *"I am Lochton, and I have been frozen far too long. Close your eyes."*

Did she imagine the hungry bite to his words?

"Why? So you can eat me? I've been told I taste terrible." Her thumb reflexively rubbed the edge of her palm, where her pinkie finger had been.

A huff. *"You are as hotheaded as Ann. Close your eyes."*

Though she bristled at the command, Sara obeyed.

The familiar darkness behind her lids transformed into a wooded glen with ancient, gnarl-barked trees. At her feet, lush, tender-green grass swayed in a gentle wind. The illusion was so real she felt a misty breeze on her cheeks, smelled the earthy shoreline of the adjacent crescent-shaped body of water, heard the soft lapping of its waves. But as enchanting as the surroundings were, Sara remained focused on the raw power radiating from the male warrior—Lochton—a mere ten paces in front of her.

Magic instinctively tingled in her palms, her bloodstones glowing red.

His deep green elysian gaze seemed to look into her soul. It was unsettling because, one, her soul was pitted with dark pockets she preferred to keep to herself, and two, he was physically striking—the exact opposite of the wizened great-great-grandfather she had expected. He appeared every ounce the warrior king his voice had suggested: chiseled face with strong jaw and chin; long black hair shimmering with hints of glossy green and strands of liquid silver; bare, muscled torso with a faint outline of scales rippling across his tan skin; and corded arms, their outer edges lined with dragon spikes from his biceps to his wrists.

He wore only a skirt of heavy, midnight fabric—indeed, stars seemed to glint in the folds. It flowed to the calf-tall grass, making it impossible to tell if he was barefoot or wearing shoes. His stare was fierce yet curious as he assessed her. And when his gaze settled on her bloodstones, his demeanor softened.

"Ann didn't survive the Shadow Mother's attack, did she?"

Sara gently shook her head. "No. I'm sorry."

His nostrils flared. In a quiet voice, he said, "I tried to save her." Lochton turned his gaze to the sky, chest expanding with a deep inhale, clenched hands shaking from grief or rage. Perhaps both.

Sara held rabbit-still. Having lost significant loved ones, she knew all too well no amount of placated condolences could comfort a ragged loss. Yet while she felt deeply for him, she couldn't put aside her need for his help.

Lochton heaved a long sigh and slowly turned to her with his all-seeing gaze. "We have both suffered. I will help you as best I can. To do so, you must understand what happened when Ann came to me."

Stars. He had read her thoughts. Any attempt to fortify her mental shield would be futile, if not outright offensive, since she had no doubt he could crack her mind like a walnut. She steeled herself and grinned, hoping it countered the fear he must smell on her. *"By all means, please proceed."* She accompanied her thought with a casual hand gesture.

A smoky laugh. "You *are* just like Ann."

This time, Sara's grin was real. It was good to know her ancestors weren't pushovers, that Lochton truly hadn't attacked Ann, and that he was willing to help her. Triple win.

Lochton stared at Sara for a long moment, eyes swirling. "I did not attack her. I was overjoyed to meet the daughter I hadn't known I had, and even more happy to know she had two daughters of her own. I had asked to meet them and see Mary—my Mary. But Ann told me of her death—of her sacrifice. My fury had been so great it summoned the Shadow Mother." Lochton's eyes flashed, his hands fisting once again. "She devoured my rage and struck back with ice. I tried to shield Ann, then used the last of my magic to return her to Ware Woods—where it was safe. I could barely crawl back to my lair before I was frozen in stasis."

Lochton rolled his shoulders, as if casting off both his rage and sleep, and began walking around Sara. His slight turn revealed a triple row of spikes running down his bare back, a shimmering outline of scales at each puncture through his skin, a greenish-gold sheen on each tip. His steps were slow, near quiet save for the shushing of the grass, his elysian eyes never leaving her.

Sara stiffened, fighting the urge to turn when he prowled behind her. The dark grimoire had said Ann provoked the Shadow Mother, yet all she'd done was visit her father. And as Gran's story implied, it had been a joyous reunion—until Lochton's rage summoned the Shadow Mother from whatever pit of Hell she called home.

Sara's mouth went dry. The epic level of Lochton's fury struck a familiar chord in her scarred soul. Sara hadn't even known Mary and had been hot with anger when Ian told her how she'd sacrificed herself to save Ware Woods from heretical normals.

From behind her, Lochton said, "Your presence tells me I have been frozen a long time, and the Shadow Mother is stronger than she has ever been before."

Sara opened her mouth, eager to explain so many things and let Lochton's rage destroy the Shadow Mother while she slipped back to Ware Woods, when the distinct whoosh of fire shot at her.

CHAPTER 31

S ara whirled, protective shield snapping into place as she pulled water from the air and doused a ball of flames aimed at her head.

Lochton continued stalking as though nothing had happened. "What is the status of the other dragons?" Pure warrior demanding information.

What the Hells? If Lochton had coughed, at least he could apologize for nearly roasting her—again.

She turned with him. Considering it best to answer his question and avoid any infamous anger, she replied, "Flat-eyes are infected with shadows and are under her control. All elysian-eyed dragons—except for three—are sleeping." His answering frown was a gut punch to her hope.

"They are not sleeping. They are frozen. She is cleverer than I thought," Lochton mused. When Sara raised a brow, he explained, "I am the eldest dragon in this world. By freezing me, she has also frozen all other elysian-eyed dragons, starting with the second oldest to the youngest. We are connected. What happens to me eventually happens to the others—a ripple effect. The three dragons you speak of must be the youngest and haven't been affected yet."

Yet. Her heart skipped a beat.

"Where are these three dragons?"

"Secluded in a lair."

Lochton rubbed his chin. "Good. They need to stay there. They are young enough that the shadows may infect them too."

Sara stilled, recalling Thomas's dragon coated in oily shadows, his eyes milky, the pain in his voice when he'd told her to run. He *had* been infected, their bond barely curing him in time. If it happened again—especially if she wasn't with him—the Shadow Mother could be strong enough to control him. And use him to destroy more than just Sara's heart.

Yellow-orange flickered in her peripheral vision, her thoughts of Thomas interrupted by two fireballs coming at her from opposite sides. She rocketed into the air above the glen, letting the fireballs collide before squelching the flames with more water and lowering back to the lush grass, not a scorched blade in sight. Her satisfaction over quickly exterminating the flames was eclipsed by the dawning awareness that the fireballs had been intentional.

She faced him, her snarl catching at the sharp glint in his eyes—the same glint she often saw in Kane during their particularly painful sparring sessions.

Lochton was testing her. But why?

Since she was fairly certain he wouldn't tell her, and since she was still a bit lamb-before-the-lion concerned he would find her lacking and prefer a dead descendant over a weak one, she dropped her snarl and simply said, "Good thing you're awake now, and you can—"

"I am frozen," he growled. His deep-chested vibrations quaked the trees, putting her snarl to shame. His bared teeth gleamed with brutal, honed points. "This illusion is all I can manage. I cannot mentally project past my cave." He threw up his hands, clawing the air with his pointed black nails, the furious gesture suggesting he was angry at his situation, not at Sara.

"Oh," she managed. For an illusion, it felt damn real. Real enough that she bet his fireballs would burn Cave Sara to a crisp.

She blinked, her presence remaining in the glen. How was any of this possible? Her headache-inducing speculation slipped into panic. Lochton could not leave his cave. He could not save the day. He could not be her secret weapon to defeat the Shadow Mother.

Wonderful. Just *freaking* fantastic. She ground her teeth, silently screaming. Why the Hells did the dark grimoire send her here and risk her paying a heavy price if Lochton couldn't help her?

Lochton paced faster, his dark skirts flowing like a celestial waterfall, a shadowy dragon tail slicing through the grass behind him.

Sara shuffle-turned with him. *Think.* Maybe he could help in another way. Maybe if he explained more about the Shadow Mother, she could garner some useful nuggets of information. Because something wasn't right. It wasn't the Shadow Mother's style to blindly attack. She took pleasure in mentally tormenting magicals, feeding on fear and any scrap of wickedness.

At the mere memory of the Shadow Mother shredding her mind, pain lanced Sara. It weakened her knees, her mind flashing with an image of Lethal and Samson sprawled on the ground, incapacitated by the dark entity's mental torture. *Never again.*

Sara hastily swept back an errant lock of hair. "Did the Shadow Mother say anything to you?" *Did she torment you?* Sara held back her latter question, deeming Lochton's loss of Ann more agonizing than the Shadow Mother's claws.

A wall of fire erupted before Sara, blocking her view of Lochton so quickly she couldn't tell if he breathed the flames or simply willed them.

The wall surged toward her, flames licking the slate blue sky. Sara resisted the instinct to fly away. If this were a test, she needed to stay her ground. Summoning a wave of ice, she pushed back the wall, letting her wave crash over the fire, obliterating it.

In a sizzle of green energy, any trace of their clash vanished, the glen immaculate. Lochton inclined his head toward Sara, a subtle approval before answering her question. "She said, '*Dragons cannot love.*'"

Sara frowned. *That* was what she'd said?

He stopped pacing and faced Sara. "All this time, I thought her attack was punishment for loving. The Mother told me to watch over Mary—not get involved. And for good reason. Our love endangered Mary's mission to create Ware Woods and my duty as an impartial overseer of the magical balance. So we mutually agreed to separate. I still watched over her from afar, but her magic was greater than my elysian eyes. She hid Ann from me, and when she created the barrier around Ware Woods, I couldn't see anything—not even her death. I thought I would never feel love again—*shouldn't* feel love again—then Ann came and told me I had a family." Silver welled in his emerald gaze as he looked Sara up and down. His family.

Every muscle in Sara's body went slack; even her bones seemed rubbery. Should she hug him? His prickly appearance and his choice of words grounded her feet. He *thought* he'd been punished for loving and that he shouldn't feel love. What did he think now?

Reading her mind, Lochton said, "Your existence has proven the Shadow Mother wrong. Dragons can love. You are my progeny, and you are in love with a dragon. I sense your bond. It is stronger than any I have ever known." He raised his hands, palms to the sky, and a ring of fire surrounded Sara.

Burning Hells! *Enough of the testing!* She unleashed a touch of her frustration—her anger at the Shadow Mother for targeting her family for generations. Witch fire sprang forth. It raced from her in an outward circle, gobbling up air, suffocating the dragon fire. And just before her fire reached Lochton, Sara panicked and yanked it back, stuffing the fire deep inside herself.

I didn't know I could do that. Sweat ran down the sides of her face, soaking the shirt beneath her jacket. With a curse, she braced her hands on her thighs and panted. Who knew you could use fire to fight fire? Apparently, Lochton. Sara scowled at him, dragon wrath be damned. He could have just *told* her fire extinguished fire. Too bad it was so exhausting.

Through verdant grass, Lochton approached her, a closed-lip smile on his face, the first smile he'd shown her. "The Mother and Father do not punish," he said, his voice soft, solemn. "I should have known it was a lie whispered by the Shadow Mother. It is love she fears, and with elysian-eyed dragons frozen, you, Sara Lochton, are her greatest threat."

Sara slowly straightened. Impossible. She'd faced the Shadow Mother before, and though she'd momentarily pushed back at her, Sara had only survived because of Jin's interference and the golden shield created by Ian and the Hills children. To permanently defeat the Shadow Mother—now that the entity was stronger and the magical balance awry—Sara needed a magical sword capable of piercing shadows or the Shadow Mother's real name, *anything* of world-changing power. Anything but herself, because Sara couldn't possibly be the weapon she was seeking.

"It is possible," said Lochton. "You have proven yourself. Your lineage and dragon mate will help you." He paused, glancing at her bloodstones and smoke stone pendant. "*Everyone* must help you. But it is your inner fire that is most important in undoing the Shadow Mother."

"I—" Sara's denial cut off as darkness rubbed against her calves, a cat demanding attention. Her feet and legs went numb, swallowed by depthless shadows.

"What's happening?" she cried, trying and failing to kick her legs.

"The spell you used to come here is wearing off." Lochton gave her another smile. This one a gently open, goodbye smile. It terrified Sara, not because of his many pointed teeth, but because she wasn't ready to leave. Not in the slightest. She needed to know more—like *how* exactly to vanquish the Shadow Mother. And, perhaps most importantly, where were the Mother and the Father? If they didn't punish, why did it feel as though Sara was being punished for something she didn't do?

Sara looked at Lochton, her eyes wide, mentally shoving her

many questions at him as the shadows embraced her torso, their cool whispers creeping up her neck.

He held her gaze, the calm swirls in his eyes soothing her. "Believe in yourself. Once you undo the Shadow Mother, all dragons will be free, and the balance will be corrected."

He made it sound terrifically easy. Too easy. Before she could ask what epic price she would have to pay—to undo the Shadow Mother and achieve her goal of peace—the shadows kissed her lips, silencing her. It was for the best, really. If she knew her end, she might curl up into a ball same as a woolly caterpillar—or set the entire world on fire like a demon from Hell. Probably the latter. She hoped to see Lochton again and hoped he knew this—that she claimed him as family.

Her vision darkened, the Lochton before her fading away similar to a dawn dream. What she could see of the wooded glen and misty body of water dissolved into the dim features of his frozen lair, the only light the soft emerald glow of his dragon eye. It winked out, and Sara plummeted into scorching-hot gloom.

CHAPTER 32

Bursts of fiery orange glowed through billowing smoke. The indirect heat of fire roasted Sara's flesh and stung her eyes while thick, downy ash flooded her nose and lungs, suffocating her. With a garbled choke, Sara pulled up the neck of her shirt and covered her face—the best she could do while falling through the Aether. She struggled to suck in a breath, her heart racing at a flashback of the witch fire that nearly consumed her after she'd killed Dorcas.

Is burning in the Aether my own personal Hell?

This was so inconvenient. She still needed to face the Shadow Mother and achieve peace. Her fear melted into anger. Now was *not* the time to pay a price—to die.

As if the Mother heard her, Sara slammed onto burnt ground, the resulting pain that ran up her legs confirming she was very much alive. The crackle of fire filled her ears, distant enough not to induce panic, yet close enough to be a concern. She healed herself and threw up her protective shield, reducing the heat level from star explosion to barely sufferable smelted lava, then took in her surroundings. Though she was no longer falling, the heat and smoke remained, veiling everything around her save for the murky silhouettes of very tall, upright trees. Too upright to be Ware Woods.

A high-pitched scream of terror, of fatal wounds and defeat, of certain death and pain, slashed through the apocalyptic surroundings.

Sara lurched ahead—toward the cry. She stumbled over deep grooves, the ground seemingly raked by massive claws and littered with glowing embers that spit and hissed against her jets of water. Attempts to blow away the curtain-thick smoke only made it worse.

The scream hadn't been Caleb, she told herself. Dorcas was *not* in this nightmare. The miserable, deceitful witch was dead by Sara's own hands.

But the Shadow Mother and Brad were certainly capable of eliciting such screams.

Sara rushed forward—and smacked into a wall, her bottom lip splitting open, the taste of metal filling her mouth. Not a wall, her fingertips discerned, but the sticky, scaley hide of a dragon. She pressed her palms against the flesh. A cold-as-death dragon. *Thomas?*

Sara pulled on their bond. Relief flooded her at the familiar warmth, at the inner golden threads, at his slight tug in return. He was safe in Jin's garden. She pushed thoughts of love and assurance through the bond, hoping Thomas wouldn't notice her distress. With no more screams to guide her through the haze, Sara turned her focus back to the unfortunate dragon before her.

The smoke cleared a smidge, revealing mud-colored scales tarred with shadows. On her right protruded a slack hind leg. Its compact foot was equipped with wickedly curved talons, the undersides bearing chunks of dirt and clothing and— Sara diverted her gaze, clamping down on the compulsion to retch. She edged away from the foot, following the wide plates of its abdomen to where it split open with a vicious tear. Gore pooled before the dragon, its heart ripped clean from its chest, discarded like a massive slimy peach pit. She bit down on her fist.

Evidently, there were two ways to kill a dragon: hit the soft spot at the base of its skull or tear out its heart. Both options were cruel, considering the dragons were infected, merely puppets controlled by the Shadow Mother. Sara glanced at the open stare of the flat-eyed dragon, her own heart heavy. This might easily be Thomas if she couldn't stop the Shadow Mother.

Sara reached for the smoke stone pendant hanging from her neck. Wherever she was, she needed to leave and get back to Ware Woods. Before fully clasping the pendant, she paused, listening for any signs of life around her.

Through the snap of distant fire drifted the far-off murmur of conversation. But from which direction? Sara squinted, grateful for the goggle-like shield protecting her eyes. She summoned a whisper-soft breeze across the ground, low and steady, carefully clearing just enough visibility without agitating the heavier smoke overhead.

Sara's blood ran cold at the sight of the scorched grove before her.

More than a dozen bodies were burnt into light-gray statues of ash, their hair and clothes frozen in the same powdery hue, each victim horrifically suspended in their final act. Some were digging into the ground in a futile attempt for coverage, some were running, some were clinging to each other. All had faces contorted in pain, mouths open in silent screams, fangs bared. An entire colony of lavishly dressed vampires. Amira's colony.

Sara approached the nearest vampire. She barely grazed the hem of his dinner jacket when he disintegrated, the ash so fine it vanished, not a speck of his existence left behind.

Her stomach knotted. This was her fault. Amira had said Brad threatened to kill anyone who sided with Ware Woods, the same threat he'd stated at the Global Council meeting. The same threat he'd delivered on by bringing Takers and dragons to Florine's site.

Sara darted her gaze around the grove, its treetops burning like torches, searching for the beautiful Elder Vampire. Another hint of conversation through the crackling wood. And there, in the distance, at the far edge of a particularly dark curtain of smoke, stood a figure.

Sara rushed for them, dodging her way through the cemetery of ashen statues. As she neared, mouth open to shout for Amira, the figure turned. Except it wasn't Amira who faced her; it was Brad.

Sara skid to a halt, white flames of energy gathering in her open palms.

Brad pressed a finger to his lips, shushing her. His red-rimmed eyes wide with warning, not menace. Her magic cooled at the distinct change in his aura; no longer piercing black, it was now a sludgy gray green—the color of unease and dead things. What happened to him? Or better yet, what deceitful mask was he now wearing? He was as slippery as they came, loyal only to his need for domination.

She stared at him, noting the sunken quality of his cheeks, the dark stains coating his hands and forearms. The spreading inky poison had swallowed the bite mark she'd given him in the hospital, what seemed eons ago. And then she heard it; a voice similar to Amira's, though a shade echoey, drawn out by a sinister undertow.

The Shadow Mother.

Every inch of Sara's skin prickled.

From the dense, churning smoke beyond Brad, the Shadow Mother continued talking in her cruel imitation of Amira's voice. "Vampires are the strongest of all the factions. Isn't that what you've said, Amira? Did you think yourself superior to me? Is this why you sided with Ware Woods, for more power? Pity. I could have given you all the power you wanted. Now your colony is nothing but ash, your soul tree is nothing but a torch, and you are nothing but a wretched creature the Mother no longer cares about. Even your half-breed daughter is nothing. She was all too easily abducted and killed, isn't that right, Taker?"

Brad broke his stare at Sara and slipped into the smoke, disappearing from view like an eel retracting into its cave. His grunted response filtered through the haze.

It wasn't surprising how the Shadow Mother salted Amira's wounds by grinding in the statement that a lowly Taker had murdered her daughter. But it was interesting how the Shadow Mother didn't bother to call Brad by name, implying he was an expendable servant and not a partner. And that Brad had lied to her about killing Kira.

Sweat trickled down the center of Sara's chest as she stood alone in the kindling grove, nothing but a veil of smoke hiding her.

She should go after Brad and end him for infecting Thomas and for so many more slights—never mind whatever just happened here. She should save Amira. She should strike the Shadow Mother now while she least expected it.

Yet Sara remained still, one of Kane's many strategy lessons clanging in her head: *A victor knows when to engage and when to wait.* Sara hated waiting, but there was no way she could face the Shadow Mother alone. Even if Lochton was right and Sara was a threat to her, without the support of the other magicals, the Shadow Mother would squish her mind like an overripe gooseberry. Besides, the Book had once warned her never to stand alone before the Shadow Mother. Plus, Brad was acting shifty and Amira was probably incapacitated. Surging into the smoke would be an epic disaster. Her entire body trembled, the vengeful monster inside her howling against her clenched-teeth will to remain silent, watchful, clever in biding a moment to snatch Amira and disappear.

"No one cares for you," hissed the Shadow Mother, her voice now genuine, raspy and dripping with toxin. For a terrifying moment, Sara thought she was speaking to *her*, the vehemence stabbing her soul even though she knew it was a lie. But then the Shadow Mother said, "You shall rot here. A slow, painful death befitting a deceitful Elder." The smoke churned, and Sara tensed, placing one hand over her glowing bloodstones and one hand on her jagged smoke pendant. If the Shadow Mother spotted her or if Brad ratted her out, Sara would have to be quicker than Death herself to grab Amira and smoke to safety.

She shifted to the balls of her feet, grinding her boots against loose bits of charcoal. The curtain of pitchy smoke paled to a soft dove gray, its color leaching out—darkness leaving the entire grove. With a wet slap, the heaviness in the air notably lifted. The change in pressure pulled up the remaining smoke, revealing only Amira. She lay on her side, eyes closed, fangs bared in a painful grimace.

Her fine dress was burnt through to her skin on one side, the bottom portion missing from mid-thigh down, presumably torn off to run faster. She was covered in blood, her face streaked with the grisly war paint. Behind her lay three dragons, their shadow-smeared chests torn open, their hearts beside them.

Shock rippled through Sara. None of this should have happened. The dragons were just as innocent as the vampires—just as innocent as Sara and Ware Woods. They were *all* being played by the Shadow Mother.

Fury exploded from Sara in the form of a wet gale, instantly extinguishing the remaining fires and blowing away all traces of smoke as well as the colony's ashen remains.

Amira cracked open her eyes, fresh blood tears veining the sides of her face. "Sara?"

She rushed to the Elder Vampire. "I'm getting you out of here. Can you stand?" She grabbed Amira's violence-slicked arm to pull her up; it was like grabbing an immoveable wet statue.

"Leave me. I have nothing left to live for. Not even revenge. She is too powerful."

"Bullshit," replied Sara to all of it. Sure, Amira had lost her colony, watched her site burn, and suffered the mind-numbing torture of the Shadow Mother, but the dramatics were Samson level, all the more so with her flowery accent; no wonder the two got along. Besides, revenge was always on the table.

Amira raised her brow at Sara in a very *excuse me* manner.

"Kira is alive and safe with Samson. I'll take you to them right now."

Amira propped herself up on her elbows, her bloody eyes wide.

Clearly she wasn't physically hurt. "I'm not sure they want to see me. They have been hiding from me. I think . . . ashamed of me."

For Amira to speak so candidly—to admit a vulnerability . . . Maybe she'd lost too much blood.

Sara crouched before her. "They thought you wanted to kill her for being half-vampire, half-witch."

Amira's eyes blew wider.

Sara winced at her own bluntness. Totally not a smooth High Witch of Legend. She attempted to wave off her gaffe. "You know, all the factional fighting and misunderstanding of half-breeds being weak when, actually, they're very strong."

Amira's brow hit her hairline.

Sara should really stop talking, yet she had to say something before looping them away. "I invite you into Ware Woods. You'll see." She laid a hand on Amira's bloody shoulder and with her other hand squeezed the jagged stone pendant. Smoke began to curl around them.

"Wait!" shouted Amira, shifting her position to face the center of the grove. "I must honor my colony."

Sara released the pendant. The smoke kept coming. "I don't know how to stop it," she cried, frantically waving at the ashy clouds.

Amira flung herself aside. She thrust her bloody hands into the hissing, charred ground and carved the looping symbol of a still circle. As smoke wrapped around them, Amira kept her gaze on the inner grove—where her colony had been. Her voice deep with soulful resonance, she chanted:

"May your souls find peace with the Father of Night,

May your magic return to the Mother of Light."

Her blessing carried across the empty grove, weighing heavily on Sara. The only solace Sara could offer was a firm grip on Amira's shoulder as the smoke swelled and swallowed them whole.

CHAPTER 33

SARA LANDED ON smooth wooden floorboards, still crouching, still clasping Amira's stony shoulder. The faint give and groan of the wood was similar to that of the treehouse, yet when the smoke cleared, Sara noted the lacquered floor of the Main House. They were in a sitting room of sorts, open doors on either side of the room offering glimpses of stately bedrooms as well as a hallway and the grand loft where the Hills children slept. Reclining on the sitting room's couch and upholstered chairs, having what appeared to be a very somber tea party, were Samson, Kira, Charlie, and Ian, delicate cups halfway to their slack-jawed mouths.

In a blink, the tea service whished away, and Samson was on his knees beside them. "Amira?"

Another blink, and Kira joined him, her hand flying to her chest. "Mom?"

A third blink, and Ian hauled Sara up, crushing her in a shared embrace with Charlie.

"What happened?" her brother asked, his body trembling against hers as though she'd come back from the dead.

Sara pulled away, feeling Ian's reluctance to let go of her. "The Shadow Mother attacked Amira's site for siding with us. We have to warn the others," she urged, her voice edged with need to save the sacred sites whose inhabitants believed in her.

231

Charlie clamped his hands on her upper arms, stopping her from levitating and flying out of the room. His gaze bored into her, a haggard beard of short, sandy-blond whiskers on his cheeks. "We will. First, tell us where you've been for a week."

Sara started. "A week?"

Ian's brow peaked, his curly hair in all directions as if he'd been tugging on it the entire time. Behind him, Kira helped Amira to the couch while Samson summoned one of Lethal's decadent bottles and a cut-glass goblet fit for a queen.

"I—I met Lochton, and then the spell took me to Amira's site. I've only been gone a few hours."

Charlie slowly shook his head, not a few hours but a week of worry in his glassy eyes.

Sara's heart shattered. The price for using the forbidden spell had been a week of her life—a price her family suffered most. She should be grateful to be alive—that the price wasn't *more*. Yet it had been her choice, her burden to bear. No one else's.

"I'm sorry," she projected to her father and brother.

"Not your fault," said Charlie, his quick reply no doubt meant to soothe her emotional state when all it did was inflame it.

Sara seethed. Her fingernails bit into her palms as she fumed over the cost of the spell, the unfairness of it ever being forbidden, and the dawning realization that *all* magicals, including Mary and Lochton, had been fleeced by the Shadow Mother—led to believe lies as truths. Lies that each faction was superior to the others, that dragons could not love and were ruthless and killed their mixed-magic children.

By planting these rotten seeds, the Shadow Mother had poisoned the central pillar of the magical balance by slowly replacing love with fear and hate. She had cultivated her lies for centuries until even dragons believed they could not love.

Until the three factions feared and hated dragons.

Until the idea of *any* mixed magical was feared and hated.

Until the fear and hatred between factions was a gaping

wound, eating away at the magical world while the Shadow Mother grew stronger.

Sara's knees threatened to give out, her father's hold the only thing keeping her upright.

From across the room came whispered conversation followed by a sudden intake of breath. "The *whole* colony?" exclaimed Samson, standing before Amira as Kira embraced her on the couch.

Sara swallowed hard. They were all in such deep, shadowy shit.

As if knowing she was spiraling down a wretched rabbit hole, Charlie locked his gaze with hers. "Did you get what you needed from the Lochton dragon?" The clipped urgency in his otherwise calm voice snapped Sara out of her daze.

Yes. No. "It's complicated. I'll tell you everything later because right now we need to warn the others. They need to know I invite them all into Ware Woods if they need refuge." Sara stepped back from her father's grasp, readying to fly off, when a sudden tug on the bond sent her doubling over.

"Sara!"

"Dad and I will warn the other sites," said Ian, his aura flaring a determined dandelion yellow that cautioned, *Don't even think about stopping me.* "We'll ask Dean and Lethal to help us while you get cleaned up and visit Thomas. He's—"

"Screaming my name," Sara finished his sentence, wincing as Thomas's frustration at not being able to leave the garden flooded the bond. She pushed reassuring warmth back at him and received an immediate sigh.

"Go to him. We'll meet up later," said Ian, his lanky strides matching those of their father as they dashed from the room.

"Please tell me you'll visit me soon, or I'll combust."

"I'm on my way." Not exactly, and he knew it, otherwise they wouldn't be having this conversation. First, she needed a moment for her legs to grow steady. The Shadow Mother's level of deceit was far worse than she'd ever thought possible.

"Thank the Father." Thomas mentally huffed. *"I heard about the spell. Now tell me you're fine and not covered in blood."*

Sara hesitated, taking in Amira's crimson-covered appearance where she rested on the couch. Transferred carnage shone on Samson and Kira, the latter sitting beside her mother, folded into her side. Technically, Sara wasn't *covered* in blood, not like she'd been when Samson took her finger. How ironic the same witch was now mouthing, "Thank you," to Sara while he poured another snack for Amira, a world of gratitude in his jet-black eyes.

Sara projected to Thomas, *"I'm fine."*

"That was an incriminating pause."

Guilty. With a slight nod at Samson, because really all she'd done was bring Amira into Ware Woods, Sara clutched the smoke stone pendant and looped to Jin's garden.

Sara's feet hit the pebbled pathway. The rounded black-and-white stones of the intricately laid pattern seemed to poke through the soles of her boots. But the discomfort was the least of her worries as she stared at a red dragon snout pointed directly at her, less than an arm's length away. The mouth parted, a blast of hot air blowing back her hair—the infinitesimal warning before she would be engulfed in dragon fire. Her protective shield was no match for this close of a range, the utter surprise of her situation robbing her of the precious moment needed to summon witch fire. Before the flames could claim her, an even faster force slammed into Sara, picking her up, taking her away from the fire. A force smelling of musk and ash.

Thomas.

His arms banded around her, his face buried in the crook of her neck as they landed on the soft grass beneath the garden's cherry tree, its branches in perpetual bloom.

She returned his fierce hug, light-blue energy sizzling at their contact. He was safe, his heart steadily beating inside his chest. From over his shoulder, she spotted Tobio and Matthew rushing toward them. Behind the shifters, laying prone on the garden floor, was Jin's massive red dragon. His tail rested in a pool of groomed-white sand, his body occupying the grand space where the tea pavilion had been. His long neck and head stretched down the pathway, his eyes closed, his fire already vapors in the partly clouded sky. A sudden heaviness threatened to crush Sara's insides—Jin's position and instinctual burst of fire unnervingly similar to Lochton's.

"Jin?" Sara questioned, not bothering to hide the fear in her voice. When she tried to lean away from Thomas, he tightened his hold, his refusal to let go a reminder she'd been gone for a week. Stars above, he must have been beside himself. She relaxed into him, their bond humming.

When Tobio and Matthew approached, Thomas released a possessive growl. The two shifters halted at a healthy distance, seemingly taking no offense at Thomas's warning.

"Jin's barely conscious," said Tobio. "We've been talking and reading to him to keep him awake."

Matthew held up the leather-bound book in his hand. The sly grin on his face, coupled with the glimmer in his amber eyes, told Sara he was determined to keep Jin awake, as well as Thomas and Tobio if necessary. Matthew would do anything for Thomas, who was like a brother to him. And, from the way Tobio and Matthew both tilted toward one another as if they were each other's sun, she knew Tobio was so much more to Matthew.

"Thank you," she mentally projected to him.

Matthew gave her the slightest of winks and asked, "Where've you been?"

"I went to visit a dragon named Lochton for help in defeating the Shadow Mother. It took much longer than expected." Sara didn't mention the details. She had no desire to rehash them. Besides, from Thomas's earlier comment, they knew about the bloody spell and likely knew that Lochton—the most powerful elysian-eyed dragon—was her living ancestor.

"Sara Lochton." Jin's voice echoed in her mind. Given Tobio's and Matthew's raised brows and the catch in Thomas's breath, Jin had projected to all of them. Sara stole a glance at the red dragon. His eyes were still closed. *"I hadn't known your last name until Ian came and explained the spell. Your shared blood must have let you into his lair—he's exceptionally reclusive, even among dragons. I'm surprised he spoke with you. He's been asleep for centuries."*

"He's not asleep. He's frozen. The same will happen to you three unless I can weaken the Shadow Mother enough to loosen her hold on all dragons."

At this, Thomas released her. His eyes blazed. "Did Lochton tell you how to do this?" He was pissed. Not at her. Never at her. But at Lochton for putting her on the front line. What Thomas didn't know was that she'd *always* been on the front line. The Shadow Mother had targeted her long before she'd even known of the magical world.

"I think I know what to do, but I'll need help from the other sites. She knows I need them and just attacked a vampire colony— punishing them for supporting us. I was lucky to save the Elder. The rest were burnt to ash."

Jin sighed heavily. His tail swished, marring the pristine sand with a deep gouge. Tobio and Matthew exchanged concerned glances while Thomas fully took in Sara, his jaw rigid, tiny drifts of smoke curling from his ears.

Like falling snow, a few cherry blossoms fluttered to the ground, one grazing Sara's arm. She looked down at herself for the first time and gasped. Her hands were caked in blood, her favorite black jacket with its angled zipper in scorched tatters, her jeans singed to her skin in too many parts, her boots melted into misshapen lumps. The only part of her untouched by the Shadow Mother's smoldering attack were her three bloodstones and the jagged pendant.

CHAPTER 34

I N ONE SWIFT motion, Thomas lifted her off her feet, placing one arm under her knees while his other arm cradled her to his chest. Sara swallowed her protest. She was perfectly fine to stand on her own, but after a long day of multiple terrors, being swept up into his arms felt pretty damn good.

Her hand fisted his T-shirt as he rushed them across the stepping stones of the garden's meditative stream, through the parted waterfall and into the cave. When he headed toward a solid stone wall, Sara shrieked and turned into him, eyes closed.

Thomas's lips skimmed her brow, his shoulders protectively hunching over her. "Relax. I'm taking you to my private chambers."

"That sounds rather . . . opulent." And a far cry from the spartan, white-paneled room Jin had once stuck her in. She opened her eyes, then opened them wider at a vast bathing room with three raised round wells aligned in its center. Steam clouded the surface of one bath; ice floated in a second; and in the middle bath, gentle bubbles frothed. A sleek vanity ran the length of one wall while a series of open showers lined the opposite wall. Hanging from the vaulted ceiling by silvery threads of varying lengths were glowing crystals of all sizes. Except for a pile of plush white towels on the vanity, everything was made of stone, the humidity in the air painting its color a deep gray.

The spa-like space was pure water-loving dragon decadence. For a moment, she wondered if he slept here before spotting an arched opening to another grand room with luminous crystals and a massive bed.

Thomas hastened to the middle bath and gently set her down on the well's wide edge. He maintained his contact with her, trailing his hands up her sides as though afraid to let go lest she vanish for another week. His touch tickled her with electricity until he stopped his ascent at her bloodstones. Thomas palmed them along with the smoke stone pendant in one hand. Either he had confidence in being a mighty dragon or had gathered from their previous embrace that the bloodstones wouldn't harm him.

She glanced down at the stones. Charlie and Ian had hugged her too, and nothing ill had happened to them. Perhaps, as Thomas once suggested—when Sara had first pressed her stone against him, not realizing it could harm—it was the wearer who decided when a stone could be wielded as a weapon. Sara shuddered at the recollection of Brad's Takers disintegrating with one touch.

Feeling Thomas's mental nudge for an explanation, Sara said, "Alice gave me Ann's bloodstone, Samson gave me his, and Kira gave me the smoke stone so I could return to Ware Woods."

Thomas frowned. "That spell was far more dangerous than Ian let on."

"I'm fine now."

"I'm not." His grip tightened on the stones, his arm shaking. "I should be by your side. Not hiding like—"

"You're not hiding," she cut him off before he could grow more agitated and sprout spikes. "You're in safekeeping until I weaken the Shadow Mother. *Then* you'll be by my side. Together we'll finish her off and her little dog Brad too."

Thomas's scowl did not budge at the smile she shot him. His blue aura was shredded with slashes of maroon, his hold on their bond ironclad. He was still stuck in the torture of being separated from her. It pained Sara. She felt his crushing agony as her own, yet she couldn't change what had happened. She could only focus on reassuring him that she was truly fine. Pungent, but otherwise physically fine.

She dipped her fingers, nails edged in gore, into the bubbling bath water. It was enticingly warm. "Do I smell worse than lake mud?"

Still nothing from him. Sometimes being bonded mates was a pain in her ass when he saw right through her lighthearted diversions. Good thing for both of them she had an ace up her tattered sleeve. If humor wouldn't work, she knew what would—a challenge.

She grinned slowly, wickedly. His gaze tightened, knowing she was up to something. Sara drawled, "Who shall whish off what's left of my clothes the fastest, you or me?" She yelped out her last word, her clothes gone.

His gaze locked on to her, his molten blue eyes blazing, appearing all the brighter as the suspended crystals dimmed. Without breaking his stare, he ground out, "Get in."

She arched a brow at him.

He released her stones, his expression softening, and rubbed the back of his head. "Sorry. I'm still on edge. I didn't mean to order you, Sara. You can shower first if you'd prefer. Do you want me to stay or leave while you clean up?"

"Stay," she blurted, voicing what they both wanted. When he dropped his arm, visibly relaxing, she sank into the water. Showering first would've been nice to get rid of the grime, but this bath was too tempting to put off for another moment. The temperature was perfect for melting worries. She ducked her head under, reveling in her lightness, the slight reprieve from the weight on her shoulders.

When she surfaced, Thomas was sitting on the bath's broad, smooth edge. He wore only knit black shorts—the ones she knew he preferred to sleep in—his lower legs dangling in the water, his hands gripping the inside lip of the stone seat. Beside him rested an assortment of bottles, soaps, and brushes. He whished her a bottle, its contents smelling of spring rain as Sara lathered her hair.

"Tell me everything," he said.

And so she did. In between rinsing her hair and brutally scrubbing every inch of skin from her face to her ankles, Sara told him about the dark grimoire, the forbidden spell that never should have been forbidden, everything Lochton had told her about the Shadow Mother attacking him and Ann, the colony's incinerated demise, Brad's unsurprising duplicity, and being terrifyingly close to losing Amira.

By the time she finished, the stone bench beneath Thomas's hands had fractured into a series of fine cracks. Dragon spikes protruded from his outer forearms.

She drifted over to him and lightly grabbed the back of his calves, relieved to feel hard muscle instead of sharp spikes. He jolted, his grip loosening. And when she proceeded to massage his calves and shins, the spikes on his forearms retreated with a soft hiss. The tension in his face eased as he studied her. "You're suspiciously calm. What's your plan, my fierce little monster?"

Sara continued her ministrations, pleased to have settled him and determined to keep him composed. In her most casual tone, she said, "The Equinox is two months away. If the Shadow Mother attacks any more sites, they'll loop to the safety of Ware Woods. In the meantime, I'll practice controlling my witch fire. Because, thanks to Lochton, I now know the Shadow Mother's weakness. Me."

She peered up at Thomas, who had gone very still. "Well, specifically, my fire. From what Lochton said, I'm meant to use my fire to attack the Shadow Mother in unison with the other Magi. With all of us hitting her at the same time, she'll weaken, loosening her magical hold on both flat-eyed and elysian-eyed dragons. Then you'll be at my side to finish her and Brad off. Lochton will come to magically restore the balance, and we can live in peace for the rest of our wondrously long lives. Easy peasy."

Thomas snorted. A wisp of dragon smoke drifted toward the crystal lights, now dim as twilight. "Your plan is brute force." He smirked. "My kinda fight."

Brute force, trickery, pleading with Death—she'd do *anything* to win. And before he could read her deepest thought on just how far she would go, she grazed her fingernails down the soles of his feet.

Thomas yelped, reflexively kicking out at her, but she'd expected his reaction and pushed back into the bath with a chuckle. "Good thing our enemies don't know they can tickle you into submission."

He growled. "Only you can ply me into submission, monster."

She lifted her foot just above the water's edge and wiggled her toes at him.

Another huff. "I noticed you didn't scrub them yet," he said, eyes trained on her foot. For someone who didn't prefer his feet to be touched, he was oddly fascinated with hers. He'd once admitted her feet and ears were deliciously tempting. She looked up at the vaulted ceiling, at what appeared to be diamonds glinting like far-off stars, and sighed. The fact that they could easily discuss war and toes was ridiculously reassuring.

"I saved them just for you."

"Did you now?" He grasped her foot and yanked her toward him.

Sara's head fell back, floating with the rest of her, while Thomas brushed and massaged her feet. She closed her eyes, humming her contentment.

"Are you hungry? I can summon anything you want," he said, his voice sounding distant, her ears beneath the water's surface.

Ah, that would explain the earlier appearance of the bath products. Like Jin, Thomas could now summon objects beyond just his clothes. Interesting. And convenient. She was hungry, but sleep was sucking her into oblivion so quickly she couldn't even project her response.

Sara woke, her limbs tangled with Thomas's, his heat enveloping her as they lay in his downy-soft bed. He was staring at her, his vertical pupils wide, the swirling blue behind them radiating a faint light in the otherwise dark room, the overhead crystals having turned midnight black. When Sara glanced down at the shirt she was wearing—his shirt—Thomas stated the obvious. "You fell asleep. And yes, I've been watching you."

Mother below! How long had she been asleep? There was too much to do. She needed to check in with her father and brother, and with Amira, and— *I should go.*

She hadn't projected it, but Thomas immediately replied, *"Stay."* The single word a resounding plea in her mind and a repeat of what she'd asked of him earlier. His voice low and husky with surrendered sleep, he said, "Charlie and Ian are more than capable of informing the others. I doubt the Shadow Mother will attack again—she made her point, and she won't risk losing more flat-eyed dragons. And I'm sure she's keeping Brad on a short leash."

Sara held his gaze. He was probably right. He'd had way more fighting strategy lessons with Kane than she'd had. Still, even if there wasn't an immediate threat, Sara was High Witch and needed to be back in Ware Woods.

"I need you," he said, pulling her closer. "Stay the night with me. Stay every night with me, because I cannot bear to be without you."

Her heart swooned. He rarely asked anything of her—of anyone, his tough exterior as unyielding as his dragon. But as bonded mates, they shared a deep vulnerability for each other, their love and magic so entwined they physically needed to be together.

"Of course I'll stay the night with you. Now and forever." She kissed his forehead, and he shuddered. The way he clung to her, burying his face into her neck, the wrenching mix of emotions squeezing their bond, she knew he was troubled by more than the week apart and the Shadow Mother's imminent arrival. He was afraid to fall asleep and never wake up. Because what if she couldn't weaken the Shadow Mother?

What if she *did* weaken her, but it didn't reverse her hold on dragons?

Sara kissed him again. "Your turn to sleep while I watch over you." She flooded their bond with love, running her hand through his hair until he relaxed and drifted asleep with a steady pulse. Pressing her lips to his temple, she breathed in his musk and ash scent for hours until the crystals overhead slowly brightened with the comforting glow of dawn.

When Thomas eventually woke—with no surprised burst of fire—he insisted she eat prior to leaving. Before she could protest, they were seated at a low table on the far side of the bedroom.

Sara squinted at the fish soup Thomas summoned and took a sip. It tasted far better than it smelled. She scarfed it down along with a cup of green tea. The meal must be a dragon thing or a Jin thing. Regardless, it was an improvement over the protein shakes Thomas often drank for breakfast. She could get used to it. She *hoped* to get used to it. A flush of adrenaline-fueled determination surged in her veins.

Sara sprang to her feet, reaching for her smoke stone pendant.

"You're not leaving in nothing but my shirt again," Thomas proclaimed, suddenly standing before her.

Fair point. "Alrighty." She drew the word out with a grin, her hand falling to her side. "Are you giving me your shorts too?" They'd fall right off.

He narrowed his eyes as if she'd challenged him, and slowly stalked around her.

Okay, this was a total dragon impulse thing. If he threw a fireball at her, she would dump him in the ice bath. "What're you doing?"

He rounded back into view, and in a puff of smoke, they were both dressed.

"Gaa!" Sara patted herself down. Her shirt, jeans, jacket, and boots were nearly identical to her old ones yet somehow softer, like a comfortable pair of slippers. Thomas wore his favored sparring outfit of black tactical pants, heavy boots, and snug T-shirt.

"I've had nothing but time to practice dragon magic," he said.

"You don't say." Oh, his new powers were definitely convenient. "I'll see you tonight." Neither of them smiled as she clasped the jagged pendant and darkness devoured her.

CHAPTER 35

WHEN THE SMOKE cleared, Sara stood in the cemetery, her new boots sinking into a fluffy layer of snow as she stared at the grave in front of her. With a flick of her finger, she straightened the pine boughs adorning the top of her mother's headstone. With another flick, she whished fresh boughs—their evergreen foliage a symbol of lasting memories—to Naomi's and Ann's graves and around the base of the oak tree for Mary.

Sara approached Ann's grave near the oak's trunk, a root embracing the lichen-dappled stone. Cold nipped her fingertips as she swiped snow from the root. "I met Lochton. He's strong and kind and loved you both very much."

The oak waved its branches, one of its lower limbs extending to brush Sara's shoulder.

"He told me I can undo the Shadow Mother, and I will. I'll suffocate her with witch fire, free the dragons, and reset the balance."

At this, the oak shook, clacking its branches in clear agitation.

Sara furrowed her brow at the tree and backed up, bumping into someone, who tried to steady her. She whirled, coming face to face with a witch in an admiral-blue jacket, a smirk pulling up the corners of his lips.

"Apologies if I interrupted your argument with your tree," said Samson.

"We weren't arguing." Father of Night, she hoped he hadn't heard her private words. "How's Amira?" she asked, redirecting the conversation.

"Hot," he said, pulling at his loose band collar, then added with a roguish gleam in his eyes, "for revenge."

Sara squinted at him. His inky-black hair was slightly mussed. "Where is she now?" Hopefully not terrorizing Ware Woods with an unchecked blood lust. Maybe she should've asked Amira to drink the sap.

"She's with Kira at the Main House, along with most everyone else for the noonday meal."

Noon! Thomas had slept in again, and those damn crystal lights were not to be trusted. Sara scowled.

"Calm down. Amira isn't eating anyone. She's quite enamored with Lethal's bloody bottles."

"Hmph. I suppose that's good news." Lethal had an extensive stock, plus they could always order more bottles of heavens-knew-what since the delivery driver wasn't on the Shadow Mother's immediate hit list. Sara's mind skipped back to Samson's previous comment. *Everyone.* "Are Charlie and Ian at the Main House?"

"They just arrived along with Lethal and Dean's pack. They asked for you, and fine Magus that I am, I came to retrieve you." He gave her an odd smile she couldn't place.

Sara folded her arms, studying him. "Why physically come when you can mentally call me? What gives?" She glimpsed the shine of silver chains around his neck, his many *black* bloodstones tucked inside his jacket. *Oh.* "Thanks for loaning me your red bloodstone," she said, snatching it and beginning to pull it over her head.

"No, Sara." He shook his head and added an eye roll for extra emphasis, as if she were insulting him.

Seriously? She let it go—the eye roll and the necklace—because he'd actually said her name and not "Rookie."

"I came to thank you for saving Amira and bringing her into

Ware Woods. It means more to me and Kira than you'll ever know. Especially since I played a part in the accident that claimed your mother." He dipped his chin, onyx eyes shimmering.

Well, this was completely unexpected. She wished he had just taken back his bloodstone. She didn't want to talk about this. Yet here they were. "I don't blame you for what happened to my mom. I mean—I *did*. I feared and hated you for it—but not anymore. Besides, my mother wouldn't want me holding on to rage and grief. She'd want me to be happy and to help as many people as I can."

That smile again. "Like saving the world?"

This time Sara rolled her eyes.

It had never been her intent to save the world. It still wasn't. She only wished to save the people she cared about and to finally have a damn moment of peace. She couldn't help that the world had gotten tangled up in her mess.

Samson gently reached out and touched his red bloodstone from where it hung around Sara's neck. In a quiet voice, he said, "This is my brother Ardeth's stone. He too was always saving other people, including me. I know he would be honored to help you save the world."

Sara's throat tightened, Samson's solemnness heavy in the chill air. Bloodstones were rare and special, and this was Samson's *only* red bloodstone. Her mind reeled, putting together the pieces of his past. Samson's explanation implied Ardeth had died protecting him. It was eerily similar to Thomas's older brothers dying to save him from Takers, leaving Thomas feeling both guilty and driven to fight dark magic. Samson had felt the same, except he'd let it consume him for a time. Perhaps, had Sara not intervened and fought to save Thomas from himself in a snowy birch grove, Thomas would have faced the same fate.

Sara's arms hung slack at her sides as she considered the witch before her. For centuries, Samson had infiltrated dark magical groups and usurped their rogue Magi. Now, Sara knew why. For the death of his beloved brother, Samson had sought to correct a wrong by resetting the balance in his own vicious way. Yet despite all the killing, all the shrewdly gained black bloodstones around his neck, he couldn't ease his guilt. He thought Sara more worthy to wear Ardeth's stone.

Since refusing such a gift would wound him more, she pursed her lips and nodded.

Samson grinned. He put an arm around her and steered her toward a path at the edge of the cemetery. "Come on, Sara. The others don't have the best news, but I'm sure you'll put a creative spin on things. Plus, we're all giddy to hear what valuable information Lochton gave you."

His confidence in her was borderline delusional. First Ardeth's stone and now this. Lochton's information wasn't exactly the tide-turning weapon they needed—at least not yet—and adding not-the-best news to the mix was akin to giving a drowning person a glass of water. She was in way over her head.

As they walked past her mother's grave, Sara caught a whiff of lilac in the faint breeze. It swirled around her, a brief, encouraging hug.

They all believed in her. She couldn't—*wouldn't*—let them down. For Thomas, for her family, for all of Ware Woods, she would dig deep into her witch fire, seize her destiny, and burn that bitch back to hell.

Sara raised her chin. If it took a monster to beat a monster, she would do it—and even enjoy it. She quickened her pace.

"That's the spirit," said Samson, reading her mind. She really ought to strengthen her mental shields. Samson chuckled. With a swirl of his hand, a plume of smoke engulfed them.

When the smoke lifted, Sara was standing in the main room, a majority of the forest seated around her. Samson ducked away to sit with Amira, Kira, Lethal, and Lily in oversized, upholstered chairs. With their intricately whorled wooden arms, the chairs appeared like thrones for the perfectly postured vampires. Indeed, Amira looked regal, her umber skin as rich as a polished tiger eye gemstone. Her oversized white shirt—possibly one of Samson's—was unbuttoned to her navel, exposing a slice of skin down her center. At another cluster of furniture sat Charlie, Ian, Ted, Gran, and Alice, with Albert resting at her feet. Sara's father and brother regarded her with bleary eyes, fatigue etched on their faces. Adjacent to the kitchen, at the longest dining table, Moira, Dean, and the Blue Ridge pack paused eating, the triplets simultaneously in mid-bite. Luke winked at Sara while Wes nervously adjusted his ball cap. Sara wished the young shifter would crack a joke to break the tension. She missed her cousin Caleb and his humor. From the kitchen, the Cahills ceased their chatter, all eyes on Sara.

She hovered, the better to see everyone and hear their distressing news. Lead filled her stomach. "What happened?"

Dean cleared his throat. "Because of the attack on Florine's site and . . . the *example* made of Amira's colony, the others are scared. Except for Florine, they have rescinded their alliance, preferring to remain neutral and avoid the Shadow Mother's wrath. Even Damon isn't willing to risk dragons igniting his site."

Burning Hells. Sara needed *all* the other Magi. Lochton had said *everyone* needed to help her. She groaned, realizing too late such a reaction was not becoming of a High Witch, much less one who needed to be legendary.

"They're cowards," snarled Alesha, the scar on her cheekbone deepening with her discontent.

"No," countered Sara, slowly shaking her head. Though a big part of her had hoped for the best, a small part had been expecting this—it was what she would have considered if their roles were reversed. "The Magi are acting reasonably on behalf of their sites. We cannot fault them for protecting their own. It's exactly what we're doing."

Charlie stood. "What they say and what they will do may

differ. Of the sites I visited, they were torn. They want to help us, and I think they will when the Equinox comes."

"Agreed," stated Lethal. "However, we cannot count on this."

Charlie returned to his seat, Lethal's statement silently understood. Everyone volleyed their attention back to Sara. Instead of defeat, hope shone in their eyes. They believed in her.

And she would not disappoint them.

Rising higher in the center of the main room, Sara said, "The other sites are acting exactly as we need them to. The Shadow Mother made her point and achieved the unrest she wanted. She has no motive to attack them again. In fact, she's probably hoping we'll fight one another before the Equinox. So we sit tight. Revisiting the sites will only make us appear weak and may make them targets. We must trust in them.

"The others know they're welcome into Ware Woods at any time to seek refuge. Without Dorcas to betray us"—Sara spat out the dark witch's name—"our barrier will hold, and everyone inside Ware Woods will remain safe."

Sara met Gran's steel blue gaze, and before her grandmother could ask, Sara answered her question. "I met the Lochton dragon. He's frozen by the Shadow Mother, as are the other elysian-eyed dragons. Jin, Tobio, and Thomas will eventually follow." At this, gasps and murmurs spun around the main room.

Sara rose a little higher still, quieting everyone. "Although frozen, he could communicate with me. He said my fire will undo the Shadow Mother—that I will weaken her enough to release her hold on all dragons. Then Lochton will come and reset the balance." She intentionally left out the part about everyone else helping her defeat the Shadow Mother. Lochton hadn't said *how* everyone must help her. Hopefully their belief in her was enough.

There was a collective sigh of relief. Sara panned the crowd, encouraged by their response, momentarily believing it would be easy until she spotted the unconvinced frowns of Samson,

Lethal, and Amira. The fearsome trio had firsthand knowledge of the Shadow Mother's insidious powers, and they knew Sara was holding something back.

Alrighty, then. She'd give just enough to appease them. "Of course, I can't face the Shadow Mother alone. I'll need the help of everyone with power outside of the wall. Which is Samson, Amira, Lethal, and Dean. Any additional Magi who show up on the Equinox can join us while everyone else remains within the Ware Woods boundary." Technically, she did say she needed the help of everyone; she just didn't specify that Lochton had implied *all* magicals. Revealing this would only incite panic, as would sharing her thoughts that the Shadow Mother had been cultivating poisonous lies and intentionally manipulating them for centuries.

"Wherever Dean goes, I go," declared Moira, her chair flanking Dean's, their hands clasped together on top of his massive thigh.

"Same," barked Luke, Wes joining him. The triplets dropped their food and punched the air in agreement.

"No!" shouted Sara. *Are they crazy?* Even with magic, they would be stepping into extreme pain—at best. If she didn't shut this down right now, more would recklessly volunteer to go outside the wall. More potential deaths on her hands.

The Main House fell silent. Moira looked as though Sara had slapped her. Fine. She'd rather Moira be furious with her than dead.

Dean scrubbed his head, his aura a troubled burnt ochre with eggplant-colored splotches. The expression on his wide face showed the same tortured pain Sara often saw in Thomas and in her own reflection—the agony of choosing between duty and love.

To spare Dean the decision, and to keep the pack safe, Sara stated, "If the pack operates as one, then Dean remains inside the wall." Dean loosed a low growl; the pack whined. Let them join Moira in being livid with her. Sara was High Witch, and this was her forest. More importantly, this was her battle to lose should things go badly. Because for some wretched twist of fate, the Shadow Mother wanted her most of all.

Lethal cut her an icy stare while Samson stewed beneath a personal churning cloud of smoke.

Wonderful. The other sites may not help, and her own team was angry with her. Fortunately, the Equinox was still over a month away; plenty of time for everyone to cool off—though hopefully not the last three dragons—and for Sara to hone her witch fire. Lochton's testing of her fire had exhausted her and facing the Shadow Mother promised to take everything she had to give. And then some. An extravagant amount of fire play would be the responsible thing for a High Witch to do, and it would unleash some of her frustration.

Before she could do or say anything else to further upset everyone, Sara announced, "I'll be in the marsh if anyone needs me." She ducked under the archway, her back skimming the wooden beam, and flew toward the wettest part of the forest, the part that secretly housed dark magic for centuries and would be the perfect practice spot for witch fire.

CHAPTER 36

Sara hovered near the middle of the marsh, creating spheres of crackling witch fire. For hours, she launched them one by one in all directions, sloppily hitting imagined targets, vaporizing snow and ice until a muddy mess surrounded her.

The sun grazed the horizon when she finally halted her destruction and pressed her heated palms into the mud. With an internal pull on the forest's energy, Sara summoned earth and water magics, restoring the marsh and even adding a light dusting of snow.

"It's about time," called out Gran as she marched across the spotless expanse, Alice and Albert with her. "We thought you'd never tire."

Sara wiped her hands on her jeans, then folded her arms. "You could have interrupted me if you needed something. But if you've come to challenge me on making Dean stay within the safety of the wall, you'll find out just how stubborn I can be."

Gran snorted a laugh. "Pure Lochton fire. No one is challenging you. You made a decision, and the pack will get over it."

I hope so. Sara withdrew Ann's bloodstone from beneath her jacket and thermal shirt. "Here, Alice. Thanks for——"

Alice stopped her, putting a hand over hers. "I want you to keep it," she said, her calm, lilting voice easing Sara's frustrations. "This stone boosted my powers and gave me witch fire. It will serve you well."

Sara studied her great-aunt, whose amber eyes glowed in the setting sun as Albert leaned into her. Though they weren't bonded mates, the giant silver wolf meant everything to Alice and vice versa. "Thank you, Alice. But since your powers are not as strong without this stone, I'll only accept it if Albert remains at your side and doesn't get any ideas about crossing the wall." Sara raised a brow at her great-uncle. He probably thought she had forgotten about him and was planning on leaping over the wall as he nearly did when the Blue Ridge pack had first shown up at Ware Woods.

Albert huffed, his breath blooming in the cool air. With a disgruntled wrinkle of his snout, he sat at Alice's side, head slightly dipped toward Sara.

"I know you want to loop off to see Thomas," said Gran, waving her hand in the air as though Jin's garden were in the sky above, "but first you'll have supper with us at the brown house. Charlie, Ted, and Ian have made your favorite pasta. Kingsley is there too. And you're going to tell us all about the Lochton dragon."

This time, it was Sara's turn to huff. Feisty grandmother. "You had me at pasta."

Sara dutifully followed them to the brown house, and over the best meal she'd had in a long while, Sara recounted Lochton's every detail and word. Well, not every word. She still omitted the part of Lochton saying she would need *everyone's* help.

"I knew it," said Kingsley, his age-lined face splotchy red, his eyes shimmering with tears. He pointed his dessert fork at Gran and Alice, white frosting clinging between the tines. "I told you girls Annie had whispered '*dark witch*' to me. I knew Lochton wouldn't hurt her. I just never understood why he didn't come to Ware Woods." Kingsley speared another bite of cake from his plate and stuffed it in his mouth. For someone who seemed to exist on sweets, he was quite slim. Then again, he was also active for a centuries-old witch, continually maintaining the Atwell island's shoreline and the cemetery beneath the oak tree. Sara had encountered him many times among the headstones, picking up brush and plucking weeds by hand despite her offer to magically do the chores.

From across the blue diner-style table crowded with food and plates for the seven of them, Charlie inclined back in his chair and scrutinized Sara. "So," he inquired, "witch fire is the key?"

"Yep," replied Sara, busying herself with arranging her fork and spoon on her empty plate. It was the truth as far as she knew, and yet she couldn't meet his gaze. She reinforced her mental shield.

"And Ryujin, Tobio, and Thomas are fine?" her father pressed.

"Well," said Sara. She wouldn't lie, yet there was no sense in worrying them about Jin's current barely conscious state. "They're frustrated at having to remain in the garden, but they're not frozen." Another truth, albeit a slick shade of gray.

From his seat against the wall, the sheer curtains drawn on the window behind him, Ian narrowed his eyes at her. "We weakened the Shadow Mother when the Hills kids and I pushed her out of Ware Woods with our shield. Why didn't that loosen her hold on the dragons?"

A good question to which Sara had no answer. She couldn't say: *Because everyone wasn't here.* With too many sharp-witted and psychic witches staring at her, Sara triple-checked her mental shield, imagining it as impenetrable as the forest's wall. On the inside, hidden from their attentiveness, fear squeezed Sara's spine. Fear that Lochton was mistaken, that no matter what she did or how many magicals helped her, dragons would remain infected or frozen and peace would never be possible. She conjured a confident smile to her lips before answering Ian. "Because Lochton said we must use fire—my witch fire."

Ian frowned, as did Charlie and Ted, who had been unnaturally quiet for the entire meal. Kingsley helped himself to another piece of applesauce cake as the grandfather clock in the living room chimed eight.

Sara held her smile. Much to her relief, Gran cut the tension by shoving back her chair and standing.

"We've kept you long enough," said Gran as she began clearing the table, Alice popping up to help her. "If anything of interest happens around here, one of us will come get you. Now skedaddle." Gran jerked her chin in dismissal before stepping toward the sink, a stack of dishes clinking in her hands.

Eager to escape before she had to tell any more half truths, Sara clasped the smoke stone pendant and gave a hasty thanks for the meal. In an attempt to shake off their concern, she smirked at Ian and mentally projected, *"You should invite Kira to our next family dinner."*

Sara caught his grinned response and Charlie's blown kiss goodbye before smoke swallowed her whole.

A marked chill in the usually temperate garden pinched Sara's cheeks, to which she heeded little mind, her chest tight at the scene before her. Jin's red dragon lay as she'd last seen him, glass-clear ice now glazing his tail, hoary frost creeping up his fiery scaled body. Huddled against his neck, behind a fan of spikes, sat Tobio, a quilted blanket over his legs, a steaming mug of blackest caffeine in his hands.

Beside Tobio stood Matthew. He sneezed before turning to Sara, giving her a panic-stricken look over the pile of blankets clutched in his arms. She knew her matching terror shone back at him.

Without warning, Thomas crashed into her. His arms wrapped around her waist. His cool lips pressed against her brow. Together they fell through a silky ring of dragon smoke, looping from the garden and gently landing on the enormous bed in his private chambers. Her jacket and boots had been whished off. She wasn't sure which of them had done it, and she didn't care. She held him tight against her, letting her body heat and love soak into him while summoning the covers up around them, cocooning their embrace. With magic warming her palms, she rubbed his back, fingertips grazing the nubs of his retracted spikes. "I've got you. Rest while I keep you warm," she whispered. *While I keep you safe.*

She remained awake the entire night, counting his breaths, counting his heartbeats. Counting the days until the Equinox.

For three days she kept the same routine—practicing witch fire during the day, watching over Thomas during the night—each vigil wearing on Sara until she collapsed mid-practice in the marsh. Just a little nap, she'd told herself before waking to a wet nose bopping her in the face.

"I'm up!" Sara scrambled to her feet. The white flames that had been flickering around her, keeping her warm, vanished.

The russet wolf before her leapt back and phased into Moira, one hand on her popped hip. "Bloody hell, Sara! Why are you *sleeping* out here?"

"I wasn't sleeping. I just . . . dozed off." She glanced from the blueberry-hued evening overhead to the wolf pack surrounding her. With a snort, Dean sat on his haunches, the rest of the pack doing the same. Given they were checking on her, and not ripping into her for *strongly suggesting* they remain inside the wall when the Equinox came, was a good sign.

Moira's fierce expression dropped, her aggressive posture morphing into distress as she clutched her hands. "How's Matty? And the others? We'd visit, but Matty warned me about uncontrolled dragon fire."

The pack whined, their concern carrying across the frigid marsh.

Ah, so this was why they were checking up on her. "Matt never leaves Tobio's side. They've been reading, enjoying warm beverages, and remaining safe in the garden." All very true. "I'll tell them you said hello, and if I can sneak up on Tobio, I'll put him in a headlock for you." She'd do no such thing; it was impossible to sneak up on an elysian-eyed dragon. She'd tried and failed many times at surprising Thomas. Besides the one snowball to his face, he seemed to see her moves before she even thought of them.

Luke howled at the swelling moon. Sara wasn't sure how to take his reaction until she saw Moira's half smile. Another good sign, and also an opportunity to politely leave. Though Thomas hadn't mentally projected to her, their bond was stretched thin with longing. "I'm going to visit them now. Is there anything else you want me to tell them?"

"Tell them we miss them," said Moira. She flung herself at Sara, embracing her in a crushing hug. "I miss you too," she added, her voice lower.

What are you talking about? "I'm right here," Sara gasped, patting Moira on the back. "Maybe not for long. You're squeezing the air from my lungs."

Moira pulled away, loosening her hold and setting her honey gaze on Sara. "Har har," scoffed Moira. "You've changed since Winter Solstice. You're even *more* serious than you were before. And you keep trying to do everything on your own. You're not alone, idiot."

Sara blinked. Moira only used the term *idiot* for those she truly cared about. While it was heartwarming to be reminded how much Moira cared for her, and though she knew she wasn't alone, Sara was High Witch, and there were many things she *had* to do on her own—like seeking dark grimoires for sketchy forbidden spells, practicing witch fire until the marrow of her bones melted, and enduring the near-paralyzing anxiety that she might not be able to stop the Shadow Mother. Everything seemed to fall on her shoulders, and Sara was secretly pissed at the Mother below for bestowing this undeserved fate on her. But a High Witch of Legend didn't burden others with her grievances or duties.

"You're right," said Sara. "I'm not alone." Her simple answer seemed to appease Moira, who gave a gentle nod. Sara stepped back and grasped her jagged pendant. As smoke coiled around her, she looked from Moira to each wolf. "I'll give the boys your best."

The pack's yipping response followed Sara into her weightless looping, their uplifting cacophony a stark contrast to the pin-drop quiet of the garden.

CHAPTER 37

SARA DROPPED TO her knees at the sight of Tobio's dragon lying beside an ice-encased Jin. Matthew leaned over Tobio's snout with open arms as if still warming him with his body. On a nearby boulder slouched Thomas, a quilt with an interlocking pattern of crashing waves draped over his back.

Sara rushed to Thomas, embracing him while wrapping them both in white flames of heat. "Why didn't you call for me?"

Thomas leaned into her, the cold of his cheek biting her face.

"He's conscious," said Matthew, his focus remaining on Tobio, his voice high-pitched, his statement weeping with denial. Tobio's eyes were shut, his sides barely moving with the long, languid inhalations of deep sleep. "He's still mentally communicating with me," Matthew choked out before lowering his voice, murmuring intimate words to Tobio.

Sara dragged her gaze from them and took in the garden. Frost nibbled the tips of every tree, shrub, and blade of grass. A translucent pane of ice shone atop the winding stream, broken only by the sluggish waterfall whose viscid descent appeared like white wax running down a purity spell candle. But it was the cherry tree that struck terror in Sara's soul. Over half of the tree's perpetual blossoms lay in pink snowy drifts beneath balding branches.

Her grip on Thomas intensified as more blooms parted, drifting to the ground with all the silent finality of sand through an hourglass.

"Thomas?" She pulled back and held the sides of his face. His eyes were half-lidded, their brilliant blue now the color of pale ice. His skin remained chilled, unyielding to her warmth. Though portions of the blanket were scorched, he remained untouched by her magic. Her pulse pounded, her bloodstones glowing.

"Cold," he whispered, his word a hazy puff.

"Don't worry. I'll warm you up." She wove white flames into what was left of the quilt, whished it over Matthew's back—beseeching the Father above to keep him and Tobio warm—then grabbed her pendant and smoked herself and Thomas to his bathing room. If flames wouldn't warm him, maybe water would. Dragons loved water.

Thomas stumbled to the steaming bath. Half collapsing onto the circular benched edge, he dropped an arm into the water and sighed. The bath, or perhaps his skin, sizzled.

"In you go," Sara ordered, whishing off his clothes.

"So aggressive," his voice rumbled in her mind. The diamond-shaped tattoos along his spine quivered, spikes rising into fleshy bumps, threatening to punch through.

Stars above, if he shifted into a dragon he wouldn't fit into the bath, not to mention possibly crushing her in the process. *Think.*

She did the first thing that came to mind. She reared back her hand and slapped him on the arse. His spikes retracted with a series of pops.

"Hey! What was that for? I'm not exactly—"

"Get in," she grunted, awkwardly hauling his legs onto the edge. His skin was much too cold. His heartbeat too slow. Showering first be damned. He was so lethargic he hadn't seen her wind up to slap him, hadn't caught her hand. He *always* caught her hand.

Instead of commenting on her order, the same one he'd given her less than a week ago, he slid into the bath without so much as a splash. Thomas hissed along with the water. Dragon scales flickered across his skin before disappearing as he relaxed on the inner bench, eyes closed, back against the stone wall.

From the adjacent center bath, Sara whished a soft-bristled brush and a red fish-shaped soap smelling of pomegranate. She dipped them into the steaming water—and promptly withdrew her hands, pain spearing up her arms, her skin now as red as the soap.

The water was scalding.

Her jaw dropped at Thomas in blissful repose. A gentle touch to his shoulder confirmed his body temperature had warmed to near normal. Through the bond, their heartbeats matched in a steady rhythm.

Alrighty. Bracing herself, Sara plunged her hands into the bath and set about tending to Thomas, brushing every ticklish nook and cranny. By the time she'd washed and rinsed his hair, her arms were blistering. She healed herself as Thomas sank farther under the water, his eyes still closed.

"Thank you," he projected, slurring his words. *"I'm just gonnarest abit . . ."* His head fell back, nearly smacking onto the stone bench before Sara managed to whish a folded towel beneath him.

In the moonlit glow of the hanging crystals, Sara watched Thomas all night. His skin never reddened or wrinkled; his position never changed. Whenever sleep threatened to claim her, Sara thrust her arms into the boiling water.

She had just healed herself from a particularly nasty burn when Matthew trudged into the room from the bedroom archway. Sara supposed he'd entered Thomas's chambers from the hallway near a far corner of the bedroom.

His presence and bruised aura told her everything, yet still she asked, "Tobio's frozen, isn't he?"

Matthew nodded, his liquid amber eyes haunted as he slumped onto the bath's bench beside Sara.

"I'll bring him back," promised Sara. "I'll bring them all back."

"I know you will," said Matthew, his swift response fueling her inner fire, inflaming it from smoldering frustration to blazing determination.

A smile ghosted Thomas's lips. *"Yes, you will. I believe in you too. Just be sure to leave the heavy fighting to me."*

"You'll have to beat Jin, Tobio, and Lochton to the party if you want a prime piece of the action." It was a challenge. A challenge she needed Thomas to latch on to, to stay awake for, and to win.

"I will. I'm fassst." He hissed his last word and drifted back to sleep—a normal sleep with a stable pulse. His cheeks were warm beneath her palms as she leaned over and kissed his mouth, a zing of electricity shooting through her.

Matthew glanced up at the brightening crystal lights and bumped his shoulder into hers. "It's late morning, Sara. I'll stay with him while you check in with the forest."

The last thing she wanted to do was leave, yet she didn't want everyone worrying about her or the dragons. As High Witch, she needed to maintain the calm and bolster everyone's hope with regular displays of witch fire. The Equinox could not come soon enough.

"Thanks." Sara took Matthew's hand in hers and gave it a squeeze. "Moira and the pack say hello. They all miss you and Tobio."

He raised his gaze to hers, his freckled face weary. "Don't tell them."

She wouldn't lie outright, and she knew Matthew knew this. He only wanted her to bend the truth, a mercy to prevent futile worry. Little did he know she'd been dancing this fine line for far too long.

She gave his hand another reassuring squeeze. "I'll be back soon," she promised, then grabbed her pendant and smoked to Ware Woods.

Sara spent most of the day pretending to inspect the stone wall when, really, she was leaning against it for support while pushing love and warmth through the bond at Thomas. Around noon, when Dean and Uncle Larry tried to approach, Sara waved at them from afar and kept moving. She stopped only to grab a bite to eat and a quick nap at the treehouse before returning to the empty marsh.

With a mountain of worries threatening to crush her, Sara closed her eyes and spread her consciousness deep into the ground. She pushed past the frozen layer, past the fine roots, past the rock and rich soil, and into the vibrant energy of the forest. For a fleeting moment, calm washed over her. Mother knew she tried, but Sara couldn't hold on to it. Her emotional storm of frustration, grief, and anger overwhelmed any semblance of calm. The current plight of Thomas, all dragons, her forest family, and all magicals—herself included—wasn't fair. The injustice raged inside her. It built and built, becoming a burning red-hot, monstrous rage that needed *out*.

With a roar, Sara freed her anger and her magic. Witch fire surged from her in concentric rings of death, decimating frozen marsh grass, leaving behind a starless black glaze. She reveled in the heady release, the destruction, the *power* to crush the Shadow Mother. She may have wept. She may have laughed. She wished the Equinox would come so she could end all of this.

Though her fire was a touch volatile, Sara kept it contained to the marsh and away from Makwa and Dorcas's foul hut. As tempting as it was to burn down the building, the dark grimoire had been helpful and surely held more valuable information.

Sara regarded the partially sunken building. Perhaps it knew where she could *find* the Shadow Mother. A wicked grin spread across her face.

Sara flew to the hut, flicking witch fire on the brimstone bri-ars. Their resulting high-pitched squeals were both terrifying and thrilling. She summoned more fire to her fingers—and stopped short at the sound of her name.

A deep voice bellowed again across the marsh, this time saying her first *and* last name. "Sara Lochton!"

She shrank upon herself. Her fire guttered out as Kane flew to her, Connor at his side wearing a navy blue knitted hat. It was the first time she'd seen Connor fly. Her wonder at Thomas's younger brother was instantly squashed by Kane's murderous expression. How long had they been watching her? Her gaze darted to the blackened field, to the smoldering edges from where they'd come. *I could have incinerated them.*

"What do you think you're doing?" he demanded. Connor, completely unfazed by his father's ire, quirked a brow at her.

She lifted her chin. She had to; Kane was levitating higher than her. "I'm practicing."

"No, you're not. You were having a *damn tantrum*, and now you're torturing the vines."

Sara stuffed her hands into her pockets. He was right. Granted, being devilish flora, the vines probably enjoyed it. She would have rolled her eyes at him, but it wasn't a very High Witch thing to do, especially with Connor watching. Kane probably brought his younger son just to keep her in line. Now she had to fight back an eye roll *and* a scowl.

"Samson, Lethal, and Charlie asked me to watch over you," he said.

Ah, that would explain why they'd graciously left her alone these past few days.

Kane continued, his voice softer. "I get it. You have a lot on your shoulders, but *behaving* like a monster to protect your loved ones is not the best method. I should know. It nearly cost me Thomas once, and I won't let you make the same mistake."

Ho ho! Her little teasing torture was *nothing* compared to how he'd treated Thomas. Maybe he was worried she was sliding down a slippery slope.

Sara sighed. Fine. She wouldn't toy with the vines or delight in destruction. However, she *would* continue pushing her fire and resolve to be as fierce as possible. That was definitely a High Witch of Legend thing to do.

Sara crouched to the ground, placed her palms on the scorched crust, and summoned nurturing earth magic until the marsh was fully restored to a picturesque frozen field. A cardinal's song floated along the forest's edge. From the hut, the brimstone briars held still, seemingly watching her every move.

Kane and Connor hovered in front of Sara, their late afternoon shadows stretching across the snowy ground. "Would you care to come for dinner?" offered Kane, a humble look replacing his typical stern appearance. "Abby still cooks as if we have a full house."

Sara's heart ached at his unspoken words. As if Thomas and Violet were still there, as if their deceased sons were still there. Her heart ached even more for having to turn him down. "Thank you, but I need to get going."

Connor brightened with a smile. She could have kissed his cheek for being a ray of joy. "Are you gonna see Thomas? What's he doing? Cool, dragony stuff?"

Hmph. She gave him a conspiratorial grin. "He was taking a bath the last time I saw him."

Connor scrunched his face.

She laughed and added, "He's looking forward to sparring with you after the Equinox." And before Kane could ask questions, Sara thanked him for his invitation—and his intervention. She touched her pendant and smoked to Thomas's bathing room.

CHAPTER 38

ER PULSE QUICKENED at the empty, steaming bath. *Please don't be frozen in the garden.*

"We're in here," called Matthew from the bedroom.

Thank the Father. Waving off the remnants of her smoke travel, Sara followed a trail of puddles and towels into the dim bedroom. Matthew sat cross-legged on top of the silken covers, a glazed cup in his hands, a tray with a pot of tea between him and a tucked-in, slumbering Thomas.

Sara felt Thomas's forehead. He was cold again.

She exchanged a grim look with Matthew. Most of his copper hair had escaped his short ponytail. Fatigue rimmed his animal-glowing eyes. His nose twitched, followed by a sneeze. When he apologized and set his cup on the tray, Sara whished the tea service—save for one of its many chocolate-dipped pastries—to the low table on the opposite side of the room. "Get some rest while I keep watch," she said before devouring the sweet.

Matthew mumbled thanks and phased into a giant, lanky wolf—on top of the bed.

Thomas didn't move an inch despite the bed's initial jolt and subsequent shaking as Matthew circled and plopped down, pressed tight along Thomas's side. Shifters. Though she knew they craved physical contact, she figured Matthew was also warming Thomas with his body heat.

She shucked off her jacket and boots and slid under the covers, draping herself on Thomas's other side. He was as cold as the stone floor, clad only in shorts.

"Thomas?"

Nothing.

"Baby?" She yanked on their bond.

The bond quivered in response, his tug weak. From what seemed like the far side of the moon, his voice echoed, *"Sara?"*

"I'm here with you. Please don't leave me."

"I'll never leave you."

Her eyes welled with tears. A few spilled onto his chest as she wrapped her arms and legs around him.

A shushing as he soothed her. *"I know you'll free me."*

"Of course I will."

A distant chuckle. *"I'll be there for you. I promise."*

"I'm counting on it."

The bond fell slack. Beneath the covers, her white flames wrapped around them—her magic seeking his. Seeking and seeking for hours until sleep claimed her.

Sara woke to a cool breeze, a jostling of the bed, and a whine.

She bolted upright, the overhead crystals peach with daybreak. Crouched on the edge of the bed was Matthew's wolf, whining in distress. Thomas had thrown back the covers and was halfway across the bedroom, striding for the hallway.

"Thomas, wait!" she shouted, jumping from the bed and whishing on her boots and jacket.

Thomas, his movements stiff, paid her no mind as he disappeared down the hallway.

Matthew phased and grabbed Sara's arm. "I know where he's going." He tugged her down the hall, through what appeared to be a wall of solid stone—she may have yelped—past the cave and waterfall, now pulled back in a curtain of ice, and into the garden.

Thomas headed toward Jin and Tobio, his bare feet leaving

prints in a sugary dusting of snow. As he neared the two dragons encased in clear ice, the garden shivered, widening with a series of high-pitched cracks that sounded of splintering glass. Spikes punched through Thomas's tattoos, scales replaced skin, claws and horns emerged as his form grew and grew into his blue dragon. The momentum of his transformation slid him onto his stomach until he was lying beside Tobio with his chin on the ground, tail slightly curled, eyes closed.

No, no, no! Sara flung herself at his cheek, patting his scaled armor, willing his eyes to open. "Thomas!" This wasn't supposed to happen. He was supposed to hang on until the Equinox. Because what if—what if weakening the Shadow Mother didn't release her hold on dragons?

"Thomas!"

He snorted a puff of white. *"Don't worry. I'll be there."* She held on to his faint words, repeated them like a mantra as their bond fell slack again, the many invisible threads connecting them cold and dark save for one golden string.

When the sun hung low with evening and disappeared behind hazy clouds, Sara released her hold on Thomas and stepped back. Frost coated most of Thomas's tail and crept up the sides of his belly. Matthew, in wolf form, lay curled against Tobio's iced snout. Beside them, Jin lay still as a sculpture.

Snowflakes began to fall. They hung in the air, lazily floating, honeybees drunk on pollen. A thick, milky layer of ice covered the garden's winding water feature. On its bank, drifts of pale pink blossoms surrounded the cherry tree. Only one living blossom remained, clinging to the end of a naked branch that reached toward the sky as if in supplication to the Father.

Sara swung her gaze back to Thomas, Tobio, and Jin—the blue, black, and red dragons aligned like a frozen fairytale. She could do nothing now except weaken the Shadow Mother enough to lift her control over them.

"Matt, we need to leave," she said, her words thick. "We need to go back to the forest. Tonight's a full moon Council meeting, and we have to tell everyone what's happened."

Matthew raised his head and shook it, dislodging snow from his fur.

Of course he didn't want to leave. Sara didn't want to either. Yet she had to tell the others, and she wouldn't leave Matthew behind with only grief for company.

She gnawed the inside of her cheek, considering. Shifters needed their pack, and same as everyone else, they also needed a purpose.

"Please," she said, "I need your help. I haven't asked this of anyone because I didn't want to create panic, *but* should something go wrong during the Equinox and the barrier breaks, I want you to gather the children and loop them here. You know the garden, and they'll need you." She extended her hand.

Matthew's ears flicked, his gaze holding hers for a long moment before he slowly rose to all fours. With a whine, he gave a parting nudge to Tobio, brushed along Thomas's snout, then phased and clasped hands with Sara. "Okay," he said, "but let's loop through the tree. The smoke from that pendant is like pepper in my nose."

Fair enough. She squeezed his hand in response.

They leaned into one another, kicking through spent blossoms as they approached the cherry tree.

"Together," said Sara. With a final glance at the dragons, she stepped with Matthew into the static hum of the trunk.

Petal-soft darkness enfolded Sara, the thumping of the cherry tree's heartwood so slow it seemed time would stop. Instead of a pleasant warm gust blowing back her hair, a frigid whisper kissed her cheeks. It was wrong. Too slow, too cold—just like the frozen dragons.

Something brushed against her leg. Not the graze of fine tree roots Sara had grown accustomed to. Something with fingers. It latched on to her calf and jerked. Her hold on Matthew slipped.

Matthew shouted her name, his hand squeezing the tips of her four fingers, pulling her toward him.

The something jerked again, and she was wrenched away from Matthew.

"Sara!" His shriek faded, quickly swallowed by the Aether.

The thing holding Sara choked out a wet laugh.

All Hells. Sara kicked and squirmed, swung and punched. She connected with nothing, succeeding only in flailing about like a manic fish on a hook. Attempts to summon magic were fruitless; she couldn't even conjure a flame to illuminate her captor. She swore. Loudly.

"Even as High Witch, you still have a filthy mouth."

Sara stiffened at the thing's voice. Though it was raspier than the last time she'd heard it, it was unmistakably Brad. "Come closer, and I'll show you just how filthy, you bastard!" She swiped at the empty darkness before her and again tried to summon a spark of magic.

Another laugh, deep and disgustingly phlegmy. It sounded the same as Samson's had been before Sara unwittingly healed him.

"Magic doesn't work in the Aether," croaked Brad.

No shit. But nothing malevolent was supposed to happen in the Aether either. Which was probably why she couldn't grab Brad and squeeze the life out of him. Had he been hanging out in the Aether for a chance to annoy her? Because apparently *that* was allowed, or . . .

"Are you taking me to the Shadow Mother?" She hoped so. She'd go willingly provided it wasn't to Brad's lair or any other such place that blocked magic. Without her witch fire, Sara would be a snack for the dark entity.

He coughed hard enough to shake her. "No. I'm here to talk some sense into you. I felt the cold shift in the balance—the elysian-eyed dragons are all frozen. Your boyfriend is *gone*. You *need* me now. Don't you see? You were always meant to be mine."

She lunged, intent on prying his hand off her ankle, yet still grasped at nothing. *Seriously!* He was such a thorn in her side.

"What I *need* is for you to let. Me. Go. You're sick. In more ways than one. And Thomas is *not* gone. I'm going to pound the shit out of your Shadow Mother and bring him back."

Brad snarled, sounding more hell hound-ish than anything remotely human. "You can't beat her by yourself. You need me. Admit it."

She went limp, letting him think he convinced her while secretly manipulating her body weight as Kane had once instructed her to do in worst-case scenarios. When Brad coughed again, his hold on her spasming, she kicked out with her other leg. The sudden movement tore her free from his grasp. But instead of howling, Brad whispered in her ear: "She's coming for you." Then he pushed her, square in the chest, sending her plummeting through darkness.

CHAPTER 39

Sara flung out her arms and legs, desperate to slow her descent, when a net of roots snagged her and bounced her up and out of the oak tree's trunk. She fell more than landed before a wide-eyed Matthew.

"What happened to you?" he whisper-shouted as if afraid someone might hear him.

Sara smacked a hand to her chest, over her pounding heart. "I was . . . propositioned. And either threatened or warned. I'm not sure."

"By *who*?"

"Brad."

A harsh inhale as Matthew scanned her unscathed appearance.

The oak clacked its branches, drawing Sara's attention to the twilight sky and full moon. A shadow, appearing like a bite mark, stained the edge of the moon's pale surface. Her breath quickened. The lunar eclipse had begun.

"We have a lot to discuss at Council tonight. Come on." She grabbed the front of his fleecy sweatshirt and tugged him with her into the oak. In a cold whoosh, they popped out of the maple tree, the Council stump stage to their left, the entire forest in the clearing before them.

Lemon-yellow orbs bobbed above the clearing, providing light and heat as well as a festive atmosphere to the gathering. Platters of all kinds of foods were heaped upon the buffet tables. Among the desserts, waiting to be cut, was a giant sheet cake with "Welcome, Amira" in drippy red icing. Children chased one another between dozens of tables filled with magicals eating, drinking, and laughing.

Sara searched the crowd. At the Lochton table sat Ted, Charlie, and Ian, along with Kira, Samson, and Amira. Her scalp prickled as she zeroed in on the table's vacant seats and the empty stage. Where were Gran and Alice and Albert?

From across the clearing, at a cluster of tables occupied by the Walkers and the Blue Ridge pack, Moira's face lit up. "Matty!" she shouted. When Matthew didn't return the cheerful greeting, her smile fell.

All conversation ceased as everyone followed Moira's gaze to Sara and Matthew.

Sara froze, her magic itching beneath every inch of her skin. All around them, the forest's rainbow of vibrant energy wavered as though shaken by an unseen force.

Something was wrong. Horribly wrong. She felt it in her bones, felt it in the very air around her like the static charge before a lightning strike. Did they not sense this shift in the forest? Was this a High Witch thing?

Dean immediately rose from his table, his bright aura switching to a worried shade of blue-gray at the sight of Matthew without Tobio.

Lethal stood from their seat beside Lily at the Atwell table. The vampire's expression sharper than usual, their eyes chips of glass.

Next rose Samson and Charlie, their previously jovial demeanors replaced with knitted brows and stiff spines. *"Firecracker?"* Their magic washed over her, reading her emotions. They strode for her, as did Dean and Lethal, knocking back chairs in their haste.

They needed answers, they all did, but first she had another pressing matter.

"Gran?"

"Sara!"

Her bloodstones pulsed. Now Kane and Abby and Connor were joining the others in rushing toward her. *"Where are you? What's wrong?"*

"We're at the blue house. The Book—"

Sara didn't wait for an explanation. She grabbed her pendant and was swept away by smoke.

In a thunderous heartbeat, Sara stood with Gran and Alice before the kitchen's farmhouse table. At Alice's side growled Albert, his amber eyes fixed on the Book rattling on the table, his silver fur on end, his lips pulled back in a deadly grimace.

A plume of smoke and Samson joined them. "What are you—" He stopped himself mid-sentence, gaze darting around the room. "Whoa. Is *this* your grimoire? Father of Night, it has more energy than—"

"Shut it!" snapped Gran, her focus never leaving the grimoire in question.

The Book jumped, clearly startled. When it landed back on the table, it slammed open to a page of swirling shadows.

They all edged closer as an image of a full moon bled through the shadows and filled the center of the page. Within the moon, scripted words appeared one by one in brick-red ink:

Blood Moon

She is coming.

She is coming.

She is coming.

Sara grabbed hold of Samson and Gran, a sudden lightheadedness making her wobble. The Shadow Mother had deceived them again. She *wasn't* coming on the Equinox, when day and night were equal.

"She's coming NOW, on the lunar eclipse," said Sara, her voice as grim as the death headed their way.

She inwardly screamed. Of course the Shadow Mother was coming now. An average full moon was rife with turbulent energy, but a blood moon—a total lunar eclipse when the moon was blanketed by the Earth's *shadow*—was when magic could turn wildly unpredictable. Apocalyptic.

Brad had warned her.

Even the dark grimoire had warned her, in its own twisted way.

Sara turned to Samson, readying to smoke him with her to the stone wall, when a low-toned discordant blare rocked the house. The single note, promising certain doom, reverberated in Sara's bones. She froze, her wide stance rooted to the wood-paneled floor despite the bleating instinct to flee. Albert pawed at his ears and howled. Gran and Alice clung to each other. The Book clapped shut and disappeared.

When the alarm stopped just as abruptly as it began, Samson straightened his jacket—a seasoned general preparing for war—and gave a half smile. "She's so dramatic."

His crack at levity broke Sara's stupor. "You used to do the same thing!" she hollered at him, recalling the blares she used to run toward. An image of his black smoke pressed against the forest's invisible barrier filled her mind. Though Samson hadn't been able to breach the wall, the Shadow Mother was more powerful than him. And she'd been growing stronger, biding her time for this moment.

Sara felt cold and heavy, as if she were already six feet under.

A sonic *BOOM* slammed the house with all the force of a hundred dragons ramming the forest's barrier. Barstools clattered to the floor, overhead pots and herbs crashed to the counter, and from the cellar below came the shattering of glass.

Albert scrambled to find purchase, his nails raking the floorboards. Sara and Samson hovered. Gran and Alice grabbed hold of the wooden counter. Everyone stared wide-eyed at each other until the quaking subsided.

"Now she's merely being a bully," said Samson, tucking back a disheveled lock of hair. The hard glint in his onyx eyes betrayed his mocking tone. Dark smoke poured from the cuffs of his jacket, and in a single clap, he looped them all back to the crowded clearing.

Atop the stump stage stood Kane and Charlie, arms pointing in all directions as they gave rapid-fire instructions to band together, similar to how they'd survived the Shadow Mother's previous attack. Overhead, the glowing orbs swung violently while the nearby bare-branched maple and surrounding forest swayed. The buffet tables had collapsed, food lay in heaps, smashed cake littered the ground.

Sara's initial shock melted into anger. The bitch had ruined their party. And Sara knew just how to make her pay—witch fire.

Her palms tingled, her magic aching for release. She didn't need the other Magi and magicals. None of them had witch fire capabilities anyway—even Alice couldn't summon the flames without Ann's bloodstone. Besides, this was Sara's fight. The Mother had chosen her for whatever fateful reason to weaken the Shadow Mother. And though Sara didn't understand why and found it unfair on the best of days, right now, in this moment, she embraced it. Now was her chance to end this—to save Thomas and all dragons, reset the magical balance, heal Ian's heart, and have some damn-bloody peace.

She levitated, rising above the chaos, white flames dancing around her. Kane and Charlie stopped directing as everyone turned their attention to Sara, who was now glowing with energy. From the crowd, Kingsley quietly slipped away into the maple. Matthew stood out among the many earnest faces staring up at her. He gave her a tight-lipped nod, and Sara called for all the children to follow him to the oak.

In a silent hurry, Matthew, Lily's siblings, and the Cahill kids filed into the maple and looped away. Sara feigned a calm demeanor as Connor and the Hills children approached the soul tree next.

She gave them an encouraging smile before sharing hard glances with Samson, Amira, and Lethal. Though she'd prefer for them to remain within Ware Woods, she knew they would meet her outside the barrier as soon as the last kid looped away. Indeed, Samson's smoky tendrils curled around him and Amira while Lethal tensed, ready to run and leap over the wall.

The clearing darkened, everyone bathed in a deep blood-red gloom as the Earth's shadow veiled half the moon.

As Connor and the last Hills child neared the maple, another *BOOM* struck the forest. Connor grabbed the younger child and ran into the trunk. The entire tree shook with such force a lower limb split off and crashed to the ground.

From all around came an ear-piercing screech, like talons and dagger-sized teeth punching into metal.

And then a mighty *CRACK* sundered the night.

It sounded of thunderbolts and earthquakes. It felt of heartache and grief. It speared Sara's soul with a pain that brought her to her knees.

The forest floor heaved, the only warning before the barrier detonated in an explosion of stones and the sky lit up with dragon fire.

CHAPTER 40

S ARA GASPED, DESPERATE to get air into her lungs, desperate to *move*, as the forest's shock and pain seized her. The roar of dragons and her forest family became a distant din. Her white flames snuffed out. The scene before her melted at the edges.

No! She dug her hands into snow and soil, grounding herself, forcing herself to remain conscious through the forest's pain as she swayed on her knees beside an overturned table, staring at the chaos.

Dozens of flat-eyed dragons swam through the hazy orange sky, spitting jets of fire. On the ground, plumes of thick smoke erupted around the clearing; from them burst a wave of Takers. Their gaunt faces, smeared with poisonous stains, were little more than skulls. Their blackened hands were laden with dark magic and deadly edged weapons. Their hollers Hells-born.

They surged for Samson, their numbers burying him while shoving back Amira and Kira. The vampires screamed, hacking and killing with raw fury. But instead of spilling blood, the wounded Takers simply vanished into wisps of shadow. More poured from the plumes of smoke, pushing Amira and Kira farther away from the mountain of Takers overwhelming Samson.

Another blare. Sara's attention shot to the sky. From the garish haze emerged a lean, glittering fluid shadow, its smooth side-to-side motion resembling a snake on the hunt. More and more of the shadow flowed forth, coiling upon itself until it was a heaving, writhing creature. Its jagged tentacles curled and uncurled in a beckoning manner, taunting.

Rage flushed through Sara, energy crackling around her, a fuse about to blow. *I'm going to set the world on fire and end you, bitch!* With a snarl, she *pulled* at the forest's energy.

The ground quaked, and Sara's bloodstones pulsed. Magic flooded her so quickly, it was as if the lake's dam had broken, releasing a torrent of power. She launched into the sky, a comet trailing witch fire, aiming directly for the undulating black mass of the Shadow Mother.

She rocketed past Kane and Abby—the pair hovering back-to-back as they frantically threw energy at flat-eyed dragons—past a frenzy of poison-tipped tails, and slammed into the Shadow Mother. It was like hitting a solid wall of black sand.

Sara bounced back. The roots of her teeth throbbed in her skull as the Shadow Mother's grainy presence blasted in all directions. But instead of fracturing, the Shadow Mother expanded in the explosive manner of ink blown on paper, the tips of her tentacles spearing toward the forest floor—toward the heart of Sara's forest family.

"Yes!" shrieked the Shadow Mother, her voice the grinding of claws on stone.

Sara bellowed in response. She threw back her arms and summoned witch fire. For Ann and Lochton and *every* magical, Sara became a living torch, her skin burning, her soul aflame, her bones kindling to the consuming blaze. And then she *pushed*.

In a furious whoosh, the flames leapt, racing along every inch of the Shadow Mother. She shrieked again as they gobbled up her darkness until nothing was left, not even a speck of sand.

Sara's unchecked rage continued fueling her fire. Flames filled her throat and lungs, choking her, burning her, controlling her.

"Stop," Thomas's voice echoed in her mind. *"Stop the fire, Sara."*

"Thomas?" She pulled on their bond. She had to have weakened

the Shadow Mother, was on the verge of burning out herself, so where *was* Thomas? He promised he'd come. Lochton had said Thomas would help her. *"I need you!"* The bond remained slack, their only connection the single golden strand stretched tight as a bowstring and covered in frost.

He hadn't spoken to her; she'd simply remembered the words he once said to help her. She seized the strand, grateful for the flash of cold and the reassurance that, although frozen, Thomas was still alive and waiting for her. She placed a hand to her chest, willing her heart rate to slow, willing the fire back into her core until she was covered in sweat rather than flames.

Far below, the battle continued with furious yells and clashing magic as Takers swarmed the forest, but there was no sign of the Shadow Mother.

Sara spun, searching a sky murky with dragon fire and the claret hue of the full blood moon.

"Where are you, you deceitful bitch? You can't be that easy to defeat. Come on! I'll shove my flames down your throat and burn you from the inside out." *Let's go!* Sara stole another glance at the battle below. She needed to end this before anyone got hurt.

"COME ON!" she roared, witch fire blazing in her palms.

"So eager to die," hissed the Shadow Mother, suddenly appearing in front of Sara.

Gone was the vile polypus creature, replaced by the curvaceous form of a naked woman made from sparkling obsidian sand. Her face was strikingly beautiful, a shade familiar even, but her eyes were vacant, soulless voids.

Sara stared too long, the distraction costing her. Jagged-edged, glittering whips lashed out from the Shadow Mother, turning her into a many-armed goddess of Hell. A wet crack rent the air. Pain instantly tore through Sara. She bit back her scream and whirled, barely dodging another shadow whip, only to be hit by two more. *Crack! Crack!* White-hot anger replaced her pain. She threw an arc of witch fire, incinerating every whip. The Shadow Mother grew more, same as a hydra.

Sara panted, trembling to keep her fire under control while mentally scrabbling for a clever strategy. The only solution coming to mind was incredibly foolish. Stupidly, deadly, assuredly foolish. Yet Lochton had said her fire would undo the Shadow Mother, and she was running out of time.

The Shadow Mother swelled, her voluptuous body and torturous whips blotting out the red moon. Agony pierced Sara as invisible talons scraped her insides. A cry escaped her.

The entity sneered, triumphant in her torment. Spitting black ash, she rasped, "I gave you time to grow stronger—to become a worthy adversary—but you are still weak. A fraud of a High Witch. Incapable of protecting others. An *abomination* like all of Ware Woods. It is why you are alone before me. No one believes in you."

"Lies!" shouted Sara, drawing on the strength of her fury. All of Ware Woods believed in her. Thomas believed in her even when she didn't believe in herself. And Florine—

Sara's thought cut short as the Shadow Mother's talons dug deeper, slicing into her mind as if intent on extracting her hopes.

"It is the truth! The others see you as the problem that you are. They are not here because they are fighting among themselves. Destroying one another, thanks to you."

No! It wasn't true. The others wanted to help Ware Woods. They were united in seeing the Shadow Mother as their greatest threat. They weren't here because they expected the Shadow Mother on the Equinox. *Right?*

Sara's rage flared, witch fire dancing around her. It didn't matter. "I don't need the others. Ware Woods weakened you before. It's why you've been gone. Now I'm going to weaken you again and break your hold on dragons. Then I'll help them send you back to Hell."

She launched herself at the Shadow Mother, slipping past her whips, and, reckless witch that she was, dove into her center.

With fingers and flames, Sara tore into the Shadow Mother, determined to rip out her heart and set it ablaze. Sara shredded gritty darkness until her hands bled, and when she found nothing beyond an empty core, she burrowed deep into her anger and burned. Her flames soared, trying to fill the void. The more she blasted, the more the void demanded, pulling at her, draining her.

"*More,*" urged Thomas's husky voice in her head. "*I'm almost free.*"

"*Thomas?*" It was him. She couldn't have imagined his voice. Instead of sounding echoey, his words rang clear as though he were beside her. Sara clenched her jaw and became an inferno, her soul screaming with pain, her magic nearly depleted. "*Hurry! I can't last much longer.*"

"*More fire, baby,*" his voice commanded.

Her heart immediately bristled. She extinguished her fire. The comment was *wrong*. She and Thomas used that term *very* sparingly and only when they were emotionally vulnerable. Thomas would never call her that to push her power.

Trick, trick, trick.

The Shadow Mother had played her for a fool.

Sara screamed into the Aether and promptly choked in pain. Everything hurt. It felt like she'd been turned inside out and broiled to a blackened husk. Her bloodstones glowed a raw shade of red, illuminating the dragon smoke churning around her and the most unwelcome tentacle wrapped around her waist. A decidedly *large* tentacle.

Laughter filled Sara's mind. It started as Thomas's warm chuckle and quickly morphed into a brittle cackle. "*Your wrath is savory. Now let me taste how delicious your fear and anguish are.*" More tentacles lashed out, wrapping around Sara, restraining her arms at her sides.

Sara clamped down her fear as the smoke cleared and she beheld the glittering Shadow Mother, now twice her previous size. The shadowy sand entity stared down at her with an alarmingly smug smile.

Sara's mouth went desert dry.

She hadn't weakened the Shadow Mother by fighting her with witch fire—she'd made her stronger. The entity had feasted on Sara's rage, glutted herself, and had become more powerful.

Her tentacles squeezed, cutting into Sara's torso.

Whatever magic Sara had left was sucked away. Even her abilities to speak and mentally project had been stripped, her many curse words clanging hollowly inside her.

The Shadow Mother's grin widened. Sara's mind raced faster than her stuttering heart, but there was no clever or foolish escape from this. There was no reasoning with the Shadow Mother—no opportunity to bargain herself in exchange for leaving other magicals alone. The cruel entity was an all-consuming tempest of death, exactly as Jin had once said.

And Sara was at her mercy.

The Shadow Mother propelled them through the dragon smoke. They skimmed just above the tree canopy, a bitter wind blowing back Sara's silvery-gray hair, until the Shadow Mother stopped at the oak and thrust Sara forward with a violent shake. "Forcing you to watch the destruction of your forest will be sweet. They cannot see or hear you. They think you already gone, yet they still fight, oblivious to their discord feeding my power." She smacked her lips, and Sara's stomach roiled.

Though she didn't want to give the Shadow Mother any more satisfaction or perverse fuel, Sara couldn't help but glance down at the forest. Below them, a translucent dome of golden light enclosed the oak tree, its upper branches scorched into crippled claws.

Despite her efforts to control her emotion, fear washed over Sara.

The children hadn't looped to Jin's garden. They had stayed to protect the forest. But that wasn't the worst of it. Outside of the protective shield, Matthew's russet wolf snapped and snarled at a mob of Takers. The shifter fought for every inch to keep them from overwhelming the kids' shield and to protect the all-too-still body of Kingsley lying among the graves.

Sara had no time to process the scene as the Shadow Mother shook her in all directions. Through winter-bare tree canopies, Sara caught snippets of the Blue Ridge pack in their wolven forms. They had been forced apart, each member being hunted down by dragons and Takers. Wes fled toward the birch grove, tail between his legs, while Luke, his furry flanks matted with blood, tussled with half a dozen Takers. Moesha, Alesha, and Iesha had been separately cornered by dragon fire and fallen trees, each sister facing a band of Takers with battle-axes. Near the Cahill common, Dean tore into a surrounding mob of Takers as Moira, in bear form, swiped and roared to get to his side.

Another violent shake, the Shadow Mother's jagged tendrils slicing into Sara's arms, and there was Lethal backed up against the lake's edge, a fanged snarl on their beautiful face, futilely wielding Kindness against a bevy of fire-breathing dragons.

Sara thrashed against her bindings, trying to break free and tumble to Lethal's aid, but the tendrils tightened. Wet warmth dripped down her forearms and fingers. The Shadow Mother grated out a cackle, the sound raking across Sara's battered mind.

"I have waited ssso long for the fall of Ware Woodsss," she hissed.

In a blur of smoke, Sara was suspended above the chaos in the Council clearing. Directly below her sprawled Samson's body, his limbs bent at ghastly angles, his onyx eyes fixed unseeing on her.

No! Impossible! Samson was stronger than Sara. He was her nemesis turned twisted mentor with *far* more experience and magical power. Hells, he even had shadow magic gifted to him by the Shadow Mother. *This can't be real!*

The bloodstone Samson had given Sara—Ardeth's stone—pulsed. Guilt racked her. Samson's beloved single red bloodstone had likely saved him for centuries. Now he was gone. And all for *nothing*.

Sara was caught, a witless fly in the Shadow Mother's web,

incapable of saving Samson or anyone else, much less the world. She'd let him down. She'd let them *all* down.

Sara internally bellowed, her anguish escalating into a raging river as a cloud of smoke erupted beside Samson. Kahn, the dark witch from the Global Council, and Brad lunged forth from the smoke. They fought one another, each trying to take the many black bloodstones hanging from Samson's limp neck. When a mass of Takers descended over them, obscuring them from view, the Shadow Mother hummed with delight and jerked Sara's attention to the stump stage.

A glacial chill flooded Sara. From atop the stage, Gran threw sizzling globes of steel blue energy, straining to hold off a drab-green, shadow-smudged dragon. Beside her, Albert and Alice, the latter also in wolf form, bit back at Takers.

More guilt stabbed Sara. If Alice had kept her bloodstone, she could have used witch fire to better protect them. On the opposite side of the stage, Charlie, Ted, and Ian clustered behind Ian's golden shield as a gray dragon, its sides rotten with infection, blasted them with fire.

Sara flailed against the Shadow Mother, whose tentacles responded by cutting to the bone. Blood ran down Sara's legs in hot rivulets. She screamed into the Aether—for Florine, for Damon, for the Mother, for *anyone* to help them.

The Shadow Mother laughed. With another whiplike tentacle, she nudged the gray dragon, redirecting its jet of fire. The flames shifted away from the stage and toward Kira, still slaughtering her way through a horde of Takers. Ian immediately projected his shield onto her, leaving him, Charlie, and Ted unprotected.

Sara stilled. *Nooo—*

The Shadow Mother flicked her tentacle and, with a crack that cleaved Sara's heart, hit Ian in the chest. He stiffened, eyes wide, hand pressing the area above his heart as though he could pluck out the Shadow Mother's splinter of ice. Everything slowed as Ian collapsed, falling to his back, gaping up at the sky.

Sara silently screamed, her grief manifesting an aura of iridescent black that clawed in vain to reverse time. Alice and Albert howled, their mournful gale startling the nearby dragons into halting their fire. Charlie, Ted, and Gran wailed. And from the clearing filled with Takers, Kira released a soul-piercing cry.

"This is your fault, Sara." The Shadow Mother yanked her until they were both high above the forest. She dangled Sara before her. Up close, her fine sand shimmered resembling black stars, her vacant eyes obsidian mirrors to Sara's all-consuming grief. "You failed them. You were never capable of facing me and correcting the balance because *you* are the problem." She spat, hitting Sara with toxic ash. It sizzled on Sara's face, yet she felt nothing, her body, heart, and soul numb. "Without you and Ware Woods in my way, I will absorb all magic until hate and darkness reign. The entire world will finally recognize *me* as they bend to my shadows." And before Sara's tears could spill over whatever was left of her cheeks, the Shadow Mother flung out a tentacle, driving her toward the ground.

CHAPTER 41

DRAGON SMOKE AND the sheer force of being shoved through the sky tore at Sara's eyes. Trees blurred in her periphery, her primary field of vision filled with the rapidly approaching Cahill common, its snowy plain marred with paw prints and smears of blood.

At least death by splattering will be quick.

Sara slammed into the center of the forest, but it was not a quick death that met her. It was pain. Wave after wave of pain as the Shadow Mother hammered her farther, deeper, obliterating all sense of time. Roots and rock and ice tore at Sara's flesh while her devastating failures and the Shadow Mother's words shredded her soul.

What had Sara been thinking? Of course she wasn't strong enough to weaken the Shadow Mother on her own. Even Lochton had told her she'd need everyone's help. And like a damn fool, she hadn't been prepared for the Shadow Mother to strike before the Equinox. She had failed Ian and Samson and Kingsley. She had failed everyone in Ware Woods.

Yet there was more. A *long* list of failures had brought Sara to this fate. Her reckless visit to the Global Council had riled the Magi. And her failure to protect her few supporters had resulted in the death of Amira's colony and the foreswearing of the other sites.

"This is your fault, Sara."

The Shadow Mother's condemnation flayed Sara from the inside out as she fell and fell and fell.

After what seemed an eternal purgatory of confronting her failures in a mercurial arctic grave, and Sara was nothing more than a raw wisp of consciousness, she stopped fighting. She let go of her guilt and grief and rage, releasing even her hatred for the Shadow Mother. If this was to be her pitiful existence—or punishingly drawn-out final moment—Sara wanted to feel her love for her family and Ware Woods.

A red glow penetrated the cold crushing darkness, its soft light an encouraging glimmer.

And oh, stars so high above, she wanted to always feel her undying love for Thomas. Whatever afterlife awaited them, she would find him.

At the thought of Thomas, there came a tug on the innermost part of her being—at the *heart* of her being. The golden thread connecting her and Thomas.

Her consciousness brewed, a bubbling potion about to reach a long-awaited remedy. Her pain and exhaustion ceased. Her torturous descent slowed.

Wait a minute. If she could feel the bond . . . *I'm not dead?*

Trick, trick, trick.

Not dead and certainly not at fault. The Shadow Mother was wholly deceit and lies, which meant whatever she said was the *opposite* of the truth.

Sara wasn't at fault. She *hadn't* failed Thomas or her family or the magical world. If the Shadow Mother feared her and claimed she was the problem, well then, Sara wasn't the problem—she was the solution. She *could* correct the balance. But how?

Her descent fully stopped, leaving her weightless. Cozy heat embraced her as a sunrise of golden light appeared in the distance. It grew and grew, forcing Sara to squint against its brilliance.

When Sara's eyes adjusted, she was standing in a resplendent garden, plush moss beneath her feet. Flowering shrubs and flitting butterflies grazed her legs as summery sun kissed her face, the nectar-sweet scent of ripe fruits teasing her nose.

She slapped her hands to her cheeks. No tears. No blood. She ran her hands over herself. Her clothes were untouched, her body injury-free. Her bloodstones pulsed with a steady beat.

Craning her neck, she took in the surrounding vast garden. Somewhat circular in nature, it was ringed by trees of all kinds, from citrus to apple and pine to willow. In front of the trees burbled a lazy brook that seemed to flow in a continuous loop, feeding itself as it wreathed the flowering garden where Sara stood.

On tiptoe, she peered over a bloom-laden shrub, catching a glimpse of the slightly elevated center of the paradise. Her entire body tingled. *It can't be.*

Needing a closer look and having nowhere else to go, Sara followed the mossy path through a swirling labyrinth of colorful shrubs and wildflowers until she reached the center. There, sur-rounded by a grassy courtyard of dozing animals, sat the Mother.

She rested on a tree-like throne, its curling armrests and splayed headrest of leafy branches a work of art. An ox and a lion flanked the sides of her chair, while an eagle perched on top. In her lap, a rabbit nestled among the folds of her multi-hued robes. Similar to the courtyard of various animals and the Mother herself, the sentries at her side were sleeping.

Sara picked her way across the court, side-stepping elk, tur-tles, peacocks, and more. Though their shared rest was a touch concerning, waking them and causing pandemonium was the last thing Sara wanted.

She stopped before the throne, her heartbeat hummingbird fast. The Mother appeared identical to the image the Book had once shown her: serene countenance, golden-chestnut skin, pert nose, cascading locks, and a gemstone-embellished crown of in-terlocking branches.

Sara's scalp prickled. What if the Shadow Mother had somehow frozen her too?

Her fear melted when a smile graced the Mother's lips. She opened her eyes, and Sara's breath hitched at her golden-flecked earthen gaze, at the nurturing energy radiating from her. Magic flooded Sara's veins with comforting warmth.

"Hello, Sara. It is good to see you."

Her voice was as rich and smooth as honey, with a bell-like resonance so befitting of a god Sara wondered if she should bow or curtsy. Instead, she froze. *What is happening here?* "You—you know my name?" she stuttered.

The Mother's smile deepened into the same expression Sara's own mother used to give her when she asked something ridiculous.

Sara glanced around the garden, half expecting—half hoping—to see her mother tending the crescent moon-shaped flower beds. And though Sara felt the pulse of her bloodstones, the zing of magic coursing through her body, and the taut bond she shared with Thomas, she asked, "Am I . . . dead?"

The Mother gently stroked the rabbit in her lap. "You are still you. Your energy has not changed, nor will it for a long time."

Not exactly an answer. Sara frowned. If she was here, where were Ian and Samson and Kingsley? What was happening to everyone in Ware Woods? And to Thomas and the other dragons?

The Mother must have read her mind, for she said, "Time has suspended for them so we may have this moment."

Well, that seemed positive. It left a sliver of possibility for Sara to go back and somehow undo *everything*. And it also seemed the Mother knew shit had hit the fan.

Pfft. Sara needed more than just a moment.

Before her manners and sense of self-preservation could stop her, she spouted, "Where have you been? Jin has searched *all* over for you. I have *pleaded* for you. Lochton has been frozen for *centuries*. How could you let this happen? How could you—" *Let Samson and Ian die? Let Thomas become frozen? Let any of this happen?* She choked up, unable to continue her tirade. Tears pricked her eyes at all the death and suffering leading to this "*moment.*"

The Mother softened her gaze even more. It was the type of gaze that cried with you, that invited you into a gentle embrace and soothed away your worries. But Sara didn't want her grief assuaged. She wanted answers and a magical way to reverse time and save everyone. She swiped at her tears and took a step back, away from the lion purr-snoring beside the throne.

The Mother rose, her jewel-toned mosaic-patterned robes fluttering in a soft breeze. She set the drowsy bunny on a cushion of moss atop her seat and descended the grassy knoll dais. "Walk with me, daughter. I have many things to tell you. Things you need to know before you make your final choice." She motioned for Sara to follow as she glided through her sleeping court and headed toward the shrubs, now swirling in earnest, changing their pattern. By the time Sara not-so-gracefully tripped past a hooved animal and joined the Mother's side, the shrubs had halted their movement, revealing a curved pathway.

"What kind of choice?" inquired Sara, leaving out the "*final,*" which sounded far too ominous.

"That is for you to decide," replied the Mother, strolling alongside her.

Hmph. Exactly. Sara hoped the Mother wouldn't be this cryptic with whatever else she had to share.

The path ended, and together they crossed the brook, stepping on stones that emerged in an exact match to their stride and then disappeared once they were on the opposite side, standing under the shade of an enormous tree.

Sara tilted her head back, then back more, gawping at the strangest tree she'd ever seen. It was both evergreen and deciduous, its branches displaying a peculiar mix of differing pine boughs as well as leaves in varying patterns and colors ranging from spring green to fall amber. Fruits, flowers, and nuts of all kinds adorned its sprawling canopy. The trunk was both gnarled and deeply grooved, and where it met the earth, thick roots grew as buttresses.

When the Mother stepped over a root and into the deepest groove, Sara hurtled after her, grabbing ahold of her silken robes as the tree absorbed them.

Instead of darkness, a warm light caressed Sara with a feather-soft touch. The rhythmic beating of many hearts thrummed in her ears and in her body. It was such a pleasant looping that Sara would have been content to remain in its ethereal void had the Mother not pulled her out to stand before a regal tree atop a grassy hillock.

A somewhat familiar tree. The Mother's robe slipped from Sara's hand as she stared up at the straight trunk and fiery foliage. It reminded her of the Atwell's black gum tree.

Sara peered at the surrounding forest. The trees and vegetation were similar to Ware Woods, yet there was no lake anywhere near them, just a valley and a river.

"Many moons ago, I created magicals to care for this world and one another," said the Mother with a sweep of her hand at the land before them. She headed for the river, floating across the valley, her long robes skimming the butter-soft grass.

Sara rushed after her. Though the Mother moved with effortless grace, as if taking a noonday walk, she was rapidly eating up the distance to the water's edge.

With a doleful smile, the Mother continued. "Over time, magicals became covetous and distrusting of one another. So I separated them into factions and was given dragons from the Aether to watch over them. But again they fought—fiercer than before. It saddened me so greatly my daughter, Mary, left our garden to wander among the magicals and beseech them to stop fighting." The Mother paused before the river as roots exploded from the angled bank, growing and twisting to form an arched bridge over the swiftly running water.

Why did she make a bridge when we could just fly—Wait. What?

"Are you telling me *my* great-great-grandmother Mary is *your* daughter?" There was a heaping dose of hysterical incredulity in Sara's voice. And yet, this explained why Mary had been exceptionally powerful and capable of mating with a dragon, and why Sara was even having this discussion.

"Yes," said the Mother, gliding onto the bridge, as though this were common knowledge. "It is one of the reasons why the Shadow Mother cannot kill you."

Sara paused. *Can't kill me?* But she could inflict *lots* of pain. So much pain Sara had thought she had died.

She put her hand to her chest, considering. As a Lochton, Ian was also descended from the Mother. Perhaps it hadn't been the Hills charm bracelet that had once saved him but his lineage. And if that were true, perhaps the Shadow Mother's splinter of ice in Ian's heart only caused pain and couldn't kill him.

Maybe Ian was still alive. Sara's own heart skipped a beat.

CHAPTER 42

WHEN SARA LOOKED up from her thoughts, the Mother was on the opposite side of the river, halfway up a steep hill. Sara flew to her, warily noting the river's fast current and the eerie quiet of the valley and surrounding forest. There were no bird calls, no susurrations of wind or leaves or grass. She reached out and grazed a honeysuckle bush. It felt real, yet didn't seem real, lacking a strong scent and rustling sound.

They crested the hill and the Mother stopped in a wide meadow, her wistful gaze directed at the center of the field where a male and female were walking toward one another.

Sara swayed. Not just any male—Lochton. She raised a hand and waved, only to have her excited greeting die on her lips as the Mother explained, "We are not present time for them. These are imprints of the past."

Well, crap. No wonder this forest felt familiar yet different. Sara dropped her arm and squinted at the faintly blurry edges of Lochton. He wore a cream-colored tunic, and his midnight skirt was shorter, kilt style, and paired with boots. His black hair, loose in back and with two braids in front, shimmered with a pine green sheen. The smile he gave the female was similar to one Thomas often gave her. A smile of pure, fervent, unconditional love. Pain squeezed Sara's heart at the thought of Thomas, their bond still frozen with ice.

The female—Mary, Sara realized with no small amount of surprise—returned Lochton's affection, running her last few paces to leap into his arms. Her aura was star-white bright, her flowing hair and long dress enveloping Lochton as she wrapped herself around him. Their kiss was sweet and passionate, a claiming and a promise. Energy flared around them.

The Mother chuckled, her mirth reminding Sara of sunflowers and citrus with an undercurrent of roses and cherries, like Naomi's laughter had once been. "I sent Lochton, my fiercest and wisest dragon, to watch over Mary. Against all odds, her kindness tamed him. They fell in love."

Sara's cheeks flushed as Lochton reverently lowered Mary to the wildflowers. As soon as he settled beside her, they both vanished.

The Mother sighed. "After a while, they separated, both believing Mary needed to focus solely on creating Ware Woods as a haven for enlightened magicals. And they both agreed Lochton's love for her made him vulnerable and biased as leader of the other dragons and regulator of the magical balance."

She turned to Sara, the golden flecks in her eyes dimming. "I should have known such misgivings were whispered lies of the Shadow Mother. But I had been so troubled by magicals fighting one another, I hadn't noticed her influence on Mary and Lochton. I hadn't noticed her encouraging the magicals' fear and deceit by planting lies that dragons killed without cause and that factions were not to mingle because each was superior to the other. She also stoked fear and hatred among normals toward any magic, making it harder for magicals to protect sacred sites."

Dark clouds gathered overhead, casting them into shadow. The ground shook with such force a stand of pines at the edge of the meadow bent back and forth, their needles brushing the forest floor. Sara's scalp prickled. She whirled to face the river as it surged and flooded the valley. Water rose with frightening speed. Her jaw dropped as a stone wall magically grew around the black gum tree and surrounding knoll, holding back the flood and creating the recessed Atwell island.

Just as quickly as it started, the ground stilled. The rising water abruptly stopped, forming the lake and familiar shoreline before Sara. She toed the water in disbelief, her mind numb with shock at the sheer destruction and the Shadow Mother's formidable level of slow-drip poisonous scheming.

Sara turned back to the meadow—her meadow—and could only stare as an imprint of Mary stretched her arms to the sky and transformed into the oak tree.

Though Sara had known Mary and the oak were connected, seeing her morph, arms becoming branches, skin becoming bark, was humbling beyond words.

The clouds waned and the sky returned to a cornflower blue as the Mother slowly floated toward the oak. Sara followed. "When Mary died protecting Ware Woods," explained the Mother, "I mourned deeply and slept often. I did not see the Shadow Mother attack Ann. I did not question Lochton entering a deep sleep, thinking he was grieving Mary as well. My despair was so blinding I did not notice the Shadow Mother growing stronger as I grew sleepier.

"When I finally realized what she was doing, I also realized I could not intervene again. By initially separating magicals, I had taken away their free will and inadvertently upset the balance. I could not do that a second time and expect different results." The Mother placed a hand over her heart. "And then you were born. A seedling with enough latent magic to reset the balance and who grew stronger with every challenge.

"Hoping for the best, I instructed my youngest elysian-eyed dragon to watch over you and foretold the day would come when you would help each other. Afterward, for the sake of you all, I let go of my hold on the balance." She dropped her hand. Her hair, shimmering with flecks of diamonds, fell forward with a slight dip of her head.

Let go? Sara's mind spun, a tornado of thoughts and emotions.

If she let go, that meant . . . A bolt of understanding hit Sara. "It was you! *You* caused the sudden shift in the balance. Not me—you!"

The Mother nodded. "Yes, daughter. I had to. Any hope for permanent peace must come from within. Magicals must band together to undo the Shadow Mother, for her shadows are many." She drifted closer to the oak. In its sprawling branches, a slightly blurry imprint of the treehouse sprouted, room by room, turret by turret, deck by deck. The stairs flowed one by one like dominoes falling around the oak's trunk. When they reached the ground, Sara startled at a version of herself ascending the staircase, her head thrown back in wonder.

"But to do this," continued the Mother, "magicals need someone to take the first step toward peace. Someone who is a mix of light and dark, who values love over hate, and who focuses on hope rather than despair."

Every inch of Sara's skin tingled. *You can't be serious.*

An imprint of Samson appeared, pacing on the main deck, his worried comportment the same as when Sara once woke from stasis. He vanished just as Dean and the pack in wolven form leapt from one edge of the meadow. Sara rushed closer to the Mother, preferring not to be trampled—if an imprint could do such a thing—as the pack bounded across the field and disappeared into the pines. Next appeared Lethal and another imprint of Sara sparring in the center of the meadow. They dissolved into a sky now cloudless blue as the Mother turned, her mosaic robes a twirling kaleidoscope, and faced Sara.

"Someone who has befriended the unlikeliest of allies and knows the strength in diversity."

The forest seemed to teeter, or perhaps it was Sara. *Is this conversation really happening?* She pinched the back of her hand. Then did it again *harder*. "You—you think *I'm* capable of leading everyone to peace? You must know the Shadow Mother just handed me my ass." She winced for swearing in front of the Mother, but she couldn't help it. This was ridiculous. "I'm young and have only known magic a mere drop of time compared to everyone else." With a frantic wave of her hand, she gestured to the previous images of Samson, Dean, and Lethal.

Much to Sara's relief, the Mother didn't bat an eye. She knew Sara well.

"It is not knowledge, power, or experience that make you capable. It is your passion—your inner fire—that makes you extraordinary."

Sara reared back. *Inner fire.* All Hells. No wonder the Shadow Mother had wiped the floor with her. When Lochton said "*inner fire*," he hadn't meant witch fire. He had meant . . .

Sara tapped her chin and eyed the Mother, unsure of exactly what Lochton had meant, but figured it was wherever this "*extraordinary*" pep talk was going.

"You have made many difficult choices and have sacrificed much to bring us to this precipice," acknowledged the Mother.

That's an understatement. Sara absently rubbed the edge of her palm where her pinkie should have been. Yet a missing digit was *nothing* compared to losing her mother and Naomi and all the chaos that just happened in Ware Woods. Chaos she *refused* to accept as real. She wished the Mother would hurry with her explanations and simply turn back time to avoid all of this.

The Mother looked to the sky above them where, like one of Florine's hazelnut spells, black-and-gold sparkles appeared in the shape of a still circle. At first, the dark voids were disproportionately larger, but then, as if inhaling, the gold swelled to equal its size.

"You, Sara," stated the Mother, "are capable of resetting the balance. I cannot tell you how to do this, for that choice is yours. But I will remind you of this: hate only begets more hate, and the Shadow Mother loves to take."

Sara raised her brow. *Okaaay.* This was a lot to take in, not to mention sphinx-worthy cryptic. Still, if the Mother believed she was capable, then so did Sara. And witch fire was not the way. Apparently, the way to undo the Shadow Mother involved inner fire and a choice—a *final* choice.

Sara frowned. "Is this the part where I sell my soul to get rid of the Shadow Mother and finally have peace? Because it seems a bit pricey if I won't be able to enjoy said peace." *Thomas will be furious.*

A faint smile twinkled in the Mother's serene gaze. "When you make the right choice, Thomas will be there for you."

Such a confounding statement. It cranked Sara's anxiety that there was indeed only *one* right choice while also boosting her hope that Thomas wouldn't remain frozen. She chewed her lip, pondering the Mother's advice. If hate only brought on more hate, then Sara needed to stuff down her revulsion for the Shadow Mother; it would be hard to do, though not impossible. And Sara already knew the Shadow Mother loved to take, and wasn't planning on letting the entity take any more from her or anyone else. But the inner fire portion of the choice was a puzzle. If it wasn't witch fire, then by deduction it couldn't be her energy spheres or other such magic.

Perhaps inner fire meant her spunk. Yet no one called her spunky. They said things like firecracker, monster, bold, reckless, wicked—and then there was Lethal's spot-on reprimand: "*You have a knack for doing the opposite of what is expected.*"

Her brow rose to a new height. Eyeing the Mother, she said, her voice high with disbelief, "By inner fire, do you mean my *defiance*?"

A twinkly smile.

Sara shook her head. "I don't understand. I'm supposed to be my normal reckless self and somehow this will save everyone?" *Because it didn't work on my last face off with the Shadow Mother.* Sara paused, recalling how she'd once stopped the Shadow Mother from choking her. Maybe her defiance *had* worked. At least to some degree. She had been too full of hate and rage at the time to take notes.

"Believe in yourself, and you'll know what to do," answered the

Mother. She glided closer to the oak, the treehouse imprint fading.

Wonderful. Her advice was an inspirational quote and eerily similar to Charlie's often-dispensed fatherly guidance for her to "trust the process" and her own mother's whispers to believe in herself.

Sara sighed as she jogged a few paces to catch up with the Mother. She had no other choice but to believe, and being reckless was a natural default. Round two was looking to be in her favor. Magic tingled in her palms. She rubbed her hands together, eager to return to Ware Woods.

The Mother gestured to the oak trunk. "You can return now, and your timing will be as it should, but you need to know the right choice is not the easiest choice. For the peace you seek requires a significant personal sacrifice. Are you prepared for this?"

Ah, the *final* part of the choice. Why was nothing ever easy in the magical world?

Sara folded her arms and pressed a fist to her mouth, holding in her snark while thinking. Based on one of the Mother's earlier responses, the sacrifice was not her soul. Thomas would be proud of her leading question, which Sara looked forward to telling him someday because the Mother had also confirmed that Thomas would be there for her. Soul and Thomas. Win-win. Any other sacrifice would be worth it to save everyone and live a long life with Thomas in peace.

"I'm ready." And before she could think better of it, Sara hugged the Mother, who felt like a summer day, warm and full of sunshine, with scents of herbs and ripe berries. Except there was an odd coolness to her hair. Sara glanced at the rippling locks as she pulled back—and gasped. Those weren't diamonds shimmering in her tresses; they were ice crystals.

Though her body shivered, Sara's voice was low and steady. "I will defeat her no matter the cost." And she would, even if it was the last thing she did. She had to. Her bloodstones pulsed, white flames springing to life, flickering around her as a second skin.

The Mother nodded, a knowing smile on her face, yet Sara couldn't tell if the softness in her eyes was sad or hopeful, the stars a muted sparkle.

When the Mother didn't comment further, Sara turned to the oak and jumped in.

CHAPTER 43

I NSTEAD OF A familiar looping darkness, golden light blinded Sara. The rhythmic thumping of the oak's heartwood sur-rounded her, filled her. Each beat like the resonant ticking of the grandfather clock she hoped remained in the living room of the brown house, untouched by Takers and dragons.

The Mother hadn't said how far into the past Sara would travel. She'd only said, "*Your timing will be as it should.*" She could have hours, or she could have seconds before the forest's barrier broke. With each beat, the thumping became a countdown and Sara a gladiator about to step into a colosseum of horrors. She rolled her shoulders, the light caressing her, and gathered every scrap of determination and defiance that swirled in her soul. And when she felt near to bursting with anticipation, the beating stopped. She stumbled out of the oak, golden light still shining on her, hopeful, until the scent of dragon smoke punched her in the face.

"Sara!"

She knew that voice. She squinted against the light, letting Connor tug her by the arm to a cluster of children. Their surprised expressions were a mirror to her own shock. Here were the Cahill, Atwell, and Hills children, the latter still emanating their protective shield over the partially burnt oak. If Sara had gone back in time, it hadn't been very far. She grappled to keep her heart in her chest, to not let it sink to the bottom of the lake.

"Are you all okay?" she shouted over the roar of dragons and a too-close snarl of death. The snarl would have to wait as she studied the children. No injuries, thankfully.

The tallest of the Hills kids spoke up. "We're fine, but Matt and Kingsley need help."

Lily's younger sister, Ophelia, pointed to the far end of the cemetery where Matthew, bleeding in wolf form, was surrounded by shadow Takers. Beneath Matthew lay Kingsley.

No! Sara flicked both hands, instantly ending the Takers with a ring of witch fire. She grabbed at the air and yanked, kinetically pulling Matthew and Kingsley inside the protective golden bubble. With another tug, she placed them on the far side of the oak, prudently away from the kids.

"Whatever happens, you all stay together under this shield." She made eye contact with every child, the tall Hills girl and Connor both nodding in the brisk manner of young sergeants. Samson and Kane had trained them well. Soon, Sara would make certain these kids could play in earnest without the threat of violence.

She rushed to Matthew and Kingsley. Placing a hand on each, she flooded them with warm healing magic. The bloody gashes on Matthew's flank closed, his pulse returning to normal, yet Kingsley remained unmoving, his heartbeat fading. *Come on, King!*

Matthew phased. He knelt and grabbed Kingsley's hand in both of his. "You put the fire out and saved the oak, old man. Now you need to come back to us." Though Matthew's voice was steady, his clasp on Kingsley shook.

"I don't know why he's not healing," Sara cried, pushing out another surge of her magic.

Kingsley's eyes fluttered open. He lifted his other hand and placed it atop Sara's, halting her magic. "'Tis my time," he wheezed. "Give Lochton my best and tell Rose and Alice their love was sweeter than cake."

"King?" Sara's throat tightened, tears blurring her vision. What was he saying? Maybe he'd hit his head too hard and was confused. Because the alternative was inconceivable. Kingsley was the oldest in Ware Woods. They needed him—a living link to their past.

Warm droplets trickled upon them, acorn-scented tears from the oak.

Kingsley shook his finger, weak as a kitten. "No mourning. I'm finally back with Annie now." His eyes closed, his hand falling to his side.

The tears stopped, and the ground *moved*.

Sara jumped up, hauling Matthew with her. Roots rose to the surface, embraced Kingsley, and pulled him into the ground. In a heartbeat, he was gone.

Sara tottered, her grip tight on Matthew. Before she could even think about processing Kingsley's passing, the oak trunk shimmered and out popped a tall, broad-shouldered male, his copper hair in a long braid, his pants and vest a supple, brown leather.

He gave the oak a curious squint, then slid his amber gaze across the kids and the new onslaught of Takers banging on the protective shield before settling on Matthew and Sara. "Matty!" he shouted, his grin ear to ear. Sara swore his canines were elongated.

"Michael? What are you—" Matthew cut off as the male tackle-hugged him.

"It's been a while, little bro," said the male—Michael. He stepped back, keeping one hand, his nails neatly trimmed claws, on Matthew's shoulder and glanced at Sara. "Florine said you needed help *now*. And do you ever." He jerked his chin at the Takers, a thick curtain of dragon smoke behind them.

A lion stepped out of the oak, followed by another and another, until a pride crowded the protected space beneath the oak branches. Sara paled as the kids cheered. The largest lion inclined his head at her, his thick mane similar to the dense cape of shaggy fur she had seen on one of the Magi at the Global Council meeting.

"My pack is at your service. The packs of my siblings and Damon are on their way as well," said Michael, drawing her attention back to him.

Sara faced the smiling shifter. Another site here to help, and more were coming. They *had* believed in her.

The dusky light beneath the oak suddenly brightened as smoke cleared from the adjacent meadow, unveiling Lily beside the lake. Her platinum hair whipped about, her arms outstretched as she commanded a hurricane, holding back a thunder of infected dragons. Guarding her back was Lethal with Kindness in their hands, ruthlessly cutting down Takers.

Lily's storm slammed into the golden shield. The Hills children stumbled and clasped hands as Takers pressed against the translucent barrier, hammering at it with fists and daggers.

The oak groaned in response, its trunk undulating as wolves and bears surged forth. They leapt past the kids, through the golden shield, and tore into the shadow Takers with the lions at their heels.

"We'll protect the kids," hollered Matthew to Sara. "I'd say good luck, but you don't need it." He flashed an encouraging grin before phasing into his russet wolf and taking off after Michael's tawny lion.

Sara stared after him. *I do need it. Ian needs it. Samson needs it.* Kingsley may have been at peace to join Ann among the stars, but Sara could not lose Ian and Samson. She grabbed her jagged pendant and smoked to the maple stump stage.

In a clap of smoke, Sara landed atop the stage, Gran beside her, a wave of shadow Takers clamoring before them. She instinctively pushed out witch fire, yet as soon as the Takers disappeared into shadowy ash, another wave set upon them.

"They just keep coming," hollered Gran. With a swish of her arms, she summoned edged arcs of steel blue energy. Another swish, and the bladed energy reaped the Takers as though they were stalks of wheat.

Oh, no. This was the exact situation Sara had left them in when the Shadow Mother forced her to watch—

"Ian!" she shouted mentally and audibly, her anguish ripping her throat raw. She turned her back to the Takers, steel blue energy flaring behind her with another threshing, her grandmother more than capable of holding her own, as Sara took in the rest of the stage.

Spread out along the stump's edge were Alice and Albert, tearing into Takers, and Charlie and Ted, bludgeoning their assailants with wooden clubs. Shadowy heads and bodies flew in all directions, dissolving into nothing as soon as they hit the ground. Sara's family was a formidable force, keeping Takers away from the center of the stage where Ian lay on his back with Kira kneeling at his side.

"They have no minds to crush," Charlie mentally shouted, clobbering a Taker who had lunged for Sara, her focus entirely on Ian, her body already in motion. *"Heal him, firecracker!"* Charlie pleaded before taking a full-body swing to protect Ted's back.

Sara slid to her brother. Her hands glowed with healing magic as she slammed them onto his chest, pouring energy into him. "Ian! Stay with me!" Her shouts were futile. His golden-brown eyes were dull, his body chilled, his heart stopped.

He was already gone. Sara hadn't come in time. And no amount of healing magic could bring him back. Not even a vampire could cheat his death now.

No. This can't be. This must be a mistake. He's a Lochton. The Mother wouldn't let this happen. Kingsley had chosen to pass, but not Ian. *Not Ian!* He had suffered all his life with the Shadow Mother's ice splinter in his heart, and this was *not* how he ended.

Sara slumped back, her limbs leaden, the chaos around them a distant clash. From across Ian's still body, Sara met Kira's gaze. Her silent understanding that Sara couldn't heal him caused her onyx eyes to shimmer, not with grief as Sara expected but with determination and something even stronger. Something Sara should know yet couldn't quite place.

Kira draped herself over Ian's chest, her silvery aura blazing and crackling with energy—with love.

Sara straightened. Not casual caring love between friends and family, but rare absolute and *electric* love capable of melting ice and kick-starting a heart. The kind of love between bonded partners.

Kira placed her hands on the sides of Ian's face, spoke an intimacy Sara could not hear, and kissed him.

A spark of magic burst from their touch. The surrounding Takers howled and shielded their eyes as more sparks erupted between Kira and Ian, bathing them in gold and silver sizzling energy.

Ian jolted, his back arching, his arms reflexively embracing Kira, his golden aura flaring back to life.

Warmth flooded Sara with such weightless relief she thought she would float away. "Thank you," she sighed to Kira and to the Mother for ordaining their bonded connection.

"Kira?" said Ian. Though his voice was thin, his eyes were nearly glowing.

Kira leaned down and whispered into his ear, their auras flaring again.

Around them came whoops of joy from the Lochton family, a marked vigor in their defenses against the relentless Takers.

As much as Sara wanted to hug Ian and Kira, she had to check on Samson and then put an end to *all* of this. Power snapped in her palms. She crouched, about to launch into the sky, when Kira grabbed her wrist.

Concern pinched Kira's face. Her other arm remained wrapped around Ian, his embrace on her equally tight. "My dad," she cried. "Takers surrounded him and—"

"I know. I'll find him," Sara interrupted her. She could not tell her what she'd seen—Samson's broken body and unseeing gaze. Because what if, by some magical miracle, the Mother somehow spared Samson too? Short on time and heedful of making a promise she couldn't keep, Sara gave Kira a reassuring squeeze and took off into the murky sky.

She hovered, grazing the underside of thick clouds that stormed with dragon bellows and flashes of energy from Kane and Abby. Blocking out the overhead havoc, Sara searched the Council clearing until she spotted Samson. He lay in the same ghastly position, the Taker horde giving a wide berth to Kahn and Brad still fighting beside his body, his many bloodstones exposed by his torn jacket.

Surprise gurgled in the back of Sara's throat, her urgency momentarily suspended by Brad's wasted appearance. Toxic stains completely covered his arms and neck. Black blood exploded from his mouth as Kahn punched him with a blast of ochre energy. Kahn, his head skull-like with sunken cheeks and rotten bruising around his eyes, the gash on his forehead now a fetid crater, pounded Brad with a series of blazing arcs, flinging him back. Brad landed in a crumpled heap, his head cracking against the ground, his body unmoving.

Kahn pivoted for Samson, a victorious sneer on his gothic lips.

Hells! If Kahn could already knock out Brad, he would be a deadly adversary with all those bloodstones.

Sara dove for Kahn. The dark witch was faster. He sprang upon Samson, snatching the bloodstones in one fell swoop—and vaporized.

Sara slammed into the ground, her force dispersing Kahn's final puff of ash, and grabbed Samson's hand. Instead of the healing glow she had summoned, a spray of white and red sparks burst from her grasp, sending her flying onto her ass.

Samson twitched. It seemed a hallucination of Sara's hopeful mind. She hadn't healed him, and only the Mother knew how long he'd been sprawled out lifeless.

She scrambled back to his side, her knees sinking into the mud. He twitched again, and her jaw dropped as his limbs realigned themselves with a chain of sickening crunches. He whistled in a breath, his chest rising, and clapped a hand to his bloodstones. "Serves you right, Kahn," he spat. "You can't take them. They must be given. Greedy bastard."

What the actual fu—

Samson laughed. Sara punched him in the shoulder. He was as lean and unyielding as usual. He laughed harder. This time, it seemed aimed at her and whatever twisted manner of relief, horror, and twice-over pissed off was scrunching her face.

"Was this a trick?" she shrieked. She was so done with tricks.

"Most certainly not. My heart stopped, but I saw and *felt* everything. Really hurt. I don't recommend dying." He sat up and smoothed his torn jacket, frowning at the missing buttons.

Sara gaped at him.

"It was our blood bargain," he explained, holding out his open palm and pointing at a thin scar. "Neither of us can die until we complete our bargain to end the Shadow Mother. Supposedly, it only works once to cheat death, but let's not test that notion." He gave a wary glance at the smoky sky and shadow Takers, who teemed around them as though oblivious to their presence. Brad must have erected an invisible protective dome to keep the others away from Samson's bloodstones.

"Why didn't you tell me this?" Her voice hit a record-high octave.

He brushed at the mud on his sleeve, avoiding her gaze, and gave a one-shoulder shrug.

Gaa! "Because there's a price to be paid, isn't there?" Would it be wrong to strangle him so soon after he'd been brought back from the dead?

"Indeed." He rose to his feet and offered her his hand.

Had he answered her question or read her mind? Probably both. She scowled at him and took his assistance. "Fine! I'll just add it to my growing tab of sacrifices. What's one more?" she scoffed.

Samson stilled, his aura suddenly as pale as moonstone. "What do you mean—"

"Sara!"

She whirled to face Brad, struggling to his feet in the muck, remnants of the buffet table strewn around him. His brow was peaked, his ink-coated hands held up in submission. Energy buzzed in Sara's palms, and from the corners of her vision, she saw Samson's shadows building.

"No. No!" Brad stammered, raising his hands higher. Tar-like blood oozed from a gash in his side. "I'm helping you. I fought to keep Kahn away. Heal me," he begged Sara. "Like you did for him." He jerked his chin at Samson. "I'll help you stop her." His red-rimmed eyes were as wild as a rabid animal about to chew off its own leg to escape a trap.

Sara put out her arm, halting Samson from attacking. So this was why Brad hadn't alerted the Shadow Mother to her presence at Amira's site. *And* this was why he'd warned her the Shadow Mother was about to descend on Ware Woods. He wanted Sara to heal him. He was dying, and he *knew* it.

The magic in her hands winked out. Healing Samson had been a providential anomaly, and he'd been nowhere near as far gone as Brad. She *hated* Brad for everything he'd done to her, yet she paused, considering the greater mercy—let Samson or the Shadow Mother end him.

He stumbled forward, then jerked, eyes wide. Stain dribbled from his mouth as a jagged tentacle punched out his belly, spilling ichor at his feet. Something wet and cold splashed Sara's face. She should wipe it away, she should move, yet she was too stunned by the tentacle tip wiggling from Brad, the remainder of the appendage extending up into the clouds behind him.

Samson stepped before her, protective, his focus on the hazy sky where the rest of the Shadow Mother surely lurked.

Brad glanced down at the tentacle protruding from him, near death smoothing his features. He shifted his attention to Sara, his eyes haunted as if he realized too late all the mistakes he'd made. The tentacle slightly curled, raising him from the ground. Brad ripped off his two black bloodstones—ill-gotten gains from Makwa and Dorcas—and threw them at Sara just before the tentacle yanked him up into the clouds.

The Shadow Mother's wicked laugh reverberated like thunder through the smoke-filled sky. A blare shuddered the forest. Brad's invisible dome that had shielded them from the Takers collapsed. Sara stuffed the stones into her pants pocket, no chance to recoil at their cold bite of power before pushing witch fire at the fresh onslaught of Takers who all looked identical to Brad. They chanted, "Heal me, Sara," their eyes vacant, their edged weapons gleaming with intent.

Sara couldn't find it in her heart to feel even remotely aghast over Brad's death. You get what you give. And this universal law was much bigger than Sara.

"Why is she toying with us?" snarled Samson, twirling and swishing his hands like a mad conductor, his shadow magic squeezing the Brad doppelgängers into wisps.

A good question. A terrifying question.

With Samson easily keeping the Takers at bay, Sara paused and swept her gaze across the bedlam. Endless Takers continued to stream in from the plumes of smoke. Many fought to gain ground on the stump stage, while others battled with Amira and the Cahills in the clearing's surrounding forest. Even in their shadowy deaths, the Takers wore vicious smiles. They were enjoying this.

Sara's stomach twisted. The Shadow Mother was savoring the violence.

In a small voice, hoping it wasn't true, but knowing in her heart that it was, Sara answered, "The Shadow Mother is feeding off our fighting. She's growing stronger."

Samson cursed.

She threw back her head and scanned the muzzy sky for any hint of the Shadow Mother. No whip tentacles, though there were more than a few dragon-sized shadows flying toward the center of the forest. Sara rose to the balls of her feet, ready to take off after them, when a much smaller shadow came flying toward her—a shadow blasting violet power through the thick air, blazing a trail through the Takers.

"She's over here!" Violet shouted, popping out of the smoke. She landed beside Sara with a thud as Caleb, Bettina, and Florine emerged from the Takers.

"The other sites are on their way," exclaimed Florine, the flowers in her hair a tad disheveled.

They were coming. All of them. Relief and fear spun around inside Sara. Was their aid enough to help her defeat the Shadow Mother? Or was their growing battle more fuel on an already out-of-control fire?

"A little help," quipped Samson, slashing his arms. A wall of Takers disintegrated.

Caleb wrinkled his nose, his eyes tightening on Sara. "You've got something on your face, cousin." He gestured at her cheek before Bettina pulled him aside to help Samson with a new horde of Takers, their gangly limbs and dripping fangs more demonic than human.

"We've got this," shouted Florine. Vines exploded from the ground, seeking and strangling more of the foul advance. "GO!"

"Thank you," Sara projected, the two words failing to convey the extent of her gratitude for believing in her, for knowing to come today on the blood moon instead of the Equinox, and for gathering the other sites to lend aid. There weren't enough words to express herself, yet the glimmer in Florine's eyes suggested she understood. With a shared nod, Sara rocketed into the smoky sky and followed a soot-covered dragon toward the Cahill common.

CHAPTER 44

S MOKE STUNG HER eyes and burned her lungs, the roar of infected dragons coming from all directions. Not good. Not good at all. Sara summoned a gust of wind, clearing the haze that filled the common, and nearly fell from the sky, her heart faltering at the destruction below.

The chestnut tree was a blazing torch, its heat scalding her cheeks, the damage to its trunk beyond salvageable. More fire burned at the Main House as a dozen dragons tore into the sprawling structure, their claws and tails flinging chunks of smoldering lumber like glowing confetti. Another dozen dragons circled the barn, their jets of fire meeting water and ice from the Atwell witches.

Sara flew for them and for the Atwell vampires and Blue Ridge pack—including Moira—who were defending them from a legion of Takers. Relief at knowing the pack had somehow overcome their separation was short-lived as Sara approached. Moira's bear and Dean's wolf were streaked with red blood while two more wolves—Moesha and Luke—kept collapsing, giving everything they had to protect the barn and distressed livestock. They were all barely hanging on.

Sara threw out her healing magic to the shifters. It had worked once before, healing Thomas, Matthew, and Tobio before Jin had taken her to his garden. It had to work now. But she wouldn't know.

Her magic hadn't landed when a serrated tentacle whipped around her middle and wrenched her through the undulating clouds and into the moon's rusty glow high above Ware Woods.

"Why won't you die!" seethed the Shadow Mother, spitting glittery, viscid tar. To Sara's horror, she had grown even larger. Her beautiful, vacant-eyed face loomed before Sara, her swollen abdomen a gaping hole of star-eating black.

With a furious rotation of her hands, Sara summoned a combination of witch fire and white energy. She forged it into a blade and sliced through the tentacle.

Three more appendages immediately shot out from the Shadow Mother. They coiled around Sara, pinning her arms to her sides.

A thick, scratchy laugh. "I'll make you watch me kill your father next. Then I'll take all your magic and leave you as a husk of a human."

Not Charlie! Not *any* of them. Sara's vision went redder than the moon. Her hands flexed at her sides, fingernails carving her palms. She didn't need her arms to summon power. Though conducting helped with speed and precision, all her practice in the marsh had made her more than proficient in using just her mind to launch deadly force.

"Take this!" she shouted and rammed the Shadow Mother with a wall of white energy.

The entity shrieked as the power exploded into a million sparks, their snap, crackle, pop battering Sara's ears. Yet the whips around Sara only grew bigger, tighter, the Shadow Mother's cry slipping into a wicked, drunken laugh.

Get control of yourself! Sara reeled in her anger, stuffed it down, deeper than ever before, the effort causing her to thrash and bleed against her bonds.

Calm. Down.

She inhaled to the count of three as the last of her sparks snuffed out against the Shadow Mother's adamantine form.

The entity grinned, her teeth pitch-black blades. With a splintering whine, frost crept down her tentacles and around Sara, stealing the breath she had just fought for. Her heart stammered against the Shadow Mother's frozen grip, her touch so cold it seared. It burned Sara both outside and inside with such vengeance she thought her core might shatter. Crystal clear ice sluiced up her torso, covering her bloodstones, stilling their inner flames.

Her body strained, craving air, craving warmth. *Is this the aching cold that froze Thomas and the other elysian-eyed dragons?*

Bound and half frozen, Sara could only stare at her tormentor as the cold sucked at her magic, slowly peeling it away from her soul. It felt as if every single one of her ligaments were being torn from the bone. She stifled her scream. *Is this how Naomi had felt before the Shadow Mother killed her?*

The tentacles tightened. Not that Sara could feel them, her body mercifully falling numb to the pain. She could tell her bondage constricted by the slick crack of ice and the sinister grin deepening on the Shadow Mother's face. A face with familiar high cheekbones and pert nose.

Sara narrowed her eyes. In her ragged heart, she knew the likeness, but there was no time to ponder this connection. She needed to find a way to stop her.

Sara racked her brain, searching and scrutinizing everything she knew about the entity. The Shadow Mother wanted her to fight back, so Sara tamped down her rage and hate. *"Hate only begets more hate,"* the Mother had warned her. She had also said, *"The Shadow Mother loves to take."* And if the Shadow Mother only told lies—speaking the opposite of what was true—then it stood to reason she'd dislike the opposite of taking.

Giving.

Sara's heartbeat steadied, a warm flush of awareness flooding her veins, pushing back against the cold. The Shadow Mother specifically loved to take *power*, and while Sara could never force the entity to give power, Sara did have control over gifting her own.

The Shadow Mother hissed. "Why don't you fight me, little witch?"

Sara remained calm, silent. Her palms tingled as she eyed the swirling black hole at the core of the Shadow Mother. A hole so fathomless, she could swallow the entire magical world, the entire normal world, and still be empty. Her cup would never be full. The realization smacked Sara, and her eyes widened at recalling what Ian had told her right before she'd broken Makwa's curse: "*Dark magic seeks out power to fill their void, but it never lasts.*"

Her jaw fell slack, her mind riffling to Jin's omen about the Shadow Mother: "*There is no reasoning with her. She is a wild darkness that thrives on discord and violence. Her entire existence is to consume.*"

Stars above. The opposite of discord, violence, and rage was . . . love.

"*Love will correct the balance,*" the Mother had told Jin.

To defy the Shadow Mother and everyone's expectations of brute force to defeat her, Sara would have to gift her love, and she was the only one stupidly reckless enough to do such a thing.

With her arms still pinned to her sides, her hands shaking with cold, her inner well of magic drained to a dangerously low level, Sara carefully drew her fingertips together. And, just as she once did to Samson, she flicked a kernel of golden magic into the abysmal center of the Shadow Mother.

The entity screamed, a high-pitched peal of shock and pain—the opposite of her ominous blare. She clawed at her middle, flinging sand and tar, trying to dig out the glowing magic. It slid deeper inside her. Just like a splinter.

"You vile worm!" she spat.

A wry smile pulled at the corners of Sara's mouth. Hope blossomed in her chest. Giving her power was *working*.

She flicked both hands, spraying more healing magic. The Shadow Mother cried out again, and the ice encasing Sara's torso shattered, her bloodstones pulsing bright red again. The tentacle bonds trembled. To Sara's surprise, they withered a fraction and extended, holding Sara farther away as though she were the pestilence.

In the glow of the full moon—a moon no longer red but pure white, the eclipse over—Sara peered down the tentacle's jagged length at the Shadow Mother. The entity's humanoid form shrank, her edges more nebulous instead of sharply defined.

They both paused, staring at one another in disbelief as the roar of dragons and battle hollers drifted up through the smoky clouds below. The Shadow Mother grinned, a nightmarish promise of torture. She inhaled, absorbing the violence below, and swelled back to her larger size. Frost tore down her whips.

Pain punched Sara. *Shit, shit, shit.* She had to somehow stop the forest from fighting and cut off the Shadow Mother's source of fuel. But how? She couldn't even *see* Ware Woods.

Gritting her teeth against the cold drain on her magic, Sara dove into her inner well and summoned a gale to clear the smoke and shadows. She held on to her power, even as the Shadow Mother hissed and something precious cracked at Sara's chest. She continued holding until the air was clear and the full moon illuminated the forest below.

Every member of Ware Woods, including Matthew and the children, an army of wolves, and dozens upon dozens of magicals she'd never seen before crowded the Cahill common. Everyone halted, even the dragons and Takers, and gazed up at her.

Sara gasped at the devastation. At the burning soul trees and houses, at the red blood on snow, at the sheer number of witches, vampires, and shifters fighting as a team, and—on her chest—at Ann's shattered bloodstone. Sara had no time to mentally project her absurd request for all to stop fighting when the Shadow Mother jerked her closer.

Exactly as Sara had planned.

"Do not stand before her alone." Sara had heeded the Book's

caution, every magical now witness as she faced the Shadow Mother, close enough to weaken her and end this.

Sara dug deep into herself, grabbing at every magical fiber of her being and *GAVE*. Witch fire and healing magic burst forth, engulfing the Shadow Mother in a golden blaze.

The entity bellowed, her fury rocking the forest, swaying trees and knocking Takers off their feet. Flat-eyed dragons roared in response. Without rhyme or reason, they spat fire and smashed into trees, as distraught as the Shadow Mother.

"Thomas!" Sara projected. She tugged on their bond. The single gold strand remained frozen. With the Shadow Mother's control slipping and no elysian-eyed dragons to rein them in, the flat-eyes were wild, even more unhinged due to the night's earlier blood moon. She mentally yelled again for Thomas while giving another wave of magic to the Shadow Mother.

The two heavy black stones in Sara's pocket cracked and disintegrated. The tentacles around her waist loosened as the Shadow Mother continued to shrink.

"Nooo!" the entity screeched, her facial features ebbing into a swirling mask of darkness.

From the forest below radiated a rainbow of lights. Sara twisted in her jagged bonds, cutting her hands as she held on to them for fear she would fall, too weak to fly, and glanced down.

There was Samson giving a ray of red magic, Gran giving steel blue, Ian and the Hills kids giving gold, the Blue Ridge pack and Walker family giving amber, and Lily, Kira, and Lethal giving silver. Green streamed from the Cahills, watery-gray from the Atwells, and a range of blues from the Sullivans. Then all magicals added their power. Their collective magic poured forth, extinguishing the Takers' shadows and the smoky plumes from where they came.

Despite her perilous position, Sara's heart soared. They had followed her lead. They were willingly *giving* their magic and weakening the Shadow Mother together. Still, Sara couldn't let them give everything. It had been her choice—not theirs—to take such drastic measures in resetting the balance. It was *her* wish for peace and *her* sacrifice to achieve it. Her destiny.

She fully let go of her hate and rage, filling herself with love and giving it to the Shadow Mother. The entity howled, yet Sara kept giving. Ardeth's bloodstone cracked and dissolved.

Time seemed to suspend, the Shadow Mother stopping mid-howl. One moment they were weightless, hanging in the glow of the setting moon, and in the next moment they were falling from the sky.

"Thomas!" She fumbled through their bond for the single golden strand. Tears pooled in the corners of her eyes, partly from the rushing air and partly from relief, as she internally grasped not one but multiple strands vibrating with warmth.

The Shadow Mother shrank to Sara's size, her tentacles gone, her shadowy form barely humanesque. She lunged for Sara, wrapping cold, nebulous hands around her throat as they both plummeted toward the forest floor. Except there was no squeezing pressure to her hold, her power having been depleted just as much as Sara's.

"How could you do this to me?" her voice hissed in Sara's mind.

Wind tore at Sara's hair, her open jacket flapping like broken wings. She remained calm as she looked with understanding in her heart at what was left of the Shadow Mother. "Because you are the Mother's grief for thinking she failed us. You are my rage. You are everyone's hate and fear. You are everything left unchecked and grown out of control." The cold around her neck slipped away with a sigh. "I see you and I accept you. I forgive you and set myself—all of us—free."

And then, because it felt right, because she finally understood the last verse of the forest's blessing, Sara recited:

> *"For I am you and you are me,*
> *we are the light so mote it be."*

A crack, and Mary's bloodstone disintegrated.

The ground was much too close. Sara ignored it, her focus on the ring of smoke overhead and the blue dragon streaking toward her like lightning.

"Sara!"

A dreamy smile pulled at her lips. When had she become so cold? It was an effort to keep her eyes open, staring at Thomas in awe. She hadn't been the only one practicing for this moment. Thomas was right; he was *fast*. The scorched top of the chestnut tree blurred into view, someone—Gran?—hollered for witches to hold their magic. Psychic grandmother. She knew Thomas wouldn't fail.

With the last of her strength, Sara reached for him.

CHAPTER 45

IN A BLINK, Thomas phased. He was under her, his arms embracing her, his kinetic energy crackling around them as he broke her fall just as he'd done so many times before.

A tremendous *BOOM* rocked Sara, and somehow she felt it shake the entire forest. She closed her eyes, the only thing she could do, her hands too shredded to hold on to Thomas, her body too racked with pain to even whimper. It hurt to breathe. It hurt to exist.

She rose and fell with each swell of his chest, his steady inhalations becoming her own. She felt his pulse, rapid and strong, his heart beating for them both as he drew her closer, pressing her back flush against his chest.

"I have you. I'll always have you," his voice sounded in her mind.

Their bond flared. An inner network of thick golden strands latched on to Sara, pulling her away from swirling darkness and into Thomas's radiant embrace until all she could feel was him. Thomas flooded her with love and magic, his warmth thawing the ice in her bones, melting her heart, and twining with her soul.

She drew in a breath on her own, heard her own heart mimic his galloping beats, and relaxed into him.

Here was everything she ever needed. Unconditional love as mighty as the sun that rose every day no matter the weather. He had always accepted, trusted, and believed in her, and she knew he always would. Knew her forest family always would as well.

Near bursting with fiery gratitude, the pain in her hands a dull ache, her body zinging with energy, Sara returned Thomas's love. She poured her heart and soul into him, reveling in their glowing bond. But try as she might, there was no magic inside her to share. Not one single flame flickered to life and stretched for him, yearning to play and entwine with his magic. She had given it all away to the Shadow Mother. She'd made her choice, and even a bonded mate could not revive her sacrifice.

Sara had no regrets, even though it felt like a part of her was missing.

Her eyes still closed, she sensed Thomas sit up, bringing her with him. His arms remained banded around her; his chest pressed against her back as he braced her between his legs. He nuzzled her neck. *"My fearless wicked little monster, with or without magic, your power is infinite."*

She wholly melted, ignoring the distinct possibility that far too many magicals were watching them. Thank the Mother she hadn't lost her ability to communicate with Thomas. Maybe it was an invariable bonded mates thing. She didn't care. *"You always know the right thing to say."*

"And you always know the right thing to do," Thomas countered. He pressed a kiss to the side of her forehead.

"Pfft. That's debatable."

A low chuckle. *"I rather liked it when you slapped my——"*

"Your what?" Snicker. Wait——Did he stop himself because Charlie was listening in? Sara tried and failed to pick up her father's presence, though she knew he had to be close by.

"Sara, you should open your eyes and see what I'm seeing." Thomas's voice was still rumbling through her as she snapped to action and followed his line of sight to the sky. A sky now blue-gray with dawn——and filled with dragons.

Her eyes widened. Swim-flying through the air in excited, playful twists and turns were two dozen flat-eyed dragons. Though their gazes were still the chilling flat stare of a shark, their scaly hides were vibrant shades of ochre. Not one dragon had a smudge of shadowy infection. Chasing them with equal fervor, clearly elated to be unfrozen, were Tobio and Jin, along with five more elysian-eyed dragons. All seven were markedly more agile and swifter than the flat-eyes. Their brightly colored scales of jade, citrine, opal, amethyst, and peridot shimmered akin to jewels. Their vertically pupiled molten eyes studied the forest, Sara and Thomas, and the crowd of magicals surrounding them.

Sara reluctantly withdrew from Thomas's snug embrace and stood with him. To her relief, everyone else remained warily enthralled with the dragons and paid them no mind.

Thomas shivered, as did the dragons, their attention all swinging to a portion of sky directly above.

"What is it?" she asked. She slipped her hand into his, wincing at residual pain.

"I think"—he tilted his head, listening—"Lochton is coming."

A billow of white clouds appeared. They whorled into an oval shape and blinked open, pushing back a portion of the morning sky to reveal a starry black midnight. Every dragon and magical halted. With a roar that rattled Sara's teeth, Lochton exploded through the eye.

Sara gawked at her living ancestor. She knew he was enormous, but to see him beside the other dragons, swimming in the sky, unfrozen, was a wonder. His jet-black scales shimmered with a green luminance, his teeth longer than her arm. The triple row of spikes running down his spine ended in a mace-style tail. Massive, gold-dusted horns curved back from his head while fans of spikes framed his face. He was significantly more magnificent and terrifying than the Book had portrayed. And he was scaring the magicals. They were nervous enough with the smaller dragons, never mind one large enough to swallow half the barn and who sounded exactly like the almighty monster he was.

"Tell him to calm down!" she shouted to Thomas over the roar.

"I will do no such thing." Thomas shook his head, looking as though he wanted to join the other dragons who were zipping out of Lochton's path and bowing to him.

Lochton stopped his roar and hovered. His liquid emerald eyes seemed to scan the entire forest while simultaneously fixing on her with a blazing intensity. *"I hear you just fine, Sara. Well done on using your inner fire to free us all."*

She jumped at hearing his voice in her head and could have sworn he smiled. Later, when all the magical world wasn't watching, she'd give him a hard time for not specifying *exactly* what type of fire.

He gave two quick gurgling chuffs, and the flat-eyes immediately streamed one after the other into the midnight eye. Another huff, this one softer, more of an ask than a command, and Tobio descended to the common. A group of vampires, including the dour-faced Elder with handlebar eyebrows, rushed out of Tobio's way as he phased and landed. Dean and Matthew immediately slammed him with a hug sandwich.

Lochton swam a figure eight pattern over the forest. Jin and the other elysian-eyed dragons followed his lead, each dragon flying the same pattern over a different section of the forest as if performing a synchronized dance. Energy hummed, tickling Sara's skin. And like the unfurling of a fern, twinkling magic rolled up from the ground and restored everything: the Main House and Cahill homes and barn; all the forest trees, including the chestnut to Sara's right; even everyone's clothes and appearance. The entire common gasped, children cheered, and more than one Cahill whooped with joy and surely relief at not having to rebuild the Main House again.

Sara glanced down at herself. Her jacket and jeans were no longer ripped, but her bloodstones were still gone. Around her neck were only the smoke stone pendant and one silver chain—where Ardeth's stone had been.

Sara glanced farther down and frowned. On the ground beside her, where the Shadow Mother had fallen, stark against the freshly restored layer of snow, was a disconnected shadow. Though it stretched out in a fashion similar to Sara's own long shadow cast by the sherbet morning sun, it wasn't connected to anyone.

In the space before the shadow, where someone should have been standing, the snow slowly began to swirl. It gathered speed, becoming a tiny tempest of glittering snowflakes. Sara took a step back, tugging Thomas with her.

The flurry stopped, and the Mother stood before them.

The surrounding crowd quieted, awed murmurs replacing their hoots of celebration as they dipped their heads in reverence to her.

Thomas choked. *Is this . . ."*

"The Mother? Yes."

Sara grinned at the diamonds—instead of ice—shining in the Mother's cascading locks, at the sheer radiance glimmering from her, more dazzling than a thousand sunrises.

With a subtle sweep of her hand, the Mother claimed her shadow, connecting it to herself where her robes grazed the snowy ground. "Thank you, High Witch of Legend." Her rich bell-like voice carried across the common for all to hear.

Sara resisted the urge to quirk a brow. *Seriously? The Mother is thanking me and . . . and—I have no idea if I should bow or hug her.* Sara settled on a respectful nod, her gaze dropping to the darkness on the ground. She bit her lip at the smudge, at the understanding. The Shadow Mother had embodied far more than the Mother's grief and Sara's own rage; she had been a monstrous compilation of everyone's fears.

A melodic note of agreement hummed from the Mother. "Shadow selves have always existed," she said. "They always will. They are a part of the balance. A part of us—the imperfect, often frightening aspects of ourselves. They must not be forsaken nor left to fester but must be acknowledged in their own right."

Silence—a touch sheepish, a touch contemplative, and a whole lot hopeful—rooted Sara and the surrounding crowd.

The Mother cast them all an encouraging smile before turning to Thomas. When she gestured to him, a bluebird slipped out of her sleeve and flitted up into the chestnut tree. "Thank you, Thomas, for rising to every challenge."

Thomas bowed deeply. As he lifted his head, he tugged on the bond. *"I can't wait to hear how you personally know the Mother. Are there any other surprises I should . . ."* His question trailed off as the space beside the Mother wavered, resembling heat waves over a bonfire.

With a whoosh, an ovoid portal to an undulating celestial darkness opened and out stepped a male who could only be the Father.

He towered over the Mother. His hair and beard shone the white silver of comet tails, his ice-light eyes flickered with an aurora of colors, and his heavy robes flowed with the same empyrean fabric of Lochton's skirts. Atop his head rested a crown of winking stars.

A huff of dragon smoke drifted from Thomas.

Another wave of murmurs rippled through the crowd. In a distant pocket of her mind, Sara heard Gran shout, *"Sara Lochton!"* as if she had unwittingly summoned *both* the Mother and the Father. But Sara was too fixated on the ethereal pull of his portal and how similar it was to the center of the Shadow Mother.

A knowing smile softened the Father's regal face, putting Sara at ease. He glanced at the dark world beyond, then back at Sara. "Darkness is the natural state of the Aether. It is our own magic that lights the way," he explained, his voice as deep as an ocean, as vast as a galaxy.

The Mother peered up at him, the gold in her earthen eyes glowing. "I told you they would come together," she said.

His answering grin was pure affection, as though she were the center of his universe. "I shall never doubt you again, my dear." He tenderly took her hand, leading her toward the portal. With a near imperceptible angle of his head at the elysian-eyed dragons and a stern yet not unkind look that cautioned, *Behave*, at all the magicals gathered in the common, he stepped into the darkness with the Mother. They disappeared, the portal shrinking until it was a mere dot that dissolved into the morning sun.

A hush fell across the forest.

"Did that just really happen?" Sara murmured, referring to the Mother and Father, the dragons, the entire awful battle with the Shadow Mother—everything. A glimpse at the ground confirmed the shadow was indeed gone.

"Aye," projected Lochton, his earnestness telling Sara she would have to school him in rhetoric and sarcasm. *"I must leave now, but I will return."* He swung wide overhead and dove into his eye-shaped portal. The elysian-eyed dragons followed in a fluid stream, all except for Jin and the jade dragon, who stayed behind. The latter wore a curious expression, flared nostrils tentatively scenting the air as they glided closer toward the common—toward Tobio.

"Sara," said Thomas, his tone softly imploring.

She turned to him, noting the concern in his tense posture and in the groove between his brows.

"Everyone will understand if you need to rest. I'll take you anywhere you want to go."

Stars above, he was the sweetest, giving her options when she'd had the shittiest night ever while also smoothly addressing her lack of magic—if he used his dragon magic to escort her, no one would realize she'd lost her powers. It was thoughtful of him and showed he wasn't disappointed in the slightest at her significant change. Even so, she already knew his love for her would never waver, magic or no magic. And now they had a long lifetime full of peace ahead of them to revel and cherish. Resting was the last thing on her mind.

A corner of his mouth turned up. Sweet devil.

She returned his grin. "There is no other place I'd rather be than right here. The day is just getting started, and I intend to thank everyone for coming. Afterward, we have a Council meeting to conclude." Everyone in Ware Woods needed to know she no longer had magic and therefore a new High Witch should be elected. "And then, I very much want to be alone with you." To personally thank him for reviving her, of course.

"Of course," he said with a sly wink, reading her last thought.

CHAPTER 46

I T TOOK ALL day for Sara to greet every magical, thanking them for coming and humbly accepting their returning praise for a peace that had once seemed impossible. Apart from Florine's site, which opted to stay longer, Sara bade the magicals heartfelt goodbyes. As they took turns looping away through the oak tree, many of the Magi mentioned continuing the Global Council and working together on environmental and normal world issues. Their mutual agreeability was more than Sara had ever hoped for.

Though none had made a sacrifice quite like hers, Sara had noticed Damon and the other shifters were a little smaller when in their animal forms, truer to natural size instead of unusually large. Lethal, Amira, and the other vampires were a little slower, their movements now a trackable blur instead of nearly invisible. While Florine and the other witches were a little less *bright*. And then there was Samson. He was still the brightest witch despite the absence of bloodstones around his neck.

Sara fingered her silver chain and, with her other hand, gestured to the half dozen chains glinting from Samson's unbuttoned collar. "Ardeth would be proud of you. For giving and for saving the world."

"Ardeth would be proud of both of us," he replied. In a move unlike him, he raked a hand through his shoulder-length dark hair and sighed. Deeply. "I'm glad the bitch is gone, but, selfish bastard that I am, I'm going to miss my shadow magic."

Sara's chest constricted. Had the Shadow Mother taken it with her, or had Samson given more than his coveted stones?

Reading her thought, he said, "I gave it. It was what helped extinguish the Takers' smoke portals." He shrugged off her wide-eyed shock. "It was also the price of the blood bargain."

She coughed at his offhanded confession, at his unintended guile, then laughed out loud.

"How is this possibly amusing, oh Legendary One?" He folded his arms.

Sara rolled her eyes at the new nickname. It felt *good* to know some things hadn't changed. "Leave it to you to bend the magical rules in your favor and nab a two-for-one deal."

For a split second, he stilled, the only indication of his surprise. A wicked grin slowly spread across his face, a dusting of red magic sparking around him. He appeared positively fiendish at realizing he had cheated the system. Before he could utter a smug comment, Amira dragged him away with a purr on her lips.

"How are you?" asked Gran as she and Charlie approached, seizing a moment to talk with Sara among the parade of people heading from the oak to the Council clearing. "From your conversation with Samson and from your missing bloodstones, I gather the bargain and defeating the Shadow Mother cost you a lot too." Her steel blue gaze was the softest Sara had ever seen. It didn't sit well with Sara. She didn't want pity, much less from Gran, who was as stoic as they came. Yet Sara needed to tell them the extent of her loss and confirm what they surely already knew. Samson had known; it was why he hadn't asked.

"I gave everything," said Sara. She averted her gaze from Gran's and Charlie's worry, focusing on the cuts on her palms that she could no longer heal.

"Firecracker." The anguish in her father's tone squeezed her heart.

She dropped her hands and plastered on a smile. "I'm fine. More than fine." Her smile turned genuine when she caught Thomas's eye as he walked and talked with his own immediate family. "I have exactly what I want, and I'd gladly do it all over again." Well, not *gladly*, but the point was the same.

The path they were following opened up to the Council clearing, and Sara halted.

"Remember," said Gran, pulling her into a rare hug, "you're made of Lochton steel, Cahill cleverness, and your own brand of fire. Nothing can take that away." She patted Sara's back, rather hard to make her point, before dabbing her eyes with a handkerchief and bustling away.

Charlie grabbed Sara next, physically embracing her while his love mentally wrapped around her. *"We're all proud of you,"* he projected. He kissed her cheek and stepped aside as Helen and Florine swooped in. The two earth witches fussed over Sara's cut palms, applying a treatment of Lochton pine sap infused with what smelled reminiscent of yarrow. As they wrapped her hands, Sara murmured her thanks, her attention drawn to the clearing where everyone milled about the tables and chairs.

The overhead glowing orbs, drifting and bobbing like dreamy stars, illuminated and heated the gathering. From appearances, it seemed as if nothing had happened. The buffet tables were piled with an array of delectable foods, waiting for them to grab a plate and begin the meeting. Even the cake was on proud display, exactly as it had been save for a top of pure white frosting in lieu of one with red icing. Her breath hitched at the sight of the cake—Kingsley's favorite—recalling his sacrifice, which had been far greater than hers.

Sara immediately started the meeting by paying tribute to Kingsley. With Lily's help, she cut a generous piece from the center of the cake for him. Matthew stood and described Kingsley's valor in protecting the oak, and when he finished, Sara recalled Kingsley's final words. Gran and Alice had a teary moment before joining everyone else in sharing fond memories about Kingsley's dedication to maintaining the lake, his love for music and dancing, his sly sense of humor that Sara wasn't altogether surprised to hear about, and his insatiable love of sweets.

When their somber laughter eventually trailed off into quiet smiles, Sara climbed atop the stump stage. With a fluttering heart, she thanked everyone for their unwavering support, and laid herself bare.

"My magic is gone," she simply stated, holding up her bandaged palms. "Although we have peace and no need to defend Ware Woods, I motion we elect a new High Witch."

The clearing erupted with objection. And that was that.

Gran shooed Sara from the stage and cued the Atwell musicians to begin a lively tune. The song was one Sara recognized from their Samhain celebration, and though they were missing their best fiddle player, the music was perfection. In so many ways, the uplifting notes were exactly what they all needed to celebrate and usher in a new reality of peace.

Thomas gently took Sara's hand, placing a kiss on her bandage before leading her to an empty table. Her insides buzzed with a hot mix of joy, relief, and easily half a dozen more emotions.

In a daze, she lazily panned the clearing. Children danced on the stage, their faces beaming with happiness. At the Lochton table before her, Charlie and Ted were handing out platefuls of cake to Gran, Florine, Alice, and even Albert. Sara smirked at the two empty chairs where Ian and Kira had been sitting. Given the energy that had lustered around them, they no doubt had sneaked off for some quality bonding time.

Thomas leaned toward Sara, his finely stubbled chin grazing her cheek, his lips brushing her ear. "I suggested they find a secluded spot if they didn't want an audience for their fireworks."

Sara snickered, one shoulder reflexively rising to his tickling touch. "How long do you think it'll be before we see them again?"

"Days. I heard Kira saved Ian's life with just a kiss." Thomas sat back, pulling their clasped hands into his lap, his calloused fingertips stroking the inside of her wrist. "Remember when we first kissed in the birch grove?"

There was such heat and devotion in his molten eyes. Their bond warmed, physically tugging Sara closer to him, their chairs and sides pressed together. "How could I forget? You were trying to kill me until I tamed you with a kiss," she teased.

He nipped her jaw, a whiff of dragon smoke in the air. "You *slayed* me with that kiss, monster."

Oh? She bit back a quip about slaying dragons when her gaze naturally settled on a table with Tobio, Matthew, Jin, and a beautiful female she'd never seen before. The poised female had porcelain skin, her black hair flowing down to the waist of her overlapping green robes.

Sara slid forward in her seat for a better view. Jade green robes with a pearl-gray iridescence, the swirling hues a match to her elysian eyes. In addition to her dark hair, she had the same broad cheekbones as Jin and Tobio. It had to be their mother—the jade green dragon.

They were all smiling, Jin and his mother revealing similarly pointed teeth. For once, Tobio was at ease, the usual tension in his shoulders gone, his arm draped over the back of Matthew's chair as the two of them spoke with her. From the relief on Jin's face, Sara wondered just how long Jin had been the only full-blooded elysian-eyed dragon awake. Perhaps that had been why he'd harbored such sadness and had been quick to shed a tear for Thomas. Jin had been lonely.

Her somber thoughts came to an abrupt end when Dean, Moira, the triplets, and Wes descended upon Sara's table. A glance at the space before the stage confirmed Luke was still dancing with Violet and two females from Florine's site.

"Hi!" gushed Moira, her face glowing. Dean stood behind her, his arms wrapped around her waist, holding her to his massive chest. A wolfish grin and two crater-sized dimples deepened on his equally glowing face.

"Uh, hello?" said Sara. Something was up. Moesha playfully punched her in the shoulder. *Ow.*

"Thanks for healing us at the barn," said Moesha, grinning widely, her cheeks plump, shiny apples.

"I'm glad it worked." Sara raised a brow. "What's really going on?" She flicked her gaze to Dean and Moira.

"We're returning to the Blue Ridge site tomorrow. Moira and Matt are coming with us," said Dean.

Ah. She had been expecting this, for the pack to leave and the twins to go with them, just not so soon. "That's great," replied Sara, drawing out her words. She always knew Ware Woods wasn't a permanent place for the pack. It could have been if they'd wanted it, yet she knew they craved their own home with more forest to roam. She glanced at Bill and Shannon Walker, who'd once told the twins they couldn't leave the forest, back before everything changed.

Moira tracked her line of sight. "My folks are cool with it, especially since they can visit my other siblings whenever they want. And Jin said he restored the Blue Ridge soul tree, so we all can come and go as we please. You can visit us, and we'll visit you."

There was a trace amount of guilt in the way Moira spoke too quickly and in the way her golden beryl eyes were searching Sara. But just because she was moving in with Dean didn't mean their friendship would change. Sara was happy for her—for all of them.

She grinned up at Moira. "Sounds wonderful."

Alesha, Moesha, and Iesha howled as one while Dean whispered an affectionate, "I told you so," to Moira.

Wes rocked on his heels and narrowed his amber eyes at Sara. "When you visit, please don't bring that giant-ass dragon with you. I damn near pissed myself when he showed up."

"Language, Jokey!" Caleb hollered from two tables over.

Sara chuckled. "His name is Lochton. And I'm fairly certain he does as he pleases."

Wes stopped fidgeting, his face slack. "Lochton, as in your name? You're related?"

"Distantly." Another day she might share who else she was related to. For now, one transcendent ancestor was enough of a surprise.

"Whoa, badass." He fist-bumped her and, before Caleb could teasingly reprimand him again, he disappeared into the dancers.

"I'll see you soon," said Moira. She bent down and gave Sara a hug before she, Dean, and the triplets strolled after Wes.

Sara swung her head toward Caleb, curious when her cousin would make a similar announcement about moving to Florine's site. The joy on his face sent Sara's heart soaring. He sat beside Bettina, the two absorbed in a lively conversation. Plates of food and a few of Lethal's bottles cluttered the table they shared with Samson, Amira, Lily, and Lethal.

As if knowing Sara was looking at them, the Death Vampire slowly turned to her, a dazzling four-fanged smile on their angelic face.

Sara froze. If she could have seen their aura, it would have been blinding.

Thomas tugged on their bond, breaking her stupor. *"Should we be concerned that Lethal is so . . . happy?"*

No. Yes. Probably.

Thomas huffed a laugh, sending up a coil of smoke. "Sara," he said, his voice low.

Heat tingled her lower back.

"You've been sitting for hours and are more tired than you care to admit. I know you're ready to go home. Pick a path, or we can loop to the treehouse. Your choice." Thomas gestured with his free hand at the maple and two paths leading into the forest beside it.

It was her turn to huff. So polite with giving her multiple

non-flying practical options. It was going to take some time to adjust to not having her magic.

She stifled a sigh. He was right; she was tired, although not *that* tired. Of course, he knew that too. Sly devil. She gave him a knowing smirk, which he instantly returned, eyes blazing.

"Excellent suggestion," she said. But instead of choosing an option, she let her gaze dance around the clearing and everyone in it. After many minutes, her eyes lined with silver, her heart full, she slid onto his lap and leaned into him.

As his arms embraced her and silken dragon smoke curled around them, she said, "All of Ware Woods is home."

EPIC EPILOGUE:
FULL OF SURPRISES

THE ROOM WAS a disaster. The couch, recliner, end tables, and massive bookcase stuffed with books and homey odds and ends cluttered the center of the living room. Even the grandfather clock had been pulled away from the wall just far enough for Sara to slide a paint roller behind it.

"There," she said, hitting the last patch of wall with another coat of straw yellow. "We're done." She peeked around the towering clock and beamed at her father, who stood on the threshold of the open front door, a late spring breeze ruffling his sandy hair. Charlie and Ted had welcomed her idea to "spruce up" the living room of the brown house. As long as she didn't touch their old recliner with the indented seat, which apparently was one of Jynx's preferred napping spots. The enigmatic cat had strutted in and taken up residence the very day Bailey left to join Ian, Kira, and the Hills kids at the Hills sacred site.

"Firecracker, you're supposed to let the paint dry between coats." Charlie shook his head, a grin tugging at his mouth. He took two steps toward Sara, the closest he could manage, before leaning over the fur-coated recliner and taking the roller from her. "I'll soak this with the brushes while you wash up and tell me what mischief you've got planned for your nearly-full-moon party tonight. You're practically bursting at the seams with anticipation."

Sara noted the canny twinkle in his eyes. He already knew *everything*. Of course he did. Charlie always knew what she was up to.

"Daaad," she groaned, ducking into the adjacent kitchen and turning on the faucet.

"Humor me," he shouted over the running tap before slipping out the front door.

Through the open living room windows, Sara spied him place the roller in a bucket of water. Similar to insisting on moving the furniture by hand and painting unaided by magic, Charlie encouraged actual conversations instead of magically assumed ones. And though Sara's muscles already ached from shoving the furniture around, she knew the wisdom in his approach. With the absence of her powers over the past few months, she'd found meditative joy in walking through the forest as opposed to taking hasty flights, just as she felt satisfaction in doing tasks with her hands instead of using magic to complete them. She grinned, pleased to have a newfound appreciation for everything magical *and* normal. Perhaps this enlightenment had inspired the curious dream she'd had a week ago.

"I'm excited because this is the gang's first get together since before Thomas and Matt went to university. And yes, I have a couple of surprises planned for Thomas as birthday gifts." The dish soap lathered up her forearms as she scrubbed at a speckling of paint.

"And?" pressed her father. The screen door bounced shut behind him. From the corner of her eye, she saw him edge between the wet walls and haphazard furniture, his gleeful expression infectious.

"Aaand I'll share another surprise with everyone tonight." Giving up on the speckles, she rinsed and grabbed the kitchen towel hanging from a cabinet handle. As she turned, drying her hands, her father stooped to remove a piece of blue painter's tape from one of her canvas sneakers.

"I know you've grown so much this past year, but you'll always be my little girl, Sara." He stood, flicked the tape into the nearby trash can, and hugged her.

"Well, that's good, 'cause you'll always be my dad." She pulled back, considering him. "You okay? Ian moving out was a big change, and—"

He waved away her concern. "I'm fine. With him and Kira coming by a few times each week to hang out, it's almost like he never left. Plus, I'm plenty busy teaching my online course." He glanced at the dining table on the opposite side of the kitchen. "I'm very happy for you and your brother. Our crowded family dinners fill my heart. Speaking of dinners"—he tapped his temple and inclined his head toward the back door—"your grandmother is adamant you come with me to the blue house before going to your party."

Hmph. So much for meeting Caleb and Bettina at the field before anyone else got there. Sara tossed the towel and jabbed her thumb toward the jumbled living room. "Shouldn't we move the furniture back first?"

Charlie bopped her nose with his index finger. "I thought you learned to slow down."

"I did."

A fatherly look. "The paint is still wet. Ted and I will move the furniture tomorrow. Come on." In a few strides, he crossed the blue-tiled kitchen floor and turned the corner into the enclosed back patio.

Sara snatched her flannel shirt—the purple plaid favorite of her mother's—off the back of a dining chair. By the time the screen door creaked open, she was right behind her father. They jogged down the rear landing and set a brisk pace for the adjacent blue house, skirting around the freshly planted garden between the two Lochton homes. One did not keep Gran waiting.

To their left, the afternoon sun nestled atop the forest's tree canopy, casting shadows that licked with a crisp coolness. Sara shoved her arms into her flannel shirt, rolled the sleeves, and tied the bottom at her waist.

When they reached the back of the blue house, the door opened. Murmured conversation and the cozy scent of baked sugar ushered them in and through the living room.

Sara stopped in the wide archway of the kitchen.

At the wooden counter, rolling out dough like a cooking show professional, stood Lochton. His hair was pulled back in a messy bun. His calf-length kilt grazed the tops of his boots. His tunic, the same deep green as his eyes, was protected by an apron patterned with black and white skulls. Sara had seen him many times over the past few months for family dinners and for the Equinox and Beltane celebrations, but never had he appeared so . . . domestic. Her great-great-grandfather, the king of dragons, baking cookies. Joyous contentment radiated off him and Gran, who pulled a pan of rectangular-cut cookies from the oven and set it on the stovetop.

Lochton gave his flattened dough one more pass with the marble rolling pin before setting it aside and facing Sara with a pointed smile. His vibrant emotion, along with his sheer size and power, elicited the tiniest of squeaks from her. She pounded her four-fingered hand to her chest, trying to pass it off as a cough, and glanced away from his elysian eyes to the front of his apron. It was so heavily dusted with flour she could barely make out the quote stitched in steel blue thread: Piss off this witch, and you'll end up in the cauldron.

Charlie, bless him, said, "Yep, that's the same reaction I had when Helen showed me this apron she made for your grandmother."

"As if she needs any encouragement," chimed in Ted. Sara darted her gaze to her uncle, who wore a pressed button-down shirt, his goatee neatly groomed. He scooted his barstool closer to Alice as Charlie claimed the empty seat beside him. Both brothers grabbed a cookie from the towering stacks on the counter.

Alice tittered in agreement and whished cookies to Albert and Jynx, lying beside each other near the brick hearth—the fireplace mercifully unlit in a room already warmed by the oven and massive dragon shifter.

Before Gran could unleash whatever comment was causing her eyes to glitter, Sara nodded her head at the open book in the center of the cookie-cluttered counter and asked, "Did the Book give you a recipe?" The grimoire had never once shown her anything food related, just spells and magical information.

"Not to me," replied Gran, the devilry in her eyes sliding into sparkling wonder. "The Book provided Lochton with this special recipe." On cue, emerald green hearts of all sizes appeared on its open page, surrounding a recipe written in elegant looping cursive. The grimoire sighed and shimmied closer to Lochton, who had returned to his circle-shaped dough, carefully pinching the edge into a scalloped pattern.

"Aye," said Lochton. "This is Mary's recipe. She made her shortbread like this to resemble the sun and cooked it over embers. I often ate the entire round before she could cut it into wedges." He chuckled, releasing a wisp of smoke smelling of earth and stone before it dissolved into the sweet scent of baked love.

Really? Now I need to have one or two—or three of these. Sara started for the counter, only to be pulled back by a familiar brazen arm wrapped around her middle. In a clap of smoke, Thomas fully appeared beside her. Another clap, and Jin materialized on her other side. The kitchen suddenly felt much too small, holding three elysian-eyed dragons. Someone, or possibly the house itself, threw open every window. Ted and Charlie stopped chewing. Albert stood at attention. Jynx merely twitched her short tail.

There was a moment of silence in which Thomas and Jin, their eyes swirling, took in the kitchen and everyone in it. Neither of them commented on Lochton's apron. Thomas bowed his head at the eldest dragon and said, "I settled the dispute at Vasile's site."

Jin nudged Sara. *"I went to the treehouse and did as you asked while he was gone."*

"Well done," said Lochton to Thomas. "You've taken to your role with ease, which is exactly what the Mother intended."

As Thomas straightened with pride, Sara angled her shoulders toward Jin, letting a curtain of hair fall forward so Thomas wouldn't see the "Thank you" she mouthed at the red dragon.

"You do realize he can see—"

"Jin!" shouted Gran. Everyone's focus snapped to her.

Nostrils flared, Jin narrowed his eyes, clearly pissed at being interrupted and likely wondering how in Hells Gran had heard his private conversation. Sara pressed her lips, stifling her cackle. Usually, *she* was the one being called out by her grandmother.

Lochton stepped back from the counter with an amused grin as Gran swept in front of him and grabbed two baskets filled with cookies. She approached Jin, thrusting the smaller basket into his hands. "This is for you and your mother."

Jin's furious expression melted. "Um, thank you." He gave her a courteous bow before reporting to Lochton. "My mother and I will check on the flat-eyes tonight. They are bored and restless, prone to creating their own trouble."

"One more month," replied Lochton, seamlessly addressing the underlying question in Jin's statement. "If they are no longer needed to assist us, I will send them back to the Aether."

Jin bowed again, then vanished, leaving behind a faint ring of smoke.

Gran handed the second basket to Sara. "This is for your party. Try not to eat all of them as you *walk* to the field. There's been enough smoke in this house for one day." Gran waved off the last wisp of Jin's departure. "Now skedaddle. Us old farts have our own plans for dinner followed by a raucous night of cards with the Cahills and a few witches from Florine's."

"I'm *not* an old fart!" cried Ted.

"Neither am I," groused Alice. "But I don't deny the raucous part." She innocently smoothed back her long white hair.

Sara lifted a brow at her great-aunt, then slid a sly smile at her dressed-to-impress uncle.

"Have fun," exclaimed Charlie as Thomas steered her out of the living room and through the open back door. *"Enjoy your many surprises tonight, firecracker."* His gleefulness danced in her mind.

Sara lengthened her stride to keep up with Thomas, tossed him a cookie—which he immediately ate—and withdrew another baked rectangle for herself. Finally. She ate half in one bite, eyelids fluttering. Magical cookie, indeed. Instead of being crisp and crumbly, it was soft and delicate, sweet but not overly so.

Popping the rest into her mouth, she mumbled, "Did you terrorize Vasile by threatening to cut off his dastardly eyebrows?"

"I'd never. Those are a work of art. Besides, it wasn't Vasile who was the problem. It was a few of the others in the colony. I spoke with them, and they agreed to accept his lover's unborn child. I didn't even have to shift. Still"—he paused, giving a thoughtful rub to the nape of his neck—"vampires are more jealous than they let on, so I'll be keeping an eye on them."

Sara slowed her pace, following Thomas through the blueberry bushes covered with small green berries, and up the hill to the Lochton pine tree. "If it comes to it, you could ask Amira and Samson if they'd welcome some vampire company at the Cypress site."

"Excellent idea, but ever since Lochton and Florine restored the grove and Amira and Samson moved in, they've been *busy*." He stopped before the pine, one side of his mouth quirked at her. "I'm sure I'll catch them sated and agreeable at some point."

Sara snorted. "Good luck with that." It didn't surprise her to hear Amira and Samson were still in the throes of rekindling their relationship, nor did it surprise her Thomas had already thought of seeking their help.

Basket swinging at her side, she reached for Thomas with her free hand. His clasp was firm as he drew her to him and into the whooshing static gray of the pine. The drumming of the heartwood filled her ears and thumped in her chest while a gentle breeze pushed back her hair and kissed her forehead. Or possibly Thomas had done the kissing. His grin deepened when they popped out of the chestnut tree. Cheeky dragon.

Overhead, a mixed flock of birds settled amid the chestnut's tender-green foliage, picking spots to roost for the coming night.

Sara started for the Main House, its interior lights shining onto the dusky common, when Thomas tugged her to their right—toward the barn and farm fields beyond. "We don't need to pick up the food. I'll summon it when everyone arrives," he said.

She hesitated. Her plan to buy Caleb more time in case he needed it had been thwarted by a dragon who was now raptly assessing her. Far too raptly. He knew something was up—had known all week—but wasn't saying anything. Cheeky *and* wise.

As soon as she'd had the curious dream, Sara had wanted to tell him—to *show* him—but disbelief and uncertainty had held her tongue. Now, after a week and a certainty the change was permanent, she planned to tell him—all of them—as a surprise.

He tugged again until she fell into step with him. When he kissed her temple, their bond heated, and in the far recess of her mind, he whispered, *"Yes, monster. I'm cheeky and wise. Same as you."*

Pfft. She pressed her side into his, the basket softly bouncing against her leg. They walked in easy silence through the common, past the barn and many garden plots sprouting fresh growth, then followed the edge of the pasture fields. At the last field of short grass, a mesmerized Thomas brought them to a slow stop.

He stared transfixed at the cherry trees filling half the field. From where they sat at the nearby weathered picnic table, Violet, Caleb, and Bettina joined Sara in watching Thomas.

"Happy birthday," said Sara, swinging their clasped hands. "They won't be in perpetual bloom like the revived tree in Jin's garden, but I thought you could enjoy them for a little while during your birthday." She wondered if it was a coincidence or the Mother's divine premeditation that Thomas's birthday overlapped with the cherry's blooming season.

"Thank you," he murmured, the blue of his eyes swirling in the same dreamy manner of steam over a hot bath.

"It was my idea, but Caleb did all the work." Sara cocked her head at her cousin, questioning him with her eyes as to why he'd only planted half the field. It seemed she should have delayed Thomas.

Caleb simply gave her a gap-toothed, fanged smile.

When Sara dragged her puzzled gaze to Bettina—wearing a corseted dress of moss green—her hazel eyes quickly looked away. Though the buxom witch sported a devious grin and jiggled with suppressed laughter, a twinge of guilt rippled through Sara. If Bettina hadn't gifted her growing magic, she could have helped Caleb cultivate the cherry trees. Soon, Sara intended to gift it back with a bit of magical interest.

Thomas pivoted to face the table and repeated his thanks to Caleb. The two exchanged scheming looks. Evidently, Sara wasn't the only one up to something. When she squeezed Thomas's hand, he offered no hint of an explanation but whished the basket of cookies from her grasp to the table.

"What do you see in the trees?" asked Violet, snagging a cookie while scrutinizing her brother with the typical Sullivan cross-examination glint. She launched a few glowing orbs into the air above them, the nearly full moon not yet high enough to illuminate their gathering.

"It's more than visual," said Thomas, his awe-filled tone the same as when he'd once explained falling snow to Sara. "It's an experience—I can smell, hear, and taste each blossom. Tobio describes it as a full-body symphony. I think of it as sensual poetry."

"That's deep, Sullivan," said Caleb, his glittery vampire eyes fixed on the gently falling blooms.

Violet's low whistle of appreciation was cut short when Lethal and Lily appeared in a twist of smoke.

"Happy birthday, you two!" sang Lily. She released the smoke stone pendant around her neck—the one Sara had given her since Lethal detested smoke travel slightly less than looping through trees, and because Lethal's many foreign estates had no magical soul trees. The Death Vampire was carrying an enormous multi-tiered cake with intricate flame-patterned fondant frosting. An assortment of unlit candles in all colors bedecked each layer.

"She spent the past two days making this cake," said Lethal. The edge to their voice could have been irritation for schlepping the behemoth or jealousy for it monopolizing Lily's time or even grievance for not being able to eat it.

Lily finished hugging Thomas before commenting. "You helped me and enjoyed every minute."

Lethal merely pushed the cake to the center of the table, fussing with it for a moment before stepping back.

When Lily hugged Sara, crushing the air from her lungs, she gasped, "The cake is amazing, Lily, but you didn't have to make it so big."

"Have you *seen* how much those shifters eat?" grumbled Lethal.

True. The pack would probably devour it with their eyes alone. Which was beside the point. "It's Thomas's birthday. Not mine too."

"About that," said Thomas, leaning toward Sara as Lily took a seat at the table with Lethal. "I told everyone we're celebrating your birthday as well."

"But my birthday was a long time ago, when . . ." She trailed off, biting down on more than just her lip.

"When you were in between Green Brier Lane and Ware Woods. Charlie told me." Thomas cupped the side of her face and swept the calloused pad of his thumb across her cheek. From the slight peak in his brow, she knew he hadn't meant to upset her. *"I hope you can forgive me for wanting us to celebrate together. Maybe this*

will sway you." He turned to Caleb and gave a nod.

In a blur of movement, Caleb rushed to the other half of the field and crouched, placing his palms on the short grass. Uniform lines of saplings sprang from the ground. With a series of wooden groans, crackling bark, and leafy susurrations, a petite apple orchard grew to life beside the cherry trees.

"Are these . . ." Sara failed to deliver, her words drowned by her watering mouth.

"Ambrosia apples," supplied Bettina as Caleb sauntered back to the table. "Yep. We planted the seeds from my site before Caleb grew the cherries. We've been barely stitched together knowing you both planned similar surprises for each other."

Thomas's polite chuckle told Sara he wasn't surprised at all. "You'll have to be patient," he said to her. "Unlike at Tina's site, these trees will only bear apples in the fall."

Sara had zero patience, and Thomas knew it. "It's perfect. Thank you." She lifted her chin to kiss him, their lips grazing before they both jerked back at Caleb's sudden, "Whoop!"

"Here comes the High Witch of the Hills!" Caleb crowed.

The trees along the clearing edge parted, and Kira and Ian emerged, hand in hand. Gold and silver sparks shimmered around them.

Ian gave Caleb a halfhearted frown. "I'm just Ian, or 'dude' to you."

"Okay then, High Witch dude."

Ian sighed.

"You'll get used to it, eventually," said Sara. The title of High Witch had felt odd to her at first too, but Ian was a natural. How they'd never put together his innate leadership capabilities with his heritage was beyond her. Then again, it wasn't until Ian had visited the Hills site with Samson and the children that his full witchy powers manifested. Now he could create a magical shield large enough to protect the entire Hills site from normal eyes and, similar to every Magus, had powers outside of sacred sites. Next month, he would accompany Sara to his first Global Council meeting—a meeting *he* organized to discuss how magicals could assist normals with widespread environmental concerns.

Before she could tease Ian by calling *him* High Witch of Legend, Kira distracted her with a birthday high five and fanged smile.

"Thank you," said Sara, shaking the sting from her hand. Yeesh, did all half-vampires forget how freaking powerful they were? "I'm glad you two could make it. Who'd you get to watch the kids tonight?"

"My mom and dad. I know. Shocker, right? They've been so occupied making adjustments to the Cypress site, I wasn't sure if they'd peel away for one night."

Lethal scoffed, while Thomas let out a quiet snicker.

Kira ignored them both as she scanned the orchard, then eyed the desserts. "Nice trees. Are we late?" she asked, settling with Ian onto the empty bench opposite Bettina and Caleb.

"You're right on time," replied Thomas before taking a few paces from Sara. Dragon scales flickered on his arms and neck, just above the collar of his midnight T-shirt, as he summoned another elongated picnic table. A huff of smoke and both tables lay laden with a variety of foods, icy buckets of birch beer, and a few bottles of Lethal's crimson spirits.

The bottles suddenly clinked together. The platters of food and many table settings trembled as the ground quaked with the telltale approach of the shifters. A curse tore from Lethal's angelic lips, the cake swaying with more abandon than Luke on the dance floor.

Tobio's dragon, his gold-dusted black scales glimmering in the early moonlight, streamed over the barn and pastures, then swooped for the tables. In a gust—which Ian held off with a protective shield—Tobio phased and landed. His jet-black hair with frosted tips hung loose, softening his characteristically cool expression. When Tobio's gaze reached Sara, his greeting smile tilted knowingly.

All Hells. Of course his ethereal eyes noticed her yet-to-be-announced surprise. She gave a slight shake of her head, silently imploring him not to comment. Without breaking his poise, Tobio swept his focus to the cherry trees, his golden eyes glowing as a veil of blossoms quivered loose and drifted to the ground. Smart and easily distracted dragon.

The forest's shaking and the thudding of paws intensified as the rest of the pack raced down the edge of the fields, dirt flying, before shifting in a flurry of excited yips.

"Sorry," said Dean, grabbing Moira's hand and plunking down at the new picnic table; the spread jolted, silverware rattling. Matthew, his loose copper hair tucked behind his ears, similarly grabbed a bedazzled Tobio. The pair sat beside Moira as Tobio dragged his gaze from the cherry trees to the birch beer Matthew handed him.

"No apology needed," replied Sara. She slid onto the opposite bench with Thomas. Wes and the triplets joined them, while Luke made a beeline to sit next to Violet at the original table.

"We were running with a group from Damon's pack and lost track of time," explained Moira as Dean loaded two plates for them.

From the other table, Luke barked a laugh.

"Running?" questioned Sara. Must be a shifter thing. When Dean bit into his burger, Sara did the same.

"Some of us were running," said Alesha. A slice of a smile plumped her cheeks. "Some of us were *not* running. Isn't that right, Iesha?"

Her sister choked on a fry. When everyone at the table turned their attention to her, Iesha calmly plucked a leaf from her lopsided puffed ponytails, her grin as wide as the lake. "I wasn't the only one," she said, voice light and playful. "Wes also made a special friend."

Wes busied himself by downing his birch beer, a flush creeping up his neck. At the other table, Bettina slapped her hand over Caleb's mouth, his eyes watering as he was forced to swallow his barbs.

For the next hour, everyone exchanged teasing quips, their merriment rolling through the adjacent orchards. They caught up on one another's activities, from Lily helping Lethal renovate the library in one of their oldest castles to Moira decorating the pack's sprawling new home. And from Caleb moving in with Bettina at Florine's site to Violet continuing her attorney studies while regularly visiting the Blue Ridge pack. Although it had been months since the Ware Woods' barrier had detonated, Sara was still restoring the stone wall by hand, piece by lichen-encrusted piece. The rebuilt wall was not an impenetrable barrier—that magic was long gone and no longer necessary in a time of peace—but reconstructing it seemed the right thing to do.

When the conversation died down, and the cookies disappeared, and more than one wolf shifter stared at the towering cake, Matthew raised his drink and led a birthday toast to Thomas and Sara. "To my witchy, dragony brother, who is happier and more content than I ever imagined he could be, and to the legendary Sara, who has surprised us all from her very first day in Ware Woods."

"Hear, hear," added Ian. Everyone raised their drink of water or beer. Or blood.

"Can we finally eat the cake?" Wes's subsequent whine was met with, "Yes, but . . ." from Lily.

She stood, patting her pockets. "I forgot the matches for the candles."

Thomas elbowed Sara. A light-blue spark of energy snapped between them.

Dragon Boy? She poked him right back, in the ribs, delighting in his jump.

"You're killing me, Sara."

"I was waiting for the right opportunity."

"Now, please, before I combust."

Alrighty then. She was near combusting herself. "Speaking of surprises," said Sara. She swung her legs over the bench and stood, all eyes on her, Thomas's gaze pure enraptured happiness. "My magic is coming back." Not all of it, but enough to have wept at the first spark that had warmed her four-fingered palm when she'd woken from the curious dream. A dream in which she'd been tending crescent-shaped flower beds when the Mother approached and offered her a teacup of liquid sunshine. Only it hadn't been tea that Sara swallowed but a kernel of magic. A gift for giving selflessly and staying true to herself, the Mother had explained.

Sara winked at Thomas, his smile more radiant than the moon. With a satisfying flick of her wrist, she sent a scattering of witch fire flames to light the candles.

Stunned faces gaped at her, the gentle crackle of flames the only sound. Life paused, the suspended moment marked for all time by the details: Moira's pearly pink nail polish—her hand covering her mouth as though Sara were going to announce a different type of surprise, one she and Dean would no doubt be expecting soon—the horned owl silently flying overhead, Ian's jaw hanging like the tree swing in the brown house's backyard, and everyone's energy flaring bright enough to cast a rainbow aurora upon the night sky.

Caleb whooped first, followed by a rally of cheers and howls, tight hugs, fist bumps, and plates heaped with cake.

By the time the moon was high among the stars, the shifters had polished off the birthday dessert, their contented groans coaxing a smile from Lethal.

Sara pushed away her plate, her belly as full as her heart. When she turned to Thomas, he gently took her hand and led her away from the tables and into the cherry trees.

"Dance with me," he said, his voice rough, eyes smoldering. Tender waves of happiness flowed from him, washing over her, tingling every inch of her being. The same tender happiness had licked in surprised eagerness at her powers all week.

"Okay," she drawled, taking his measure, their bond blazing hot. "But there's no music, and you know I can't dance."

"Not true." Thomas picked her up by her hips, set her canvas shoes atop his booted feet, and pulled her in close. "Listen," he whispered, lips caressing her ear, his chest pressed against hers, their hearts beating as one.

Sara melted into him, letting him sway her body. As their magic twined and they slipped into each other's minds, she heard the delicate tinkling of bells, wondrously accompanied by the soft drifting of stringed instruments. An orchestra of cherry blossoms. "It's beautiful," she breathed.

His responding kiss to her forehead was slow, his lips pleasantly branding her skin. "All the beauty in the world bows to you, my love. My heart. My monster."

Sara ignited. White flames kindled to life, enveloping them both. Energy sizzled, and above the dreamy trees, light-blue sparks exploded in the night sky.

From the tables came a wave of swift goodbyes. In a blink, everyone dispersed.

Thomas's amusement rumbled Sara's soul. She leaned back, gazing into his elysian eyes while flooding their bond with her unending love for him. All around them blossoms fell like snowflakes.

He nipped her jaw. "Peace, magic, a quiet night alone. Whatever shall we do now?"

Smartass. She wove her fingers into his hair and tugged. "How about we enjoy the hot spring for two that Jin added beside the treehouse? The one you can stop pretending you don't already know about."

Silken dragon smoke wrapped around them. "I thought you'd never ask."

Laughter rang through the woods.

LEAVE A REVIEW

If you enjoyed *Spells & Shadows*, I would be extremely grateful if you left a review at your online retailer of choice. And heck yeah, you can leave the same review at multiple locations and then bask in the good karma. Thank you ~ Sonja

Review links can be found at:
www.sonjafblanco.com/s2review

Reviews are important to this author and help spread the word so other readers may discover and enjoy this series. Sharing your review on social media or around the proverbial water cooler and shouting from the rooftops is also encouraged.

Thank you!
Caleb-sized, crushing hugs to you

DISCOVER MORE

Get your FREE copy of *Witch of Ware Woods – Flood & Fire*, the series prequel where magic, love, destruction, and sacrifice combine in the spellbinding creation of Ware Woods.

Free download at www.sonjafblanco.com/f2

Stay in touch for more fantasy novels coming your way!

Get writing updates, sneak peeks, giveaways, and insider info by subscribing to Sonja's newsletter at:
www.sonjafblanco.com/subscribe

WARE WOODS BLESSING

Mother below and Father above,

I give my true self unto your love;

To feel the earth and touch the sky,

I choose to live before I die;

For I am you and you are me,

We are the light, so mote it be.

AUTHOR'S NOTE

While the Witch of Ware Woods story started as a dream, with vivid images of Sara and Thomas in a snowy birch grove, snippets of dialogue, and shadowy impressions of a sly-grinned character in a top hat, I would be remiss if I didn't mention four of the biggest influences on this series.

WITCHY HISTORY

In 1720 central Massachusetts—almost thirty years *after* the infamous Salem witch trials—a young woman named Mary was hung as a witch. She was my ancestor. Needless to say, her family—my family—was devastated, her father in particular. From that day forward, as a means to protect his heart and to honor his beloved daughter, he asked that no one else in the family be named Mary.

When my grandmother informed me of this bittersweet ancestry, I was stunned. Still am. You'd think people would have learned a lesson from the Salem trials. Some did. Some have. Yet, sadly, persecution in many forms continues to exist the world over.

Since I couldn't go back in time, change certain events, and roll more than a few heads, I did what I could. I imagined a different outcome for Mary: What if she and others allegedly like her found refuge in the woods?

Speaking of others, Tituba and Dorcas are two victims of the Salem trials. Tituba evaded execution and eventually disappeared from the public eye—a feat that baffles me, considering her pivotal role. Unfortunately, Dorcas, who was only four during her imprisonment, never recovered from the horror she suffered. She avoided execution only to live as a troubled indentured servant.

SACRED SITES

Throughout the world, there are special trees, such as Major Oak in England and General Sherman (redwood) in California, and there are sacred groves. These groves, sometimes referred to as sacred sites, are rooted in centuries of cultural reverence. Many are said to have magical properties. Most are protected. Some are on ley lines. More than a few are outright forbidden to the general public. And all are respected as natural sources of energy.

I find it fascinating that in pockets all over the world, throughout centuries of time and among different cultures, these groves are held in similar awe. Coincidence? I think not.

In case you're wondering, the Blue Ridge site is "fictionally" located in the Appalachians, the Hills site is in South Dakota, Florine's site is in Italy, Amira's site is in France, and Damon's site is in Germany.

THE QUABBIN

Less than a hundred years ago (from the time of this publication), the Swift River was dammed and four towns in central Massachusetts were intentionally flooded to create a reservoir, now known as the Quabbin Reservoir, providing drinkable water for the growing population of Boston. Many families were forced from their homes and farmlands, historic churches and buildings were moved by flatbed trucks, and thousands of graves were dug up and the dead reburied above the new waterline. My grandfather, a teen at the time, helped relocate many of the dead.

As a child, during summer visits with my grandparents (I see what you did there, Mom), we'd hike and fish in the Quabbin. I have fond memories of sucking on starlight mints while searching for orange newts. As an adult, I can't help but stare at the reservoir and envision the imprints of past lives at the bottom of the water.

Though the tragedy of this landscape transformation will never be forgotten, the Quabbin Reservoir is now a protected and thriving habitat. If you are ever in central Massachusetts, I encourage you to visit the Quabbin. Drop by the visitor center, take a scenic hike, and wander the cemetery. Perhaps you'll find a ghost. Or a newt.

THE AMERICAN CHESTNUT TREE

Like most stories, Ware Woods was inspired by a different story. A heartwood-breakingly true story—a memory—shared by my father, whose love of the land certainly influenced my own. (Brace yourself for another shocking history lesson.)

When my father was only four years old, his father took him to visit a "special tree." As they looked up at the towering giant with vibrant green leaves and spiky burs containing edible chestnuts, my grandfather told him to remember this tree, as it was one of the last of its kind. Such a Lorax moment.

Within a few years, by the end of the 1940s, over four billion American chestnut trees had died from a fungal blight accidentally brought from Asia. The chestnut blight has been called the greatest ecological disaster to strike the world's forests in all of history. And yet, not many people know about it.

Fortunately, there are tree lovers fighting to save this grandeur from extinction. Through crossbreeding, biotechnology, and biocontrol techniques (like mudding), they hope to someday repopulate the forests. I hope so too.

If you would like to learn more about this effort, please check out chestnut conservation groups such as the American Chestnut Foundation. There are many ways you can help, including planting and protecting chestnut seedlings, such as the four my father currently cares for on his property.

ACKNOWLEDGEMENTS

As I write this, it still hasn't hit me that *Spells & Shadows* is the final book in the Witch of Ware Woods series. These characters and this world have filled my mind, my heart, and my soul for many years. In some part, I know they always will. As Thomas would say, "This isn't goodbye, just 'see you later.'" Because that's the magic of books, isn't it? The comforting reassurance that you can revisit and escape into the pages at any time. A world literally at your fingertips. *snicker* Couldn't help myself.

In all seriousness, Sara's story and the pull of Ware Woods were always much bigger than me. Hells, Lethal alone is much bigger than me and would not "calmly" stay inside my mind. And having Sara, Thomas, Lethal, and a massive cast clanging the bars overwhelmed my little head. Thus, I am over-the-moon thankful for the many people who have supported me in getting this story out of my imagination and into your hands.

To my husband, David—Thank you for taking on the Costco runs, for making most of our dinners, and for your continuing support. Fork 'em Devils!

To my children, Mia and Jason—You are my biggest joys. May you always be surrounded by the unconditional love of friends and family. And may you always have the courage to believe in yourself and let your inner fire blaze. Thanks for humoring my jokes and life advice. Some day, far in the future, you'll find it endearing.

To my parents, Don and Donna—I can't thank you enough for all you have done for me. This series exists because of your love, from showing me how to plant trees and garden when I was little to reading my messy first drafts and taking my calls to discuss my latest bookish news and so much more. I love you to the moon and back.

To my brother, Chris—Thanks for chuckling at my puns and for not salting my milk at the dinner table. Perhaps I spoke too soon . . .

To my frister, Tami—Thank you for your honest comments and enduring support. Our friendship means so much to me.

To my cousin, High Priestess Lady Jesamyn Angelica—Thanks for jumping on board at the very start of this series, for lending your witchy expertise, for providing your editing insight, and for all your love. Sharing this story (Gran, the blue and brown homes, Charlie . . . Gaa! All of it *sniff*) with you has been truly magical.

To my long-time bestie, Bower—Can you believe this?! Me neither. Thanks for getting me through HS, giving me kickass feedback on this series, and now being my gluten-free sister in arms. The best is yet to come.

To my beta readers, Tamra, Jesa, Danielle, Regan, Merrit, Rosalyn, and Alice—Thank you for eagerly agreeing to be my early readers, for taking precious time to carefully consider all aspects of the story, and for providing your honest comments. You are my trusted court, and I am eternally grateful for you.

To my sensitivity reader, Brigid—Thank you for examining this story from multiple angles, for paying close attention to my diverse cast, and for your discerning comments. I am extremely thankful for your assistance with this series.

To my editors, Hannah and Kelly—Many thanks for your genuine love of this series and for helping me polish this story into a shiny gem. Your patience and hard work are greatly appreciated.

To my international design team, Stef, Maria, Marina, David, and Tonia—Your creativity and digital art skills are SO appreciated! Many thanks for your patience and guidance and brilliance.

To my writer friends and social media peeps—THANK YOU! Writing and publishing can be (okay, it IS) exceptionally challenging, but I know you always have my back and I always have yours. Our community is a blessing, and I am profoundly grateful to be a part of it. Special thanks to Ashley Alexander, Merrit Townsend, Darin Nagamootoo, Katrina Tortorici, Jennifer Sargent, Ali Mills, Jessica Dodge, Jess De Smedt, Otto Schafer, Alexis Henricks, Stephanie Whitfield, Sherry "S. L." Anne, Dani Hoots, Rose Fairchild, Laura Quinn, Alice Hanov, Rosalyn Briar, Kacey Rayburn, T. J. Bateman, Marla Azinger, Elana B., Cassie Sanchez, Miranda Lyn, and Debbie Gonzales, to name a few. Totally had to reel myself in from lengthy gushes over every one of you. You get me. I am beyond grateful for your support and friendship.

Thanks to all the scented candles, coffee, tea, and Three Musketeers bars that helped fuel this final installment. And thanks to my noise-canceling headphones because the new Hell Hound snores like a boar.

As always, thank you, Universe, for the magic. I couldn't have done this without you.

Like an epic epilogue, I saved the best for last. Thank YOU, dear reader, for taking a chance on my debut series. For letting Ware Woods "whish" you away. For taking this journey with Sara, and with me. Every kind comment, purchase, review, word-of-mouth praise, and social media highlight is noticed and greatly appreciated. Caleb-sized crushing hugs to you! Keep dreaming and reaching for the stars. And do stay in touch, for I have plenty more wickedly magical stories to share.

ABOUT THE AUTHOR

Sonja grew up in New England, where she ran barefoot through the woods, chased lightning bugs, tapped maple trees for syrup, and built towering snow castles.

Having an ancestor who was hung as a witch, Sonja is naturally drawn to all things magical and fantastical—trees and cemeteries in particular.

At 5'2" she is often caught climbing tables, chairs, and small children to reach the upper shelves. She likes coffee and tea equally, both of which most certainly contributed to her diminutive stature.

Witty comics easily amuse her, as do heavily jowled Hell Hounds that talk in their sleep.

She writes fantasy as if it were real, because believing makes it so.

Get writing updates, sneak peeks, giveaways, and insider info
by subscribing to Sonja's newsletter at:
www.sonjafblanco.com/subscribe

Follow and connect with Sonja at:
Goodreads: goodreads.com/sonjafblanco
Instagram: @sonjafblanco
Facebook: @sonjafblanco
TikTok: @sonjafblanco
Twitter: @sonja_blanco